# STAR

# SPLITTER

# STAR SPLITTER

## MATTHEW J. KIRBY

DUTTON BOOKS

# DUTTON BOOKS

An imprint of Penguin Random House LLC, New York

First published in the United States of America by Dutton Children's Books,
an imprint of Penguin Random House LLC, 2023

Text copyright © 2023 by Matthew Kirby

Visit us online at PenguinRandomHouse.com.

Library of Congress Cataloging-in-Publication Data is available.

Printed in the United States of America

ISBN 9780735231665 (hardcover)
ISBN 9780593619643 (international edition)
2nd Printing

LSCH
Edited by Julie Strauss-Gabel
Design by Anna Booth
Text set in Arno Pro

*For those who ask what might have been*

That telescope was christened the Star-Splitter,
Because it didn't do a thing but split
A star in two or three the way you split
A globule of quicksilver in your hand
With one stroke of your finger in the middle.
It's a star-splitter if there ever was one,
And ought to do some good if splitting stars
'Sa thing to be compared with splitting wood.
We've looked and looked, but after all where are we?
Do we know any better where we are,
And how it stands between the night tonight
And a man with a smoky lantern chimney?
How different from the way it ever stood?

—FROM "THE STAR-SPLITTER,"
ROBERT FROST

# STAR

# SPLITTER

# 1 — OS *Liverpool,*
# Earth's orbit

## BEFORE

I DON'T CARE HOW MANY PREP CLASSES YOU TAKE, or how many counseling sessions you go through, or how many waivers you sign, none of it actually prepares you to be burned apart by a laser, atom by atom. But Jessica Mathers was one of the most prepared travelers I ever had the privilege to meet. Not eager, but prepared.

I've seen pretty much the full spectrum of human reaction to teleportation and talked countless travelers through their emotional and psychological barriers. I have a pretty spectacular record, too, with a voluntary abort rate of 8.2 percent; my department average usually hovers near fifteen. Some people just can't be talked into the machine come departure time.

I've been a traveler liaison with ISTA for eleven years, and each year, the job gets harder and busier. As more and more destination ships reach their targets, interstellar teleportation goes up. Last year I sent 322 passengers a combined distance of nearly 6,500 light-years. I admit I don't remember them all. But some travelers stay with you. You find yourself thinking about them years later, wondering where they are and what they're doing out there among all those pinpricks of light. For me, Jessica Mathers was one of those passengers.

She was an unaccompanied minor, back when I was assigned to the OS *Liverpool*. I was late meeting her in the reception area at the shuttle dock because it had taken thirty extra minutes to coax a twitchy atmospheric engineer into the teleporter. I hate being late, because it often makes my job harder. If I'm not there to put the traveler at ease right away, their mind goes to work. Stress and anxiety go up. I have to spend time bringing them back down to baseline, or I can almost guarantee they'll abort their trip.

But Jessica Mathers wasn't anxious. She just looked mad.

At first I wondered if she might be mad at me. Anger is a common stress response.

"I apologize for being late," I said, extending my hand. "And I apologize for the cold fingers. Blood doesn't circulate as well up here, with only partial Earth gravity."

She stayed seated as we shook, but her scowl softened. "It's fine."

"How was the trip up from the surface?"

"Just what the brochure promised." She stood to face me and smiled, appearing and sounding completely at ease. "Are you my liaison?"

"I am," I replied, somewhat taken aback by her sudden calm. The anger I'd seen on her face had vanished, like she'd put it away somewhere for safekeeping, and I realized it hadn't been directed at me. It was just something she carried around. I puzzled over who or what could make her mad enough that it seemed to distract her from any fears she had. "My name is Jim Kelly."

"And you're here to keep me from freaking out?" she said.

"If I can. I'll be at your side for the next two hours. It's a pleasure to meet you, Jessica."

She nodded.

I gestured toward my office. "This way. And watch your step. The simulated gravity takes some getting used to."

When we got there, she took a seat in one of the chairs facing my desk. Instead of sitting down opposite her, with the desk of authority between us, I sat down next to her.

"So is this the point of no return?" Jessica asked.

"Not yet." I pulled out my tablet. "You'll know that point when it arrives."

"Then I already passed it. Back when my parents signed me up for this." Her tone hardened, and in that moment the reason for her earlier anger became clearer.

"I take it this trip wasn't your idea?" I asked.

"No. It was not." She cocked her head, and her auburn hair fell to one side. "Do you meet a lot of seventeen-year-olds who want to leave their life on Earth behind to live on a barren rock?"

"Carver 1061c isn't barren. It's simply coming out of a global extinction event." I paused. "But I realize that's not your point."

"You're right. That's not my point."

"Your parents are scientists, correct?" I pulled up her file on my tablet. "Your mom's a geologist, and your dad's a biologist?"

She sighed. "Yep."

"And you take after them? Your math and science grades are excellent."

She shrugged. "I guess."

"I've spoken to them, you know. Your parents. They'll meet you in orbit above Carver 1061c. I believe they're coming from the New Beijing colony? They should complete their teleportation right about the time you do. They seem very excited to finally have you with them."

"They're excited about having a free research assistant."

I thought about letting that go, but I also worried her resentment might still interfere with her willingness to travel. "Is that the story you tell yourself?"

"It's the truth."

"That's not the impression they gave me when—"

"Look, Mr. Kelly, I—"

"Jim."

"Okay. Jim." She leaned toward me. Her green eyes had streaks of blue in them, and her lips were a bit dry and chapped, indicating that she would need some rehydration before departure. "I know what your job is, and family therapy isn't part of it. So don't feel like you have to say something to make me feel better about my parents, or leaving all my friends. You're here to get me into the teleporter. You don't need to worry about anything else. I'll be fine."

I felt taken aback by her for the second time, and all I could say was "Okay."

She nodded and leaned away. "Thanks."

So far, her emotional and verbal responses had been so atypical, I began to doubt my usual script, so while I figured out how best to approach her and her teleportation, I defaulted to the formalities of paperwork.

"Your parents have already signed most of the necessary documents," I said. "I know you're ready to go, but I do need to review a few things with you."

"Sure. Let's do that."

"Some of this—probably most of this—you'll already know from your pre-travel counseling sessions. But I have to review it anyway. For legal purposes."

"I get it."

"Okay. Can you state your full name for me, please?"

"Jessica Havilland Mathers."

"Date of birth?"

"May fourth, 2182."

"The names of your guardians who authorized this travel?"

"Which guardians? My grandparents that I live with? Or my parents?"

"Your parents."

"Sharon Havilland and Stephen Mathers."

"And your final destination?"

"The extremely fascinating and once-in-a-lifetime research opportunity that is Carver 1061c."

I smiled. "Thank you." Then I took a breath, looked down at the tablet, and set it aside. "Everything necessary for your teleportation is prepared. The destination ship is ready to receive your data. We have your complete pre-scan loaded. The machine will use it as a map for the final bio-scan, and everything has been double-checked and triple-checked and quadruple-checked. Teleportation remains a vastly safer form of travel than even low-atmosphere aircraft or ground vehicles."

"Got it."

"Once you're comfortable inside the teleporter, the sedative will put you into stasis. It's important that you try to be as calm as possible leading up to that, because you'll arrive at your destination in the same state of mind you left. A calm departure means a calm arrival."

She nodded. "Okay."

"Remember, when you arrive, you will be you. You'll feel like you. You'll think like you, with all your memories and personality intact. You'll be exactly who you are now, down to the atom."

She inhaled and looked away, the first slip in her confidence that I'd noticed. "Right."

"You will step into the machine here, and nine days from now, after your body has been established at your destination, you'll step out of the printer on the . . ." I checked her forms. "The DS *Theseus*. Another liaison, like me, will be waiting for you the moment you wake up. Possibly your parents, too. Then, a year from now, the OS *Clarke* will enter orbit around Carver 1061c and pick you up. I went through training with the liaison on that ship, Jason Lau. Ask him to tell you about his cat. He'll set up your scan and send you back here. The process of both scans will destroy your reference body. Do you understand and accept this?"

This time, her answer came after a slight hesitation. "I do."

Hesitations almost always mean reservations, which are better addressed sooner rather than later. "Do you have any questions or concerns you would like to bring up at this time?"

"No."

But I knew there was something on her mind, and I knew which question had put it there. I decided to press that button again, just to see how sensitive it was, and whether it could be a problem later. "After your reference body has been destroyed, your complete scan will be maintained in a secure data facility until your next teleportation. At that point, the new scan will replace the old one. If the worst should happen out there, we can always reestablish you here using the backup. You will only lose the memories and experiences since your last scan."

She nodded, but absently. "Uh-huh."

The safety of her data didn't seem to be the source of her agitation. But I still had the impression that her thoughts were circling something to do with her reference body. "Any concerns about the scan itself?"

She looked at me and bit down on her chapped lip.

I shrugged and leaned back in my chair, settling in. "It's better to bring it up now. Trust me on that."

She glanced at the framed image on my desk. The one I keep oriented so travelers can see it.

"Do you get to see your family often?" she asked.

"Probably more than my kids want. I spend three days a week up here. Travel takes up a day. Then I'm home for three."

"So you're away a lot like my parents. Except they've been gone for six years."

She said it flatly, without blinking. I already knew that from her file, of course. I couldn't imagine being away from my kids that long. "That's quite a sacrifice," I said. "It shows their dedication to humanity's future."

"It does show what they're dedicated to," she said.

I shifted in my seat. It wasn't necessary, nor was it my job, to venture deeper into this minefield of childhood abandonment with her. And she was right. I wasn't a therapist, and I tried to think of a way to get us back into safer territory. But then she did it for me.

"Will it hurt?" she asked.

I sighed. "Oh. You mean the scan."

"Yes."

"No, it won't hurt." That was a fairly common question, but one that should have been answered before she got this far. "You'll be in chemical stasis. You won't remember—"

"No, not me . . . her."

"Who?"

"My reference body." Her eyes flicked up to the ceiling and back. "This body."

It was the first time someone had ever asked me that question.

People wonder all the time if it will hurt *them* to undergo the scan. They still think of the reference body as *their* body. But Jessica Mathers had already made the Big Leap. Not the leap of teleportation, which is a common misunderstanding of the term by people outside the industry, but the mental leap that is in some ways even harder than interstellar travel. The Big Leap is the moment when you accept that you are not defined by that one specific body in which you were born. That consciousness is a quantum expression simply housed in a brain. Those who voluntarily abort their teleportation usually do so because they can't make the Big Leap. Those who go through with it usually don't complete the Big Leap until they wake up safely at their destination, feeling just like themselves.

But somehow, Jessica Mathers had already made the Big Leap and landed on the other side. But she did worry about the suffering of the vessel she would leave behind.

"The reference will be in stasis during the scan," I said. "Insensate. No pain."

"But how do you know?"

"What do you mean?"

"I mean, no one has ever asked a reference body if it hurts, because there's nothing left to ask. They get burned up by the scan."

"That's true. But we monitor neurological activity the entire time. If we detect activity in the brain, we abort. We can't scan active neurons. And besides, we scan the brain first, before we process data from the rest of the body, so even if the body were vulnerable to pain, there would be no brain to receive the signal."

She nodded, appearing only somewhat reassured, and since it was my first time answering that question, I didn't have any other responses prepared; I wasn't sure what more I could offer.

"I hope you're right," she finally said.

I used my confident tone. "I am."

"Okay." She shrugged, and I saw doubt in it, but also acceptance. "Any more legal stuff we need to cover?"

I decided to let the matter go. "There are a couple of disclosures I have to run through. First, we guarantee that your teleportation will comply with all the requirements of the International Clone Regulation Treaty. Because of that, if we discover any medical anomalies during your scan—"

"You can't fix it."

I nodded. "We'll notify your parents, of course. But we do not engage in medical alteration or treatment. You'll be reestablished at your destination exactly as you are now. Additionally, the technology that makes teleportation possible is highly regulated by legal, ethical, and moral standards and procedures. At ISTA, we comply in every respect. Throughout the process, your body will never be in a simultaneous condition. In any given moment, there will only ever be one of you. In the extremely unlikely event that a duplicate is created through human or technical error, we follow international statutes to resolve the redundancy."

She nodded again. "Got it."

"That concludes the legalities. Do you have any other questions for me?"

"I don't think so."

"Then let's get you hydrated. Are you hungry?"

"A little."

"I can offer you the best reconstituted food available anywhere in high-earth orbit."

"Sounds delicious."

I led her from my office toward the cafeteria. She seemed to have adjusted fairly quickly to the *Liverpool*'s centripetal gravity. "I believe Carver 1061c has a slightly greater mass than Earth, doesn't it?"

"That's what my parents tell me," she said. "But they are very quick to add that it's within the 'adaptable' range on the Human Gravity Index." She used air quotes. "So I guess I'll get used to it."

"You will."

"And if I ever get back to Earth, I'll be super strong."

"*If* you ever get back to Earth?" We'd arrived at the cafeteria, and I swiped my badge to open the hatch. "Your parents said it's only a one-year survey."

"Right. And they were only supposed to be gone for two years." She stepped through the hatch.

I found myself wondering how two years had turned into six as I ushered her over to the counter, where she picked out some food with disinterest, and I made sure to load her up with fluids and electrolytes. We talked about life with her grandparents, Gram and Pop-Pop. We talked about her school, her friends. She mentioned a girl she liked, someone named Annie, I think. Or maybe it was Abbie. I'm not sure, but I kept things light until it was time for her to go. She walked with me to the teleporter room without any apparent reluctance and used one of the changing rooms to put on her magnetized teleportation suit.

"So, this is the point of no return," Jessica said after she was all prepped. "The one you were talking about."

"Yup, this is it. You okay?"

"I haven't gone spacey yet."

"I hope not. You haven't even left Earth orbit. It's called Deep Space Syndrome for a reason."

"I guess that means I'm still okay."

And she was. I could see her breath had become more rapid. I'm sure her blood pressure and her heart rate had risen, too. But she wasn't even close to panic. I was impressed, and I told her so. Then I opened the hatch, and we entered the zero-gravity environment of the teleporter room. Jessica laughed with delight as we pushed off and floated over to the scanning chamber. It was a common response to zero gravity, but not necessarily for a first-timer in the moments before teleportation.

She climbed into the machine without any hesitation, and I helped her get into position.

"Thanks, Jim," she said. "This wasn't as bad as I thought it would be. Believe it or not, I was pretty nervous about it."

"I couldn't tell. Maybe I'll see you when you come back through?"

"Maybe."

"You ready?"

She took a deep breath and then let it out. She nodded. "Ready."

"Safe travels."

I pushed off from the machine before she could change her mind, or ask any last-second questions, or ask for a glass of water, which I have actually had grown adults do. But Jessica said nothing as I sailed away from her, and a moment later I was through the hatch, back in the *Liverpool*'s artificial gravity. Then I closed the hatch and hit my comm to let the engineers know their traveler was prepared, and they took over from there. Through the narrow window I saw the scanning chamber engage. Jessica couldn't see me, but I watched her face for any signs of fear as the clamshell closed around her. Her eyes were open wide, her breathing still heavy, but otherwise, she seemed ready. More ready than almost anyone I had put in that machine before, or since.

I waited until she was in stasis, wondering how the reunion with her parents would play out. I sure as hell didn't know what I would do or say if I had left my kids for six years. Later, I got the alert on my comm that her reference body had been scanned, and she was on her way.

# 2 — Hades

## AFTER

I WAS THE FIRST THING I REMEMBERED.

Me.

I was me.

And I was there. In a tube of glass, lying naked on a warm, contoured metal plate.

Then I remembered the moment just before that, back in the teleportation room on the *Liverpool*. Jim had just tucked me in, and then the scanning chamber had closed. The stasis drugs had obviously started working almost immediately, because I had no other memories until I opened my eyes in the body printer, and I remembered myself.

The DS *Theseus* didn't look how I expected it to. What I could see of it through the glass, anyway. The room was dark, except for three rays of light punching through the portholes. It seemed I was alone, too, which meant my destination liaison was late, just like Jim, and I guessed my parents hadn't been fully established yet, either. I thought it was strange that I didn't see any medical staff, or at least an engineer or two. I also really wanted to get dressed. But all I could do was cover myself with my hands and wait.

As I lay there, I took inventory of my body, flexing each of my muscles, one at a time. Even all the little muscles around my eyes, my lips, my fingers, my toes. My teleportation counselor had said repeatedly that it was impossible for there to be any errors in the transmission, but I still worried that between the scan of my reference body and the printing of this one, they might have misplaced an appendage, or an organ. But everything seemed present and accounted for.

Except for my liaison. Or anyone else. Which seemed stranger with each moment that passed in darkness and silence.

"Hello?" I called. My voice echoed loudly inside the confines of the body printer. "Can anyone hear me? Maybe come let me out?"

No one came. No one answered me over a comm. The room stayed dark.

I waited a few more minutes, until my breath fogged against the curved glass, and I decided that I had somehow been forgotten. Then I pushed against the chamber's lid.

It didn't budge.

I pushed harder. I even lifted my knees up and strained against the glass, smearing the condensation, but I couldn't open the printer. Greta had tested me for claustrophobia before I left, and I had passed, but we hadn't covered a scenario like that.

"Hello!" I banged on the glass, and panic tightened the air in the chamber. "Somebody help me! Let me out!"

Still no one came, and that was the point when I started to worry that things weren't just strange. Something was wrong. I was on a ship in deep space, orbiting a planet 13.82 light-years from Earth. People don't just forget about the body of the girl they've been printing for the past nine days. Someone had to be running the machine, or I wouldn't be lying there in it. But that someone wasn't around, and the room was dark, and I was stuck.

I decided I had to find my own way out, and it didn't seem like I'd be able to open the lid by force. So I closed my eyes and took deep breaths and thought back to the safety videos they'd shown me during my orientation. That was when I finally remembered the emergency lever, the one they'd told me I'd never have to use, and I felt stupid for freaking out.

I felt for the lever at my side, and a couple of moments later I found it. When I pulled it, the lid released with a dull pop and a hiss of air, and then the glass shell opened easily. I sat up in the darkness and squinted to get a better look at the room around me.

The place had been trashed.

Panels were torn from the walls, exposing bundles of tangled wires, and some of the ship's guts had been ripped out. Cables hung from the openings and snaked across the floor. The few scattered pieces of equipment I could see looked dented and damaged. Even the bulkheads appeared crooked, their edges no longer perfectly joined in the corners.

Then I saw the bed on the floor.

A chill crawled across my shoulders and down my back. It looked like a nest between an outer wall and a control console. There were blankets and a few other random items, like a flashlight and a pile of empty food ration packages. It smelled like a bed, even from across the room. Not terrible, just the familiar, musty odor of sheets that needed to be changed. But that only made it creepier, because it meant that someone had been living in there with me while I was being printed.

That wasn't how destination ships were supposed to run. This was not how a destination ship was supposed to look. I wondered if there had been a mistake, and they'd sent me to the wrong place, some abandoned or derelict ship, possibly light-years from where I was supposed to be. That could explain the awareness spreading through every newly printed cell of my body that something was off, physically. Something I couldn't quite identify.

I looked for anything close by that I could use to cover myself, and right next to the body printer, on a narrow table that pulled down from a bulkhead, I saw underwear, a tank top, and a jumpsuit. Someone had folded them neatly and left them there. For me. A pair of utility boots waited in the shadow of the pull-down table, along with a pair of compression socks.

I slid down from the body printer to the floor, where I felt and heard the gritty scrape of sand beneath my bare feet. There wasn't supposed to be dirt on a spaceship, either. But I hurried, shivering, to pull on the underwear and tank top, then snatched up the jumpsuit and unfolded it with a shake. It wasn't the most comfortable thing, but it was durable because, like all things brought into space, it was meant to be used for a very long time. After I'd put it on, I tugged on the itchy socks and the boots and looked down at myself, toward the floor, and I froze.

The gravity felt wrong. There was too much of it. That was what I had been sensing. It wasn't until I was standing that I was able to iden-tify the slight but persistent pressure on my feet, the pull on my spine. Stronger gravity could only mean one thing, and I scrambled to the nearest porthole in a panic to look outside.

I saw hills. Low, jagged hills covered in purple vegetation.

I wasn't in space. I was somehow on the surface of another planet, but which planet, I had no idea. It could be Carver 1061c, assuming Carver 1061c had purple plants. I'd been way too angry to read any of the material my parents had sent me, so I didn't know for sure.

I looked around again at the chamber, at the bedding and the ra-tions. It wasn't just a very weird destination ship. It was a planetary habitat. Or at least, that's how it was being used. But it sure as hell didn't look like the habitats I'd seen in my parents' pictures. I had no idea where they were, but I needed them to find me and tell me what was going on. Or I needed to find them.

The room only had a single hatch. I moved toward it, and through its window I glimpsed a narrow passageway that looked a lot like the corridors back on the *Liverpool*. Except this one curved away into dark-ness, illuminated only by its dim red emergency lights. I looked at the control panel to my right, and after a moment of hesitation, I used it to open the hatch.

The air in the passage felt looser and smelled less stale, and now I could hear deep, metallic groans and distant pops from elsewhere in the ship.

I called out. "Hello?"

My voice echoed down the passageway. No one answered.

I held my breath and slipped through the doorway, then eased along the corridor one careful step at a time, listening and squinting in the rusty light. Several panels there had also been torn away from the walls, baring the ship's innards. I saw deep gouges in the metal and plastic. I passed three open hatches on my right, but the rooms were pitch-dark and empty, or at least I hoped they were as I hurried by them.

The corridor eventually ended at another closed hatch. When I reached for the control panel, I noticed a few dabs of dark stain on the buttons, and a partial, ruddy handprint on the wall. I stared for a moment, feeling a prickle at the nape of my neck, before finally opening the door.

Natural light poured over me into the passageway. Not ship light, sunlight. I shielded my eyes for a moment, and after my vision adjusted, I found I had reached a juncture where my corridor met with three others. The one to my left seemed like an external air lock. Then I noticed the walls, and my throat tightened.

Handprints painted the panels of the juncture in reddish-brown smears that definitely looked like dried blood. Leathery, crackled puddles of it covered the floor, as if a body or bodies had broken right there, at that spot. I smelled decay in the air and swallowed, finding it hard to breathe as I tried not to imagine the violence that must have taken place there, hoping my parents were okay, wanting suddenly to get out of there.

One of the few things I did know about Carver 1061c—if I was on Carver 1061c—was that it had a breathable atmosphere, and I stumbled toward the air lock. I had no idea what waited for me outside, but I knew I didn't want to stay on the ship, so I opened the internal hatch, entered the air lock, and then opened the external hatch.

A warm breeze rushed in, smelling faintly of old pennies and moss, but clean, and it brushed a few grains of sand against my cheek. I inhaled, able to breathe clearly again, and stepped over the threshold onto dark, alien dirt flecked with gold and green.

The broken and uneven landscape spread out in all directions. Brown hills rose and fell in sharp folds, covered in patches of the purple vegetation that I'd seen through the portholes. They reminded me of ferns. I took a few steps away from the hatch, wanting to get a better look at the ship from the outside, hoping for a clue to figure out where I was and how I got there, but then I saw the volcano, and I had the answer to the first question.

Mount Ida. The killer of Carver 1061c.

I couldn't tell how far away it was. With something that big, normal scale doesn't apply. Its base spread over most of the horizon. Its volcanic slopes rose through several layers of clouds, reaching an altitude so high that I had to crane my neck to see its conical peak. The mountain ruled over the landscape so completely that it seemed to have its own demanding gravity, and I found it hard to pull my eyes away from it, back to the ship.

When I did, I discovered I was right before. It wasn't the DS *Theseus*. At least, not all of it.

The large letters on the battered skin of the vessel told me I had emerged from the port side of one of the *Theseus*'s landers, but huge chunks of it seemed to have been ripped off. Other parts had been caved in, deforming its teardrop shape with massive dents. The areas of its belly that I could see bore the scorch marks of atmosphere reentry, and some of the heat shielding had been torn away. Whatever had brought it down here from orbit, the trip hadn't been easy. It didn't even look like the landing gear had deployed.

I looked up at the sky and wondered if the lander's parent ship was still in orbit, and if my parents were still on it. I stared into that blue void so long my eyes watered, and I got dizzy running through the reasons an evacuation of the *Theseus* might have been necessary. An emergency of some kind, for sure, but something very, very bad. There weren't that many possibilities, according to the safety presentation on high-orbit and deep-space ships that ISTA had made me watch. Externally, an asteroid strike or a solar flare could do it. Internally, one of the main systems would have to malfunction in a catastrophic way, like a reactor failure.

I looked down at my hands. If something had gone wrong with the reactor, the body that had just been made for me might have been bathed in radiation while it was still being printed. I had no idea what that would mean, but my guesses ranged from cancer to mutant monster, even though I looked and felt fine.

A cloud passed in front of the sun. I figured that's what I might as well call the star in the sky. The deep shade gave me chills as it glided over me, the lander, the ground, and then the sun came back. I decided to circle the lander, just to see if I could find any more clues about the catastrophe that had brought it down, and I moved toward the rear of the ship.

As I came around the back, I saw the deep furrow the lander had carved in the skin of Carver 1061c as it crashed. That trench must have been a mile long, and I had to climb down into it and back out again, pulling against the planet's extra gravity to reach the opposite side of the ship. The damage there looked a lot like what I had seen on the first side, but I found the greatest destruction at the front, where the cockpit had been completely crushed. I knew the pilot's body couldn't have survived the impact.

As I returned to the side of the lander I had come out of, something caught my eye a short distance away. It looked like a mound of soil, but its shape was too regular to be natural. I moved toward it, already somewhat out of breath from the walking I'd been doing. The planet's gravity had been slowly getting to me, growing more insistent. My feet felt heavier. My whole body felt heavier, and I moved more slowly be-cause of it.

When I approached the mound, I saw three more just like it nearby. Each was about a meter wide, and about two meters long, the dirt dry and packed hard. Then I noticed the signs, and my stomach turned. Someone had attached name badges, like the patches on uniforms, to pieces of scrap metal from the ship and placed one at the head of each mound. Each grave.

I made myself read them.

> *Rebecca Sharpe*
> *Evan Martin*
> *Elizabeth Kovalenko*
> *Amira Kateb*
> *Alberto Gutiérrez*

The last plaque was different from the others. No badge, no mound, just a name scratched into a piece of metal, marking a flat patch of dirt next to the others. I sighed, relieved that none of the names belonged to my parents, and that none sounded familiar. Then I felt a bit guilty, because even though I didn't know those people, someone had cared enough about their broken bodies to bury them.

"What happened to you?" I whispered.

I shivered and turned away. Cemeteries had always freaked me out because graves were for your last body. They were terminal. I hurried back toward the broken nose of the lander, but as I moved around it and down the side of the ship, something rustled the purple ferns on my right.

I jumped and spun to face it but saw nothing except the plants swaying a few meters away. Their stalks only came as high as my knees, so whatever was out there, it was low to the ground.

I kept my back against the lander, watching the ferns as I slowly inched toward the hatch. Not that I wanted to go back inside the ship, but that seemed better than staying outside it with some kind of alien. I'd never seen an extraterrestrial life-form before, but I *had* just seen five graves, so it was easy to imagine something deadly lurking out there. Something with fangs. Or claws. Or venom. Or all three. Or something completely alien and far worse.

Or it could be totally safe, like a puppy. If I had read the shit my parents had sent me, I might have known what it was. But I hadn't read the shit my parents had sent me, so I crept away from it, refusing to blink or breathe, watching.

I'd moved a few meters when the thing burst through the ferns toward me. I almost bolted, but then it stopped, still hidden in the vegetation, clearly able to see me or sense me in some way.

I tried to reassure myself that its behavior might not be hostile. It might instead be evidence of curiosity, or even its fear of me, and its need to observe me in case I was the kind of threat I feared it to be. But since I had no way of knowing its intent, I continued to hurry down the side of the ship toward the hatch, expecting it to follow me.

But the ferns didn't move, and I wondered if the alien was still watching me, or if it had simply decided that I was neither interesting nor a threat. Then something stirred the plants much closer, directly in front of me, scratching in the dirt and snapping stems and fronds.

There were two of them.

"Stay back!" I shouted, without even knowing if the things had ears. "Both of you!"

"There's only one of them."

I flinched at a very familiar voice. An impossible voice.

She stood in the doorway to the air lock, one foot in, one foot out. She wore the same boots I wore, and she wore the same type and size of jumpsuit, though her clothes were dirtier than mine. She wore my face, though it was dirtier, too. She wore my hands, and my body.

She was me.

Not metaphorically. She didn't look like me. She *was* me.

A horrified shock immobilized every muscle, my mouth stuck in the open position. In that moment I lost every thought that had been in my head. I lost Carver 1061c, and I lost the alien somethings. I lost myself, even as I was looking at myself.

"They live underground," she said with my voice, nodding toward the ferns. "Come inside. I'll explain everything else."

# 3 — DS *Theseus*

## BEFORE

I AM THE FIRST THING I REMEMBER.

Me.

I am me.

And I'm here. In a tube of glass, lying naked on a warm, contoured metal plate.

Then I remember the moment just before that, back in the teleportation room on the *Liverpool*, when Jim tucked me in, and the scanning chamber closed. The stasis drugs obviously went to work almost immediately, because I don't remember anything else. Now I'm here in the body printer, remembering myself.

The room beyond the glass is filled with a gentle light that isn't too warm or too cold. I can see people moving around at the edges of my vision, maybe doctors, or technicians, and I cover myself with my hands. At that point, one of the figures turns, then approaches me and smiles down through the glass. She presses a button on the controls, and I hear her voice through a speaker near my head.

"Jessica, welcome to the DS *Theseus*. My name is Amira Kateb, and I'll be your liaison." She speaks with a slight French accent, looks like she's in her late twenties, and has gorgeous skin. She's wearing a white jumpsuit, her name embroidered on a patch in blue. "I'm going to open the printer so you can get dressed, okay?"

I nod, grateful.

There's a gentle pop, and the hiss of releasing air, and then the glass lid lifts away. Amira helps me sit up and wraps a blanket around me. I'm not cold, but I'm glad to not be sitting there naked, even though the other woman and two men in the room don't seem to be paying any attention, their faces lit by harsh computer screens and consoles that are much more interesting than me, apparently. Then again, they've been watching my body printing from the inside out for the last nine days. Not much left to see after that.

This room, with its sleek walls the color of ash, is much smaller than the scanning chamber on the *Liverpool*. But the technology to read my data is completely different from the technology needed to turn that data into a living body. In addition to the printer that established me here, there are three others. They're empty.

Amira supports me as I climb out, and my bare feet touch the cold, smooth floor. With my first steps I realize the gravity here is still only partial-Earth, but I manage to walk to a narrow changing booth without stumbling too much. Inside, I find underwear, a tank top, and a jumpsuit like Amira's, all of which I put on. The suit isn't comfortable, but it's durable, a quality I should probably get used to out here.

When I'm dressed, Amira finds me some boots in my size.

"How do you feel?" she asks.

"Fine," I say. "Like . . . myself. I assume that's a good thing."

She chuckles. "Yes. That is a very good thing."

"Where are my parents?" I glance at the empty printers. "I thought they were supposed to be here."

"Yes, your parents." She nods and tries to usher me toward one of the hatches. "There has been a delay."

I don't budge. "A delay?"

"Everything is fine—I assure you. No cause for alarm. The scanning chamber at New Beijing needed a minor repair before they—"

"A repair? For what?" A few of the techs finally look up at me.

"Only a minor technical issue. They didn't elaborate. The point is, your parents are now on their way, and they should be established here in two days."

"Where are they now?"

"We used the printers on the *Theseus*'s landers, to spare you seeing their bodies before full arrival. It can be . . . upsetting."

She's probably right.

"They will be here soon," she adds. "In the meantime—"

"It's your job to keep me entertained." I smile, remembering Jim. "I get it."

"Entertained?" She shakes her head with a slight frown. "No, not quite. It is my job to show you around and make sure you have what you need. I'm sure you'll be glad not to have a babysitter."

I am, and yet, I'm not sure what I'll do with myself for two days on board a strange ship until my parents arrive, especially as Amira gives me the tour and I realize how small the *Theseus* is, even with the two landers that function as living space when they're attached to the ship like barnacles. But we don't enter those, for obvious reasons.

The corridors are tight, the ceilings are low, and the rooms are cramped. Amira shows me my cabin, and it's not much bigger than the bed that pulls down from the wall. The only place on the ship I can really stretch out is the common room, where the tour ends.

"This is where the crew and passengers heat their food," she says. "And we gather here to socialize."

I see they have an entertainment console. The shows and the games are probably old, but the menu lists a shooter I liked a few years ago, so at least I'll have that to play.

Amira crosses to one of the common room's far walls and presses a button. I hear the hum of a motor, and then several large panels slide up toward the ceiling, revealing an array of wide windows.

I gasp and step my nose up to the glass. "Whoa!"

Outside the ship, I see the forward length of the *Theseus* stretching ahead into space, like a rocket taking off. It's spinning, and the stars are rotating with it in a slow arc. Then my perspective shifts as I realize I'm the one who's moving, with the ship's gravity-simulating rotation. The *Theseus* is basically a barrel rolling around a central axle, and I'm standing at the edge of the inside lip, staring into the endless space that lies beyond the end of the ship. The view is breathtaking and dizzying.

"Whoa," I repeat, mouth open.

Amira nods. "The stars have inspired both awe and terror since the beginnings of humanity." Then she tilts slightly in my direction. "My educational background is anthropology and psychology."

"Why were the windows closed?"

She shrugs. "Some people find the motion gives them vertigo. Most rooms don't have windows, and those that do can be closed, if it bothers you."

"It doesn't," I whisper.

She nods and then turns her back on the view to face the common room. "All the crew come and go here, so I am sure you will meet everyone before too long."

"How many are there?"

"On the ship? Fifteen. There's a command crew, an engineering crew, and a few scientists. You already saw Dr. Gutiérrez. He was there when you came out of the printer, along with two of his technicians, David and Liz."

I glance down at myself. "Yeah, I was kinda trying not to make eye contact."

"Naturally." She bows her head. "Our captain is Rebecca Sharpe."

The name is familiar to me, and then I remember it from a novel I read in English class.

"You might be interested to know her son is with her," Amira adds.

"So I guess I'm not the only space brat out here."

"No." She seems unamused by the term. "His name is Duncan. He's about your age, sixteen."

I wonder if this Duncan guy's mom gave him a choice about living on a spaceship, or if he chose to come out here. I hope he isn't weird. He'll be the only person my age I get to talk to for a year.

"You'll find food here, when you're hungry." Amira shows me the cupboards where they keep the ration packs. "Try to limit yourself to three meals a day, plus a snack."

"Okay."

"The lighting on the ship creates an artificial twenty-four-hour cycle of day and night. We're set to SST, and . . ." She looks at the comm on her wrist. "It's just after three in the afternoon. Do you have any other questions?"

"Yeah. Where's the planet?"

"Carver 1061c? It's on the other side of the *Theseus*. We face most of the living space away from it."

"Why?"

"A fixed object that large can make the vertigo worse." She draws a spiral in the air with her finger. "The best way to observe the planet is from the ship's hub, in microgravity."

"I'm allowed to go there?"

"Yes. You're allowed anywhere on the ship except for the Belfry and the reactor module at the rear of the ship."

"The Belfry?"

"The forward command module. And for the time being, I think it would be wise to avoid the landers."

"Yeah, you don't have to worry about that."

"I didn't think so. Oh, you can use any of the computer terminals here in the common room, in addition to the smaller unit in your quarters. All the files you wanted to bring with you are here. Do you remember the username and password you set up?"

"Yes." But that reminds me of something. "Amira, what—"

"Ms. Kateb, please."

"Oh." So not a first-name-basis kind of liaison. "Okay, Ms. Kateb, what if I want to send a message back home?"

"We open the Tangle twice a day, at midnight and noon. If you wish to send a message, simply get it queued before those times."

"Okay, thanks."

She nods in a final kind of way and checks her comm again. It seems she's eager to be rid of me. Jim might have been eager to get rid of me, too, but he didn't show it. I don't know why her impatience irritates me, but it does. After all, I've just traveled almost fourteen light-years, my parents aren't here yet, and I'm all alone on a strange ship.

"Am I keeping you from something?" I ask.

"Actually, there is another matter that requires my attention. Do you need anything else from me?"

"A bedside manner?" I say, but not quite far enough under my breath.

"Excuse me?"

I pause, then shrug. "Never mind."

Her brow descends. "Is there something you need that I haven't addressed? Have you found my services unsatisfactory in some way?"

"It's not that." I don't know why I'm irritated with her. It's not her fault I'm here. "Sorry. It's just . . . my last liaison was different."

"Jim Kelly, wasn't it?"

I nod.

"Well." She folds her arms across her chest. "We don't all have the luxury of an assignment in Earth orbit with the ability to go home and see our families on a regular basis. I'm sure that would do wonders for my bedside manner, too."

I hadn't thought about that. I guess I'd assumed that everyone out here volunteered, like my parents. I feel my cheeks getting hot and drop my eyes to the floor. "I'm sorry."

"If you need anything else, please don't hesitate to ask." Her pleas-
ant tone is a makeup-thin veneer I can see right through. "That is, after
all, what I am here for. Now, if you'll excuse me, there really is something pressing that requires my attention."

With that, she turns and leaves me alone in the common room,
and I stand there for a moment or two feeling like shit. Then I cross
to one of the armchairs and slump into it, somewhat awkwardly in the
lower gravity, and face the black expanse of the entertainment console's
screen. In its dark reflection, I see myself and the stars behind me. I
imagine that I'm looking into a dim parallel universe where a different
me is leaving the *Theseus* and heading back to Earth.

But I'm not going anywhere. I'm trapped.

The glass-and-metal skin of the ship suddenly seems very fragile
and thin against the void of space, and I feel a growing sense of real
panic, the first since I left my grandparents' house to come here. My
teleportation counselor, Greta, talked me through concepts like "iden-
tity permanence" and "body transience," but we never talked about
what interstellar travel would actually be like. Now I'm here, orbiting
a planet that's orbiting a star that's nothing more than a speck of light
when seen from Earth. I'm so far from home, my mammal mind still
fails to hold the distance and scale in a thought that makes any sense.
My heartbeat is fast, and my breathing is shallow. It feels like the time I
got lost in a house of mirrors for six whole minutes when I was a little
kid, but instead of a carnival tent that Pop-Pop promised would be fun,
this is the fucking universe.

Maybe I'm starting to go spacey.

I think about playing a game or watching something to take my
mind off everything, but I doubt any show is that good. I'm here, and
there isn't anything I can do to change that, and I can't even yell at my
parents about it. Not for another two days.

The muscles in my legs are restless, wanting to coil up tight. I bounce my knees, but it's not enough to relieve the stress, maybe because there isn't enough gravity pulling against me. I have to move, so I get up to go explore more of the ship.

On my way out of the common room, I bump into a bald man not much taller than me. He has the build of a tree stump, and his jumpsuit is stained and looks worn out. His name badge reads EVAN MARTIN.

"Pardon me," he says, backing up. Then he moves aside, allowing me into the narrow corridor.

"Thank you."

I slip through the hatch, and when I'm out of the way, he steps halfway into the common room before turning back toward me.

"You're the traveler," he says. "Mathers?"

"I am."

"Your parents are studying the volcano, right? Mount Ida?"

I glance at the ceiling and sigh. "Uh-huh."

"What, you don't like volcanoes?"

"I don't have anything against volcanoes. Unless they are about to blow up. Or they're on an uninhabited planet that my parents want to study."

He grins. "Well, I think volcanoes are magical mountains." Then he winks.

"Uh, okay?" He's acting weird, but his words have nudged a memory.

"You know that game?" he asks.

I do, but I haven't thought about it in years. I used to love it, and I would have played it every night with my parents if they had been willing, which they weren't. But I've never met anyone else who's even heard of it.

"How do you know about that game?" I ask.

"My daughter used to like it. She's about your age. I just appreciated the fact that it was an actual, old-school board game we played sitting around the table. I'm Evan, by the way. Engineer." He pats the bulkhead between us. "I keep this place running."

"Ah, so it's your fault there wasn't a malfunction that prevented me from teleporting."

He holds up his hands. "Hey, don't blame that on me. Teleportation has its own team. But everything else is mine and my crew's, from the spheromak to the command console."

"The sphero-what?"

"Spheromak. The imposed-dynamo current drive. The ship's nuclear reactor is my responsibility. Along with most everything else. Except for the teleporters."

"In that case, can you tell me how I get to the ship's hub? I want to see the planet."

He leans back out into the corridor and points with his whole arm, like he's sighting along it. "Go down this passageway until you come to your first intersection. Turn to the right and look for the spoke that connects the drum to the hub. You can't miss it."

"Thanks."

He gives me a flick of a salute with a couple of fingers. "Welcome aboard, Mathers."

Then he goes into the common room, and I follow the gentle curvature of the corridor's floor leading down and up away from me. When I reach the first intersection, I turn to the right, and about five meters along that passage, I come to a ladder marked D2, which disappears through an opening in the ceiling. As I step closer to the ladder's base, I look up into a very, very long tube that can't be much wider than a meter. From where I'm standing, the far end is little more than a distant dot, and I don't think a person would need to be claustrophobic to find the tunnel intimidating. I grasp the rung at eye level, take a deep breath, and start climbing.

After I've put several meters behind me, the grip of the simulated gravity weakens. I feel myself going weightless, which makes the climbing easier. My breathing echoes up and down the tube, and several meters later, I'm in microgravity, and this ladder doesn't have an up or a down anymore. I'm just floating, pulling myself along it, gliding and flying like a superhero as I remember the training I had to go through before teleportation. I occasionally catch a rung with the toe of a boot, and that throws off my form, or I bump a shoulder into the side of the tube, but for the most part, I keep it graceful. Before long, I reach the hub at the end of the tunnel, and the vertigo Amira talked about finally hits me.

I'm basically clinging to the inside of a spoke that connects the rolling barrel of the ship to the stationary hub, but this close to the center, I'm whipping around and around like I'm on an amusement park ride. I know that if I just kick off from the ladder and sail into the center of the hub, the world will stop spinning. But this is worse than anything from my training, and my body simply won't let me. I grip the ladder's rungs until the spinning tingles my cheeks and turns my stomach.

"You just have to go for it," I hear someone say. A guy's voice.

I look around for the source, and I glimpse a boy my age just off to the side, around the edge of the hatch inside the hub. As fast as I'm moving, I can't get a good look at him, but I assume he's the other space brat. Duncan, the captain's son. I'm afraid if I open my mouth to answer him, I'll throw up.

"Seriously," he says, "just kick off from the ladder. It's only hard the first time."

I have to do something fast, so I bring my knees up and brace my boots on one of the highest rungs, and then I launch myself like I'm going off a diving board.

I shoot into the hub, but I guess I used too much force, because I fly right past Duncan, through the middle of the ship. I'm about to collide with the opposite wall, close to the edge of the tube I just escaped as it swings around to meet me.

"Fucking inertia!" I shout, flailing, then brace myself with my hands and forearms in front of my face.

Before I smack into the wall, I feel a hand around my ankle, and it gives me a sharp tug. It's enough to slow me down so I don't hit the wall as hard as I would have, and I'm able to stop myself with my hands. I push off and spin around.

Duncan floats nearby, one hand holding on to a rail that runs along the wall. He's not a big guy, but he isn't small, either. He has dark hair and a long face, with a sharp jaw, and blue eyes that are just a bit close together. None of his features are particularly attractive on their own, but they go together pretty well. He's wearing a jumpsuit like mine.

"Next time, a gentle push will do the trick," he says, not laughing at me, but almost. I can tell, and it pisses me off.

"Aren't you the one who told me to just go for it?"

"Not like that."

"I had it under control."

I didn't, but he lets that go. "I'm Duncan."

"Jessica," I say, looking around. "Jess."

The hub is like a dark subway tunnel, about ten meters wide and hundreds of meters long, full of shadows and lit by sharp and infrequent lights. Storage lockers and crates line the walls, all strapped down tight, and the windows near me offer a view of the inside of the ship's barrel as it rolls around us. I would have thought the rotation of the spokes would be noisy, but it just sounds like the *Theseus* is whispering to itself.

"What brings you to the hub?" Duncan asks.

"They told me I could see the planet from here."

"Not here." He points to my right. "You have to go forward, toward the Belfry."

"Thanks." I tip my head to the side. "What about you? What are you doing here?"

"Depends." He pushes off from the wall, sails past me, and lands on the other side, and I think I'm supposed to be impressed. "Usually I just want to be by myself. There aren't a lot of places for that on a ship like this."

I twist and pivot to face him. "How long did you stay mad at your mom? Or are you still mad at her?"

"What do you mean?"

"I mean for dragging you all the way out here."

He pauses. "She didn't drag me out here. I asked her to let me come. She actually wanted me to keep living with my dad."

"Wait." I close my eyes and shake my head. "You mean you chose to leave Earth and live on a spaceship?"

"Yeah, I did."

I'm baffled. "Why would you do that?"

He looks equally confused. "Why would you *not* do that?"

The answer to his question is so obvious that I don't even know how to reply, but before I can, he looks over his shoulder toward the Belfry and says, "Come on." Then he pushes off, sailing headfirst down the middle of the hub, gliding in and out of the spotlights.

That's the direction I wanted to go anyway, so I follow him, but not quite as elegantly. He flies a straight line, while I ricochet off the sides, but he doesn't say anything and barely glances back. It takes a few minutes for me to remember my training and figure out the way my body moves in micro-g. I start to get the hang of it as the hub brightens and we come out from under the shadow of the barrel.

Duncan glides up to land against a window, but when I try to join him, I don't stop where I plan to and bump hard into his shoulder. Before I can apologize, I look out the window and see Carver 1061c for the first time. I mean, really see it. Because pictures don't count. They don't prepare you.

There's a whole planet down there that isn't mine. I can see through the swirls and stripes of cloud that it has oceans, and reddish-brown continents, but they're the wrong shapes, and I'm surprised that I suddenly miss the familiar contours of Earth.

"Just look at that," Duncan says.

But he doesn't need to say it, because I can't take my eyes away from it.

"Less than one percent of the earth's population gets to see anything like this." His head is close to mine as we both look through the window. "My mom works for ISTA, and that makes me one of the lucky ones. That's why I'm here." He turns to glance at me. "But you're even luckier."

"I am?"

He nods toward the planet. "You get to go down there."

# 4 — Hades

## AFTER

I STOOD THERE OUTSIDE THE LANDER, FROZEN AND confused.

I wondered if I was dreaming, still lying in a body printer on the *Theseus*, not yet fully established and awake. No one had told me whether it was possible to dream during teleportation. I hoped it was, because no other explanation for coming face-to-face with myself would make me feel better about it. But unlike my childhood nightmares, this dream didn't collapse when I woke up. This one kept going.

A moment went by, and when I didn't follow her back through the hatch, she reappeared, and her face jarred me again.

"This isn't a dream," she said. "This is real."

I felt dizzy. "How did you know—"

She sighed, sounding exhausted and impatient. "I'm you. You're me. Now come inside."

She disappeared again, and this time I found myself trudging after her through the hatch. Instead of turning to the right, which would have brought us back to the room with the body printer, she strode down the corridor straight ahead. I walked behind her into unknown ship territory, keeping a safe distance between us, studying her. In a disorienting way, I recognized her walk, the movement of her hips, though I had never seen myself from this angle. I felt self-conscious and tried to walk differently from her.

We passed a few storage lockers and then came to a hatch on the left. She opened it and disappeared into a darkened room.

I stayed outside in the corridor, waiting. No way was I going in there. But a moment later, she switched on a portable lantern, and I saw that she stood in what appeared to be the lander's narrow galley. I stepped through the open hatch, and the air inside the room was musty and stifling. There was a very small counter for preparing food, and a table in the middle of the space surrounded by chairs, all bolted to the floor. A couple of thick, round columns supported a low ceiling, and two black screens stared at me from the far wall.

"Are you hungry?" she asked, voice flat, then walked toward the counter without waiting for my answer. "There's plenty of food."

I barely understood her question. It was far too normal to fit what was happening, and when I didn't reply, she looked at me for a moment. Then she sighed again.

"Right." She gestured for me to sit. "Let's talk first."

I glanced at the open hatch and corridor a few feet away, then picked the chair closest to the exit and moved slowly and deliberately toward it, keeping my eyes on her as I sat. She took the seat directly across the table from me, and I got my first really good look at her face by the cold light of the lantern between us.

She wasn't exactly like me, after all. Or at least, it wasn't like looking in a mirror. Her nose seemed off, just a little bit. Same with her eyes, which appeared red, maybe from crying or lack of sleep, and her cheeks and forehead bore smudges of dirt and grease. And I noticed a small scar near her hairline that I didn't have.

"It's weird, right?" she said, her voice stale, her words a bit slow. "I've been watching you print for nine days, so I had a head start at getting used to the idea. Sort of."

I still couldn't think of what to say, but I didn't want to talk anyway. It felt as if speaking to her would turn the whole situation into something real.

"You can see it in the nose." She pointed at the middle of her face. "I figured out it's because a mirror actually reverses everything. So right now we're seeing what other people have always seen when they look at us."

"I . . ." Nothing else came out.

She leaned toward me, propping her folded arms on the polished white table, and waited.

But I had nothing more to give her. Too many questions clawed and competed to be asked, climbing over each other in the nest of my head. *Whats* and *hows* and *whys*, all cutting one another off before I could ask any of them.

"Okay," she said. "How about I just answer some of the questions I know you'll eventually get around to asking. Sound good?" She glanced around the room. "You've probably figured out this is a lander from the *Theseus*. I was established on the *Theseus*, just like I was supposed to be. On schedule. But Mom and Dad were late. So I had to wait around for them a couple of days. Before they finished printing, there was an accident. I'm still not sure exactly what it was. Something to do with the reactor. Evan tried to—" She paused. "Evan was the ship's engineer. He tried to fix the reactor, but he couldn't. So we evacuated. You saw the graves."

I thought back to the name badges and the mounds of dirt, and I nodded slowly.

"Evan's body broke in the crash. He was in the cockpit." She tossed her words on the table like cards, with all the dispassion of a blackjack dealer. "He volunteered for that because he said his body was broken anyway, from the radiation. But everyone else broke, too."

"M—" I cleared my throat, finding my voice at last. "Mom and Dad?"

"They never arrived."

I didn't know if that made me feel better or worse. "So . . . is it just you? You're alone here?"

She nodded.

"That means you buried them." I tried to imagine myself doing something that daunting and couldn't.

She paused. Then nodded again.

I thought of the dried blood I had seen, and I knew, however bad I imagined it had been, it was probably worse for her. "I'm sorry."

"Thanks." She leaned back in her chair. "I've been here for two weeks. But I've had the lander for shelter, and like I said, there's plenty of food. The passive water reclamation system is working." She unfolded her arms and gripped the edge of the table. "What's not working is the distress beacon. It got damaged in the crash. I thought it was just a power supply problem, so I started going through the ship, trying to see if I could reroute energy to it from another system."

"You know how to do that?" I asked. I didn't know how to do that.

"I've picked up a few things. But clearly not enough. I blew out the power in some parts of the ship." She looked down at her hands. "And that did something to the body printer."

I leaned forward. "What happened?"

"I don't know for sure. I never used that room, and I wasn't in there when the power surge hit. The body printer just activated itself and pulled up your data. I think you were about a day and a half into your printing before I discovered you, and I didn't even know it was you until I figured out how to read the display. That was a few days in." She reached up and scratched her forehead, still staring down at the table. "It was an accident."

"It?" I asked. "You mean me. I'm the accident."

She nodded.

I didn't feel like an accident. I felt like myself. I was me, and I knew that as surely as I knew I had been on the *Liverpool* with Jim Kelly. But the girl sitting across the table from me had also been on the *Liverpool* with Jim Kelly. Because she was also me. Her time on the *Theseus*, the evacuation, and everything since the crash, those memories were the only differences between us. A few weeks. That was all.

"The lander's distress beacon still isn't working," she said. "ISTA doesn't know we're down here. They may not even know what happened to the *Theseus*."

I wondered what had happened to the other passengers and crew members, the ones whose graves I hadn't seen. "And Mom and Dad are . . . ?"

"Like I said, they never arrived."

"Can we pull up their data? What if we just establish them here?"

"I thought about that, so I checked the printer while you were outside exploring."

"And?"

"It's dead. Must have used up whatever power it had printing you."

I couldn't tell if she meant for that to sound like an accusation. It felt like one. But I hadn't asked for this. Who would choose to be a clone? Because that's what I was. I had come second, so according to the law, I was the simultaneous condition that Jim had said could never happen. I wasn't supposed to exist.

My chest tightened, and I felt a stabbing pain, right in the center.

"Sorry," she said. "I know this is a lot."

My heart raced and skipped, out of control, like it was about to explode. I gasped, unable to breathe, and my vision went blurry at the edges.

"Hey." She leaned toward me. "Are you—are you okay? You look really pale."

I couldn't answer her. I thought I was having a heart attack, my clone body already breaking down. Suffocating. Dying.

She got up from her seat. "Just breathe, okay?" Then she took a step around the table toward me. "I think you're in shock—"

"Don't touch me!" I scrambled out of my seat to get away from her. I didn't want her anywhere near me. I ran through the hatch, almost blind, turned right, stumbled down the corridor to the intersection, and then burst through the air lock.

My boots hit the dirt outside hard, and I skidded to a stop a few paces from the ship. I leaned forward, hands on my knees, sucking air deep into my lungs. Then I turned my face up to the sky, closed my eyes, and counted inhales and exhales, slow and even despite the pounding of my heart in my ears and throat.

The breeze helped to calm me, and the panicked tingling all over my body gradually subsided. After a few moments, I lowered my chin and opened my eyes on the purple ferns.

"It'll be okay."

She stood behind, and I spun around to face her. "How can you say that? How can this ever be okay? You and me—" I made a frantic gesture back and forth between us. "This isn't supposed to happen! Ever!"

"Maybe not," she said. "But maybe—maybe when you look closely, a star you thought was one star is actually two."

"What the hell does that mean?"

She shook her head. "I don't know. Nothing. I just know I thought about this the whole time you were printing, and I am not this body. You are not that body. We're the same person, like the same flavor of ice cream in two different cones. Our memories are ninety-nine percent the same. We were both mad at Mom and Dad because we didn't want to come here. We both have a crush on Avery. We were both sad we wouldn't get to see her unicorn costume for the party, where we had planned to tell her how we feel."

The mention of Avery grounded me, because no one else in the universe knew how I felt about her. She was going to send me pictures of her costume over the Tangle. She was something real, something from before my teleportation, and it hurt to think about her.

"What about when we go back?" I asked.

"What do you mean?"

"Which one of us gets our life? We can't both be Jessica. You know that—"

"I don't know that!" Her sudden anger surprised me, and it seemed to surprise her, too, because she closed her eyes and held still for a moment before continuing. "What I *do* know is that I could have pulled the plug on you." She took a step toward me and pointed her finger at the middle of my chest. "I could have shut down the printer before it finished establishing you here, and I didn't."

"Why not?" I asked.

"Do you really want me to answer that question?"

I didn't like thinking about not existing, but I said, "Yes, I do."

She adjusted her stance, folded her arms, and stared hard at me. I knew that look, but it was weird to have it directed at me. It was my look when I wanted someone to know I had made up my mind. "No," she said.

"What do you mean, *no*?"

"No. I won't answer that question."

"Why not?"

"Because I want you to think about it. You're me. Imagine I'm inside the printer, but my heart is already beating before you realize I'm there. I'm alive. Tell me what you would do."

So I did. I imagined myself as the sole survivor of a horrific crash, standing over the body printer, watching another me being made, cell by cell, layer by layer of bone, muscle, and skin. I imagined myself doing what needed to be done, putting an end to the process, terminating the life growing inside the machine. That wouldn't be considered murder by any cop or judge, but somehow it felt like murder to me, which meant I apparently wasn't as far along in my body dissociation as Greta thought I was.

"Well?" she said. "Would you do it?

"No," I said quietly, and thought about my reference body.

"Okay." Her voice softened. "Then no more of this talk. This subject is banned from Hades."

"Hades?"

"That's what I named this planet. It just didn't feel like a Carver 1061c to me. And also, this place is hell."

I nodded. "Okay, then. Hades it is."

"And remember, we are both Jessica. Equally."

"You mean like half-and-half? Then I get the half with Avery." I smiled to show I was joking, but I also wasn't. I knew that whenever we got off that planet, we would have to deal with the fact that we couldn't both fit in the same life, the same ice cream cone. "So now what?" I asked. "Do you—"

The thing in the ferns rustled again, and I flinched away from the sound. "What *is* that?"

"It's okay," she said. "It's harmless."

"But what is it?"

"They look like a mix between a mole and a snake. They live underground. I think they eat the worms that live in the roots of the ferns." She pauses. "They're big worms."

I did not like the description of the alien being part snake, or the mention of big worms, and stared into the purple vegetation. "You sure they're not dangerous?"

"Yeah," she said. "They're everywhere, so if they were, I think I would have found out by now."

I finally lifted my attention from the ferns to the surrounding landscape. "What else have you seen here?"

She shrugged and gazed outward with me. "Not many other life-forms. I think the mole-snake, the ferns, and the worms are all pioneer organisms."

I didn't know that term. But she did. I looked at her with a frown, wondering about that 1 percent of memories we didn't share.

"Pioneer organisms are the first to bounce back after a mass extinction," she added.

I detected a hint of condescension in her voice, a casual superiority I recognized in the same way I knew her posture. She was doing to me what I'd done to others when I knew something they didn't. But I didn't want her to take any satisfaction from it. "So do you have a plan?" I asked. "What are we supposed to do now?"

"We need to let ISTA know what happened."

"But you said the beacon is broken."

"It is." She turned around and pointed at Mount Ida. "But ISTA landed a habitat farther up the base of the volcano for Mom and Dad. It's just sitting there, waiting for us, and it has all the supplies we would need."

"Does it have a beacon?"

"Even better. It has a Tangle."

If I had paid better attention to the information my parents had sent me, I might have thought of that. I tried to take in the mountain again, but its size still confounded me. Back on Earth, I would have assumed something that high in the sky was a weird cloud, not a volcano. The impossible scale of it made it hard to estimate how far away it was.

"How long will it take to get there?" I asked.

"I don't know."

"So it could take a long time."

She nodded. "It could take a very long time."

"That means we don't know how much food and water to pack. And maybe we won't even be able to find the habitat. And there might be other aliens out there that you haven't seen yet."

She paused. "I guess so."

I raised my right eyebrow at her in obvious skepticism, a movement she would surely recognize. Then I said, "What if we stayed here? In the lander?"

She rolled her eyes. "We can't."

"Why not?

"Because we can't."

"But we have shelter here. We have food and—"

"No!" Once again, her raised voice startled me. "We can't stay here. You don't know shit, okay? You're just a—you're a liability. That's not your fault. But for now, you just have to trust me."

"A *liability*?" I knew how unprepared I was, but the disdain in her voice shocked and hurt me, even as I had begun to sense that something wasn't right with her. I tried to keep my voice calm. "I just want to know why we can't stay," I said. "Is it dangerous here?"

"No." She turned away, hugging herself. "You just . . . you don't know what it's been like for me. I would have left a long time ago, but I was waiting for you. And the others are counting on us. Mom and Dad are counting on us."

I knew that was the simple, undeniable truth of it. "Then when do we—"

The ferns parted, silencing me, and a mole-snake emerged. It didn't look anything like the creature I had imagined, based on the name she'd given it. I would have called it something different. I had pictured scales, or lizard skin, but this creature seemed to be covered in short, white fur. It was more like a large ferret, although its wide, flat head did resemble the shape of a snake's. It stared at us with small, black button eyes, like a stuffed animal, and it nodded its head up and down, as if answering yes to a question someone had just asked. It had delicate, feather-like whiskers, and long claws on its feet, but the rest of its sinuous body remained hidden in the ferns.

"Whoa," I whispered.

"That's the first extraterrestrial life-form you've seen." She offered me a slight smile, but there was still something patronizing in her expression that I couldn't read.

"It's kinda cute," I said.

"Really?" She cocked her head to the side and regarded the creature for a moment, then shrugged. "If you say so. Now, back to your question."

I wondered briefly how we could look at the same creature so differently if we were the same person. "My question?"

"You were going to ask when we should leave."

She was right, I was.

"I think it'll take us a full day to organize and pack," she said. "So let's plan on heading out the day after tomorrow."

"Oh—okay," I said. That felt very soon. But I nodded and noticed that the ferret, or the mole-snake, had retreated back into the ferns.

# 5—DS *Theseus*

## BEFORE

I FLOAT IN THE HUB NEXT TO DUNCAN, LOOKING down at Carver 1061c. "I don't *get* to go down there," I say. "I *have* to go down there."

"You mean . . . you don't want to?"

I hear the judgment in his voice. I got it from lots of people back on Earth when they found out I didn't want to go. Teachers, guidance counselors, and even some of my friends. First, they would accuse me of being selfish and ungrateful, and sometimes they would add lazy, shallow, or entitled to the mix. They typically followed that up with an offer to go in my place, and I would tell them they were welcome to. But before I can play out the usual routine with Duncan, he nods.

"I don't blame you," he says.

I wasn't expecting that. "You don't?"

"No. I mean, if I was as unprepared as you seem to be, I wouldn't want to go down there, either."

So he's not sympathetic, at all. He's even more judgmental. "What makes you think I'm unprepared?"

"I can tell. I see a lot of travelers." He leans back a bit and looks me over. "But being unprepared isn't really about you. It's about the rest of us, including your parents. Because out here, you can die in more ways than you can imagine, and when you come unprepared, you become a liability."

"A *liability*?" I try to sound outraged, but I'm also aware of how clumsy I look floundering in micro-g.

"Yes. You put the rest of us at risk with your—"

"Listen, space brat. I'm not an idiot, and I can take care of myself. Just because I don't want to live on an empty planet doesn't mean—"

"Empty?" He points through the window. "Do you know anything about that planet?"

"I know that according to the ISTA survey, there's nothing down there. And there's nothing wrong with me wanting to stay on Earth. That's where my life is."

"An ISTA survey only captures a fraction of the planet's surface. It's a guess, based on probability more than anything else."

"What is the probability that you'll stop lecturing me?"

He narrows his eyes. "Carver 1061c isn't an empty planet. There's life down there, and it fought its way back from an event that almost wiped out the whole planet when—"

"When the volcano blew up. Yes, I know all about that."

"Really? You know all about it?"

I shrug. "I know what I need to know."

"Okay, then. How big is it?"

"How big is what?"

"How big is the volcano?"

I really don't care how big it is, but he does, and I don't want him to know that I have no idea. "It's big. Who cares how big it is."

"It's almost fifteen hundred kilometers across at the base," he says. "It's bigger than Texas. And it's three times taller than Mount Everest. We have no idea what kind of species it wiped out, or how evolved they were. You might even find evidence of advanced extraterrestrial life."

"Uh-huh." He sounds like my dad. "And?"

"And?" He shakes his head. "Don't you want to know? Don't you want to see it?"

"Sure I do. I'm curious. Who wouldn't be? That doesn't mean I want to go down there to live in a cramped habitat, eating rations and drinking reclaimed water with nothing to do for a year but catalog soil samples for my parents."

"Why not?"

I stare at him. "Because I have a life. I have friends. Maybe there's nothing back on Earth for you, but there is for me."

His posture deflates and he goes silent, and I can see I've gotten to him. But I didn't mean to actually hurt him with something true. I don't know anything about his life on Earth. I just wanted him to back off from judging me.

"Look," I add. "This life just isn't for everyone. That's all I'm saying."

He runs his fingers through his hair and goes still for a moment. "You're right. It's not for everyone. But I'd take your place if I could."

And we're back to the routine. "Be my guest."

"I'm serious. As soon as I'm old enough, I'm applying to be a colonist. Maybe here. Maybe some other planet. But somewhere."

"That's great. We need people like you." I want it to sound sincere, but it comes out patronizing, and I almost wince at my own words.

"People like me?" He laughs through his nose. "You mean the people on this ship who have all sacrificed their comfort and safety for the good of humanity?"

"I didn't mean—"

But he turns away and kicks off from the wall, straight toward one of the circling hatches. As it swings by him, he latches onto it and gets carried around the hub a short way before he gracefully slides into the tunnel feetfirst.

Before his head vanishes, he stops himself and says, "Even if you're not 'people like me,' you might still want to know something about the place you'll be living for a year. That's just basic survival. For all of us."

I open my mouth to say something back but come up with nothing, and then he's gone. He's the second person on the *Theseus* I've somehow offended, and now I want nothing more than for my parents to finish printing so we can get off this ship and I can get on with the business of resenting them for the next year.

I take another look at Carver 1061c, with its strange oceans and continents. Then I attempt my best imitation of the Duncan Maneuver leaving the hub, and I'm glad he's not here to witness how badly I do. But eventually I'm gliding along the ladder in the spoke, feetfirst. As the other end approaches, gravity starts to kick in, and I feel myself pulled toward it. The ship has an up and a down again by the time I reach the rungs at the bottom.

It takes me some time, and a few wrong turns, but I manage to find my way back to my sleeping quarters without meeting or insulting any other members of the crew. Then I sit down at my computer terminal and log in to my files.

It's all here, just like Ms. Kateb said it would be. But now I'm thinking about what Duncan would say if he looked through it, and I feel pretty stupid. Unprepared. ISTA gave me a data limit on what I could bring, and I mean, really, how many times am I going to watch this video of a guinea pig riding around on the back of a goat? And why did I bring so many selfies? I should have brought more pictures of my friends. And I should have brought more music, because I can already tell it won't take long to get sick of listening to what I have. I was in a bad mood when I picked these songs, and I mostly chose them based on how much I thought they would annoy my parents.

Gram always says that you shouldn't shop for groceries when you're hungry. There should be another rule that you shouldn't pack for outer space when you're mad.

I shake my head and close up my personal stuff, then switch over to the files my parents sent to help me prepare for life on Carver 1061c. There are summaries of climate, geology, and the different life-forms recorded by previous scans. I'm relieved there doesn't seem to be anything obviously lethal to humans down there. The pioneer organisms are all benign, though Duncan's comment about ISTA surveys and probabilities has left me a bit unsettled.

There's a whole document on the mass extinction, and the theory that Mount Ida caused the event when it erupted 3.7 million years ago, filling the atmosphere with ash and toxic gas. It's a beast of a mountain, as big as Duncan said. It started out life as a shield volcano, like Mauna Kea on the island of Hawaii. But somewhere along the way, it had a midlife crisis and turned into a stratovolcano that makes Vesuvius and Mount St. Helens look like babies.

That's why my parents are coming here. Before Carver 1061c can be settled by humans, potential colonists understandably want to know for sure what killed 93 percent of life on the planet, and whether the murder weapon is still loaded. My parents are the detectives sent in to solve the case. I guess that makes me their bumbling sidekick.

My dad wrote most of the stuff I'm reading. I can tell. There are way too many bad puns to be anyone else, and it looks like he wrote it just for me, which must have taken him hours. So I try my best to read through it, but I have a hard time digesting it all. And my anger still distracts me whenever I think about the fact that I shouldn't even be here.

But I am here.

Reading all this stuff is making that fact very real, and I'm finally starting to accept that I can't change it. And Duncan is probably right. How stupid is it to carry such a grudge that I was going to land on a planet without knowing anything about it? That's like going outside in the winter without a coat just because my parents told me to wear one. So I probably owe Duncan an even bigger apology than I thought.

But now I just feel overwhelmed, so I close the Carver 1061c stuff and switch back over to my personal files. Then I sift through my photos, looking for my favorite pic of Avery. It's a little blurry, because she was laughing so hard.

A few of us had gone to this place after school that serves cheap, crappy pizza. While Avery was chewing on a huge bite, she sneezed, and somehow a piece of green pepper found its way up her nose. It was just sitting there in her nostril like a big booger. And that was the moment that made me like her. It was her confidence. She laughed at herself so comfortably and easily. She even let me take the pic, which I finally find and open.

But it's not Avery.

Or not only Avery.

I don't know how the file got ruined. The quantum channel is supposed to give perfect data transfer. But it looks like there's a second image behind her, trying to force its way through. I can't even make out what it is, but it's disturbing. A mass of horns or claws or teeth or something.

I open a few more pics, just to see, and lots of them are ruined in the same way, and I'm back to being angry. Really angry. That was my favorite pic of Avery. A favorite memory. I brought it with me for a reason, to have it with me for the next year, and now it's fucked up, and I have no way to replace it.

I sit there raging silently for a few minutes, bouncing my knee, just staring at the screen, until I make myself take a deep breath to calm down. Maybe I can find someone on the ship who'll help me clean up the file.

It's probably time to eat some dinner anyway. I'm not really hungry, but my cabin is feeling cramped, so I close up my files and flip the bench back up into the wall. Then I try to find my way to the common room, but the ship's geometry is doing weird things to my brain.

I'm used to things being flat. I mean, sure, back on Earth, if you leave point A and travel in a certain direction, you'll eventually end up back at point A. But you have to go around the entire planet to do that. On the *Theseus*, I can leave point A and be back at point A in minutes. I can literally walk in a straight line but end up traveling in circles, which is what I think I'm doing right now.

"Can I help you?"

I turn to see a tall woman marching with purpose in my direction down the slight curvature of the corridor, and I know right away she's Duncan's mom. She has the same close-set eyes, and the same dark hair, which she wears almost as short as her son's. But unlike his angular features, her face is round. Her jumpsuit is like mine, and all the others, except for the silver bars embroidered on her shoulders to mark her position.

"Hello," I say, trying very hard not to piss off anyone else, especially her. "Are you captain of the *Theseus*?"

"Yes, Rebecca Sharpe," she says without slowing her pace toward me. "You're Jessica Mathers, correct?"

"Yes."

"Where are you headed?"

"I'm trying to find the common room."

"You're far afield." She reaches me and smiles, but continues right on by. "This way."

"Oh—okay." I fall in beside her, and I stumble a bit as I try to keep up with her in the low gravity of the ship.

"I move quickly," she says. "I spend so much of my time in the microgravity of the command console, I need to fit in exercise when I can. Have you settled in?"

I'm already breathing harder. "Yes, ma'am."

She waves a hand. "Please, not ma'am. I'm just Captain."

When she says the term, it sounds more like a nickname than a rank. "Yes, Captain."

"Your parents should be established shortly, yes?"

"Yes."

"Do you need anything until then?"

"Actually, is there someone who can help me with my files? I think some of them got corrupted."

"Really?" She cocks her head slightly and frowns. "That's unusual. But Liz Kovalenko should be able to help you sort it out. She was probably there in the Print Shop when you emerged."

I do remember the name. "The Print Shop is the printer room?"

"Yes, that's what we usually call it. Liz is a computer engineer. But if she's busy, you can also ask Duncan, my son. He's inclined toward computer programming, among other things."

But after what I said to him, I doubt he'd be inclined to help me, and I'm not inclined to ask.

"Have you met Duncan?" she says.

"I . . . have."

"I'm glad. We don't get many travelers his age on the *Theseus*. He's been going through a rough patch." She adjusts the short collar of her jumpsuit. "Truthfully, I'm not always sure I'm doing the right thing having him out here with me. But it's what he wants."

I don't know why she's telling me this, but at least she's concerned about her son. My parents sure don't seem to care.

"In fact," she adds, "Duncan would probably volunteer to live on Carver 1061c and assist your parents, if that was an option."

"My parents would probably prefer to have him than me."

"Why do you say that?"

I shrug. "He just seems . . ." I struggle for the right words. "More inclined."

She accepts this with a nod and points down the corridor. "Common room is just up here."

Moments later, we step inside, and I notice the sweet, tinny smell of packaged spaghetti, which is nothing like the aroma of Pop-Pop's sauce as it simmers on the stove all day. There are a few new faces, but I also recognize some of the crew members from earlier. The three people from the Print Shop sit together at a table, and one of them must be Liz. Near them, Ms. Kateb sits at a table with two women wearing jumpsuits that look as worn as Evan's, and I assume they must be part of the engineering crew. Duncan sits by himself; the room's big windows are closed behind him.

Everyone looks up as we enter, and as one they all call out, "Captain," but there's more affection in it than formality.

The captain nods. "Good evening, everyone." Then she guides me over to the food prep station. "Are you hungry?" she asks as she goes to a cupboard labeled LUNCH/DINNER and pulls out a package.

"Not really," I say. "But thanks."

"Well, why don't you go sit with Duncan. I'll join you in . . ." She checks the label on the package. "Two and a half minutes."

It's not where I would have chosen to sit, but now that she's made the suggestion, it would be weird if I didn't. So I nod, then turn and start walking slowly toward him.

He looks up from his bright red spaghetti as I approach. "Oh, do you sit with people like me?"

I glance around to make sure no one else is listening. "I didn't mean it like that. And besides, I'm just following the captain's order."

He glances at his mom, then regards me for a moment before he puts down his fork and nods at the chair across from him. I slide into it, feeling awkward.

"Then what did you mean?" he asks.

I take a second, then answer. "I meant that you're . . . unique. Like one of those arctic explorers. I was just telling your mom that my parents would probably rather have you helping them than me. You're much more like them than I am."

"I'll take that as a compliment."

"You should." I relax a little and lean toward him. "I also wanted to tell you that you were right."

"I know. But you'll have to remind me what I was right about."

His self-certainty annoys me. But I tighten my lips and manage to keep going. "You said I should know about the planet where I'll be living for the next year. You were right, and I've been reading up on it."

"Good," he says. "It's a fascinating world."

"You seem to know a lot. Maybe we could compare notes?"

He smirks and shakes his head as he picks up his fork. "I don't think so."

"Why not?"

"I stopped doing other people's homework a long time ago."

"That's not—" Now he's really pissing me off. "You think I need you for that?"

"Isn't that why you're being nice to me all of a sudden?" He shovels a clump of pasta into his mouth.

I'm about to lay into him, but his mom is suddenly there at the table. She sets down a small tray with a fried rice dish and some dried fruit and says, "I'm starving," as she takes a seat.

"I'm finished." Duncan wipes his mouth on his sleeve and gets up to leave.

"Where are you going?" his mom asks, but with a captain's authority. "I haven't seen you all day. Sit down with us." She gestures toward me. "Talk with Jessica."

"Yes," I say, and flash him a fake smile. "Sit with us."

He lowers back into his seat with a scowl, but his mom is eating and doesn't notice.

"What have you done today?" she asks him.

"I read some," he says. "Spent some time in the hub. Not much."

"What were you reading?" I ask.

He turns toward me. "An article on natural selection. It's about how some species can't adapt when their environment changes, and nothing and no one can help them, so they basically just curl up and die."

"That sounds pretty grim," his mom says.

"That's the universe we live in." Now he's the one smiling at me.

"Did Jessica tell you about her files?" The captain chews into a piece of unidentifiable fruit. It stretches and takes some effort for her to tear the bite away with a snap.

"What files?" he asks.

I did not want to bring that up with him. "It's nothing. I can ask Liz—"

"Some of her files are corrupted," the captain says. "Isn't that right, Jessica?"

I nod. "That's right."

"Corrupted how?" Duncan asks.

"Really, it's nothing," I say. "I just— When I opened my files, some of them had gotten messed up."

He shrugs. "You must have uploaded a bad file when you—"

"Nope." He really seems to think I'm stupid. "I didn't."

He leans back in his chair. "Well there's no way our system did it."

"How do you know?" I ask.

The captain answers, "Our system doesn't have permission to directly access or alter your personal files." She's already finished her meal, apparently as efficient at eating as she is at walking. "We just hold it for you. Not even I can open your data."

"Then maybe something else went wrong," I say. "Something with the quantum network . . ."

"The Tangle?" Duncan shakes his head. "Not possible."

"Well something went wrong—I know that."

The captain gestures toward one of the computer terminals. "Maybe you should show us. Show Duncan."

But I don't want to do that. They're my pictures, my music, my private memories, and I don't want him to see them.

"Can I take a look?" he asks.

I want to say no. But just like everything else about this situation, I can't think of a good enough reason.

A few moments later, I'm sitting at the terminal, and Duncan is looking over my shoulder. I know what he must be thinking, so I scroll as quickly as I can through all my selfies and pictures, searching for that image of Avery.

"Wouldn't it have been easier to just bring a mirror?" he asks.

"Just—" I feel heat in my cheeks, and I use my elbow to give him a little shove. "Back off. Quit looking."

He chuckles, but he stops leaning over me, and I scan photos until I find the green-pepper-booger picture. When I open it, the same spiky, toothy distortion appears in the image, and I find it just as unsettling as before.

"What is that?" Duncan asks, leaning in again.

"I don't know." I frown in disgust and hold out my palm in front of the screen to block it. "But I know it didn't look like that before. Something happened to the file after I uploaded it."

"Can I sit down and take a look?"

His demeanor has completely changed. He cranes his head forward in curiosity, and he sounds earnest now. He believes me.

"Please do," I say, getting out of the chair, hoping he can recover my original file. I need that picture of Avery back.

# 6 — Hades

AFTER

SHE SHOWED ME THE REST OF THE LANDER, OR AT least, the places that hadn't been destroyed in the crash, like the cockpit where the engineer had broken. I thought about the amount of damage to the ship that I had seen from the outside, and I thought about the graves she had dug, and tried very hard not to imagine what had been left of the bodies to bury.

With the few hours left before sundown, we gathered supplies and piled them in the common room. We pulled bedding from the sleeping quarters, a variety of tools I didn't know how to use from the different utility compartments, lanterns and flashlights, a portable water reclamation unit, a tent, a few medkits, and anything else we could think of that we might need.

The work of loading it all into one place wore me out more quickly than I would have expected. The extra gravity on Hades made everything feel just a bit heavier than it should have, including my feet. That extra weight only got heavier as I worked, and I was breathing pretty hard by the time we'd finished and I slumped into a chair at the table.

"How are we going to carry all of this?" I wiped sweat from my forehead.

"We're not." She stood over the gear with her hands on her hips, surveying it. "Tomorrow, we'll prioritize. Pack only the essentials. You hungry?"

By that point, I was.

"Keep in mind," she said, "we don't have any power in here to heat the food, so choose accordingly."

We crossed the room to the kitchen area. I looked at the available options and reached for the spaghetti at the same moment she did. I figured that was probably because we both remembered standing in front of the open refrigerator after school, eating Pop-Pop's leftovers right from the container.

In keeping with that tradition, I didn't even bother with a plate or bowl. I just sat at the table and dug my fork into the open package. The pasta was too soft, the sauce was bland, and the meat was indefinable, but I was grateful to have food. Stories of marooned space travelers typically didn't feature plentiful ISTA rations.

"Not as good as Pop-Pop's," she said, attempting a smile.

I found it comforting, and also a little threatening, that she shared my thoughts and memories. "No one makes spaghetti as good as Pop-Pop's."

She pointed her fork at me. "True." Then both her smile and the tip of her fork fell.

"What is it?" I asked.

"I miss him."

For her, it had been weeks, and she had been alone for much of that time. But Pop-Pop and Gram had both hugged me when they dropped me off at the orbital shuttle just twelve hours ago. Or that's how it felt, according to the unreliable timestamps on my memory.

"Hey," she said, "do you remember that one time—"

"At Mill Park?" I knew exactly what had come into her mind, because it had come into mine at the same moment, and I laughed out loud at the memory. I'd only been living with Gram and Pop-Pop for a few weeks, and that poor girl he grabbed in a bear hug *did* look like me. I remembered the horrified expression on Pop-Pop's face when she started screaming and kicking, and he realized his mistake.

She laughed with me. "He was so embarrassed."

"So was I."

"And I was like, 'Stop! What are you doing to that girl?' "

We both laughed for a few moments more, followed by a sudden, deep silence during which neither of us looked at each other. I ate another bite of bad spaghetti, poking at the soft noodles with my fork as if I could stir up some flavor.

"It's weird," she said. "That used to just be my memory. But now it's ours."

"Yup." We both claimed it. Equally. Not as two people with individual memories of a shared event, but two people claiming the same whole memory of one person. "That's what I was talking about earlier," I said. "How is this going to—"

"Stop. We're not going there. We decided."

I closed my mouth. Then I took another bite of pasta, and another. After we'd eaten, we decided to go to bed. It was early, but I was completely exhausted, physically and emotionally, and without consistent power, the inside of the ship had grown very dark with the setting of the planet's sun. She led me down a narrow corridor bathed in the red glow of emergency lights to the lander's tiny sleeping quarters and pointed at one of the open hatches.

"You can take that one." She hitched a thumb over her shoulder. "I'll take this one."

I remembered the nest of blankets in the printer room where she'd been sleeping, but I decided not to ask about it.

"Bathroom is two doors down, on the left," she said. "The toilets still work."

"Good to know," I said.

We turned away from each other to go into our opposing rooms, but she stopped.

"You know," she said, "this might sound crazy, but . . . I'm glad you're here. Until now, I've been the only person on this whole fucking planet."

"You're still the only person on this whole fucking planet," I said with a grin.

She cocked her head a moment and then caught my meaning. She laughed, and we said good night. I entered my room, where I closed my hatch, then pulled the bed down from the wall and fell into it. The sheets crinkled beneath me, smelling of plastic, and the thin mattress wasn't much softer than a yoga mat. But I must have been even more tired than I thought, because the next thing I heard was a knocking on the door to my quarters the next morning.

"Yeah?" I mumbled, eyes closed, face buried in my flat pillow.

"Sun is up," she said through my door.

I remembered where I was, and my eyes shot open.

"We should be up, too," she added. "We've got work to do."

She sounded like Mom. I was pretty sure that I never sounded like Mom. "Okay."

The extra gravity on Hades made it hard to heave myself out of bed, but a few moments later, I lumbered into the kitchen, and about a minute after that, I discovered that cold scrambled eggs are nowhere near as edible as cold spaghetti. But I tried to swallow some of them down with the help of coffee made from dehydrated crystals that didn't dissolve well in cold water.

"We'll start by getting organized," she said from the floor, where she sat cross-legged with a clipboard in her lap and a lamp at her side in the middle of all our gear. "I think we should group things into three categories. Essential, important, and comfort."

"Sounds good." I left the kitchen and carried my eggs over to join her. "Food and water will obviously be essential."

She looked down at the clipboard. "Right. So we definitely need the water reclamation unit."

"But Hades has water, though, right?"

"Lots of it," she said. "Most of it's underground around the volcano. It seeps down into the old lava tubes and stuff. But even if we find water, you know what most pioneer organisms are, don't you?"

"What?"

"Microbes."

"Oh." I was reminded again that she knew things I didn't. "Don't drink the water. Got it."

"As for food," she said, "I haven't eaten anything that didn't come out of a package. I don't know if the ferns are poisonous, or if we can eat the worms, or the mole-snakes, or anything else."

"Um, I'd rather not eat worms, even if we can. So let's just bring rations."

"Yes, but how much?" She seemed to be asking herself, not me.

I knew that how much depended on how far, so I decided I needed another look at the volcano. "I'm going to step outside," I said.

I took my eggs and left the small common room, still stumbling a bit with sleepiness and the planet's extra gravity. As I stepped through the air lock and external hatch, the ferns rustled in a way that told me I'd frightened at least one of the ferrets back into hiding.

"It's okay," I called in the soft voice I used on puppies and babies. "I won't hurt you. So maybe don't hurt me?"

The Hades morning felt fresh and cool, but not cold, like a late-spring morning back on Earth. The dewdrops glistening on the ferns reassured me that the reclamation unit would be able to pull plenty of water from the air. I stepped away from the lander, toward the ferns, until I had a clear view of the volcano behind me, hazy and blue in the distance. I thought back to the farthest I had ever walked in a single day, an all-day hike through redwoods that covered about twenty kilometers. I tried to visualize how that distance would map to the ground between the lander and Mount Ida but quickly gave up.

"That's the stratovolcano." She emerged from the hatch to join me and pointed at the peak. "It grew on top of a shield volcano, which is unusual, apparently. But they're part of the same mountain."

I turned and looked at the landscape around us. "Then that means we're—"

"Yes, we're already standing on Mount Ida, technically. The outer edge of it is like five hundred kilometers away."

"You must have read that stuff Mom and Dad sent."

She shrugged. "I got bored on the *Theseus*."

"How bored?" I chuckled, assuming she was joking. "I can't imagine how bad it would have to be for me to read one of Dad's reports."

"Evan tried to land us as close to the habitat as he could." She shielded her eyes against the sun and looked up at the volcano's peak. "But I think we're at least thirty kilometers away, and that's just a wild guess. Do you remember that hike in the redwoods?"

"If you do, I do," I said, but as soon as I said it, I wondered if that was always true.

"Right, of course." She shook her head. "Based on that hike, we're looking at two days, minimum. The gravity will slow us down, too. Then, once we reach Mount Ida, we'll have to find the habitat, and that could take a long time." She paused. "I think we should plan on bringing two weeks of food, just to be safe."

"Okay," I said, looking down at the package of eggs in my hand. That sounded like a lot to me, but probably necessary, and a bit overwhelming to think about.

"I know where an Earth-metric scale is." She turned back toward the hatch. "I'll go weigh the rations."

When she was gone, I looked up again at the volcano, which somehow seemed even bigger than it had just a few minutes before. Then I heard the ferns rustle behind me, and I turned around. Two black eyes in the purple caught glints of light like smoky glass, and I could see patches of white fur through narrow breaks in the foliage.

"Hello," I said.

The ferret didn't move.

Something about the way it watched me seemed intelligent, but I remembered enough of Mr. Stamitz's xenobiology class to know that I really had no idea what this creature was thinking, or how it thought, or even if it thought at all in the way we used the word.

Mr. Stamitz used to say all the time that according to the universe's accountant, life is cheap, but intelligence is priceless. Colonists had found life on lots of planets, with fungi and viruses competing for the panspermia prize. But so far, none of that life possessed what we recognized as advanced cognition, let alone civilization. Mr. Stamitz always put particular emphasis on the word *recognize*, and I think he'd be glad to know I took something from his class.

"Hey," I said to the ferret. "Are you secretly a genius? You can be honest. I won't tell."

It just stared at me.

I looked down at my scrambled eggs, and I did what I had always done, ever since I was a kid, when trying to get a wild animal to approach me. The thing the signs always told me not to do. I offered it food.

"Here you go." I dumped the eggs in a pile at the edge of the ferns, then stepped a few meters away and waited. "It's okay," I said, trying to coax it toward the food.

The purple ferns stirred. The ferret seemed to be creeping closer, and I imagined it was curious about the food, but it never left the safety of the foliage to investigate. I wondered if the slightly sulfurous aroma of the eggs would smell good to it. Then I wondered if it even had a sense of smell. Maybe it detected things in its environment differently. Maybe those weren't even eyes staring back at me.

"You coming?" she called from the air lock.

"Coming," I called back.

I waited another moment, then backed away toward the lander, keeping a close watch on the eggs, but the ferret never emerged from the ferns to eat them.

As soon as I entered the common room, she said, "I think we should only take dried rations. If we take hydrated rations, like the spaghetti, we're basically carrying unnecessary water weight. That's what the reclamation unit is for, so we don't have to carry water."

"But what if something goes wrong with the reclaimer before we get to the habitat? We won't have any water, even in our food."

"That's true. I guess we should take a mix of rations?"

"Sounds good to me."

So we picked out seven days' worth of dehydrated rations, and seven days of hydrated rations, three meals a day. The dehydrated rations weighed less than a hundred grams, but the hydrated packages weighed over three hundred. That brought the total weight to eighteen kilos, nine kilos each. In Hades gravity.

"That seems like . . . a lot," I said.

"It is. But we'll be eating it along the way, so the load will get lighter. There will be plenty of food waiting for us on the other side."

"Are you sure about that?" It would be a disaster if we got there and found no supplies. "Like, a hundred percent sure?"

"Yes, a hundred percent." She seemed to be avoiding looking at me. "Next item. The water reclamation unit weighs about three kilos when it's empty. That's a bit more than the tent weighs, so I'll take the reclaimer, and you carry the tent."

"Why are you taking the heavier one?"

"Because I've been here longer and I'm stronger than you," she said. I knew she meant that word in ways beyond physical strength, and she was right, so I didn't argue.

We spent the next few hours sorting other gear. Blankets and bedding quickly and obviously fell into the comfort category. Hades didn't get cold enough at night to justify bringing them, and I gave up any hope for good sleep until we reached the habitat.

We also set aside most of the tools. They weighed a lot, and we weren't bringing anything with us they could help to repair. If the reclaimer broke, it would stay broken, because neither of us could fix it even if we had the right tools. So we selected only the most basic things that might be useful for general purposes, a couple of knives and a plier multi-tool. Then we grabbed some utensils for eating, and we debated whether to bring two medkits or just one, ending up with two.

"We should bring a couple of empty flasks," I said. "To store water from the reclaimer that we don't drink right away. They don't weigh much."

"Good idea. And I think as long as we each have a flashlight, we can leave the lanterns."

I looked around the room. "So that's it, right? We're done?"

She let out a deep breath. "I think so. Let's see what it all weighs."

We each took a pack and loaded up our rations and equipment. Mine came in at just over sixteen kilos, Earth-metric, including the weight of the pack. Hers pushed past seventeen. I hefted mine like a dumbbell to test the weight and then slipped my arms through the straps to take on the full burden. The load felt closer to twenty kilos in Hades gravity, and I gasped.

"It'll be rough at first," she said. "But it will get easier."

I hoped so, and we set our packs aside to eat a late lunch.

After we'd finished our cold spaghetti, we decided to take another walk through the lander, just to make sure we had thought of everything we might need to bring, and spent a couple of hours poking through every accessible room and storage space one more time. We found plenty of comms and other devices, but without power or access to the lander's mainframe—which was probably damaged, anyway—they were all useless. By the time we reached the rear of the ship, near the chamber with the body printer, our search had uncovered nothing worth adding more weight to our packs.

I hadn't been back to that room since waking up. Curious, I moved toward the hatch.

She stepped into my path. "Where are you going?"

"Um—" It seemed she was trying to block me. "I just wanted to take a look?"

She didn't move. "I would rather you not go in there."

"But I've already been in there. I kinda came from in there."

She already stood close to me, but she took a step even closer. "Just don't."

"Why?"

"You don't need to know why."

I looked directly into her eyes. "I think I do. What is it you don't want me to see?"

She said nothing, and I moved to step around her, but she reached out her hands to grab me. I dodged aside and lunged for the door.

"Don't!" she cried out, and the desperation in her voice stopped me. "Please." Tears filled her eyes, then rolled down her cheeks, mixing with the grime on her face.

I didn't know what to think. She seemed not only desperate, but afraid. And I knew she wasn't faking it. I tried to think of what could make me feel that way, what I would need to hide so fiercely, even from myself, and came up empty. I wanted to know what was in that room, but I wasn't ready to get into a physical fight with her over it, so I decided to wait for another opportunity.

"Okay," I whispered, and stepped away from the hatch. "I won't go in there."

She sighed and scrubbed the tears from her cheeks with her palms. "Thank you."

I nodded, and we headed toward the galley.

"I think I need some air," I said.

"I'll join you," she said, but as an announcement, not an offer.

When we neared the juncture, I looked at the old blood smears on the walls and imagined things more sinister than I already had. We turned to the left and climbed through the external hatch, then emerged outside.

Evening had fallen over Hades. The sky where the sun had gone down looked similar to an Earth sky at sunset, and the purple ferns blushed a deeper red. The eggs I'd left for the ferret were gone, and I saw no signs of the creature anywhere.

We stood next to each other in the exact same pose as the light grew dim, and then we both sighed, almost in the same moment.

"I'm sorry about—" She nodded her head toward the lander. "Back there."

"It's okay."

She looked at her feet. "I probably seem crazy."

"You seem . . . like you've been through something."

She turned to look at me, but she seemed to see more than me. She was remembering things, and I could tell she was on the edge of crying again. I thought maybe she wanted to say something.

"What is it?" I asked.

She opened her mouth, then looked away, shaking her head. "We should go to bed so we can get an early start tomorrow."

"Okay, but I—"

She walked off and left me standing there.

A moment passed, and then I followed her. We went to our cabins, but I wasn't tired, and I lay awake thinking about where I was and what I was about to do, wishing I could go back in time and stop myself from getting in the scanner at all. I wondered what Jim would have done if I had simply refused, like a lot of travelers probably do.

Then I realized that wouldn't have prevented the accident on the *Theseus*, and Mom and Dad would still be in limbo, only no one would know. That thought made me feel sick. It was one thing to die because you'd never been scanned, or because you'd decided not to be printed again. It was another to have your data stored somewhere, but not have your body established anywhere. A nowhere death.

I squeezed my eyes shut and told myself that Mom and Dad would be fine. We just had to reach the habitat and use the Tangle.

Eventually, after lying there for a while, I grew tired and drifted, but before I fell asleep completely, I heard the hatch open and close across the hall. I thought she was probably using the bathroom, but I never heard her come back. That's when I started wondering what she could be doing, and whether it had something to do with whatever was in the printer room that she didn't want me to see. Even though she was me, and I was her, I didn't really know how far I could trust her, and that distance seemed to keep getting smaller.

I stayed in bed a bit longer, battling with myself over what to do, before I made my decision. I slipped out of bed, tiptoed to the hatch, and opened it a crack. I saw nothing in the red light of the corridor.

But then I heard a distant moaning, a deep and injured sound that seized my bones and chilled my skin.

It was coming from somewhere inside the ship.

# 7 — DS *Theseus*

## BEFORE

DUNCAN SPENDS ALMOST AN HOUR DIGGING through code, but he doesn't find any answers and eventually gives up on the photo in frustration. I feel a bit of satisfaction in his defeat, which isn't very mature of me. And I do still want my photo back the way it was. But at least I've been vindicated, and he and his mom know I'm not an idiot.

"We'll have to see if Liz can figure it out tomorrow," he says.

Most of the crew have gone. Those who have stayed settle in to watch a movie together. Their mood seems light and relaxed, like any other evening at home with family and friends, and not at all how I'm feeling. Duncan joins them, and I can tell by their inside jokes and familiarity that these are his people. They are like him. They invite me to watch with them.

It's a horror movie about a serial killer who erases his victims' data before he murders them, so he can tell them before they die that they will never be printed again. I've already seen it a few times, and I'm feeling tired, so I decline. No one seems to mind.

When I'm back in my quarters, alone, I stare at the tiny cabin for several moments and decide I don't want to go to bed yet. I leave in search of a shower, and I soon find the bathrooms Ms. Kateb showed me during the tour. The shower stall is smaller than a closet, and I bump my elbows against its cold walls as I step inside and turn around. The door seals shut with a hiss when I close it, and then I hear a gentle flow of air as the suction drain engages at my feet. I turn on the water, which falls and crawls over my skin more slowly than water back on earth. It looks and feels very strange at first, almost as if it's alive, but after a few minutes, the slowness of it relaxes me. The suction drain gurgles, and I close my eyes, enjoying the heat and the steam for a while before I turn on the cleansers, and then the water smells like lemons. After a quick rinse, I turn off the water and turn on the dryer. A current of warm air rushes over me and drives any remaining water down the suction drain, toward the reclaimer.

I head back to my quarters feeling refreshed and finally ready for bed, my hair still a bit damp. I try to read some more of the stuff my parents put together about Carver 1061c, but I don't get very far before my eyes want to close.

The next morning, I don't make myself get out of bed, because I don't see the point. My parents won't arrive until tomorrow, and I have nothing to do, so I just lie there.

Eventually, I hear a knock at my door. "Yeah?" I say without opening my eyes.

The voice is too muffled to understand.

"Hang on." I roll out of bed, slowly, and then stagger the two steps to open the hatch. "Yes?"

Duncan stands in the corridor. "Hello there." He glances up at my hair, which feels like it dried funny because I went to bed with it wet, and I think I catch a bit of a smirk. He's probably one of those people who never sleep in. "The captain sent me to make sure you're alive."

"Well, as you can see, I'm alive." I move to slide the hatch shut. "Thanks for your—"

"The captain also wants me to try and get you out of your cabin."

"Do you ever just call her Mom?"

He pauses. "So this is me trying to get you out of your cabin."

I give him a thumbs-up. "Good effort."

I've almost got the hatch closed when he suddenly adds, "Oh, and Liz took a look at your files."

Shit. He's got me. I reopen the hatch, just a bit wider than a crack. "And?"

He turns away and strolls down the corridor. "You'll have to ask Liz," he says over his shoulder.

"Damn it," I say under my breath as I watch him go. "Good effort."

I use my fingernails to at least attempt to part my hair, and then I leave my quarters. I'm not exactly sure where to find Liz, so I head back to the Print Shop, where I saw her working yesterday.

When I enter the room, I see my printer, now empty and dark. It reminds me that this body has only been fully alive and conscious for a day, and in the days before that I wasn't technically alive at all. But I'm not supposed to think those kinds of thoughts. I'm supposed to remember that I am not this body, or the next. I'm the me that connects them all in a continuous line of memories and experiences.

Liz isn't in the room, but Dr. Gutiérrez is. He's a sturdy man, with a broad smile, a square jaw, and twinkly eyes.

"What a coincidence," he says. "I am just finishing up your arrival documentation."

"You're still working on that?"

"I am always working on that. Teleportation is ninety percent paperwork and safety protocols, ten percent body printing." He sighs with a shrug. "How are you feeling today? Did you sleep well last night?"

"Maybe a little too well. I just woke up."

He chuckles. "No, that's good. Teleportation is hard on a person, emotionally and intellectually. You need your rest. And you might be hungrier than normal, so be sure to eat. Doctor's orders."

"Thanks."

He glances down at his screen. "Your parents are right on schedule. Soon, you'll be a pioneer on your very own planet, writing the history of humanity in the stars." He waves his hand in a wide arc. "And, constant stars, in them I read such art as truth and beauty shall together thrive."

"That sounds like Shakespeare."

"Very good. It is 'Sonnet Fourteen.'"

"Uh-huh, you and my dad will get along great." I glance around. "But do you know where I can find Liz?"

"Ms. Kovalenko?" He looks around, almost as if just then noticing she isn't in the room. "Oh, yes, that's right. She said something about running diagnostics on Brad. Or she might be eating an early lunch."

"Brad?"

"The ship's computer. Ms. Kovalenko calls it Brad."

"I see." As far as anthropomorphizing goes, that's oddly boring. "And where is Brad?"

"In the hub, near the command module."

"Thanks." I turn to leave.

"Safe travels, pioneer." He gives me a salute.

I decide then that he is sincere, if also overly dramatic. I smile and salute him in return.

Then I leave and walk the corridors until I find one of the spokes that will take me to the hub. I make the climb and the flight along the ladder a bit more gracefully than I did yesterday, and when I reach the end of it, I carefully launch myself into the open microgravity vault. From there, I turn upship toward the command module, and this time I do a fine job flying. I almost wish Duncan were here to see it.

I pass through the same areas of the hub I crossed yesterday and eventually reach the place where I stopped to get a look at Carver 1061c. We're over a different part of the planet now, with different oceans and continents. The sight of it is still overwhelming, but I feel slightly less intimidated now that I've read more about what's down there.

After a few minutes, I leave the window and push ahead. The hub is brighter past that spot, and free of storage. Arrays of instruments and displays line the walls, and I reach a couple of crew members. They're pulling away a large panel that would probably weigh too much for them to manage under normal gravity, exposing a nest of wires and conduits behind it. They notice me and nod as I approach.

"Do you need something?" one of them asks.

"I'm looking for Liz?"

"She's up ahead." He points in the direction I'm already floating.

"Thanks."

I glide past them and come to the end of the hub, or at least, the end of this section of the hub. There's an open hatch, and I pull myself through it into a juncture with five more hatches, four of which surround me, with one overhead.

The hatch to my right is open, and through it I can see a spherical chamber. Liz sits in the middle of it, strapped into a chair in front of an imposing computer terminal. I move toward her, but before I enter the room, I rap my knuckles on the bulkhead.

She glances over at me. "Oh, Jessica. Come on in."

I nod and carefully pull myself into the round room. Dozens of screens and thousands of blinking lights surround me, and I hear the rush of circulating air. It's pretty cold in here, and it smells aggressively metallic. I can almost taste it. "So, uh, this is Brad?" I ask.

Her attention has already turned back to whatever she was working on when I came in. "This is Brad."

"Is Brad the name of an ex-boyfriend or something?"

She chuckles. "I spend way too much time with this thing to name it after an ex-boyfriend. It's from a Robert Frost poem. 'The Star-splitter.'"

"You all really like your poetry out here, don't you."

"Have you read it?"

"No."

"Oh, it's great." She turns toward me again. "See, Brad is a farmer, but he's not a very good farmer, and he doesn't actually want to be a farmer." She's talking pretty fast, but I get the impression it's her normal speed. "What he really wants is a telescope to satisfy a lifelong curiosity about our place among the infinities, as the line goes. So, he burns down his house to collect the insurance money, and he uses it to buy a telescope." She pauses, looking at me with raised eyebrows, waiting.

I think I'm supposed to get something, but I'm missing it.

"Brad is us," she finally says. "He literally burned up his old life so he could see the stars. Like everyone on this ship when we climbed into the body scanner."

"Oh, right." Now I get it. "And what does the title mean? 'The Star-splitter'?"

"That's what Brad names the telescope, because when you look closer, what you thought was just one star becomes two. It's a great poem."

"I'll have to read it."

"You should." She resumes work at her station. "So, what can I do for you?"

"Duncan said you looked at my files?"

"Yeah, I did. Really bizarre. I still don't know what happened."

"But were you able to fix it?"

"No. Didn't Duncan tell you?"

"He didn't tell me anything."

"Oh. Well, when I realized I couldn't restore your corrupted files, I asked ISTA to resend your whole package."

I sigh, feeling relieved. "That's great. Thank you."

"You're welcome. Sorry you came all the way up here. Duncan was supposed to let you know you could access your files from your cabin again. Or any common terminal."

"He neglected to mention that."

"He's been a bit distracted lately. But with everything going on in his life, I can't say I blame him. He's a good kid. He deserves better."

I don't know what she's talking about, but I remember the captain mentioned him going through a rough patch when I first met her, back in the corridor. "Uh-huh," I say.

"I don't mean the captain. She can be strict and by the book, but she's a good mom. I mean all that stuff with his dad."

"What stuff?"

"His dad's an anti-teleportation guy. Annihilation of the soul, and all that crap."

"He's Antimat?"

"I don't know if he's a card-carrying Antimaterialist, but he would probably feel comfortable at one of their rallies. That's why he divorced the captain when she took the job with ISTA, and why he doesn't want anything to do with Duncan. Can you imagine if your own father didn't think you were you anymore?"

I can't imagine that. It's awful, and it's honestly more than I wanted to know.

"Duncan burned up a lot to be out here. He—" She stops herself, looks at me, and then looks down at her keyboard. "Sorry, maybe you don't want to hear all of this. It's a small ship. You get used to everyone knowing everything."

"It's fine." I push away, back toward the hatch. "But I should let you get back to work."

"Oh, yes. Of course. The exciting work of running diagnostics, because I do still need to figure out what went wrong with your first data package."

"I hope Brad cooperates."

"Thanks."

I smile and return through the hub the way I came, feeling really bad for Duncan, and also guilty for saying his life back on Earth must suck for him to want to live out here. I wouldn't have said that if I'd known his dad hated him, and now I don't know what to say to him at all. It's weird to know something like this about someone when they don't know that you know, and they may not even want you to know.

I reach one of the spokes and climb in, taking the ladder slowly, and by the time I'm back in simulated gravity at the other end, I'm feeling hungry, so I head for the common room. It's still lunchtime, and when I get there, I see several crew members eating, including Ms. Kateb and Evan.

I haven't had breakfast, because I slept in so late, so I choose an egg and hash brown scramble from among the options, and after I've heated it up, I sit down at a table by myself. The big windows are open, offering a view of the spinning stars, and I watch them as I take a few bites of my steaming food. Then Duncan enters the room. He sees me right away and puts on a face of mock surprise as he walks toward me.

"Wow, you're up! Did you, uh, talk to Liz?"

"Mm-hm. It seems that someone forgot to tell me I could access my files from my room."

"Yes, I probably should have mentioned that." He sits down across the table from me. "Got you up and out of your room, though, didn't it?"

"I guess you can tell the captain mission accomplished."

"I already did."

I think about his dad, then look away from his eyes and take a bite of my eggs. "You and your mom seem close."

"You're not close to your parents?"

"I was. When I was younger. But they've been gone for a long time."

"Oh, right," he says. "Sorry, stupid question."

"No, it's fine." I put down my fork. "It's just hard to stay close over a quantum channel, you know?"

He nods, listening. So I go on.

"When they left, I was scared at first, and I was sad. But mostly, I was just really mad. Back then, it took even longer to establish your body, so

I didn't hear from them for two weeks. When they finally called, I told my gram I didn't want to talk to them."

"How come?"

I haven't even thought about any of this in a long time, and I certainly can't remember talking about it with anyone. I'm not really sure why I'm telling him about it. Maybe I just want things to be even somehow. "I guess I wanted to hurt them back? I was only eleven. Pop-Pop—he's my grandpa—he tried to get me to come to the terminal, but I refused. I could hear my mom crying from the next room." The memory sucks me in for a moment. But I blink it away.

Duncan nods like he understands, and maybe he does, at least partly. But I've told him as much as I want to. Maybe more. I gather my napkin, utensils, and plate of uneaten eggs, and I stand up.

"I think I'll go check out my files now," I say.

"Right. Better make sure it's all there."

I was just making an excuse to leave, but now that I've said it, that's what I really want to do. I toss my garbage and utensils into the recycler, and I leave the common room. When I reach my cabin, I sit right down at my computer terminal and pull up my files. I find and open the photo of Avery with the pepper booger, and it's just the way it's supposed to be. I can almost hear her laughing, and I make myself stare at that picture until it hurts.

Then I'm crying.

But it's not just Avery that I'm crying about. I'm crying about all my friends. I'm crying about missing Gram and Pop-Pop. I'm crying about the teleportation, and my life on Earth that got burned up. I'm even crying about Duncan and his dad, and the thought of a year of bad spaghetti, but more than any of that, I'm crying about my parents bringing me out here, and I'm crying because they left me behind in the first place. I'm crying like I cried when I was eleven, and I decided I *did* want to talk to them, but the quantum channel had already closed.

It feels like one of those self-sustaining cries that could go on forever if I let it. But I clamp it down and get it back under control, and as I work my way through the leftover hiccuppy breaths, I feel the first twist of a headache that will turn head-splitting if I don't do something about it. So I fold up the bench and pull down my bed to rest and close my eyes. I don't plan to fall asleep, but I do, and when I wake up, I feel disoriented, like I slept through the night.

I check the time and realize it's only been a few hours, but it's almost past dinnertime, and I consider just staying in bed until the next morning. A moment later my stomach tells me I'm way too hungry for that.

The scene that greets me in the common room is pretty much the same as the evening before. The crew hangs around together, talking and laughing, a movie on the screen. Duncan sees me walk in, and as I move toward the kitchen, he gets up and joins me there.

"Everything okay?" he asks.

"Uh-huh. I fell asleep and . . ." An enormous yawn takes over my mouth that lasts long enough to be embarrassing, and it leaves my eyes watery. "Sorry. I don't know why I've been so tired. I guess it's the teleportation."

"It happens to most travelers," he says. "It happened to me. You'll probably feel better by tomorrow."

"That's good to know." I open the cabinet and decide to try a burrito.

Duncan nods toward the movie on the screen. "Do you want to watch with us?"

I look, and it's another movie I've already seen. But that's probably true of all the movies they have, and I know the movie selection isn't really the point. I look at the crew, and I notice Liz sitting with Dr. Gutiérrez. She sees me and gives me a little wave, and then cups a hand beside her mouth.

"I put a copy of that poem in your files," she calls across the room.

I mouth *thank you* in reply.

Then Duncan asks, "What poem?"

" 'The Star-splitter.' "

"What's it about?"

I can't resist repeating his own words back to him. "You'll have to ask Liz."

It takes him a second to get that I'm teasing, but then he smiles, and he nods his head toward the screen. "Movie?"

"Sure. Just let me heat up my burrito. And save me a seat."

"You got it."

He walks away. I wait for the numbers on the microwave to count down.

# 8—Hades

THE MOANING SOUNDED AWFUL. AND FAMILIAR. Deeply, disturbingly familiar. It sounded like me. Like her. But the lander's corridors distorted her voice, twisting it into something lost and surreal. It wasn't the sound of something in pain. It was the memory of pain.

I didn't want to leave my room, but I had to. I had to know. And if I was in danger, my cabin didn't provide any real protection anyway.

Still, I waited a few moments before creeping out into the corridor, and then I forced myself to turn toward the sound. It seemed to be coming from the rear of the ship, near the printer room, and I took myself in that direction through the dim, red passageways, my breathing shallow and halting, taking each step deliberately and cautiously.

At times the moaning swelled, loud and bone-jarring, followed by retreats into eerie silence that left behind only the creaking of the ship. And even though I expected the voice to return, it raised the hair across my scalp every time it did.

When I finally reached the printer room, I stood in front of the hatch and stared, afraid to open it, my hands trembling, my body tense and ready to bolt. But then, from the other side of the door, the wail arose, closer and louder now that I stood so near, but also clearer and very me. I heard desperation and anguish in it that squeezed my stomach in sympathetic pain. She was hurting in there, and I realized I knew that sound better than anyone else could.

I hit the button, and the hatch opened.

The red emergency lighting from the corridors filled the room, but not well. I stepped across the threshold, eyes straining in the darkness. To my right, I could see that someone had demolished the same body printer that had printed me. Chunks of it lay scattered on the floor, the whole unit opened up like a carcass left behind by a pack of wolves on a nature show.

The moaning came from my left, near the pile of bedding I'd seen the last time I was in there. Now that pile seemed to be moving, writhing in the shadows on the floor between two computer consoles, near a bulkhead.

"J-Jessica?" I whispered.

The groaning continued, unbroken.

I took a step closer. "Jessica?"

Still nothing.

I took another step. Then another, walking over wires and other debris with my bare feet.

As my eyes adjusted to the darkness, I could see she was sleeping, but she was caught in a nightmare. When her wailing reached its greatest intensity, her arms flailed, and her face contorted into a grimace.

I didn't know what to do. I'd heard somewhere you weren't supposed to wake a sleepwalker, but this wasn't sleepwalking. It also wasn't normal, and I couldn't stand the sound she was making. So I waited for another lull in her moaning, and when her body settled, I moved in, quick and light on the balls of my feet. Then I crouched down next to her, and I laid my hand on her shoulder.

"Jessica," I said, close enough to see the beads of sweat on her forehead. I gave her shoulder a gentle nudge. "Jessica."

The moaning stopped. Now she whimpered, eyes squeezed shut, still sleeping. "Nuh—" she said.

I nudged her a little harder. "Jessica, you're dreaming."

"N-no . . ."

"Jessica." I shook her, hard enough for her head to wobble. "Jessica, wake up."

"Not him!"

"Jessica!" I raised my voice. "Wake up!"

"No!" Her eyes shot open. Then she screamed and scrambled away from me, all tangled in blankets. She ended up against the bulkhead behind her, curled into a defensive ball.

"It's me," I said, trying to sound as soothing as I could, holding up my empty hands. "It's okay. It's just me. You were having a nightmare."

She peeked at me, and her wide eyes blinked. Then her shoulders relaxed, and I could tell she recognized me.

"It's okay." I slid closer toward her. "It wasn't—"

She lunged toward me.

I flinched, raising my hands to fight her off. But she just threw her arms around my shoulders, grabbing me into a hug, and then she started sobbing. It took a few seconds for my shock at the physical contact to pass, and then I hesitantly reached my arms around her. Around myself. But it wasn't me, because her body felt a bit harder and thinner than mine. Her chest heaved, her crying uncontrollable and frantic. I felt her hot tears on my neck.

"It's okay," I whispered, confused and almost dizzy.

She shook her head fiercely against my shoulder, like she was burrowing, and then her frame gave out. She slumped in my arms, still crying, gasping and clinging to my jumpsuit, and I did the work of holding her up.

Several moments went by like that, and I felt helpless. I wasn't Mom. I wasn't Gram. I'd cried in both of their arms when I was younger, and they usually told me exactly what I wanted or needed to hear. But I had never cried like she was crying, and I didn't know what to say to her, even though it occurred to me that I should know what to say to myself. But instead of talking, I just held her.

She draped against me until her sobbing eased and she'd worked her way through some little, hiccuppy breaths. Then she propped herself back upright and wiped her face with her hands and sleeves, avoiding eye contact with me. She sniffed, staring down into her lap, and I waited for her to speak first. When she finally did glance up, she looked away again after only a second.

"Sorry," she said.

I assumed she meant her crying. "Don't be. You—"

"No." She nodded in the direction of the broken body printer, and I took a quick look at what she had done. "I got so angry," she said. "I just . . . exploded."

I couldn't remember ever being angry enough to do that, and I was surprised I hadn't heard the destruction. But that was apparently what she didn't want me to see. "It's okay," I said. "I mean, it was dead anyway, right?"

A moment went by. "Right."

"So . . . why are you sleeping in here?" I asked.

"I was scared."

"Of what?"

"It's hard to explain." She glanced around the room. "I don't want to leave the lander." Then she made a sound that was halfway between a laugh and a sob. "How crazy is that? I look around and I hate this place. So much. But I also really, really don't want to leave it."

"It's not crazy." I actually found it reassuring that a part of her didn't want to leave the lander after all.

She looked up at the ceiling. "But we have to." She closed her eyes. "We have to. If we don't contact ISTA, then Mom and Dad, and all of the crew . . ."

"I know. We'll find the Tangle. We'll bring them back."

Her smile was faint, but it was there.

I circled back, trying to figure out what had scared her. "What were you dreaming about?"

"Nothing." She pulled away and got to her feet. Then she snatched up one of her blankets, shook it out, and began to fold it, using her chin to hold it in place against her chest. "It was just a nightmare."

I stood up next to her. "That didn't seem like just a nightmare."

"Well—" She pulled, creased, and slapped the blanket into shape. "I guess it was a very bad nightmare." She had turned flat and shut down again.

"You were also talking in your sleep," I said.

"Oh?"

"*Not him.* That's what you said." I watched her face for any sign of recognition.

She only shrugged. "Okay?"

"What does that mean?"

She shook her head. "I don't know."

"Really?" I crossed my arms and cocked my head so she would be sure to notice my skepticism. "You don't remember *anything*? The sounds you were making shook the whole lander. You were totally—"

"I believe you," she said. "So believe me. I would answer your questions if I could."

I studied her for the same tells that gave me away whenever I tried to lie to the people who knew me best. But she wasn't holding a breath, and she didn't seem to be trying extra hard to look me directly in the eyes.

"You should go back to bed," she said. "There's only a few hours left until morning, and we have a long walk ahead of us."

"What about you?"

She looked down at the blanket in her arms, which she had just folded. "I'll . . . try to get back to sleep."

I looked around, at the spot on the floor where she had been nesting, and at the damaged printer. "What, here?"

She nodded.

"Um . . ." That room reminded me of a zoo, like the cage of a wild animal. It creeped me out, and I had a very strong feeling that it would not be good for her to stay in there. "I think you should sleep in your cabin," I said.

"Why?"

I came up with a good reason that wasn't the real reason. "Because you have a long walk ahead of you, too. You need your sleep just as much as I do, and I don't think you'll sleep well on the floor."

"Well I know for sure I won't sleep well in my cabin."

"Why not?"

"I just won't."

"Then sleep in my room with me."

"What?"

I didn't know why I had just offered that. It was an impulse I immediately regretted, but I stuck with it anyway. It felt safer to keep her near me. "Come sleep in my room."

"It's too small."

"I think we could both squeeze in the bed."

"Are you serious?"

"Sure, why not?" But it was a ridiculous question, with an obvious answer: because it would be very weird. Of course, the entire situation was already weird, so I wasn't sure how much weirder sharing a bed with her would make it. "It's not like the tent will be much bigger," I added. "We might as well get used to it."

I was a bit surprised at how hard I was trying to get her out of that room, and a part of me hoped she would refuse. Then I could leave knowing that I had done everything I could. But a moment later, her mouth formed a half smile.

"Good effort," she said quietly.

"What?"

"Okay." She tucked the blanket under her arm. "It's weird, but so is everything else about this situation, right?"

She'd read my mind. Or just read her own mind, I guess. "That's exactly what I was thinking."

"Might as well get used to that, too." She stepped toward the door. "It's probably going to happen a lot."

I followed her to the hatch, where she paused with the obvious intention of letting me go through first, which I did. She came out into the corridor after me, closed the hatch, and then turned away from it in the same way I turned away from someone I was trying hard to ignore.

We walked back to my cabin, and on the way there I tried to figure out how this was going to work. We both slept the same way, on our right side, which would make fitting on the bed easier, even though we would basically be spooning. I opened the hatch, and we stepped into the small room, where the bed looked even smaller than I'd just been imagining it.

"Hopefully the tent is bigger than this," she said.

I agreed. But neither of us moved. We both stood there in the weak emergency lighting, staring at the bed.

"Yup," I said, "this is weird."

"I guess we just have to embrace it."

"Literally," I said. Then I sighed, resigned, and lay down on the outside of the bed on my right side, facing the bulkhead. That would put her on the inside, and I wouldn't have her at my back, which felt safer. But she didn't move.

I looked up at her.

She glanced over her shoulder at the hatch. "I need to sleep where you are. But facing the room."

That meant she didn't sleep on her right side anymore, and I wondered if she needed to face the door. I had done that when I was six or

seven and I couldn't sleep with my back to the monsters that lived in
my closet. But I had outgrown that, which meant she had, too, or so I
would have assumed.

I decided not to fight it and rolled over, then scooched my back
up against the bulkhead as closely as I could, facing the room. She lay
down next to me, and it seemed like she was as near to the edge of the
bed as she could get without falling off. Several moments went by as I
stared at the back of her head, at the shape of her shoulder and the dip
of her waist, all cast in red, until I became disoriented. Like I was outside my body, looking at myself, nothing more than a camera. None of
my body-transience counseling had prepared me for that.

The whole idea behind body transience was letting go. Letting go
of your reference body. Letting go of the belief that you even were your
body. Accepting the idea that you had never been more than a divot of
data, nothing but a tiny, temporary impression in the quantum fabric
of the universe. That was all necessary if you planned to step into a teleportation scanner.

But now there were two of me, and letting go wasn't an option. Instead, and against all my counseling and training, I had to hold on to
myself. To the body that was me.

"Thank you," she whispered.

Her voice brought me back. "For what?"

"For not leaving me in there."

I watched her stillness. "You're welcome. I'm sorry you were so scared."

She said nothing, and I knew she was still afraid, but I didn't understand it. The threat from the accident on the *Theseus* had passed. The
lander had already crashed. Nothing on the planet posed a danger that
I knew of, according to what she'd told me earlier. Unless she hadn't
told me everything. Unless there was something I didn't know about.

"What are you afraid of?" I asked for the second time. "What are
you afraid will come through that door?"

Several long moments went by. "Nothing."

"Does it have to do with your nightmare?"

"No."

"Then why do you have to face the door?"

"I just do."

"But why—"

"Maybe you would understand if you'd been trapped on a ship in space with nowhere to run and no way to escape."

It was hard to argue with that.

"Good night," she said.

"Good night," I whispered, and then I added something Pop-Pop used to say before bed. "Enjoy sleep, the main course in life's feast, and the most nourishing."

She sniffed. "That always made sleep sound like something delicious. But then I found out where he got that line."

"*Macbeth.* Right after he murders someone."

"And that's Pop-Pop. Right after he gives you a hug and a kiss on the forehead."

We both chuckled, and then we fell silent. I kept my eyes open, staring at the back of her head, missing Pop-Pop.

A few moments later, she started crying again. She was trying to hide it, but I could tell, and I guessed that she missed Pop-Pop more than I did. It was like I could sense it in the subtle shake of her shoulders. I could feel her loneliness and her pain, and it moved me, naturally and automatically.

I slid toward her. She had her arms and elbows pulled in tight against her chest. I smelled her musty, greasy hair as I reached my right arm over and around her. She noticed, but she didn't stop me, and I didn't hold her too tightly or pull her too close. But it was enough. I felt and heard her sigh against me, and within moments, she was asleep, her breathing slow and deep.

I did not fall asleep right away, but in the hours that followed, I drifted.

I imagined myself back on the *Liverpool*, but without Jim Kelly at my side. I stood by myself in the teleporter room, and then I climbed up into the chamber, only to find that I was already in there. Or she was already in there. I tried to shout and scramble back out, but she grabbed me and hauled me inside with her. She was so much stronger than me. I kicked and thrashed, but I couldn't escape her grip. Then the chamber closed, sealing us in. I pounded my fists against the shell, calling for help. She squeezed more tightly, and I saw sparks. Then a weakness washed through me, and my arms became useless. I recognized the effects of the stasis sedative. But something was wrong. It was enough to paralyze me, but not enough to knock me out, and I could hear the low hum of the scanner warming up. I knew the chamber was about to burn my body away with a laser—layer by layer, cell by cell, atom by atom—and I was still awake. I was still me. But I could only scream inside my mind as the temperature in the teleporter chamber plunged.

A maze of frost spread across the inside of the shell. My teeth couldn't chatter with the statis drugs, but I felt the cold deep in the roots of my molars. I would feel everything that was about to happen to my body.

She wasn't squeezing me anymore, but she held on to me, and in my fear I realized I wanted her to. I was cold, and she felt warm against me, and I didn't want to be alone. I closed my eyes.

Then I opened them, awake.

I was back in bed, in the lander, with no idea how much of the night had gone by, or whether I'd just been dreaming or imagining or something in between. She was still asleep next to me, and I still had my arm around her. I left it there. Then I slept again, deeply, until she awoke me in the morning when she moved and slid down off the foot of the bed to get up.

"Today's the day," she said, on her feet and yawning.

I propped myself up on my elbow and nodded, rubbing my forehead, eyes barely open.

She turned to the hatch and opened it. "Breakfast first." Then she was gone, as if she'd already forgotten about the strangeness of the night.

I decided that I would also like to forget about the strangeness of the night, so I said nothing about it as I joined her in the galley. We ate a large breakfast of foods that should never be served together for any meal, and after that, we had no reason to delay any longer. We each picked up our pack. I lost some of my breath under the weight of mine as I hoisted it onto my shoulders.

She led the way down the corridor and through the air lock. We stepped outside into a Hades dawn, and I inhaled the chill in the air. Then I pointed myself toward Mount Ida, which was easy to do, since it took up half the horizon.

"This way, right?" I said.

I was kidding, but she missed it. She was staring back at the lander. "Uh-huh."

"Hey, are you okay?" I asked. "Are you ready for this?"

"Yeah." Her gaze lingered for another moment, and then she turned to face me. "It's weird. I guess it just feels like I should do something to say goodbye."

I wasn't sure what that would look like. "Do you—do you want to visit the graves?"

"No." She shook her head as she cinched up her pack's shoulder straps. "Those are just bodies that got broken. The people are only dead if we don't reach the Tangle."

"Then let's get to the habitat," I said.

"Okay." She pivoted, squaring off against Mount Ida with me. "Let's go."

With that, we set out and left the lander behind.

# 9 — DS *Theseus*

## BEFORE

I'M SITTING ALONE IN THE COMMON ROOM WHEN Liz walks in and announces that my parents are almost established. "They should be coming out of the printers in about an hour," she says. "Do you want to be there?"

"When they come out?" I think about my own experience waking up and decide I really don't want to risk seeing either of my parents naked. "Maybe not *right* when they come out."

Liz nods with a knowing smile. "Understood. I'll come get you when it's time."

"Sounds good," I say, and she leaves.

I settle deeper into my chair, watching the slow rotation of the ship and the stars, imagining what it will be like to see my parents again. I've talked with them over the quantum channel, and they've sent me videos and photos. But this is the first time in six years that I'll be in the same room with them, and I don't know how I feel.

I know how I'm supposed to feel. They're my parents, so I'm supposed to be happy and excited to see them, and I'm supposed to be glad they made it safely, and I feel those things, I do. But I also feel angry at them, and not just for bringing me out here. Ever since my talk with Duncan yesterday, I've been feeling mad at them for leaving me in the first place, back when I was a kid. I feel mad that I'm apparently still mad about that. I'm also scared, but I don't know what I'm scared of.

For a while I sit there by myself in the common room feeling all of that at once, until I can't anymore because it's too overwhelming, and I just let myself slide into neutral, staring out the windows, switching my perception back and forth between a spinning ship and a spinning universe.

Eventually, and inevitably, Liz comes back, smiling in an annoying you-must-be-so-excited kind of way.

"Are you ready?" she asks, which is a really stupid question.

But I stop myself from saying that and offer a flat lie. "Yes."

"Good."

I get up, and she leads me out of the common room. To give my mind something to do for the next few moments, I concentrate on counting my steps as we walk along the *Theseus*'s corridors. *One, two, three, four* . . .

Liz keeps talking. "Your dad arrived before your mom. He wanted to be with her when she emerged from the printer."

*Fourteen.* "Okay," I said.

"Amira is with them both now. They're on *Lander One*, where we established your mom, which works out well."

*Twenty-three.* "Why is that?"

"*Lander One* is yours tonight. Well, yours and your parents'. You know, to give you some privacy. For family time."

I can't even concentrate on counting after that. But I keep walking.

"It's got everything you'll need," she says. "Your own restroom and a galley. And in a day or two it'll take you down to the surface."

"Uh-huh," I say, but I'm still stuck on the other thing. I do not want privacy for family time. Private family time is all I'm going to have for the next year, and I'll probably be sick of private family time for 364 of those days. I'd rather hang out with Duncan and the crew while I still can.

"Is everything okay?" Liz asks.

Another stupid question I have to bite my lips against answering. "Yup."

"Are you sure?"

Now she's watching me as we walk, but I keep my focus on the passageway ahead. "I'm fine."

Several steps later, she gives up with a head shake, and I try to go back to counting, but the numbers scatter as soon as we arrive at the lander. The hatch is in the floor, because the lander attaches to the outside of the *Theseus*'s barrel, and it's open. I look down at the hole, and then we descend a ladder, through a short air lock in the lander's ceiling.

The corridors on the smaller ship are narrower, and after we've passed through a couple of junctions, Liz brings us to a halt. We're standing before a closed hatch, and I am intensely aware that my parents are on the other side, just a few feet away. I manage a deep breath as I prepare for Liz to open it.

But she doesn't.

I glance over at her, and she gestures toward the control panel.

"When you're ready," she says, like time is endless, and no one is waiting for me, and my heart isn't pounding out every second I've been standing here.

I guess I appreciate that she's not trying to force me into this last step, but the control panel is doing its best to stare me down, and I know I don't really have a choice. I manage to hold out for a few more seconds, then hit the button.

The door opens, and there they are.

They look at me and rush toward me before I can really take them in. And then I'm rushing toward them before I've told my feet I'm okay with it. We collide after a few steps, and our hugs are uncoordinated, arms landing where they land. I'm holding my mom, and her shoulder is pressing into my throat, choking me a little as she squeezes me, hard. I squeeze her in return, and I feel my dad wrap his long arms around both of us.

I forgot a long time ago what it felt like to hug them. I thought it would come back to me, but there is nothing familiar about this. My mom feels bony, and she smells only of the laundered jumpsuit she's wearing. My dad is rounder than he used to be, and shorter. Or maybe I've simply grown out of his hug like I grew out of my old fleece pajamas with feet.

My mom shifts, like a signal to end the hug, only she doesn't let go, and I realize she's crying.

I am not crying, the way a dam is not a river.

My dad tightens his embrace around us for a moment and then pulls away. Then my mom allows me a partial release, holding me at arm's length by my shoulders. We're the same height now. I might even be taller. She smiles, and that expression, at least, is something I know well.

"My god," she whispers. "Jessica."

She looks older than I expected. It's only been six years, but maybe it's just a weariness that I never saw across the quantum channel. Her face is thin, with wrinkles at the edges of her eyes, and a lot of her brown hair has turned gray. She has it cut short, like the captain's.

"Hi, Mom," I say.

She lets go of my shoulders and brings her hands to her face, hiding her mouth with her fingers. Over her shoulder, my dad wipes his eyes with a thumb, his other arm around my mom. His hair isn't as gray as hers, but I hadn't realized until now just how much of it he had lost. But I've seen pics of Pop-Pop when he was Dad's age, and he was basically bald.

"Hi, Dad."

"Jess, you—" He clears his throat with a grunt, his cold blue eyes standing out against his weathered, olive skin. "This is—this is overwhelming. I don't quite know what to say."

Neither do I. This isn't a moment I could have prepared for, no matter how long Liz had let me stand in that hallway. I notice she's gone, and Ms. Kateb isn't here, either. I'm alone with my parents in what looks like the lander's galley. There's a kitchen area to one side, and a table in the middle surrounded by chairs. My mom follows my gaze.

"Would you like to sit down?"

"Sure," I say, even though that's not what I was thinking, but as we each take a seat, I'm glad she suggested it.

My mom sits next to me, and my dad sits across the table from both of us. She lays her hand on my forearm and leaves it there. The three of us smile at one another, but we don't say anything for long enough that I feel the need to shovel something into the silence.

"I'm glad you made it safely," I say.

"We're so—" she says.

"And we—" he says.

They stop. My dad smiles and gives my mom a nod, clearing the way, and then she says, "We are so excited to have you with us."

I can feel she means it. But it's not what I want to hear. If they really missed me that much, they could've seen me any time they wanted. All they had to do was come home. But instead they're glad that I'm the one who traveled fourteen light-years to be with them.

My dad leans toward me. "I am so happy to see you."

"And we hope you're at least a little happy to be here," Mom adds.

"I am . . . happy to see you, too," I say with a fleeting glance, and leave it at that, because I don't want one of the first things I say to my mom after six years to be a lie.

"I have a surprise for you," Dad says.

"What is it?"

"Wait here. I'll be right back."

He pushes himself to his feet and hurries from the galley, and I aim a quick, questioning glance at my mom.

"You'll see," she says. "This was all his idea. And it took some doing."

Now I'm even more curious.

A few moments later he returns, hiding something behind his back as he approaches us, his smile wide and eager. When he reaches the table, he sets down a long, flat box in front of me, and I gasp as soon as I see it.

"Magical Mountain," I whisper.

"It seemed fitting," Dad says. "Though I don't expect Mount Ida will be home to many kobolds or dragons."

I hear him, but I'm barely listening, because I'm staring at the box. It's not just a copy of the game. Somehow, it's *my* game. I can see my name in faded green marker on the side of the box, exactly where my mom wrote it when I was six, before she let me take the game over to my friend Lien's house.

But it can't be my game. Resources out here are too precious to print anything but travelers and replacement parts for the ship, and it would take fourteen years at the speed of light to bring the game here from earth, and since no ship travels that fast, the game would've had to start its journey here before I was born.

But it's here, right in front of me, and eventually I let myself pick it up, feeling the texture of it against my fingertips. Then I tip the box, and the wooden game pieces slide and rattle inside. The sound does something to me. It cracks me open, and suddenly I'm six years old, carrying the game into the living room before bed, hair still wet from my bath, teeth brushed, warm in my pajamas.

Now I do feel like crying, and I keep my gaze fixed on the box, at the image of the castle on top of the mountain. "How did you—"

"I had Pop-Pop scan the original," Dad says. "Then Dr. Martin used one of his engineering printers to establish it here."

Now I understand why Evan mentioned the game the first time we met. "Isn't that illegal?"

"It's against regulations," Mom says. "Especially on a ship this small. So don't mention this to the captain. We don't want to get Dr. Martin in trouble."

"I won't," I say. "But why would he—"

"He's a father," Dad says. "And we few, we happy few, we band of brothers take care of each other out here when we can. And there really isn't a lot of mass to that game."

He's right about that. It's just a flimsy cardboard box filled with little game pieces and air, but somehow it feels like the first solid thing I've touched since Jim Kelly put me into the scanner.

"Thank you," I say.

"You're welcome," Dad says.

He puts a hand on my shoulder, and I can't help but turn to look at it, like I can't decide if it belongs there. Parents aren't supposed to feel like strangers, but that's almost how he and my mom feel to me, even after this gift. I don't know how to deal with that, or talk about it. Maybe I'll figure it out. But for now, I'd rather just leave it alone, so I turn to something I do still remember.

"Do you want to play?" I give the box a little shake.

"I was hoping you would ask," he says, and resumes his seat across the table.

I set the box down, and the cardboard chirps as I lift the lid away. Inside, the game even smells right, like old books and wood. I unfold the board and set it up, placing the glass gems and the dragon in the cave, along with the stack of riddle cards and the vaguely humanoid player pieces.

"You still remember where everything goes?" Mom says.

"Of course," I say. "Don't you? I made you play it pretty much every night."

"Yes." She sighs. "You certainly did."

I claim the red player piece, obviously. "You want green?"

She nods. "I see no reason to break with tradition."

"But you do see a reason to mess with me?" Dad says.

"It's not our fault you're color-blind," I say.

"Oh, don't worry," he says. "I can tell your pieces apart just fine."

"You can?" I scowl a bit. "Since when?"

"I don't know." He shrugs, looking upward. "Must be the lighting in here."

Mom holds her piece up a few inches in front of her nose. "What are these supposed to be? Trolls?"

"They're kobolds," Dad says.

"They're what?"

"Kobolds." He picks up the yellow piece and places it on the board, at the base of the mountain with ours. "They're a kind of mythical figure from German folklore. Like a leprechaun, I think."

"Let me see the picture." Mom reaches for the lid, like she doesn't believe him.

But I know he's right. The random quirkiness of the game was always one of the things I loved about it, even though Lien thought it was weird and didn't ever want to play it again.

"Okay, who goes first?" I ask.

My dad bows his head dramatically. "I think that honor belongs to you."

I pick up the die. "I'm not going to argue with that." Then I roll a four and start my kobold up the path.

Mom is still frowning at the lid. "Where did we even find this game?"

"Chicago," Dad says, and rolls the die.

Then my mom takes her turn, and after a few times around the table I start to feel more at ease. I wouldn't say I'm comfortable yet, but this at least feels somewhat normal. Maybe even a bit nostalgic.

"So what have you been up to?" Dad asks. "Our liaison said you arrived a couple of days ago."

"Yeah," I say. "I've just been, you know, hanging out. There's a guy here, Duncan. He's my age."

Mom rolls the die. "Oh?"

"He's the captain's son," I say.

"Well that's a nice surprise," she says. "You don't find many children out here."

I want to point out there's a reason for that, and also that Duncan and I aren't children. But I don't.

"At least you've had the company of a peer," Dad says, taking his turn. "Before you . . ."

I guess he decides not to finish that statement. So I finish it for him. "Before I become a hermit for a year?"

He exhales. "Before you have this experience."

"You've met the captain, I assume?" Mom says, clearly trying to change the subject.

I nod, roll the die, and move my piece into the mountain's cave to answer one of the dragon's riddles and collect some gems. "She's nice. The crew members all like her."

"That says something. Your father and I have dealt with our share of tyrants. The stress gets to them."

"I've been saying for years that ISTA should reduce the length of a ship command." Dad leans back in his chair and folds his arms, a gesture that matches the dinner-table memories deep in my mind. "Five years is too long. Captains shouldn't serve more than three years in deep space."

"What about scientists?" I ask, because he and my mom have been gone for a lot longer than three years.

"The pressures of being a captain are very different," he says.

"Not for their families back home."

With that, the mood in the room shifts, growing heavier, like the *Theseus* has increased its rate of spin and gained more gravity.

My dad looks at me with his blue eyes, and I can't tell if they're teary again or just shiny in the light of the lander's galley. "We know it's been hard on you," he whispers.

"Do you?" I ask.

"Of course we do." He unfolds his arms and leans closer. "It's been hard for us, too. There were times we weren't sure we could endure it. But one day you'll realize that some sacrifices simply must be made. That's one reason we brought you out here. We want you to see and understand why we chose—"

"To leave me?" I look back and forth between them, feeling my throat tighten, confused about how we got here so quickly when I hadn't meant to bring this up. "So you're saying that you made me come all the way out here just so you can try to convince me that you made the right choice when you left me?"

"I wouldn't put it that way," Dad says.

I raise my voice. "Then how would you put it?"

"I would say—"

"Stephen, please. We agreed." Mom fixes him with a fiery glare, and it's another look that I recognize. Suddenly I'm a kid again, standing in my mom's office surrounded by the shattered remains of a large chunk of amethyst that I just dropped. Her glare terrified me back then, and it silences my dad now. She turns to me and says, "Jessica, you have the right to feel whatever you are feeling. Your father and I respect that. We're going to have a lot of time to work through it all together, and we know those conversations will be hard. But I don't want to spend our first night together fighting." She glances at my dad again.

"I'm sorry, Jess," he says.

I'm not sure what he's sorry for. Not for bringing me out here, I know that.

"Whose turn is it?" Mom asks, but she doesn't wait for an answer. "I think it's mine."

We talk less over the next hour as the three of us make our way up the mountain. Dad manages to reach the castle first, but in the end I have more gems and riddle cards, so I win the game.

"I think you have those cards memorized," he says.

I know he's just trying to tease me, to lighten the mood, but it sounds like an accusation.

"That was enjoyable," Mom says. "I'd forgotten—" She yawns, long and wide. "Oh goodness, excuse me."

"Teleport lag," Dad says. "We should turn in early. You need your rest."

"How about you?" Mom asks.

He looks down at his hands. "I do feel a bit off."

"Off how?"

"I don't know. Just . . . off."

"I'm sure you'll feel better after a good night's rest," she says.

With that, we all rise from the table. I leave the game where it is, and we claim our cabins just down the hall. My mom and dad each take their own room, because the beds aren't big enough for two. But my mom says that's how most beds are out here, so she and my dad have gotten used to sleeping apart. We say good night, and they pull me into another group hug and tell me they love me. They tell me they're happy I'm here. Then they let me go.

THE FARTHER WE WALKED ACROSS THE SURFACE OF Hades, the weirder it felt to be here. The increased gravity was a part of that, and I was still getting used to the new heaviness in my feet, and the tightness of the compression socks. They were supposed to help with circulation, to stop the planet from pulling my blood into my legs and feet, at least until my heart caught up with the new demands. Before we'd even walked a kilometer, the socks felt scratchy and I felt out of breath. We weren't walking very hard or fast.

"You doing okay?" she asked me, after a little while.

The worry on her face annoyed me, especially since she seemed to be breathing just fine. "I'm good," I said.

She watched me for a moment, like she didn't believe me. "Just let me know if you're going to pass out or anything."

"Yeah, you too." It seemed she was even stronger than I'd thought she was, and that pissed me off. Or maybe it just disturbed me to see such a difference between us.

But it wasn't just her and the gravity that felt off. The oddness of the alien landscape that surrounded me made my brain itch as badly as the socks chafed my calves, mostly because I couldn't pinpoint exactly what was wrong with it. The disorientation went beyond the purple ferns, or the size of Mount Ida, or the metallic colors in the rocks and soil. It wasn't any one thing on its own. It was the whole picture, a thousand alien details that my mind added up to mean I simply didn't belong there.

It also didn't help that the ground we covered wasn't as flat as it had looked from the lander. We climbed up hills and down through gullies, into the coppery wind. We even crossed a couple of shallow streams, which might have been reassuring if we could drink the water, but I wasn't about to risk getting a space parasite. Pop-Pop had made me watch enough old science fiction movies to know how that would end.

After a few kilometers, we finally settled into a rhythm, just walking and thinking our own thoughts. I wondered how many of those thoughts were the same.

Later that morning, we came across something new to both of us. It looked like a cross between a cactus and a palm tree. It wasn't very tall, maybe two meters, but it was fat, and the frond leaf things coming out of the top drooped low, almost to the ground, creating a canopy. We stopped for a minute to look at it, and then something rustled the ever-present ferns behind us.

"I hope that's just one of those ferrets," I said.

"You mean a mole-snake?" She glanced over her shoulder. "There's nothing else it could be."

"Nothing? On this whole planet?"

She didn't answer. She just set off again. "Let's keep moving."

I took another glance at the ferns, saw nothing, and followed after her.

Even though we walked for that whole day, Mount Ida didn't seem any closer by the end of it. Before the sun went down, we picked a level spot to set up our tent, in a clearing free of the ferns, near a cluster of the cactus-palms. The tent went up easy, mostly because Hades wasn't trying to bake us or freeze us, so we didn't have to hassle with any of the climate control systems.

After that, we set up the water reclamation unit and sat down on the ground to eat our cold dinner. I was trying not to show it, but I felt completely exhausted. My legs had gone boneless, and I was pretty sure my shoulders would have permanent dents from the straps of my backpack. On a positive note, I was hungry enough that the packaged food tasted way better than it had back at the lander.

The sun continued to light up the top half of the mountain, even after it had disappeared over the horizon. I watched as a tide of shadow rose from the ground and wiped the golden glow away until it reached the tip of the peak, and then that last bit of light also went cold, like a blown-out birthday candle on top of a cake.

Then the stars turned on, and there were more than I had ever seen. But it looked different from the sky on Earth.

"Think of all the new constellations up there," I said.

"There aren't any constellations up there," she said.

"What do you mean?"

"There's no one on this planet to name them."

"Okay, fine. But do you remember what Dad used to say? A constellation is a story we write with stars." I looked up, and without searching very hard, I found a familiar shape. "See that bright star there?" I said, pointing. "That is the tip of a unicorn horn. If you follow it, you can see the eye and the nose. That constellation is called Avery."

She looked up, but she said nothing.

It occurred to me that my parents had probably seen skies like this many times. Maybe they had even named their own constellations. Maybe the stars were one of the things that made it all worth it to them. Because there had to be something.

I'd often wondered what was so great about space exploration that my mom and dad had been willing to trade me in for a career with ISTA. They would never put it that way, of course, but that's basically what they had done, and as I thought about that, sitting there without them on Hades, I got mad, in spite of the pretty stars.

"You're fooling yourself," she said next to me. "There aren't any unicorns up there. There's no pattern. It's all just random chaos." Then she stood and brushed the dirt off her backside. "We should get some sleep."

That was fine with me, so I followed her to the tent. We arranged ourselves in that cramped space like we had in my bed the night before, close to each other, but not touching. For a moment or two I lay there in the dark, listening to the winds of Hades gently buffeting the tent and stirring the ferns, but I fell asleep quickly and stayed that way until morning.

When I first opened my eyes, nothing hurt. But then I tried to move, and all my muscles complained at once, some just whining, others shouting and swearing at me. I swore back at them, and not under my breath.

"I know," she said next to me. "I'm sore, too."

"You're just trying to make me feel better."

"I'm in too much pain to think about your feelings."

I looked up at the domed roof of the tent. "I'm hungry. But if I want to eat, I have to move, and I never want to move again. How long does it take a person to starve to death?"

"You'll loosen up." She grunted her way through a slow sit-up, rolled onto all fours, and opened the front tent flap. "I'm going to check the water reclaimer. We need to know if it's working."

She crawled outside. The chilled morning air that reached into the tent felt good against my face. I closed my eyes, took a few deep breaths, and then repeated her sit-up-and-roll maneuver at about a third her speed with twice as much groaning.

When I left the tent, she was standing by the water reclaimer and gave me a thumbs-up. I nodded, aware of the fact that a broken reclaimer at this point wouldn't be a big deal. We could just hike back to the lander. A broken reclaimer several days into our hike, on the other hand, would be a much bigger problem.

I went to my pack and pulled out some food for breakfast, which I ate standing, gazing out over the Hades dawn. A beautiful peace held the ferns and the rolling hills like it was a painting. Then a breeze stirred

it all up, and the painting came alive, as if the artist was still at work. I
sighed, smiling at the view.

I had always wanted to go camping with Mom and Dad, but they
had never taken me, and then they were gone. And camping certainly
wasn't something Gram and Pop-Pop had any interest in doing. Lien
had asked me to go with her family once, but they went in a big RV with
a built-in espresso machine, and that wasn't what I'd had in mind. I had
wanted what I somehow enjoyed that morning on Hades, muscles sore,
eating terrible food in the cold as I watched the planet wake up.

"Mole-snake," she said.

I turned toward her. "What?"

She pointed with her fork, one cheek round with a bite she hadn't
finished chewing.

I looked and saw two black eyes sparkling at me from the ferns
about five meters away.

"Or a ferret, or whatever you call them." She drew a disinterested
circle with her fork in the air before plunging it back into her packet of
food.

I watched the creature for a moment. I had no way of knowing
whether it was the same ferret I'd given my eggs to back at the lander,
but I wanted to believe it was. I took a step toward it, expecting it to
disappear, but it didn't. It stayed right where it was, its unblinking eyes
locked on me. I knew that would probably change if I got too close, so
I crouched down where I was and spooned some of my food out onto
the ground.

"Here you go," I said.

"What are you doing?" she asked behind me.

I kept my voice soft, without looking away from those two black
eyes. "What does it look like I'm doing?"

"It looks like you're feeding some of our precious food to a wild
animal."

"Relax," I said. "It's just a few bites."

"I think you'll wish you had those bites if we can't find the habitat."

I ignored her. The ferret hadn't moved, but it also hadn't run away, and I could see its feathery whiskers twitching.

"How do you know you're not poisoning that thing?" she asked.

"It wouldn't eat it if it was poison."

"Yes, it would. Remember Bradley Whittaker?"

Prior to that moment, I hadn't, but as soon as she said that name, I did. I recalled the gasps and the sight of a tank full of dead fish in Mr. Shapiro's third-grade classroom, some of them floating on their sides at the surface of the water, some of them lying milky-eyed on the blue gravel at the bottom. Bradley was crying. He'd earned the privilege of feeding the fish the day before, but instead of the usual flakes, he'd accidentally given them the little pellets of plant fertilizer that Mr. Shapiro kept nearby for his orchid. The fish ate it anyway. The jars were about the same size, and I could have easily made the same mistake.

I took another look at the ferret, and then I tried scooping the food back up into my pouch, feeling foolish, wondering why she had needed to remind me of those dead fish.

"Sorry," I whispered to the creature, hoping I hadn't already killed one of them.

"Do you want to break down the tent or the reclaimer?" she asked.

"Um. Tent, I guess."

She nodded, and we turned to our work for the next several minutes. She finished well before me and then helped me figure out the infuriating geometry needed to bend and fold the tent away. It wasn't long before we were ready to leave our campsite behind.

I gasped in pain as I pulled on my pack, my body done for the day before we'd even started.

She took a deep breath next to me. "Ready?"

"No," I said.

"Me neither." And then she set off.

I looked for the ferret but didn't see it anymore. If it was the same ferret I'd given the eggs, I hoped it would go back home. I felt guilty for having fed it, not just because I didn't want to be Bradley Whittaker, but because I didn't want it to follow us thinking it could get more food.

As I pulled my gaze away from the ferns, I saw something small on the ground near my feet. I picked it up, but then I could only stand there staring at it, completely bewildered.

"Everything okay?" she called back to me, already several meters away.

I couldn't answer her. I couldn't make sense of the thing in my hand, an odd little piece of painted wood. I knew what it was, but another part of my brain refused to believe that it could possibly be what it was, where it was.

"Did you find something?" she asked.

"Magical Mountain," I whispered.

"What?"

I looked up at her. Then I looked again at the yellow kobold between my fingers. "It's a piece from Magical Mountain."

Her hand went instantly to a pocket of her jumpsuit. She dug around for a moment, and then her eyes got big. "Shit," she said.

# 11—DS *Theseus*

## BEFORE

I WAKE UP IN THE MIDDLE OF THE NIGHT. FOR A moment I'm disoriented, wondering where I am, and then I remember I'm on the *Theseus*, sleeping in the lander, and my parents are in their own rooms next to mine. But as that initial confusion fades, I'm left with a nagging sense that something woke me, like a noise. But the ship is quiet.

My mind is not.

I roll over. There's someone in my room.

I let out a yelp and scramble into the corner of my bed, away from the dark figure looming in the corner, but in the next moment I recognize him.

"Shit! Dad—" I lay a hand over my beating heart with a nervous laugh. "What the hell are you doing?"

He just stands there, silently.

"You scared me." I flip on the small reading light. "What's going on?"

He's looking at me, still half concealed in shadow. His stare is odd, cold, but not lifeless or vacant. He's seeing me, but I can't tell what he's thinking.

I lean forward a bit. "Is everything okay?"

He blinks, but otherwise his rigid body doesn't move.

"Dad, seriously. You're starting to freak me out. What's going on?"

He's still staring at me without saying a word, and I wonder if maybe he's sleepwalking. I think I remember hearing somewhere that you're not supposed to wake up a sleepwalker. I don't know if that's true, but if it is, it leaves me kind of stuck, because the room is too narrow for me to get around him easily. And he's blocking the door anyway.

The longer he stands there, the less he seems like my dad, and the more like a dad-shaped container holding something . . . else. But the truth is, this could be totally normal for him and I wouldn't know it, because I don't actually know him that well. It's entirely possible that in a few hours, I'll mention this little staring contest over a breakfast of space rations, and my mom will chuckle and tell me it happens all the time.

That would surprise me, though. Because this is fucking weird.

I'm getting to the point where I'm about to shout for my mom and risk whatever happens if I wake him up, but before I do, he turns and leaves. He doesn't nod or say a word. He just vanishes into the dark corridor, leaving my door open. I hop out of bed and peer out into the hallway after him.

He's walking away slowly, silently, lit from below by the pale night lighting along the floor, and then he disappears around a corner. For a moment, I wonder if I should follow him, to make sure he's okay. But that's not something I'm particularly eager to do, and so I manage to convince myself he's not in any real danger. It's not like he can just sleepwalk out into space through an air lock. But I think maybe I should wake up my mom, just in case. So I step out into the corridor, toward her room.

He reappears suddenly from around the corner, and he's walking toward me. I gasp a little and retreat into my room, ready to close my hatch and lock it if he tries to follow, but he stops at his room and goes inside.

I wait a few moments, watching. He doesn't re-emerge, so I assume he must have gone back to sleep in his bed like a normal person, and I shut my door. Then I lock it.

The next morning, when I enter the lander's galley, I find my mom already sitting at the table, holding a mug of steaming coffee that has filled the room with its toasty aroma.

She looks up and smiles. "Good morning."

I smile back. "Morning." Then I go to the small counter to find some breakfast and make some coffee of my own. "Is Dad up?"

"Not yet." She raises her mug with both hands and takes a sip. "I guess he had a rough night."

"He's not the only one."

"Why do you say that?"

"He was sleepwalking."

"What?"

"Yeah." I throw a waffle into the microwave. "I woke up, and he was standing in my room. Scared me half to death. Then he was wandering around the lander."

She sets her coffee down. "Are you sure it was your father?"

"Um, I know it's been a few years, but I do know my father when I see him." I heat some water for my instant coffee. "So yeah, it was him."

She scowls, but I don't get the feeling it's in response to my sarcasm.

"I guess he's not usually a sleepwalker?" I say.

"No." A moment goes by, and then she shakes her head and sighs. "Must be the teleportation. It can disrupt biorhythms, like sleep patterns."

I nod, keeping my comment on the weirdness of this disruption to myself. When my food is ready I take it to the table and sit across from her. I notice the Magical Mountain game has been put away nearby, which my mom must have done.

"Other than being awakened by your father's adventure," she says, "did you sleep okay?"

I shrug. "Fine, I guess."

"I slept like lead," she says. "I was so tired."

We both sip our coffee. She hunches around her mug, like she's warming herself with it. "This ship runs a little cold, I think."

"I wouldn't know," I say.

She nods, and a moment goes by.

"Did, uh, did teleportation make you tired?" she asks.

"Yeah." I take a bite of my spongy waffle, its fake maple flavor baked in.

"Teleportation fatigue is pretty normal," she says.

"That's what I hear."

"Do you feel like you've recovered?"

The squishy sound of my chewing is obnoxiously loud, even to me. "I guess so."

Another moment passes.

"How long have you been established, now?" she asks.

"Three days."

"Ah." She nods, like that means something. But none of her questions go anywhere. They're the small-talk questions you ask a stranger.

"I actually sleep better in partial gravity." She wiggles a bit in her chair. "Less pressure on my back and hips."

I take another bite, and then another, trying really hard to chew quietly in the silence of the room. Neither of us speaks for a while, but when the break in our conversation grows wide enough that one of us needs to say something, she just smiles at me again. It's the kind of forced smile you give someone when you don't know what to say to them. I smile back, because I know that's what she needs, but I resent having to reassure her. She's the one who wasn't there for all the mornings we could've had before school and work. She's the reason this is uncomfortable.

Things get more uncomfortable when my dad lumbers in yawning and rubbing his face like it's made of clay.

"What a night," he says, heading right for the coffee.

"Jess was just telling me," Mom says.

He hooks a coffee mug with a finger and pulls it from the cupboard. "Telling you what?"

"Apparently, you were sleepwalking."

He sets the mug down and looks at me. "Sleepwalking?"

"Well, you didn't seem to be awake," I say.

I tell him everything I saw him do, and he finishes making his coffee as he listens. Then he joins us at the table, his eyebrows pressed low under the weight of his confusion.

"I don't remember any of that," he says.

"I'm sure it's just a side effect of the teleportation," Mom says.

"Hmm." He taps his coffee mug with a fingernail, making a little chiming sound.

"You could talk to the ship's doctor," Mom says. "Just to be on the safe side? I can't remember his name—"

"Gutiérrez," I say.

She nods. "Right."

"I might mention it to him," Dad says. "But I don't want to waste his time over nothing."

He shrugs, then claps his hands together. "So what's on the docket for today?"

Mom eyes him for a moment and then says, "Review the latest Carver data from ISTA, then wake up the habitat and run a remote systems check."

"Okay," he says. "But let's just keep it to the critical systems."

She shakes her head. "Full diagnostics."

"That'll take a lot of time."

"That's protocol," she says. "It's been down there, unoccupied, for eighteen months."

He turns to me with a smirk. "You can always count on your mom to bring up protocol."

"Protocol exists for a reason," she says.

"I know," he says. "And that reason is an ISTA bureaucrat who's never left Earth orbit, but somehow knows how things should be done out here."

Now Mom leans toward me and smirks. "You can always count on your father to bring up ISTA bureaucrats."

This isn't exactly a fight between them, but it also isn't friendly. Whatever it is, I get the sense that it has played out many times before without me, but now that I'm here, they're both looking to me as if I'll take their side.

"A full diagnostic will take at least twenty-four hours," Dad says.

"At least," Mom says.

He sighs. "I guess that means we're on the *Theseus* for another day. Sorry, Jess."

"That's okay," I say. I am not feeling impatient to leave.

"We'd better get started." My mom takes a long drink of coffee and then stands. "I'll go shower."

My dad nods, and she leaves the galley. Then he turns and looks at me, and I feel the awkward weight of his expectation. Before he can ask me anything, I fold the last, big bite of waffle into my mouth, so I have an excuse not to talk.

"Is it what you thought it would be?" he asks anyway, and with my mouth full, he guesses at what my follow-up question would be. "I mean this," he says, glancing around the galley. "Outer space. Is it what you expected?"

I shrug and keep chewing.

"Oh, not easily impressed?" he says, trying to tease me. "Is my daughter that kind of teenager?"

He'd know the answer to that question if he'd been around, so I keep him waiting. But eventually I finish chewing and swallow the last of the waffle. "It's not about being impressed," I say.

"Then what is it?"

I shrug again, even more deliberately. "I didn't know what to expect. I've never really thought about it."

"You never— You mean you haven't imagined what it would be like? To be out here with us?"

"No." It's too early for this conversation. "I haven't."

"Really?"

"Really," I say, a bit surprised that his surprise seems genuine.

"Huh."

He's frowning at me in disbelief, waiting for me to elaborate and explain myself, but the truth is pretty simple. "Mostly I've imagined what it would be like to have you back home," I say.

His mouth opens just enough to suggest that he would say something if he had the words, but he ends up staring down into his coffee instead.

"I mean, of course I've thought about you and Mom," I add. "A lot. I've imagined you out here, exploring. But I've never pictured myself as a part of it."

"I wonder why," he says, still looking down.

"I don't know. I was a kid. To be honest, I kind of assumed you didn't want me to be a part of it."

"Why would you think that?"

"Maybe because you left me behind?"

He falls silent again, even as things fall into place in my mind, and I realize something.

"Oh," I whisper. "Wow. Now I get it."

He looks up. "Get what?"

"Why you brought me here. The whole time you've been gone, you assumed I was just sitting at home, wanting to be out here with you."

"I—" He pauses before continuing. "Yes, I guess we did. But even if we were wrong, you're here now, and I can't bring myself to apologize for it. I'm too happy to see you."

"I'm . . . happy to see you, too." That much, at least, is true.

"But I am now sorry for one thing."

I look hard at him and wait.

"I'm sorry we didn't ask you," he says.

Hearing that from him means more to me than I would have expected. "Would my answer have made a difference?"

He seems to consider this for a moment, then finally says, "I don't know."

I appreciate his honesty, but it's a little late for him to be having this kind of basic insight about his own daughter. I'm here now, and I don't match the version of me my parents have in their heads. They've been telling themselves a story about me for years, but it isn't true. It'll probably take time to correct it. And I guess I've been telling myself stories about them, too.

He sighs. "'For of all sad words of tongue or pen, the saddest are these: "It might have been!"'"

"You sound like Pop-Pop."

"Well, before he was your Pop-Pop, he was my dad."

"Was that Shakespeare?"

"Longfellow."

"He usually—"

"No, wait. John Greenleaf Whittier." He waves his hand. "One of those Fireside guys."

"What guys?" Mom asks as she enters the room, her hair wet from her shower.

"Poets," Dad says. "Some of Pop-Pop's favorites."

"Ah." She reclaims her coffee mug from the table and goes to make a second cup.

"That was a fast shower," I say, trying to change the topic of conversation.

"You got that right," Dad says, using his fake cowboy accent that I had almost forgotten. "Your mom here takes the quickest shower this side of the Milky Way."

"We have to conserve resources," she says. "ISTA recommends taking three to five minutes. Just think of a favorite song about that long and sing it in the shower to time yourself."

I realize she's talking to me now. Giving me space-shower tips.

"I use 'What a Wonderful World,'" she adds. "It's only about two minutes long, which gives me a bit of time to spare. If I want it. And it puts me in a good mood."

"Uh, thanks," I say, standing up.

I do not take an ISTA-recommended shower of three-to-five minutes, and by the time I return to the galley, my mom has left to see Liz and get started on the habitat systems check. My dad is working at a computer terminal.

"Make sure your stuff is all okay," I say. "At least one of my files got messed up."

"Really?" He keeps his eyes on the screen, clicking through files and folders. "Messed up how?"

"I don't really know. One of my pictures got scrambled with an image of . . . something."

"What was it?"

"I don't know. There were these horns or claws or something. I didn't really want to look too closely. It freaked me out."

"So far everything looks good with our stuff. Did they get yours figured out?"

"No. Liz just had them resend the packet."

"Huh. Spooky."

"It was."

"If it happens again, your mom might be able to figure it out. She's picked up some impressive computer skills over the years."

I had never once thought of my mom as a hacker, and that just reminds me of how long they've been gone. A few moments pass, neither of us talking while he works. I'm not sure quite what to do with myself, so I just sit there.

"You know, this is going to take me a while," he finally says. "I'd love your company, but it won't hurt my feelings if you want to find something more interesting to do."

I hadn't really planned anything, but now that he's brought it up, I realize I do want to hang out with Duncan a bit more before we leave. But it feels a bit weird to just leave my dad alone when I haven't seen him in six years.

"Are you sure?" I say. "Because I can stay . . ."

"I know." He looks over his shoulder at me. "And as much as I'd like to give you my attention, I need to focus on this boring crap. Besides, I think it would be good for you to load up on human interaction. Why don't you go find the captain's son, uh—" He snaps his fingers. "What was his name?"

"Duncan."

"Yeah, Duncan. Why don't you go hang out with him? I'm sure he'd enjoy your company. But maybe come back and have lunch with me."

I finally smile and agree. "Deal."

He nods, and I leave him to his work, but on my way to the ladder, I spot the yellow kobold piece on the floor near the table. My mom must have missed it when she put the game away. I pick it up and slip it into my pocket with a grin.

"Thanks, Dad," I say.

He spins his swivel chair around to face me. "What for?"

"For giving me Magical Mountain." I point at the box sitting on the table. "The game. Not the volcano."

He chuckles. "I was worried you'd think it was dumb."

"Why?"

He shrugs. "Because you're older now. I know you're not that little girl in pajamas anymore."

"I kind of am," I say. "A part of me is."

He smiles. "I'm glad." Then he swivels back to scanning files, and I climb up through the hatch.

Duncan isn't in the *Theseus*'s common room, so I head for the next most likely place I think he'll be, and that's the hub. As I ascend the ladder and then glide along the spoke, I decide I've finally gotten the hang of getting around on the ship. The tightness of the tunnel doesn't even bother me much anymore, and when I reach the hub, I execute a perfect kickoff in the microgravity and land exactly where I want to. From there I sail upship, toward the command module, looking for Duncan.

I find him at the same window we looked through the other day, and he seems surprised to see me as I float up next to him.

"I thought you'd be with your parents," he says.

"They're working."

"Working? How long has it been since they've seen you?"

"Six years."

He shakes his head with a chuckle. "They sound like my mom."

"Parents are all the same, I guess."

"Not all parents."

I think I hear sadness and anger in his voice, but I might be imagining it because I know about his dad.

"And at least you have both of yours," he adds.

It seems like he wants me to open the door on the subject. "Your dad is back on Earth?"

He nods, eyes aimed out the window.

"What does he think about you being out here?"

"If he thinks about me at all, he thinks I'm dead." His voice is flat, his face empty. "As far as he's concerned, I died the day I got into the scanner."

"Liz kind of mentioned something about that. I'm sorry."

"Thanks," he says, but there isn't any feeling behind it.

"So . . . is he Antimaterialist or something?"

Duncan shakes his head. "He's not out protesting. He's not one of those people who thinks ISTA should be charged with murder. He just can't accept that I'm the same person who got into the scanner. He thinks only God can put a soul in a body." He turns his head and looks at me. "He wrote me a goodbye letter before I came out here. A real goodbye. Terminal."

I swallow. "What did it say?"

"Probably what you'd expect." He shakes his head at the memory, like it's lodged somewhere he doesn't want it to be.

"And you came out here anyway," I say. "That makes you brave."

He frowns, and I worry he thinks I'm making fun of him. But I'm not.

"Duncan, you are." I put my hand on his shoulder. "I don't know many people who would do what you did. I know I'm not that brave."

"I'm not brave," he says. "I just knew he wasn't ever going to change his mind, and I decided I wasn't going to spend the rest of my life on Earth to please him."

I pull my hand back. "You make it sound simple." But simple doesn't mean easy, and I imagine his teleportation experience was probably very different from mine. "Has he ever—"

An alarm blares, jolting me. Red lights flash up and down the hub, and then a very calm and slightly mechanical voice speaks over the ship's main comm. *"Code blue, code blue."*

"What's that?" I ask.

Duncan looks upward, listening. "Medical emergency."

"Medical emer—"

"Shh!"

*"All medical staff to* Lander One. *Repeat. Code blue, code blue . . ."*

"Shit!" I kick off and shoot toward the nearest spoke. "I left my dad on *Lander One*!"

# 12—Hades

## AFTER

I TURNED TO FACE HER, STILL HOLDING THE IMPOS-sible little wooden game piece. "What do you mean, *shit*?" My mind sped through possibilities, but I couldn't think of a single way that piece could be here on the surface of Hades. But I knew it must have come from her. "Do you mean I wasn't supposed to see this? Were you hiding it?"

"That's not—" She looked away, off into the distance somewhere, tapping the pocket where she'd just gone looking for it. "Yes," she finally said. "I was hiding it."

"Why?" I gripped the piece in my fist and shook it at her. "What is this? How is this even here?"

She shut her mouth and said nothing, which infuriated me. I charged a few steps toward her, kicking and snapping through purple ferns. But she didn't move or flinch, and I stopped short a pace away. Because what was I going to do? Hit her? I figured she could probably hit me back even harder. I relaxed my fist and opened my hand, and found I'd squeezed the shape of the kobold into my palm.

"Why were you hiding this?" I asked, trying to sound calm, and hopefully stay calm. "And what else are you hiding from me."

"I'm not—"

"Don't bullshit me. You can't bullshit me, not *me*."

She sighs. "If you really believe I'm hiding something from you, do you really think I would tell you just like that?"

That both denied and admitted nothing, while also reminding me that she had all the power. I couldn't force her to tell me anything. Or do anything. I had been forced to trust her since I'd stepped out of the printer. I'd had enough of that imbalance. I had to take back some power of my own, which meant using the few things I did know against her.

I took a deep breath and sat down cross-legged on the ground, my sweaty hands resting in my lap. It was a pretty risky move, letting down my defenses like that. My muscles stayed tense, poised to fight, even though I tried to look calm.

"What are you doing?" she asked.

"Nothing," I said.

"Then stand up. We have to get moving."

"I'm not going anywhere with you."

She snorted. "Stop acting like a child."

"You realize you're only a few weeks older than me, right?"

"I guess those weeks make all the difference."

I shook my head and looked down at the yellow piece. I'd never met anyone else who had even heard of Magical Mountain, so the chances seemed pretty slim that someone else had brought a yellow kobold all these light-years from Earth. It hadn't come the slow way, I was sure of that.

"Who printed this?" I asked.

"What do you mean?"

"You know what I mean. Or are you suggesting someone shipped this to Hades in the mail?"

Her lips thinned, and I could tell she was thinking about how to answer me, or maybe whether she would answer me at all.

"The ship's engineer printed it," she said.

"That's illegal."

"It's not illegal. It's against regulations."

"Did you ask him to print it?"

"No."

"Then why would he do it?"

She sighed and shrugged. "I suppose it was out of the goodness of his heart."

"You're telling me some engineer broke the law, or the regulations, or whatever, just to print a wooden piece from a random board game for you? Without being asked?"

"I never said he did it without being asked."

"You just said—"

"I said that I didn't ask him."

She had to hate word games like that as much as I did, which meant she was doing it on purpose. "Fine. Whatever. Then who asked him to print this thing?"

She said nothing.

I raised my voice. "Who was it?"

She glared at me, and I could tell she was getting angry, too.

"Tell me!" I shouted. "If you don't, I swear I'm not going one more step—"

"Fine. It was Dad, okay?" She paused and brushed something from her cheek. "Dad asked him."

I could believe that. It was surprising, but at least it made some sense. "And why did the engineer print it for Dad? Were they friends or something?"

"I don't think so."

"Then why would he—"

"I don't know!" She threw her hands up. "Dad said they're a . . . a happy band of brothers out here in space, or something like that, and they take care of each other."

That sounded like something Dad would say. But then I realized he had never said anything like that to me. "Wait." The hair on my arms stood up. "When?"

"When what?"

"When did Dad say that?"

I heard her breath catch as a brief look of realization crossed her face and then turned to panic. She hadn't meant to tell me that, just like she hadn't meant for me to find the game piece.

"You said they never arrived," I whispered.

She raised her fingertips to her temples, eyes wide, staring at me and through me. "No, no, no, this can't be happening . . ."

I felt too vulnerable sitting on the ground, so I slowly rose to my feet, keeping my eyes on her.

"You did see him," I said. "You talked to him."

She ignored me, almost bouncing in agitation, shaking her hands like they'd just come dripping from the sink.

"Why—why would you lie about that?"

She turned away from me, hugging herself, muttering to herself, while I quickly reassessed my situation, what I actually knew and didn't know, since I could no longer trust anything she had said.

I was on Carver 1061c. I knew that much just by looking around at the purple ferns and the ferrets. I also knew she'd been printed before me. Beyond that, I couldn't say I knew much. I didn't actually know how and why the lander had crashed. I didn't even know if the *Theseus* had really been destroyed, or if it might still be in orbit above me, and I wondered if my parents were still on it. I also couldn't say for sure how long it had been since Jim Kelly had put me in the scanner back on the *Liverpool*. So I didn't actually know how long before me she'd been printed. It could have been weeks. It could have been months.

I didn't really know anything, other than knowing that I was myself. And she was me.

"Jessica." I had to get some answers, so I made my voice as powerful and angry as I could. "Where are Mom and Dad?"

She still had her back to me, but she lifted her head. "Broken," she said.

"How do I know you—"

"You just have to trust me." She turned around, and she sounded confident again, like she thought she was back in control. "You don't have a choice. That's the only way forward. You have to trust me that we need to do this. The habitat—"

I laughed, even though I found absolutely nothing about the situation funny. "You think I'm going anywhere with you?"

"Yes. Because we have to."

My laughter died instantly. "We?"

"Yes, you and me." She pointed her finger back and forth between us. "Literally the only two people on this planet."

"You do what you want. I don't have to do anything—"

"Just stop. This isn't—" She squeezed her eyes shut and shook her head. "Just—just listen to me."

"Why?" I held up the yellow kobold. "Why would I listen to anything you—"

"Just listen, you asshole! Look around! Do you see where we are? You don't. Have. A choice!" She threw one of her arms out straight, stabbing her finger toward the mountain behind her. "That is where we are going! That is the only option!"

"That's not my only option."

She opened her mouth like she was about to yell even louder, but she stopped herself and brought her hands together in a wedge above her nose. She inhaled deeply. "Okay, then. What other option do you think you have?"

"I could go back to the lander, for one thing." I didn't particularly like the idea of returning there, but I was pretty sure I could find the crash site again, and it seemed like a better idea than going anywhere with her. "Maybe I can get the beacon working again. Or maybe you lied about that, too."

"I didn't. The beacon was destroyed."

"How do I know that?"

"Because I know it."

"I'm not you—"

"Goddamn it! Yes, you are! Would you stop being so fucking stubborn?"

"Me? If I'm you, then you're just as stubborn as I am!"

She stared at me and blinked. Then she put her hands on her hips and studied her boots, and after a few long moments had dragged by, she kicked a small rock. "You make a good point. You are exactly as stubborn as I am, and I can't physically drag you all the way to the mountain."

"Nope," I said, annoyed that she'd even considered it. "You can't."

"So that means one of us has to give."

"It sure as hell won't be—"

"Me," she said. "I'm the one who's going to give."

I wasn't expecting that, maybe because I had no intention of backing down. "What does that mean?"

She slipped out of her shoulder straps and let her backpack fall to the ground with a heavy thud. "It means this is on you now."

"What?"

She marched directly toward me. "If you won't go with me, then go by yourself."

"Wait, you—"

"Only one of us has to reach the habitat and turn on the Tangle. Only one of us has to tell ISTA what happened."

"But I don't even know what happened!"

She had almost reached the place where I stood, and her determined gaze forced me out of her path, but she walked right on by, away from me and away from the mountain. "Go," she said over her shoulder. "Take the gear."

I couldn't figure out what she was doing. I looked at her pack, lying where she'd dropped it, the water reclaimer and her rations still inside. "What about you? Where are you going?"

"Back to the lander."

"The lander?"

"Yes." She stopped and looked back at me. "I get the lander, and you get the Hades Hotel."

I was still trying to figure out her motive for doing this, but to really understand that, I had to know what she had been hiding. "There's always door number three."

"Which is?"

"You could just tell me the truth."

She turned away without a word and resumed her march.

"Wait!" I called, but not because I didn't want her to go. I wanted answers, and I wouldn't get them if she left.

But she kept walking.

"Wait!" I shouted again, feeling even more helpless as I thought about being alone on a planet I knew almost nothing about. "Just stop!"

She did, and when she turned around toward me, I saw tears running down her cheeks.

"What?" she asked, distant and harsh. "What do you want?"

I just stood there, taken aback. "You—you know what I want."

She rubbed the tears from her face with the heel of her palm. "That's never going to happen. There are things only one of us can know." Then she turned her back on me and marched away.

"What does that mean?" I asked, but I could tell by her pace and the angle of her shoulders that she wouldn't stop again. I called to her anyway. "Jessica, what the hell does that mean?"

"Don't follow me!" was all she shouted back, and I could only stand there and watch her until she disappeared over one of the low hills.

# 13 — DS *Theseus*

## BEFORE

I RICOCHET DOWN THE LENGTH OF THE NARROW spoke toward the main body of the ship, banging hard into the walls as I wrench myself along the ladder. But none of it hurts yet. I'm only thinking about my dad.

"You're going the wrong way!" Duncan shouts. He's right behind me, his voice echoing on all sides.

"No I'm not!" I call back.

I know the way, and I'm flying fast. But then I feel the ship's simulated gravity taking charge, and I realize what Duncan was trying to say. I dove into the spoke the wrong way, and before I can stop myself, I'm careening into a headfirst free fall to the floor below.

I flail to grab onto something, but before I can, Duncan seizes me by my ankle. I yelp, he grunts, and I bang my forehead against one of the rungs.

"I got you," Duncan says.

I look up at him, blinking away the sparks and the pain in my head as I hang upside down.

He's perched like a monkey, with his legs tucked up against the ladder, holding on to me with one hand, the elbow of his other arm wrapped over a rung. I don't know what kind of acrobatic space maneuver he had to pull to get into that position and grab me at the same time, but I'm glad he did.

"Can you flip yourself around?" he asks, straining.

"I think so."

I latch onto the ladder, and then try to fold myself up so I can get

my other foot under me. It's awkward, and I only manage it because I
don't yet have the ship's full gravity pulling on me.

"You got it?" Duncan asks.

I grunt. "Yeah. You can let go."

When he does, I flail a bit and bump the sides of the spoke as I twist
the rest of the way into position. Then I climb down as fast as I can
and leap from the ladder as soon as I've cleared the corridor's ceiling.
Duncan hits the floor right after me, and then we're racing toward the
lander. It's the first time I've run in the simulated gravity of the ship, and
I stumble a bit.

"*Code blue, code blue,*" says the ship's perfectly calm computer voice.
"*All medical staff to* Lander—"

"We hear you!" I shout over her.

When we round the last corner, I see a couple of crew members
standing above the lander's hatch. Evan is with them, and he looks over
as I barrel toward him. His eyes go to the top of my head.

"Are you okay? You're—"

"I'm fine." I skid to a stop and touch my head where I hit the ladder
rung. My fingers come away red. "Where's my dad?"

"On the lander." Evan points downward. "He had a seizure—"

"A seizure?"

I push past him and the other crew members and scramble down
through the hatch and the air lock. When I reach the galley, Dad is
sitting at the table where we played Magical Mountain. He's slumped
down in his chair looking dazed, with wide eyes and slow blinks. Mom
stands next to him, biting a thumbnail, her other hand on his shoulder,
while Dr. Gutiérrez monitors an instrument hooked up to his arm with
tubes and wires.

I rush forward. "Dad, are you okay?"

He turns toward me, but the movement of his eyes lags the movement of his head. "Jess," he says. "You're bleeding."

I'm relieved to hear him talking, even if his words sound groggy. "What happened?" I ask.

"Just tired," he says.

"You sleep when you're tired," Mom says. "You don't have seizures."

"It wasn't . . ." He waves her off with a weak shake of his wrist. "We don't even know for sure that's what it was."

She leans away to get the right angle on him for a full Mom glare. "Stephen, please." She points in the direction of the computer console where he had been sitting when I left him. "When I came in you were convulsing on the ground. And I don't even know how long you'd been there."

"The ship's security footage can tell us," the captain says.

I turn and see her standing nearby, hands clasped behind her back. Duncan is next to her. He leans toward me and hands me a small towel he must have grabbed from the kitchen. I accept it with a nod and press the towel against my head.

"I'd like to review that footage," Dr. Gutiérrez says. "To see the onset of the episode. In the meantime, blood pressure and oxygen levels are both a bit low. We should get you into a medbed, Dr. Mathers. Do you think you can you walk?"

"I think so," Dad says.

"No he can't," Mom says. "Or he shouldn't. And he certainly can't climb the ladder."

Dad leans forward, hands on the table, and heaves himself to his feet, like he's trying to prove her wrong. But he wobbles a bit once he's up, and Mom and Dr. Gutiérrez reach out to stabilize him.

"Stephen, you—"

"Just give me a second," Dad says, his breathing heavy.

"Let me help." I step closer, and Dr. Gutiérrez moves aside so I can slide in under my dad's arm to support him.

"Jess." He looks down at me. "You're bleeding." He says it exactly like he said it a few moments ago, and I worry what it means that he's repeating himself.

"Let's get you to a medbed, okay?" I look at my mom. "I'm sure that's protocol, isn't it?"

She nods. "Absolutely."

"Protocol." Dad chuckles. "We wouldn't want to ignore protocol."

With that, we lumber together from the galley toward the air lock, my mom on one side and me on the other. Dr. Gutiérrez hurries in front of us to lead the way, while the captain and Duncan follow behind. Evan and his crew lower a harness, and after we've buckled my dad in, they lift him up from the lander to the *Theseus*. I see the worry on the faces of the crew as I climb up after him, and I don't like it. It tells me this kind of thing doesn't happen often.

From there, the doctor leads us to the medical bay, a room right next to the Print Shop. Inside there are two medbeds that look a lot like the body printers. Dr. Gutiérrez indicates the nearest one as it lowers to the floor so we can lay my dad on it.

"Dr. Mathers," he says, "I'm pleased to offer you the most comfortable bed on this ship."

"That, I can be . . . believe," Dad says. "My bunk was . . ."

He goes quiet. Then he goes limp.

The sudden weight almost pulls me to the floor, and my mom gasps on his other side. We both struggle to find our footing while trying to hold on to him and stay upright. Then he starts to twitch and convulse. He's having another seizure, and I'm about to lose my grip.

"I got him," Duncan says behind me, and I feel some of the weight lift.

I slip out from under my dad as Dr. Gutiérrez rushes up, but I stay close by as they lower him into the medbed.

"Stephen?" Mom says. "Stephen, can you hear me?"

His eyes roll back. Quick grunts and groans punctuate his ragged breathing. The medbed shakes a little with the thrashing of his arms and legs.

"Stephen?" Mom leans over him, her hand on his forehead, her face close to his. "Stephen, it's going to be all right. Can you hear me? It's going to be—" She looks up at Dr. Gutiérrez. "Can't you do something?"

But he's already there with a hypo, and a few moments after the injection, my dad settles with a sigh. His eyes close, and his breathing evens out. The doctor puts down the hypo and circles the medbed, hooking up fingers and arms to different clips and sensors, and then he stretches a white mesh cap over my dad's head. The graphs and charts on the screens behind the medbed come alive with moving lines and glowing dots. I don't know what any of it means, but Mom scans it frantically, like she understands, or she's trying to. Dr. Gutiérrez gives all the displays a quick glance and then sits down at a computer near the medbed.

"So that's two seizures," the captain says.

"It would seem that way." Dr. Gutiérrez studies his screen, that friendly twinkle in his eye turned fierce. "But that was not a typical seizure."

"What do you mean?" my mom asks.

"Seizures have consistent electrical patterns. That's how we diagnose them." Dr. Gutiérrez glances from the computer toward my dad. "There is something else going on here."

"Is?" I'm still holding the bloody towel to my head. "You mean it's still going on?"

Dr. Gutiérrez nods and returns his attention to the screen. "I needed to get a reading of the event. The injection I gave him simply shut down his muscle movement."

"How is it atypical?" the captain asks.

"The pattern doesn't correspond to any episode or condition in the medical database. It also appears that his body is mounting an immune response to something."

"To what?" my mom asks.

"No pathogen I can identify. It might be autoimmune." He gets up from the computer and circles the medbed, rechecking all the clips and sensors. "I'll record as much data as I can before the Tangle opens. Hopefully ISTA can give us some answers."

I move closer to my dad and glance down at his hands, his face. On the outside, he seems calm and peaceful. But apparently there's an electrical storm raging inside his head, even though he looks like he could be sleeping. But that gives me a thought.

"Maybe this has something to do with his sleepwalking," I say.

Dr. Gutiérrez looks up from the computer screens. "Sleepwalking?"

My mom nods. "Jessica thinks her father was sleepwalking last night—"

"I don't *think* he was. I know it."

"We could check that on the security footage as well," the captain says.

Mom hugs herself like she's cold. "Can we access that from here?"

"Not directly." The captain moves toward the exit. "That system is on a secure command server. But I can go up to the Belfry and make the footage available to Dr. Gutiérrez here. It shouldn't take long." She steps through the hatch, and then she's gone.

In the quiet that follows, the medbed beeps and clicks and breathes, and Dr. Gutiérrez goes back to studying whatever data he's getting on his screen. The rest of us watch my dad as he lies there and does nothing, or we cast brief glances at each other. Duncan offers me a half smile that's sad but lets me know he's here and he's not going anywhere. I say thank you with a slight smile of my own.

Then Ms. Kateb enters the room, out of breath. "Is everything okay?" she asks. "I heard the code blue and went to the lander, but no one—" She sees my dad in the medbed. "What happened?"

"Seizures." My mom exhales sharply. "Have you seen this before, Doctor?"

Dr. Gutiérrez looks up. "What, seizures?"

"As a side effect of teleportation," she adds.

He taps his chin. "Not as a side effect of teleportation, no. Though I did once treat a traveler with a prior epileptic condition made worse by teleportation."

"My husband has never had a seizure in his life." My mom makes eye contact with me and asks the doctor, "What about the sleepwalking? Could that be a side effect?"

Dr. Gutiérrez leaves his computer and comes to stand near the medbed. "General sleep disturbance is quite typical, of course, predominantly fatigue, but occasionally insomnia. Theoretically, somnambulism could be possible, but quite rare."

"Theoretically?" I say.

"I've never heard of it happening." He adjusts the white cap over my father's head. "But I'm not saying it's impossible. I can ask ISTA for a survey of the latest research the next time we open a quantum channel."

"Has he gone spacey?" Duncan asks.

Mom scowls, and Dr. Gutiérrez frowns.

"I don't care for that term, Mr. Sharpe," he says. "But no, seizures are not a recognized feature of Deep Space Syndrome that I'm aware of."

"Then what about what Jessica said?" Duncan looks at me. "Could the sleepwalking and the seizures be connected?"

The doctor taps his chin again. "There is a relationship between fatigue and seizure activity, so it's possible they're related." He pauses, then also turns to look at me. "I'd like to examine your injury now."

"I'm fine," I say. "My dad is more—"

"Let him take care of you," Mom says.

She's worried about me, too, I guess, so I let Dr. Gutiérrez sit me at the end of the second medbed. Then he uses a roll of gauze dipped in a solution of some kind to gently wipe and dab away the blood from my head. It stings, but I manage not to flinch.

"How did you get this?" he asks.

"Superman imitation," I say.

"Isn't Superman invincible?"

"It was a bad imitation."

He chuckles. "Well, the cut will patch up easily, but it might leave a small scar."

I don't care about that right now, and as soon as the skin patch is done, I thank the doctor and return to the side of my dad's medbed. "How long will it take to get the data you need?"

"Hard to say," Dr. Gutiérrez replies. "It could be—"

The room's comm pings, and then we all hear the captain's voice over the speaker. "I've sent you the files, Doctor. You should be able to open them and review the footage. I'm on my way back."

"Thank you, Captain." The comm goes quiet, and he heads toward his computer.

My mom moves to the doctor's side, and so do I, along with Duncan, and the three of us lean in to look at the files. There's quite a bit of footage, from the various cameras and angles, but we use the timestamps to watch them in a logical order.

The sleepwalking plays out on the screen just like I've been saying, except the cameras caught even more than I was aware of last night. My dad was up walking around for a while before he came into my room. He spent most of that time shuffling up and down the lander's corridors in the dark, appearing aimless. Several times, he just stopped and stared at the wall, or at nothing, and he paused outside my door a couple of times before he opened it and stepped inside. There isn't any footage of what he did in my room, because there aren't any cameras in the private quarters, but the timestamp shows he was in there for thirty-six minutes before he came back out. Shivers crawl up my neck when I realize how long he was standing there while I slept.

Next we open the footage of the first seizure. There's only one camera in the lander's galley, near the hatch, so the view of my dad is from behind as he sits at the computer. Dr. Gutiérrez skips the recording to the point when I left him alone. Nothing really happens until the moment my dad's posture suddenly goes stiff, then limp, and he falls from the chair onto the floor, convulsing. It's disturbing, and I look away from the screen.

"Hmm," Dr. Gutiérrez says. "I wonder if . . . I think I can zoom in on the file he was looking at when his seizure began."

"What are you thinking?" Mom asks.

"Some visual stimuli can trigger seizures, like strobes." Dr. Gutiérrez rewinds and manipulates the image, speaking almost absently. "Perhaps something in one of the files caused—" He stops. "What is that?"

I look at the screen, and I see a familiar image, but magnified and grainy. It's the same thing I saw in my picture of Avery. Something with horns or spikes or claws ripping through the screen, shredding the image there. I turn toward Duncan as he turns toward me, and I know he recognizes it, too.

"This is disturbing," Ms. Kateb says, hand at her mouth.

"What is disturbing?"

The captain has returned from the Belfry, and as she joins us, Duncan nods toward the computer screen.

She looks at it for a moment. "This is the second time we've had file corruption in the last seventy-two hours. That is not supposed to happen with the Tangle. Ever." She raises her wrist comm. "Liz Kovalenko, please report to medical. Liz, come to the medical bay." Then she turns to Dr. Gutiérrez. "Could that image have somehow caused the seizure?"

"I can't imagine how," he says.

"It didn't cause any of us to have seizures before," Duncan says.

He's right, which might suggest that it was only a coincidence that my dad had a seizure while looking at it.

"I will continue to monitor," Dr. Gutiérrez says. "He's stable now, and he'll stay that way while he's on my watch."

That is not as reassuring as I think the doctor hopes. But I know the sedative is the only reason my dad is stable, and I know his brain is doing something the doctor has never seen before, so there's a limit to the reassurance Dr. Gutiérrez can give me.

"My god," Mom whispers, and everyone turns toward her. She's looking at the computer screen and leans away from it. For a second, I worry that she's about to have a seizure, too.

"What is it?" the captain asks.

"I think I know what this is." She shakes her head. "But it doesn't make any sense."

"What do you think it is?" I ask.

"I—I might be wrong," she says. "I'm probably wrong. The survey only found a few fossil fragments, but this . . . it looks like a species from Carver 1061c."

"Wait." I point at the screen, at the horns and the claws. "You mean those things live down there?"

"No," she says. "Or at least, not anymore."

"Not anymore?"

"The volcano," Duncan says. "Mount Ida."

"Exactly." Mom points at the screen. "I think this is an image of an alien creature that went extinct almost four million years ago."

# 14—Hades

## AFTER

I STOOD THERE A LONG TIME WATCHING THE HORI-
zon for her return. A part of me wanted to see her coming back, but a
bigger part of me didn't. I didn't trust her anymore, which was a frightening and confusing thing to realize, because that was like saying I
didn't trust myself. But she had lied to me, and then she had abandoned
me on an alien planet facing one hell of a decision, with only three options that I could see.

Option one: I could make my way to Mount Ida and search for the
habitat alone, but the volcano was still a long way away, and it scared
me to think of crossing the surface of Hades by myself.

Option two: I could catch up with her and go back to the lander,
but she'd told me not to follow her, and I was pretty sure she meant it.
I also didn't really feel safe when I thought about being in the lander
with her.

Option three: I could stay right where I was and do nothing.
That was certainly the easiest option, but also the stupidest, because
I would eventually run out of food, assuming the water reclaimer
didn't break down first, and I wasn't about to eat those worms she'd
told me about.

I decided on option one. When enough time had gone by that I
was sure she wasn't coming back, I pulled my attention away from the
horizon and walked over to her backpack. I transferred the most important gear to my pack, which included the water reclamation unit,
her flashlight, and some of her food packets. I didn't find any more hidden pieces from board games, or any other clue to help me figure out

what was really going on. But I took the clue I did have and tucked that yellow kobold into one of my jumpsuit's zippered pockets.

When I lifted the pack onto my back, the added gear felt like it doubled the original weight, which had already strained me to my limit the day before. I didn't know how I'd be able to carry both her stuff and mine in Hades gravity, and when I added that thought to my other doubts, it broke me a little.

I dropped to the ground and lay there like a helpless turtle on my back. My lips quivered, but I pressed my fingers hard against them, refusing to cry.

I looked up into the Hades sky and focused on the clouds sliding overhead. They looked just like Earth clouds, and I imagined myself back home, sitting in one of the weathered Adirondack chairs that Pop-Pop refused to replace. I focused on the sky and nothing else, believing that if I were to lower my eyes from the clouds, I'd see Pop-Pop pruning a tree and Gram kneeling in front of one of her flower beds, wearing the khaki explorer hat she put on to work in her garden. I could almost smell the warm soil. I held on to that illusion for a while, until the grief of it threatened to defeat my efforts not to cry, and then I forced it away by looking right at Mount Ida.

I couldn't stand up with the pack on my back, so I rolled out of it in a way no turtle could leave its shell and got to my feet. Then I tried again to hoist the pack onto my back. The weight of it still staggered me, but I found that if I leaned forward and kept my feet moving, I could stay upright with a kind of stumbling momentum.

I set off again, and as I walked, the ferns around me swayed with a persistent breeze. I flinched at every noise, every snap and rustle of vegetation, still not convinced the planet was empty, and that tension and fear soon exhausted me as much as the physical exertion.

I don't know how many kilometers I walked, but eventually the red sun came close to setting, and I realized an entire day had somehow gone by. I halted at an open spot in the ferns where I could set up my tent, and I just kind of tipped over, like a bicycle when you stop moving.

I lay there on the ground, breathing hard. The endorphin numbness started its retreat from my shoulders and legs. Then the pain set in. I knew I didn't have long before I wouldn't even be able to set up my tent. So I forced myself to get up, and after fumbling with my gear for several minutes, I raised my sloppily assembled shelter.

I didn't even bother to eat. I just collapsed inside and fell asleep, and when I woke up the next morning, the sun was already well above the horizon. I could see its muted spotlight through the fabric wall of the tent, and I sat up, whimpering at a soreness that reached every joint and muscle in my body. My throat burned, dry as sunbaked sand, and I wished I had drunk some water before I crashed.

That's when I realized I hadn't set up the reclaimer.

"Oh no," I said out loud, my voice hoarse. I felt stupid, especially because I was sure she wouldn't have made that mistake.

For the reclaimer to work, it needed humidity, time, and temperature fluctuations, but it wouldn't have any of those things unless I decided to stay put for a day, which I didn't want to do. I knew I had some water left over from the day before. After I dragged myself from the tent, drank a bit, and used a little more water to rehydrate my breakfast, I had just under a liter remaining, which would have to do. I decided to get moving and stop early that evening to let the reclaimer have extra time to do its thing.

A few swear words and a lot of grunting later, I had my tent packed up and I was back on the road, except there wasn't a road. There was only the uneven Hades ground, the purple ferns, and the volcano.

With time, my muscles loosened a bit, and their complaints changed from protest to painful acceptance. The day unrolled much like the one before, but a bit warmer. I worried what the sweat beading at my hairline would do to my rate of dehydration, so I eased up on the pace, taking the surface of hell at a stroll.

Around midday I came upon another stream, this one a few meters wide, flowing along a sunken bed with steep banks, but as thirsty as I was, I still couldn't bring myself to risk drinking it. The water wasn't deep, so I found the shallowest spot and just plowed across it, my water-resistant boots keeping my socks mostly dry. As I reached the other side and started to climb the embankment, I heard a little splashing behind me and spun around.

One of the ferrets swam toward me from the opposite side, like it was following me. I wondered if it was the same ferret that I'd given a taste of ISTA egg rations, which should have been enough to scare it away, but had apparently turned it into a little tagalong instead.

"You're pretty determined," I said, watching it slither and glide over the water.

The stream's current wasn't very strong, but I wanted to be sure the ferret made it across safely, so I waited. If it was there because of me, or at least because of my food, that meant I was at least a little bit responsible for it. So I watched until it emerged safely from the stream and shook the water from its glistening white fur and whiskers.

"You're welcome to keep me company," I said, then nodded toward the volcano. "But that's where I'm going, just so you know."

The ferret stayed at the water's edge, watching me as it folded its length nearly in half to groom its belly fur.

"That's a volcano," I added, "in case you didn't know. So what I'm saying is, if you decide to come with me, and that thing blows up, you can't blame me later. Understand?"

Those little black eyes just stared.

I had to get going, so I moved slowly away from the ferret, resuming my march to Mount Ida. I wondered if it would follow me, and before I'd gone far, it did. When I moved, it moved. When I stopped, it stopped. It stayed in the ferns most of the time, which turned the rustling of the fronds into something reassuring, rather than threatening. But I was glad it kept its distance. There were lots of cute animals on Earth that would scratch you or bite you or give you a disease if they got too close. But I liked having the company, and the ferret kept pace with me throughout the day.

That couldn't have been very hard to do, because I made poor time and stopped when I ran out of water, with plenty of daylight left. But I figured it was more important to get the water reclaimer working than it was to cover a few more kilometers of ground. I set it up before I did anything else.

Even though it was early, I felt hungry, but the reclaimer needed time to do its thing. I choked down one of the ISTA packets dry, not even sure what it was supposed to be, and then I put up the tent. The ferret watched me from the edge of the clearing, disappearing occasionally to go take care of its ferret business. But it always came back.

After that, I decided to rest in the tent, and my muscles thanked and berated me at the same time. Before long I dozed off and had a vivid nap dream about the ferret where it could talk. But all it did was criticize how little I knew about the planet and tell me how much of a liability I was. But I couldn't say anything back because I knew it was right. When I woke up, it was evening, and the reclaimer had dribbled out a bit of water. I gulped it down as I stood outside the tent in the burnished light and wiped my mouth with the back of my hand. Then I noticed the ferret tucked away in the ferns nearby.

"What should I call you?" I asked it. "If you're going to stick around, I need to call you something."

Its feather-whiskers fluttered, and I remembered the name from my dream.

"How about Duncan?" I'd never known anyone with that name,

and I wasn't sure what made me think of it, but it felt right. "Yes, I think I'll call you Duncan."

The ferret vanished, I assumed because it had grown tired of waiting for me to feed it and had gone to find ferret food, and not because it disliked the name I'd just given it.

"Duncan," I said again, to myself.

The sound of distant thunder drew my eyes to the horizon, where a wall of charcoal clouds had risen without warning, and I watched it barrel toward me. The clouds brought an early nightfall with them, and I retreated into my tent as the first drops of rain fell, but I didn't close it. I sat near the opening, listening to the snapping and tapping of the big droplets against the fabric of my shelter and the nearby ferns. The wet Hades soil smelled earthy, and I felt the temperature drop to the coolest it had been since I'd woken up on the lander. Goose bumps rose on my arms as thunder rumbled overhead, but I felt reassured that the reclaimer would soon have more water than I could carry or use.

A little way from the tent, I spotted Duncan curled up in a white ball under the shelter of the ferns. I wondered why it hadn't gone underground to escape the rain, but we both sat there in our shelters, surrounded by the storm, and I hoped the other me, the not-me, had made it back to the lander.

A heavy mist rose up, and then darkness closed in, until I couldn't see much farther than my tent. I pulled out my flashlight, and with a click I flooded the patch of ground and ferns in front of me with light, but the mist pushed back against it. Two specks of gold glinted in the night, Duncan's eyes watching me.

I switched the flashlight off and plunged back into a darkness that seemed even deeper than it had been just a moment ago. The sound of the heavy rainfall had become a deafening static, and the storm had smothered the stars. The cold, damp air felt heavy in my chest, and a sudden loneliness caused an ache that made it hard to breath. I thought back to what she had said to me before she left.

*There are things only one of us can know.*

I still had no idea what that meant, but it seemed to suggest that she had some kind of plan for me, and that freaked me out. It also seemed that our fight had not been a part of her plan. But then I thought maybe it *was* a part of her plan, and I was exactly where she wanted me to be, heading to the habitat for both of us.

I wished I knew where my parents were, but I took comfort that they were somewhere. Or at least, I knew they had been somewhere, because she had seen them and talked to them. They had been established. But I didn't know when or where, or what had happened to them after that, and I knew that even if I'd asked her, she wouldn't have told me, because there were things only one of us could know.

The storm outside filled the night with an intense and growing fury. I used the flashlight to take one last look at Duncan, who seemed surprisingly untroubled by the rain, and I closed up the tent. I knew I shouldn't waste the batteries, but I was all alone, and the storm shook my tent, so I left the light on for most of the night.

# 15—DS *Theseus*

## BEFORE

EVERYONE STARES AT MY MOM. FOR SEVERAL MOments, the silence in the room competes with the beeps and clicks from Dad's medbed. I assume we're all having the same trouble processing what she just told us.

"Extinct," the captain finally repeats, not quite as a question.

"Yes," Mom says. "This organism died out after the last supereruption."

I glance at the image again, and I swear that thing is staring back at me with whatever it has for eyes. But I don't look away this time, even though the horn-claw-teeth baste my stomach with cold and rotten dread. Because if this thing did something to my dad, I want to know what it is, and what exactly it did.

"Well that explains it," Dr. Gutiérrez says. "Two images from your files must have somehow become superimposed."

Mom shakes her head and points at the screen. "We don't have an image like that. No one does. The only pictures we have of that species are of its fossil fragments."

The room falls silent again.

"Then what is it?" Duncan asks.

"It's a ghost," says Ms. Kateb, and everyone turns to look at her.

"A ghost?" I glance at my mom. "Does that word mean something different out here?"

She frowns. "No."

The captain folds her arms. "I would not have pegged you for Antimat, Ms. Kateb."

*THESEUS*                                             **147**

"I'm not—" Ms. Kateb holds up her hands. "I am not an extremist, or a radical."

Mom scoffs. "Then why bring up ghosts?"

"I don't mean ghosts in an exonatural way."

"What other way is there?" Mom asks.

Ms. Kateb forms her mouth into a thin, straight line. "One does not have to be Antimaterialist to conclude that materialism doesn't have the answer to every question—"

"Yet." Mom finishes for her, using the word like a blade to cut her off.

But I doubt that's the word Ms. Kateb was about to say. She ignores the interruption and continues. "We might be able to solve certain mysteries, if only scientists would allow themselves to pose the right questions."

"What are you suggesting, Amira?" Dr. Gutiérrez asks, his tone much gentler than my mom's.

"Consider human history," she says. "Nearly every culture in the world has, or had, a spirit tradition—"

"Some of those same cultures also thought the world was flat," Mom says, out of the side of her mouth. I doubt I'm the only one who feels uncomfortable with her obvious disdain and irritation.

"Please, Amira," the captain says, "continue."

Ms. Kateb sighs. "We don't truly understand the way the universe works at the quantum scale, where the classical laws that govern our perception and experience, and which seem inviolable to us, become irrelevant—"

"Why should we be able to understand it?" Mom asks. "The universe isn't under any obligation to make sense to you."

Ms. Kateb accepts this with a nod and continues. "If I am not mistaken, time is understood mathematically to exist all at once. It is only our limited perception that creates the illusion of a past, a present, and a future." She pauses, and when my mom doesn't argue with that, she goes on. "There is also a law within quantum physics regarding the conservation of information. Information cannot be destroyed—"

"That's true," Mom says. "But that isn't—"

"Please, Dr. Havilland," Ms. Kateb says, "allow me to finish. What if something, some trace of our consciousness, or remnant of information about us, remains behind at the quantum level when we are gone, existing across time?"

A moment passes.

"You mean a *quantum* ghost?" Duncan asks.

"Exactly," Ms. Kateb says.

I get the chills as I imagine a universe haunted at the subatomic level, everywhere around me, even flowing through me.

Mom smacks a nearby terminal with her palm, startling everyone. "This is absurd! Am I the only one hearing this?"

No one answers her. I've never seen this side of her, and I don't understand why she's acting so angry and hostile. But I also don't know much about quantum physics, and I don't think Ms. Kateb does, either. What I do know is that my dad is unconscious, and there's an extinct alien staring at me from a computer screen, and no one else has suggested an explanation for it.

"Such a remnant wouldn't necessarily be exonatural," Dr. Gutiérrez says. "Scientists who study the mind have suggested that consciousness might be rooted in a quantum function. A fundamental property of *all* matter, like mass."

"When we send our information over the quantum channel," Ms. Kateb says, now mostly to Dr. Gutiérrez, "there is already information down there. Is it possible the old information could interact with ours?"

"No!" Mom says, sounding exasperated. "That's not what information means! You don't— You're not physicists! None of us are. This is all wildly speculative, it's irresponsible, and most importantly, it doesn't do a damn thing to help my husband!" She ends at an almost frantic pitch, her voice on the edge of breaking.

Dr. Gutiérrez bows his head. Ms. Kateb goes silent.

A moment goes by, and then I force myself to walk over to my mom to do what a daughter is supposed to do, even though it doesn't feel comfortable yet. I put my arms around her.

She just stands there for a second or two, and then she puts her arms around me and squeezes me hard enough to take my breath. "I'm sorry," she whispers in my ear. Then she pulls away, wipes at her eyes, and says, "I'm sorry," but louder, to the whole room. "I'm not handling this well."

"There isn't a right way to handle something like this," the captain says. "But please know I have faith in my people. They will do everything they can to help Dr. Mathers."

Mom nods, her tired eyes like wet ice, and suddenly I can see how fragile and scared she really is. "Thank you," she says.

The hatch opens, and Liz comes in. She looks at all of us, but before she can ask any questions, the captain pulls her toward the computer terminal and explains the situation in low and murmuring tones. Mom watches from a distance and doesn't even try to interject. I think maybe she's starting to shut down.

"I'll get right on it," Liz says, after the captain has finished. She marches from the medical bay quickly but gives me a reassuring nod on the way out.

Ms. Kateb inches closer to us, and then she speaks to my mom. "Dr. Havilland, I truly didn't mean to add to your distress—"

"My distress is not your fault," Mom says. "I disagree with your hypothesis, but—but I know you're trying to help. I appreciate it."

Ms. Kateb nods, and my shoulders loosen a bit as the tension between the two of them eases.

"I'm needed in the command module." The captain turns to Dr. Gutiérrez. "The Tangle will open soon. Let's give ISTA everything we have."

"It's ready to go," he says.

The captain and Ms. Kateb leave the medical bay, and then it's just Duncan and Dr. Gutiérrez with me and my mom, and my dad, lying there with a brain on fire. I don't want to say anything to upset my mom again, but I'm still a little frightened by Ms. Kateb's alien-ghost theory. It occurs to me that photos aren't the only kind of information we send over the quantum channel. ISTA basically sends people.

I look down at my dad in the medbed, and I wonder if his data got corrupted like the pictures, and maybe that's why he's sick.

Then I look at my own hands, my skin, imagining something alien tunneling through the code of my DNA, and I sit with the horror of that for a few moments. My data came here the same way as his. But I force that thought away, telling myself that I feel fine, and that my mom is right. That's not how quantum physics even works, and Mom knows more about this stuff than Ms. Kateb.

"Oh, Stephen." She lays her hand against my dad's forehead, and the intimacy in the gesture makes me feel like she's forgotten any of us are here.

I look directly at Dr. Gutiérrez, and I keep my voice calm, but sure, so he knows I want the truth. "Is he in pain?"

"No," he says without hesitation.

I'm glad for that, at least.

Duncan walks over to me and leans in. "Can I get you anything? Are you— Do you want something to eat? Drink?"

I'm not even thinking about that right now, and I shake my head. "I'm fine."

He leans away.

"I could use a coffee," Mom says. "If it's not too much trouble."

That straightens Duncan's back and lifts his shoulders. "No trouble. I'll be right back."

He takes a couple of long strides across the room and leaves through the hatch, and when he's gone, I turn toward my mom.

"He just wanted to be helpful," she says. "He needed a job."

That hadn't occurred to me. But then I watch my mom hugging herself and shifting on her feet. Her darting glance takes regular laps across the medbed's displays, and whenever Dr. Gutiérrez comes over to check something, she looks over his shoulder and asks what he's doing, and if everything is okay. He's patient with her and answers her questions, but I wonder if she needs a job, too.

"Did you finish checking the habitat?" I ask.

She blinks. "You mean the systems check? No, I—I was interrupted."

I wait a moment. "We still need to do that, right? For when Dad's better?"

Her lips part, and I think she's going to say something about that being a low priority right now, but after a pause, she nods instead. "I suppose we do. It makes sense to get the diagnostics running. That way, we'll be ready to go when your father has recovered."

"Exactly," I say.

She looks around the room. "But I can't do that from here."

"I'll stay," I say. "If anything changes, I'll come get you."

She shakes her head against the idea, until Dr. Gutiérrez speaks up.

"Dr. Mathers is stable," he says. "Your presence or absence won't change that."

"Are you sure?" She already seems more settled by the distraction of a task. "Because I can—"

"It needs to be done." I smile. "It's protocol, and protocol exists for a reason."

She smiles back at me. "I can't wait for your father to hear you say that."

Before she goes, she leans down and kisses my dad on the cheek, then plants a peck on my cheek, too, but it's quick and automatic, like she didn't quite mean to, and it seems to catch us both a little off guard.

"I'll be with Liz," she says, and heads for the hatch. "Come get me if there is any change."

"I will."

She leaves, and I notice Dr. Gutiérrez looking at me over the rim of his glasses with a grin. "Nicely done." His nod takes in the medbed displays. "Your mother knows just enough to worry about the right things the wrong way."

The blinking lights and fluctuating numbers mean nothing to me, so I worry about other things instead. Maybe the wrong things. Like ghosts.

"Dr. Gutiérrez," I say. "Do you really—"

The hatch opens, and Duncan enters the medlab. "I didn't know if you wanted cream or sugar," he says, his full attention on the blue coffee mug he carries. "I brought both."

"Thanks," I say.

He looks up, then glances over his shoulder, like he's in the wrong room. "Where did your mom go?"

"Jessica put her to work," Dr. Gutiérrez says.

I lift the mug from Duncan's hands. "I'll take her coffee, though."

"Not sure how hot it is," he says, and offers me the powdered creamer and sugar packets.

I sit down next to Dr. Gutiérrez, and in the weaker gravity of the ship, the white dust falls slowly from the packets into the mug, like snow. The flakes melt when they touch the surface of the coffee, and after giving it a stir, I take a sip.

"How is it?" Duncan asks.

It's still warm, but not enough to be considered hot. The flavor is what it is. "You make a mean cup of space joe."

He steps closer toward my dad. "Any changes?"

"No," Dr. Gutiérrez says. "But that coffee looks good."

"Oh." Duncan looks at the hatch. "I'm sorry, did you want—"

"No, no," Dr. Gutiérrez says. "I'll get it. I could do with a stretch. Will you two be okay for a few minutes?"

I say yes, but I feel a bit nervous about it, even if he'll be right back, and I have to remind myself that he said my dad is stable. That probably won't change in the time it takes Dr. Gutiérrez to get a cup of coffee, but he's gone before I can voice my reservations, anyway. Then I'm alone with Duncan.

My head is starting to throb and pull against the patch Dr. Gutiérrez applied to my skin. I feel around the rough edges, where a tender bump is swelling up underneath, and I wince at my own touch.

"Does it hurt?" Duncan asks.

"A little."

"Hang on." He walks over to a supply cabinet and opens it. Inside are a bunch of small boxes, and he scans them until he seems to find the one he's looking for. He pulls out the box and then takes a vial from inside it, which he inserts into the hypo like he's done it many times before.

"What's that?"

"Anti-inflammatory," he says. "Basic painkiller."

He moves toward me and raises the hypo, but I put up my hands and lean away from it.

"You sure you know what you're doing with that thing?"

"Of course," he says, and I believe him, but he waits for me to give him a consenting nod before he steps up close and puts the hypo to my neck.

I feel the slight pressure and prick of the hypersonic spray like a needle. Within a few moments, the pounding in my head eases up, but maybe I'm just imagining that.

Duncan looks into my eyes. "How're you doing?"

"That's better, thanks."

"Good." He leans in a bit. "But how are you doing?"

"I—I'm holding up."

"I'm sure your dad will be fine."

I look at the medbed. "Me too."

"We'll figure this out."

"I know." I glance at the computer terminal, where the image of the alien still leers at the room. "What do you think about the whole quantum-ghost theory?"

"I don't know if I'd call it a theory yet. It's just an idea. But I think there might be something to it." He steps away and puts down the hypo. "Did you ever hear about that scientist who tried to calculate the weight of the soul?"

"The soul? No."

"It was a long time ago. He weighed people before they died, and then right after they died, to see if there was a difference. He tried to claim the soul weighed twenty-one grams, but other scientists proved he was wrong."

I remember what he said about his dad. "Do you believe in souls?"

"I don't think so." He pauses. "But I guess there has to be something that makes us who we are, right?"

"I don't know why there has to be something." I go for the coffee he brought for my mom, which is now cold, but I sip it like it's hot. "I think my experiences make me who I am. My memories. My choices. My DNA. That seems like enough without bringing the soul into it."

"I guess that's true."

We're both quiet for a few moments, and then Dr. Gutiérrez comes back into the room.

"Everything okay?" he asks as he walks over to the medbed. He squints a bit as he sips from his mug and surveys the displays. Then he seems to notice something, and his posture tightens. "I need to give him another motor blocker," he says, setting his coffee mug down, and then he crosses to the supply cabinet where Duncan found the pain reliever.

I look at the displays, wondering what he saw there, and what it means that my dad needs another motor blocker. "Is that bad?" I ask.

"It is neither bad nor good." Dr. Gutiérrez changes the vial in the hypo. "It's just a bit sooner than I was expecting, but—"

My dad twitches, first his hand, then his arm.

"—we're in time." Dr. Gutiérrez says.

He holds up the hypo as he returns to the medbed, ready to administer it, but as he leans in, my dad's arm flails high and knocks the instrument from the doctor's hand. The hypo bounces across the floor.

"Damn it." Dr. Gutiérrez grabs my dad's arm and holds it down. "Duncan, can you—"

"Sure."

Duncan moves to pick up the hypo, but then my dad's other arm twitches, then his whole body starts to jerk, but much more violently than before. Dr. Gutiérrez can't hold him down by himself, so Duncan turns back to help, pinning my dad's other arm.

"Jessica," Dr. Gutiérrez says, grunting. "The hypo."

My dad's eyes are open, and he's staring at me with the same emptiness I saw last night, even as his body writhes and bounces in the medbed.

"Jessica!" Dr. Gutiérrez shouts.

I flinch at the bark of his voice and rush for the hypo, but when I pick it up, even I can see it's damaged from the fall. I hurry it to the medbed, getting as close as I can without looking into those empty eyes, and I wag the hypo in front of Dr. Gutiérrez.

"Shit," he says, sweat across his brow. "You need to get a new one."

"But I don't know how—"

"I'll explain it to you! Just hurry!"

But I can't hurry. I don't know what's wrong with my dad, and I don't know if that's even him, and I don't know anything about hypos, and I need to get my mom, and that's all a traffic jam between my brain and my body. But I manage to get to the cabinet, and now I'm staring at hundreds of hypo cartridges in boxes.

"Look for a blue box with a red hexagon," Dr. Gutiérrez says. "But first you need—"

A sound between a howl and a roar erupts from my dad's mouth. I turn around, and he's arching his back so high I hear his spine cracking, like it might break under the strain.

"Jessica!" Duncan shouts.

He and Dr. Gutiérrez are barely holding on. I spin back to the cabinet and fumble for the first blue box I see, but my hands are shaking so bad I spill the cartridges. Dozens of capsules bounce off the counter and scatter across the floor. I dive to try and scoop one up, but before I can, my dad makes a shrieking sound. I look up as he breaks free, throwing Duncan backward against the bulkhead and knocking Dr. Gutiérrez to the floor.

"Dad!" I shout.

He leaps from the bed, snarling and ignoring me. Then he snatches the doctor's mug, splashing coffee across the floor, and breaks it against the medbed. As Dr. Gutiérrez struggles to his feet, my dad leaps on him, driving him hard into the floor. Duncan shouts something, and then the hatch opens.

It's Ms. Kateb, and her mouth is open. "What—"

But my dad flies at her, knocking her back into the corridor. She cries out, and I rush to the hatch, where I see her sprawled on the floor, looking stunned as my dad bolts away.

"No no no," Duncan says behind me.

I hear a strangled, bubbling sound as I turn around to see Duncan kneeling on the floor in an expanding pool of red. Dr. Gutiérrez lies on his back next to him, arms and legs spread wide, as if to make a snow angel. His foot twitches, and he sputters and gags through the blood overflowing the sides of his mouth. There's something sticking out of his throat, and then I notice the handle. It's a shard of his broken coffee mug.

Duncan takes hold of the doctor's blood-slicked hand. "It'll be okay," he says. "We'll reestablish you. It'll be okay, Dr. Gutiérrez. Don't worry—"

"Duncan," someone says behind me, and I turn to see Ms. Kateb in the doorway. Then Evan appears over her shoulder, peering in.

"Jesus," he whispers.

Ms. Kateb hits a comm on the wall. "Code blue!" she shouts. "Code blue in the medical bay!"

Evan pushes into the room and falls to the floor at Duncan's side, while Ms. Kateb tears through cabinets until she finds some bandage rolls wrapped in plastic. But then she just stands there, clutching a fistful of gauze that I know won't help, and I think she knows it, too.

Dr. Gutiérrez suddenly opens his eyes wide. He lifts his bloody chin a bit, pointing it at the ceiling, and he holds it there for a moment. Then he seems to relax, then sag, until he goes completely still, and I know he's gone. Ms. Kateb's hands drop to her sides, still holding bandages, while Duncan bows his head, eyes squeezed shut.

"What . . . happened?" Evan looks around the room. "What—"

Duncan glances up at me, still holding on to Dr. Gutiérrez's hand.

"It was my dad," I whisper, in shock and disbelief. "He . . . he did this."

# 16 — Hades

## AFTER

THE NEXT MORNING, I WOKE UP FEELING A little better than the day before. My muscles weren't as sore, probably because I hadn't walked as far, and the waterproof tent had kept me dry. The sun shone, and I wondered what I would see when I went outside. So much rain had fallen during the night that I almost expected to find everything around me washed away. But Hades didn't look very different than it had before I closed my tent. The purple ferns still swayed in a clean-smelling breeze, though the water had carved deep tracks through the soil in some places and piled up low, smooth dunes in others. But everything was much drier than I thought it should be. I saw no puddles, and very little mud, and I wondered where all the water had gone.

I looked for Duncan but couldn't see him anywhere, and I hoped he was okay. Then I saw the reclaimer, and I gasped.

It lay on its side, half buried in the dirt. At some point during the night, the wind had tipped it over, emptying its reservoir onto the ground with the rain. But I wasn't worried about the lost water.

"Shit," I said out loud. "Shit, shit, shit."

I rushed over and tried to lift the reclaimer onto its feet, but the rain had submerged it so tightly in sediment that I had to dig it out first, clawing at the soil with my hands. I didn't know much about reclaimers, but I knew they were very sensitive and should not be buried in mud.

When I finally got it unearthed and standing upright, my dread rose to panic. Silt and grit choked the reclaimer's gills and membranes, and I could tell it was broken. Useless.

I checked the reservoir and found a little less than a hundred milli-liters inside, barely an afterthought of all the water I had lost. I drank it down in a couple of gulps. Then I turned away from the reclaimer, resisting the urge to kick it over out of anger at myself for being stupid enough to leave it out in the storm, and I stomped back to the tent to sulk and re-evaluate my plan.

Without clean water, the mountain and the habitat lay an impos-sible distance away. I was already thirsty, and I briefly considered drink-ing the Hades water, but that came with huge risks I wasn't willing to take, which made my choice a simple one. I had to go back to the lander for a new reclaimer. I was furious with myself for that, because in her eyes it would confirm everything she'd said about me.

I still had a few hydrated rations, so I ate a packet of cold spaghetti for breakfast before I packed up, thinking my body would get a bit more water from it. Duncan returned as I knelt on the ground to roll up the tent, on time for his breakfast.

"And where were you?" I asked. "Somewhere dry?"

His head did the bobbing thing up and down, like he was nodding yes.

"And I assume you came back for more of my eggs?"

Another yes.

"Well, even if I gave them to you, you'd be disappointed. Without water, they're just powder. But I'm going back to the lander, so you—" Saying those words out loud stopped me, and I looked down at the tent for a few moments. "Can I be honest with you, Duncan? I don't want to go back. I don't trust her. I feel like I should know her, but I don't." I glanced at the ferret. "And that scares me."

Duncan's feather-whiskers twitched.

"How screwed up is that? We're supposed to be the same, right? Exactly the same. Because she's me." I gathered up the canvas in my clenched fists and shook my head. "Except she's not. Somehow, she's just not." I didn't look to see whether Duncan agreed.

After that, I kept my head down and finished packing. Then I retraced my steps from the day before as best I could through the rain-washed terrain, feeling very thirsty. Duncan followed, still my furry white shadow, and when I reached the stream I had crossed the day before, I realized where all the missing water had gone.

"Whoa." I turned to Duncan. "Does this happen every time there's a storm?"

Overnight, the riverbed had filled to overflowing. The steep banks I had just recently climbed now lay submerged under deep, muddy water, and the distance to the far side seemed to have grown wider. I looked up at Mount Ida and the heavy clouds draped over its massive, rain-catching slopes.

The current didn't look too strong, but I decided against trying to swim across, which meant I'd have to wait for the water to subside. I let my backpack slip to the ground and sat down facing the river. Duncan looked at me with just enough twinkle in his little eyes for me to imagine him asking what the hell I was doing and where was the food.

"Might as well get comfortable," I said.

I stayed there for a while. But I saw no change in the width or height of the waterline, and my thirst somehow bent the laws of physics and stretched that time into hours. I ate another packet of spaghetti, but I was still thirsty as hell. I decided that only someone who had been stranded at sea could understand the torture I felt staring at an endless supply of undrinkable water.

Duncan came and went during the hours I sat there, no doubt questioning the intelligence of my species. By the afternoon, I doubted it, too, or at least doubted the intelligence of my plan. The river hadn't changed at all, but I had grown more dehydrated, and I still had a day or two of walking ahead of me before I'd make it back to the lander. I was pretty sure I wouldn't die of dehydration in that amount of time, but only if I could get across the river soon, and I had no way of knowing how long that would take.

Eventually, I turned to Duncan. "I'm thinking of doing something very stupid," I said, and my voice sounded as scratchy and dry as my throat felt. "No, I'm not going to drink the water. But I am going to swim in it."

Duncan bobbed his head with a bit too much enthusiasm.

The river had no rapids, no violent whitewater. It was just a constant, steady flow. I expected the current to be strong, and I expected the swim to be a struggle, but I felt sure I would eventually make it across. Even if I came out somewhere downstream, I figured I could just follow the river back up to the point where I got in. That seemed like a better choice than drinking the murky runoff or continuing to wait around for something that might not happen anytime soon.

I took a deep breath and said, "I guess I'm doing this."

But I had never done anything like that. The water I usually swam in was chlorinated, and the only current came from the slurping filters along the sides of the pool. I knew I had to leave the heavy pack behind so it wouldn't drag me under, but I wondered about the tent. I still had at least one night, maybe two, before I would reach the lander, and I didn't like the thought of sleeping outside, especially if another rainstorm hit.

I pulled the tent from the pack and tested its weight, which seemed light enough to risk bringing it with me. The rest I left on the ground in plain view as a marker that I'd be able to see from the other side.

I took off my boots, compression socks, and outer jumpsuit. I hesitated before taking off my underwear but reminded myself that there wasn't anyone else on the planet to see me naked except me. I wrapped all my clothes up inside the waterproof canvas of the tent, along with a flashlight, a multitool, and a few ration packets, and I strapped the bundle to my waist so I wouldn't lose it in the river. Then I walked barefoot over the warm Hades dirt to the water's edge, and something about that connection between the soil and the toes and soles of my feet made the planet feel a bit more like Earth.

I stepped into the water and felt the current pushing hard against my ankles. The river wasn't as cold as I expected it to be, and I was grateful for that. I turned and looked back at Duncan, who appeared quite unconcerned with whatever I was doing.

"I hope you're smart enough not to follow me. I'll be back for my pack in a couple of days, if you want to hang around here. But I guess this is goodbye, for now."

He started to groom himself.

I turned my attention back to the river, and my next step plunged me up to my waist. I yelped as the water almost knocked me down, but I recovered my footing, aware that the steepness of the bank meant I'd be swimming with my next step.

I looked over my shoulder and saw that Duncan had already moved in to investigate my pack. "What's mine is yours," I said. "But eat the food at your own risk. See you later, Hades ferret." Then I faced the muddy water, suddenly hoping it didn't hide a Hades alligator, or a Hades python, or Hades leeches. "This is a bad idea," I whispered to myself.

I took a deep breath and lunged into my best freestyle crawl, but the current fought back instantly. The river grabbed me by the tent around my waist and rolled me over, far stronger than I thought it would be. My head went under, and I came up sputtering and gasping with just enough time to catch one last glimpse of Duncan, who watched me with his little eyes as the current sped me away. Then the river dunked me again.

I flailed and kicked, scrambling to keep my head above water and claw my way toward the far shore, but I got nowhere. It felt like the river had lured me in and then seized me with hidden torrents that roared in my ears every time they pulled me down. The tent strained against my waist, and the straps bit into my skin. I thought about releasing it, but it had my clothes and my shoes inside.

I tried to keep sight of where I was and where I needed to be, but the river kept pulling me under and flipping me around. Every time, I came up weaker and more disoriented, until it took everything in me just to break the surface and catch a breath.

I knew I would drown if I didn't do something fast, and I also knew clothes wouldn't matter if my body broke. I ducked underwater and loosened the straps from around my waist, then offered the tent to the river, hoping to appease it. The current snatched it away.

I felt a bit lighter after that, but not light enough, and I wondered if it was the Hades gravity that made it so much harder to swim. My frantic thrashing accomplished nothing, except to exhaust me, and I felt myself approaching the edge of surrender.

"Help!" I screamed to nobody, desperate, and then I saw the darkness up ahead.

I didn't know what it was, at first, but as the current swept me toward it, I realized it was an opening, a cave, and the river seemed to be flowing right toward it.

Fresh panic roused me to one last, useless effort, and then I felt a change in the water, a deeper tug and a speeding up. The mouth of the cave widened before me, drinking down the whole river, and I went helplessly with it into the dark.

The cave squeezed the water, and the water squeezed me. For the next few moments, I couldn't see anything. I couldn't hear anything except the pounding inside my ears. But I felt the rock walls scraping my skin as the river tried to grind me to nothing against the sides of the cave. My lungs begged for air, burning up inside my rib cage until I saw their fire behind my eyes, and then everything around me opened back up. The water fell away, and I felt cool air rushing over my skin. Then I realized I was falling, too.

A second later, my feet slammed into a wall of water that folded up around me, then let me go. I was in someplace deep, a pool or a lake, and I scrambled upward until I reached the surface. I gasped, and then I let my limp and battered body float there, faceup, eyes closed, just breathing. I don't know how long I did that, but when I finally opened my eyes and lifted my head, I couldn't see much.

I knew by the distant echoes around me that I was in a vast cave. The only light came in with the river through the opening high above, a pale and misty column that hammered the surface of the water behind me. I'd splashed down in an underground lake, its water frigid and black, with no obvious way out. But I was alive, and I'd also solved the mystery of where a lot of the rainwater had gone.

That relief did not last long. As my eyes adjusted to the low light, dark forms took shape around me, huge and looming. They seemed to rise from deep under the lake, and at first, I thought they were boulders or stalagmites. But as I drifted closer to the nearest one, I decided it was far too smooth to be natural. Then I noticed the large, round windows, and I realized it was a tower. Something had built it.

I hadn't just landed in a cave. I had discovered a sunken, alien city. But as far as anyone had told me, Hades had no cities. Hades had never had cities. And yet the drowned ruins of one surrounded me. I shivered, and my teeth started to chatter. I kicked my feet a bit more frantically at imagined cold hands or tentacles in the water beneath me, and I wondered what else we had wrong about this planet. It was hard not to think about the pale, blind fish with razor-teeth that lived in the deepest parts of the ocean back on Earth.

I needed to get out of there. I just didn't know how. I certainly couldn't climb out the way I'd fallen in. The cavern to my right seemed a bit less dark, with shadows and pale threads of reflected light that I thought might be a shoreline. A subtle current even seemed to be moving in that direction, so I swam that way, trying not to disturb the water too much with my movement.

Slowly, I drew closer to what I hoped would be dry land, but as I neared another tower, a small lump appeared to break away from it, drifting into my path without making a splash.

I froze, barely treading water, squinting at the thing to see what it was, feeling as though the cold water had seeped into my bones. I listened, but the thing made no sound I could hear over the waterfall some distance behind me. It seemed to be moving toward me, or I was moving toward it, but it gave no sign that it was aware of me.

I worried I would draw its attention if I tried to swim away. But I also knew that if I didn't move, I would eventually bump right into it, and I really didn't want that to happen. I decided to just see how far away I could get with the minimum possible motion and fluttered my hands under the surface. But that didn't move me far enough, fast enough, and I expected the thing to notice me any second.

The floating lump came closer and suddenly took on a familiar shape. Then I glimpsed a bit of color and realized what it was. My tent had floated down the river with me, its waterproof canvas keeping it afloat. The current had carried it in the same direction as it had carried me. My sigh was quick, almost a laugh, but it was loud, and I covered my mouth. Then I snagged the tent and resumed my slow swim.

When I finally approached the shore, the light from the waterfall was hidden by the towers and too far away to do much good. My toes brushed hard stone, and a few moments later, I could stand. I staggered up a smooth ramp until I was out of the water, then I dropped to my knees and huddled over my bundle. Dripping, shivering, I opened the tent roll and found my clothing still dry inside.

I dressed quickly and checked to see if the Magical Mountain piece had made it safely, and it had, still zipped in its pocket. Then I picked up the flashlight, but I paused before switching it on. I worried the light would draw the attention of anything that might be in the cave with me. But it only took a moment to decide that was a risk I would have to take if I wanted to find my way out of there.

When I turned it on, the bright beam landed on a jumble of huge rocks above the waterline, at the base of another broken tower. Beyond it, an imposing wall climbed higher than my flashlight could reach and spread out of sight to the left and right, pitted with what looked like dozens and dozens of windows. Rolling dips and swells in its surface made the stone look like a fossilized ocean, with ledges or balconies swelling outward like bubbles and breaking waves. The ramp I stood on pointed straight at the wall, almost like a street, where it met the entrance to a large tunnel.

I turned around and shined the light behind me into the water, and beneath the surface, the road rolled away gradually until the lake depths swallowed it. Then I swung the light to either side and saw that the broken shoreline followed the wall a short way in both directions before it also disappeared into the lake, leaving the water to splash right up against the smooth, vertical stone.

There was only one way I could go. I turned to face the tunnel.

## BEFORE

THE CAPTAIN RUSHES INTO THE MEDICAL BAY, FOL-
lowed by Liz and my mom. Mouths open, eyes wide, all three of them
take in the destruction with the same horrified expression, but the captain seems to suppress her shock almost immediately, turning somber
and clinical.

"Where is Dr. Mathers?" she asks.

Duncan glances up at his mom and then looks at the hatch.

The captain speaks into her wrist comm, her voice blaring throughout the ship. "Attention! All personnel! This is Captain Sharpe. We have a
security threat, level one. I repeat: We have a security threat, level one. All
personnel are ordered to initiate lockdown measures. This is not a drill.
Secure yourselves and check in with the Belfry. Captain Sharpe out."

"Security threat?" Mom says. "Are you saying—"

But the captain holds up her hand, then speaks into her comm
again. "Captain to the Belfry."

A second passes, and then a somewhat distant voice says, "This is
the Belfry."

"I need a location on Dr. Mathers. He was last seen in the medical
lab. Get back to me when you have him."

"Right away," the voice says, and as soon as the captain signs off, my
mom is there, almost in her face.

"You can't seriously be suggesting that my husband—"

"Yes," the captain says. "Your husband did this."

With a loud clunk, Liz closes the hatch to the medical bay and
locks it.

Mom backs away from the captain. "I don't believe that."

I don't want to believe it, either, but I know what I saw.

"It's true." Duncan stands up, his voice very quiet, and angry. "Jessica saw it, too."

My mom turns her whole body to face me, her posture almost accusatory, and I can tell she's expecting me to take her side and defend my dad. But I can't.

"It was bad," I whisper.

She raises an eyebrow and points down at Dr. Gutiérrez. "You saw your father do this?"

"He did do this," Duncan says, "and no one could have stopped it." He's looking right at me, and I know he's trying to make me feel better about fumbling the hypo. "Nothing could have stopped it."

"No." Mom folds her arms, shaking her head. "Stephen doesn't have a violent bone in his body. It's just not in him to—"

"I was there," Duncan says, his voice quavering now. "He . . ." But he doesn't finish, and I don't want him to.

"I'm sorry," Mom says. "Duncan, is it? I don't know you, but I do know you're very mistaken—"

"Mom!"

She snaps her glare at me.

"He did it, okay? He did it. But it wasn't *him*."

"What do you mean?" the captain asks.

"When he looked at me, it was—" I recall his eyes and shudder. "It just wasn't him. Like when he was sleepwalking in my room. It was like he was someone else."

"Like a dissociative episode?" Ms. Kateb asks.

Before I can answer, the captain's comm pings.

"Reporting security status," says the distant Belfry voice. "All crew accounted for and locked down."

I feel quite a bit of relief at that news, knowing everyone is safe.

"Do you have a location for Dr. Mathers?" the captain asks.

"Still looking for him."

"Keep on it. Captain out."

"We need to find him." Mom glances at Dr. Gutiérrez on the floor. "And clean this up."

She says it with a mix of irritation and disgust, like she's talking about spilled milk, and I feel sick to my stomach. I've never seen a dead body. I don't know if it's shock, or the metal tang in the air from all the blood, but I feel light-headed, and my cheeks are tingling.

"Dr. Havilland," the captain says with icy authority, "you are speaking about a member of my crew who deserves more respect."

"I have the utmost respect for your crew," Mom says. "But I shouldn't need to remind you, Captain, that this is not Dr. Gutiérrez." She points at the floor. "This is a broken body. You can print him a new one."

No one answers her, to agree or disagree. But I know she's right. I remember my training and my counseling sessions. I know how I'm supposed to look at Dr. Gutiérrez now.

Evan goes to one of the cabinets and pulls out a thin white blanket, which he drapes over the body. Crouching next to it, he asks, "How old is his data?"

Liz looks up at the ceiling. "Let's see . . . a little over two years, I think."

Everyone in the room knows what that means.

"Two years." Duncan bows his head. "He won't know me."

"He won't know any of us," Ms. Kateb adds. "I don't think any of us had served with him before he arrived here."

Another silence follows, this one heavier, and even my mom seems to soften a bit. I realize then that the cost of the star splitter from the poem is not a one-time deal. To be out here, you have to be willing to burn up your life again and again, and that makes me wonder how many times my mom and dad have been printed.

The captain breaks the silence with a sigh. "I guess we can all look forward to meeting him again. It's like that saying goes. Out here, we're lucky enough to get a second chance to make a first impression."

"He was scared." Duncan is looking down at Dr. Gutiérrez, where bloodstains bloom in the white blanket from below. "He was in pain."

Evan rises and puts his arm around Duncan's shoulder. "He won't remember that, either."

Liz brushes something from her cheek. "I'll prep the printer as soon as we—"

"No." The captain says it with the force of an order, drawing everyone's attention. She looks around the room at each of us. "Dr. Mathers is clearly not himself. For now, we operate under the assumption that something went wrong when he was established here. As captain, I'm treating this as a quarantine situation and suspending all printing—"

"But, Mom," Duncan says. "What about—"

"Dr. Gutiérrez will be reestablished, but not until we know it is safe to do so, and according to his print orders." The captain looks hard at her son, like he's just another member of her crew. "Understood?"

I can see Duncan's jaw muscles working. "Yes, Captain."

"What is your plan?" Mom asks.

"Containment." The captain glances at her wrist comm. "The quantum channel has already opened and shut. That means we're at least twelve hours away from the possibility of any answers or guidance from ISTA. Our next task is to find and secure Dr. Mathers. When he is no longer a security threat, we'll turn our attention to figuring out exactly what the hell went wrong."

"How will we secure him?" Duncan asks. "He's strong."

The captain pauses and then lifts her chin. "I'll open the armory in the command module."

I don't like the sound of that, and Mom looks like she's about to object, but before she can, the captain adds, "Nonlethal weapons, only. Tasers and chemical deterrents."

"In all the years I've worked for ISTA," Evan says, "I've never seen the inside of a ship's armory."

I didn't even know ships had armories.

"Let's hope we never have the need again," says Ms. Kateb.

"How do we contain him?" Evan asks.

"There's a storage space up near the Belfry," the captain says. "ISTA designed it to function as a brig, during an emergency. We'll secure Dr. Mathers there."

"A brig?" Mom presses her fingertips against her temples, and I can't tell if she's shocked or angry. "Captain, my husband needs medical treatment, not—"

"For what?" The captain's face reddens. "What is his condition? What is the treatment?"

She waits for an answer, but my mom is silent.

The captain spreads her arms. "Please, if you know the answer to those questions, do enlighten us. I'm sure Dr. Gutiérrez would have appreciated that information—"

"Mom," Duncan says, quietly.

The captain looks at him. A moment passes. Then she sighs. "Dr. Havilland, it's obvious there is something very wrong with your husband. But we don't know what is wrong with him, and the crew member most qualified to make a diagnosis paid a very high price for our ignorance. I'm not going to repeat the same mistake twice. Whether you want to call it a brig or not, we will secure Dr. Mathers as our first order of business and consider treatment options from there."

My mom doesn't argue, but her nod is tight-lipped. I wonder if she'd feel more comfortable locking up my dad if she had seen what I just saw. I certainly don't feel safe with the idea of just putting him back in a medbed.

The captain looks around the room, and at Dr. Gutiérrez's body. "This isn't an ideal place to lock down. I'd like to move all of you." She says it like she's referring to everyone, but I think she's mostly thinking of Duncan and me.

"The common room isn't far from here," Liz says.

The captain nods and speaks into her wrist comm. "Belfry, I need that location."

"We just found him," comes the reply.

The captain lifts her wrist a bit closer. "Where?"

"Corridor D, near *Lander Two*."

"That's good," Evan says, nodding. "Corridor D is good."

If I remember correctly, corridor D is on the other side of the ship.

The captain orders the Belfry to keep an eye on my dad and signs off. Then she marches toward the hatch and turns to face us before opening it. "Okay, people, let's move to the common room. Stay close together."

"He's fast," Duncan says quietly, and he looks scared. "Really fast."

"We'll go quickly," the captain says. "Ready?"

We all nod, and she opens the hatch.

My mom takes my hand, and I look down, surprised. I remember she used to do that whenever we went anywhere crowded, and it always embarrassed me. It made me feel like a child, which I was, and I would try to shake her off or pull free of her. But I never could, and in this moment, I don't want to. I give her hand a squeeze, and she squeezes mine back. Then we all file out through the hatch and hurry along the corridor. I'm listening and looking over my shoulder, and every time we come to a junction, I hold my breath until I know my dad isn't lurking around the corner.

We manage to reach the common room without any difficulty, and Evan stands in the hallway keeping a lookout in both directions while the captain ushers us inside. But she doesn't follow us.

"You will all lock down here," she says.

My mom spins around, and Duncan asks, "Where are you going?"

"The armory. Evan and I will—"

"I'll come with you, Captain," Mom says. I assume she wants to be there when they find my dad, but as she approaches the hatch, the captain lifts her arm like a bar to block the way and shakes her head.

"I'm afraid I can't allow that—"

"Yes," Mom says, "you can."

The captain doesn't budge. "But I won't."

"You will." Mom presses ahead like she's going to shove her way through, but a sharp bark from the captain stops her.

"Dr. Havilland! I have tried to be patient, but I will not tolerate any further insubordination from you. As long as you are on my ship, you will respect my authority. I have made my decision, and it is an order."

Even I catch the meaning behind that statement. If my mom keeps arguing, I'm betting the captain would throw her into the brig with my dad. I think Mom understands it, too, because the fight seems to go out of her.

"Please," she whispers to the room. "He's my husband."

"I know." The captain's voice softens. "It is because he's your husband that you must wait in the common room with your daughter. In a security situation like this, the protocol is clear. Your involvement would be a liability, and I refuse to compromise the safety of my crew, yourself, or your daughter."

"Dr. Havilland," Evan says from the corridor. "You can trust us to do right by your husband." Then he looks at me. "I promise."

I already believed that they would, but I'm grateful to him for saying it, and even though my mom's bottom lip quivers, she finally nods in agreement.

"Lock the hatch," the captain says. "Until I give the all clear over the comm, don't open it. For anyone."

She isn't looking at my mom, specifically, or me, but I know that's meant for us, in case my dad comes banging on the door.

"Yes, Captain," says Ms. Kateb. "Let us know when you reach the Belfry."

The captain nods. Then she looks at Duncan. "Stay safe."

"I will," Duncan says, and after she leaves, he's the one who secures the hatch.

I let go of my mom's hand and turn to face the common room, with its black screens and wide expanse of windows. They're open, but for the first time, I would prefer them closed. The past few hours have turned my previous awe of the infinite stars to dread.

"Are you okay?" Mom asks me.

"I'm fine, just . . . overwhelmed."

"That is very natural." Ms. Kateb walks to the sink and fills up a glass of water. "I suspect we're all dealing with a bit of shock." She comes over and offers me the glass, and I take it, even though I'm not thirsty.

Liz speaks to Duncan. "How are you?"

"Holding up," he says.

His eyes have a vacant look, like he's paying more attention to what-ever is playing on the movie screen in his mind. It's probably pretty close to what's playing on mine. I see my dad convulsing, I see a skit-tering hypo, I see blood, and I see the handle of a coffee mug where it shouldn't be.

"I suggest we all sit down," Ms. Kateb says.

A moment goes by, and then we all trudge over to the couches and chairs near the entertainment console and collapse into them. We sit there without speaking, and I feel the cold and hostile weight of the stars bearing down on me. It's like I've learned the truth about what it really means to be out here. We're stranded light-years from home or any help, and our insignificant little ship is floating over a bottomless abyss of empty space. A sudden vertigo seizes me, and it's more than just dizziness from the spinning view.

"Can we close the windows?" I ask.

"Uh, sure." Duncan gets up and works the controls, and the panels slide into place, containing us against the void. When he sits down again, he leans toward me and says, "It'll be okay. Whatever is wrong with your dad, they can fix it. Liz and Evan and my mom. Even if they have to reestablish him—"

"They can't," Mom says.

"Why not?" I ask.

She leans forward in her chair, rubbing her eyes, and doesn't answer me.

"*Why not?*" I ask again.

"There was a problem with their scanning chamber," Ms. Kateb says. "You may remember I mentioned it to you when you arrived?"

I do remember that. "You said it wasn't a big deal."

"It wasn't," Liz says. "Or at least, we didn't have any reason to think it would be a big deal. After your parents arrived, the scanner that read their data needed a repair, and during that repair, they lost its memory cache. Now, that wouldn't normally be a problem. They only initiated the repair because we confirmed that we had your father's data here—"

"Then why is it a problem?" I ask.

"It is . . . unlikely that we will be able to use that scan," Ms. Kateb says. "His data may have been corrupted."

"Like the photo?" Duncan asks, and Ms. Kateb offers a slow nod.

I feel a squeezing in my chest. "So, then you . . . can't you just use a different backup? From the scan before that?"

"There is no other scan." Mom finally lowers her hands and looks at me with wet eyes. "Before New Beijing, the last time your father and I were scanned was back on Earth. When we left."

"But I thought . . ." This doesn't make any sense to me. "But you guys have been out here for so long—"

"We've been surveying a star system," she says. "We were on one ship the whole time. Local travel. No scanning until we came here."

I know what that means, and suddenly I understand why my Mom has been acting so desperate. If we can't fix my dad, and if we have to reestablish him using his old data, then he will lose all his memories from the last six years.

# 18—Hades

THE TUNNEL INTO THE UNDERGROUND CITY WAS round, like an enormous pipe five or six meters across. My footsteps echoed as I entered it and left the lake behind.

All around me, intricate patterns covered the walls and ceiling with glinting mazes and swirls. When I examined the lines more closely, I found they were made of what appeared to be some kind of inlaid metal, like wires or electronic circuits embedded in the polished stone walls. The beam of light from my flashlight wasn't strong enough to push very far ahead of me. Impenetrable shadows massed just beyond its reach, ready to close in the second I turned off the light.

A short distance on, the tunnel opened into a larger, circular chamber several stories high and sculpted out of the same smooth material as the corridor. Sinuous walkways spiraled and crisscrossed up and down around the walls, like ribbons of stone, and numerous windows and doorways looked down on me, dark and forbidding. At the bottom level where I stood, I counted six smaller corridors leaving the chamber, radiating in different directions like spokes from a hub, and even though I was pretty sure the markings on the wall near each exit would have meant something to the aliens who built the place, those squiggles meant nothing to me.

I tried to imagine who the builders had been. They were obviously intelligent, by any of the definitions that Mr. Stamitz used in his xenobiology class. The physical dimensions of their city so far suggested a roughly human scale. So the aliens were probably about our size. But I had no idea what it meant that I hadn't seen a single corner or sharp edge. Everything looked rounded, like melted wax, and it gave that place the feeling of a burrow, or a hive, though I definitely preferred to think of it as a burrow. A burrow that would hopefully lead me to the surface, if I picked the right tunnel.

In considering which path to take, I eliminated the dozens of openings above me, because I didn't trust the ancient walkways not to collapse. That just left the six corridors in front of me. I walked around the chamber and shined my flashlight down each one, studying and listening, and each returned my silence with a silence of its own. Four of them seemed to slope downward, leading deeper underground, which was the not the direction I wanted. Of the remaining two, one smelled like mildew and wet stone, while the other felt much less damp, which I assumed was a good thing, so that was the tunnel I chose.

The same inlaid wires still covered the walls, and I decided they must have served some purpose beyond decoration. Maybe a network for energy or communication. Whatever their function, they gave no indication I could pick up that they were working anymore.

In the darkness, it was hard to know how far I walked, but after what felt like a hundred meters or so, I entered another large chamber almost identical to the last one. The same ribbon walkways climbed the walls, and another six corridors spread out like the legs of an insect. Again I picked the driest tunnel, which led away to my left, and I followed it to a third chamber that was like the first two. The burrow or the city or whatever it was seemed to have a honeycomb design of connected chambers.

In that third hub, a solid-looking ramp rose to a doorway that didn't look too high up, and I was curious enough that I dared a tentative climb. When I shined my flashlight inside, I glimpsed a smaller version of the larger chamber outside the door. Several small, round rooms surrounded an open space at the center, containing what I guessed to be furniture. Pedestals and tables grew out of the floor, made of the same waxy stone, some sections of it also traced with the metal inlay.

It felt like an apartment. A home. But I remembered enough from Mr. Stamitz's class to know that was a very human assumption to make, and for all I knew, this alien structure had been used as a dissection lab, or an alien clown school, or for some other purpose that I couldn't imagine. But somehow it felt like a house. An empty, long-abandoned house; if I was in an old movie, there would've been alien ghosts haunting the place for sure.

That superstitious feeling was enough to discourage me from exploring any higher or deeper into that apartment, so I descended the walkway to the relative safety of the ground floor. After that, I avoided looking up at any of the windows and doorways and kept my flashlight aimed straight ahead.

I passed through a dozen more large hub chambers, all nearly identical. The city felt like a maze in which I could easily get lost and walk in circles, so I tried hard to keep track of my turns.

Then I found a body.

It seemed to lunge at me when the light from my flashlight landed on it, and I yelped. But I quickly realized it was dead, and it had been dead for a long, long time.

It appeared to be a skeleton. The bones and joints were much thicker than a human's, encased in a layer of some kind of glittering, crystalline cave growth that reminded me of snow. A mass of horns protruded from what seemed to be its skull, which was shaped like a broad, pointed shovel. I couldn't see any openings for eyes, but the mineral coating made it hard to know for sure. And that was assuming the thing even had eyes, or that I would recognize the eyes it had.

I counted three pairs of limbs, each set a different size. There were two sets of limbs up near the shovel-skull: a long, outside pair that looked thick and powerful, and a shorter, thinner inside pair. A third, stout pair of limbs emerged from its backside, next to a thing that looked like a tail. The mineral growth had fused it all together and blunted the ends of each limb with a crystal boxing glove, so I couldn't tell if the alien had fingers or even hands. Taken all together, the skeleton didn't look that different from the bones of an ice-age sloth I'd once seen in a museum. Except the alien was smaller, and it had those horns and extra limbs.

I actually felt a bit disappointed by it, after my initial shock had worn off. I'd been expecting something a lot weirder. An alien so strange I might not have even recognized it for what it was.

When I moved on, I found a second alien body not far from the first, caked in the same mineral crust. The second one appeared to be smaller than the first, until I noticed it was missing pieces. I swung my flashlight and located the rest of its bones strewn a couple of meters away. A flutter of dread shortened my breath as I wondered how, or why, it had been dismembered. That was usually the work of predators and scavengers back on Earth.

But then in the next chamber, I found a massacre. An enormous tower of bones rose as high as the third level of windows and doors, surrounded by a skirt of bones that covered the floor. Hundreds and hundreds of alien bodies had been torn apart and mashed together. There were skulls of different sizes, all without horns, and some small enough they could have belonged to babies. Limbs protruded at odd angles from the centers of bodies that had been folded, twisted, and broken. Fine, pale crystals covered the skeletons like frost, binding them all together. That meant the minerals had grown over the bodies *after* something had assembled them that way. The scale of it stunned me, and I stared, transfixed by its brutality and horror. A sparkling monument of death.

I had only been walking through that alien city for a short while, but I had seen enough of its elegant lines to believe that bone tower was not how the city's residents would have chosen to bury or remember their dead. It wasn't a cemetery. Something cruel had been done to them with malevolent purpose, in their homes. All that killing and mutilation may have taken place millions of years in the past, but I could still feel the evil of it, and I had to get away.

I couldn't go anywhere without walking and climbing over the bones, which I was not about to do. Instead, I retreated to the previous chamber and picked the next tunnel to my right, hoping to find a way around the carnage.

After that, the city felt even more haunted, and I couldn't shake off the chills or the sense that something was watching me. I kept the flashlight pointed at the floor, looking out for more bodies, and when I found them, they didn't startle me quite as badly as the first had. Instead, they turned my stomach, and so did the second tower of crystal bones that loomed over the next hub I came to.

I backtracked again, choosing a new spoke, where I found a third bone tower blocking my path. And then there was a fourth.

I could only stand and stare up at it, struggling to comprehend the meaning of the thousands of bodies I had seen, and the way they had been butchered. It seemed I kept coming up against the boundary or border of a death zone, and I had no idea how far back I would have to go to get around it, or even if I could. The batteries in my flashlight would run out eventually.

I knew I was already lost, in a way, but I didn't feel completely lost yet because I had picked a direction. If I wanted to keep moving in that direction, it seemed I would have to cross the death zone and go through the bones. So I decided that's what I had to do.

I swallowed and took a cautious step forward, then another, approaching the tower of skeletons like it might collapse if I breathed on it the wrong way. By the time I took my first step onto the skirt of bones that surrounded it, I was sweating, eyes wide. My heart pounded as I heard and felt the gritty crunch of crystal beneath my boot.

Before I gave the bones my full weight, I tested my footing, just to make sure the skeletons weren't more brittle than they looked. But they held like stone, and a moment later I stood with both of my feet upon the dead.

From there, I picked my way toward the spoke that would keep me on track, leaving a trail of crushed mineral dust behind me. The unevenness of the pile caused me to stumble a few times, and some of the more delicate bones occasionally cracked and gave way. Every time I felt the ground shift, I braced myself and cast a worried glance upward, expecting the tower to come crashing down.

Halfway across the room, I came to a raised ridge in the bones, and I stopped. It stood a meter or so taller than the surrounding mound, and it ran from the tower to the edge of the chamber. To keep moving forward, I had to climb over it.

I did not like that idea. I did not know how to climb over the skeletons without touching them, and I didn't want to touch them. So I tried to high-step my way up onto the wall, hands outstretched for balance. I made it most of the way, but at the top, a slender bone snapped beneath my heel, and I lurched forward, tumbling down the other side of the ridge.

I didn't roll far, but wherever my bare skin brushed against the bones I felt a thousand tiny razor blades of crystal slicing into my face, my neck, my hands. When I finally hit the bottom, I froze, holding my body still. For several moments I just lay there, grimacing and coughing on the dust I'd stirred up.

I could feel the powder burning deep in my lungs, and I could taste its fine grit on my lips like moldy chalk. I had to work hard to keep myself from panicking at the thought that I had inhaled something toxic and deadly. But then I turned frantic when I realized I'd lost my flashlight in the fall.

I scrambled to my feet, looking all around the bone pile. I could see the flashlight's indirect glow coming from within the tangled skeletons.

It had fallen through the gaps in a mass of skulls, out of my reach. The alien heads seemed huddled together, lit from below, glaring at me without eyes and daring me to try to reclaim what they had taken. I realized then that I had also lost my tent somewhere, along with the rations inside it.

I kicked at the bones, trying to crack them so I could reach the flashlight. When that didn't work, I started jumping on them. I raged against them until I was exhausted and my knees and my ankles wanted to give out in pain. But the bones won, and for a long while after that, I just stood there, bloody and raw.

The corridor I had been aiming for opened only a few meters ahead, but it may as well have been light-years away. I knew I would never escape that alien city without my flashlight, and I could only watch as it flickered and dimmed.

I was thirsty. I started to wonder what it would feel like when my body broke. I assumed dehydration would be what did it, until I realized the bone-crystal dust had poisoned me.

The burning and stinging from my cuts had started to fade, but then a weird tingling, humming sensation spread across my skin. Then my thoughts started to go fuzzy, and I saw sparks and thin curls of white flashing in my vision. I would have probably freaked out more if I hadn't already been doomed.

Then the flashing curls began to stick to the edges and outlines of things, turning my vision of the chamber a bit squiggly, like a rough cartoon. I felt dizzy and decided it would probably be a good idea to get off the skeletons and sit down, so I headed for the corridor. The curls thickened and multiplied as my boots scraped against the bones. But I made it to the doorway and slumped to the floor next to it with my back against the wall, facing the tower. After that, the squiggles seemed to settle.

I tried to make myself feel better by reminding myself that I could always be reestablished back on Earth. Like Jim Kelly had said.

*If the worst should happen.*

I was stranded and poisoned in an underground alien city with no hope of ever being found. It seemed like the worst had happened. I closed my eyes and imagined what it would be like to wake up in a body printer as I had on the lander. It would feel like I had just climbed into the scanner. I wouldn't remember anything about Hades. But I would be me. I would be alive.

Time went by. I didn't know how much time, but it seemed like hours. My throat burned. The room grew dimmer and dimmer as the flashlight's batteries dwindled, like the sun setting over a horizon of skulls. Then the light went out completely.

I had never seen a darkness like that before, and for a long while, I didn't move. I just stared into it, and my mind filled it with shadow memories of what I knew was there. It was a thick, oppressive darkness that seemed to have weight and substance, and I felt an urgent need to move, to get out from under it.

When I shifted, the curling lines returned, outlining the black hollows of the tower, the bones, contours of the chamber. I blinked, shaking my head, and the squiggles faded again. I tried to hold still to keep them from coming back, but then I had to cough, and when I did, they blazed brighter than ever. My throat was on fire, so the coughs kept coming, and so did the squiggles, even though I was holding still. I realized that they didn't light up with movement, but with sound. Then I noticed that the squiggles didn't move with me as I moved. They stayed fixed, like they were somehow marking the physical locations of the walls, the bones, and everything else in the chamber.

I got to my feet, and as an experiment, I turned to peer down the corridor next to me. I stomped my foot, and the loud sound echoed down the tunnel, lighting up the shape of its walls with wavy white lines. I assumed it was an effect of the crystal dust messing with my perception, turning sound into visual information. Like a kind of synesthesia.

I didn't know how long it would last, or if the dust was poisoning me, but I didn't want to just sit there waiting to find out.

I glanced at the sketchy outline of the bone tower again, and then I walked from that chamber down the corridor. I took my steps slowly and carefully, scuffing my boots along the ground to keep making sounds, but also to make sure I didn't trip over anything the squiggles didn't show me. The experience felt strange, like a stylized, abstract VR game. But I was back on the move, even without my flashlight.

# 19 — DS *Theseus*

## BEFORE

I SIT THERE TRYING TO IMAGINE EXACTLY WHAT IT would mean if my dad lost six years of memories. For him, it would be like he never even left, except for the fact that he said goodbye to an eleven-year-old daughter, and now I'm a teenager. The loss of his memories would probably be a lot worse for my mom, though. She and my dad have spent a third of their marriage out here. Of course, I wouldn't lose much, because I never had those six years with him to begin with.

"Teleportation is supposed to be safe," Duncan says.

"It *is* safe." The ISTA liaison in Ms. Kateb looks personally affronted. "Statistically, teleportation is the safest form of—"

"But this isn't the same as a plane crash or a car accident, is it?" Duncan's knee is bouncing, and he's fidgeting with his hands. "Those can only hurt your body. They can't . . ." He bows his head, shaking it, and doesn't finish his thought.

But he doesn't need to. I suspect we all know what he's thinking, even if we would all probably come up with a different word for it.

"My husband is the same man he has always been," Mom says. "He is gentle, and he is kind. He is the sort of man who remembers his daughter's favorite childhood board game. If there is a problem, it is with his data. It's just code, just qubits in superposition. It is a medical problem. We can sort it out."

It sounds like she's just giving herself a pep talk, but I still want to believe it's true.

"I am certain we will," Ms. Kateb says. "The captain will do everything she can to help Dr. Mathers—"

"Stephen," Mom says. "Please, call him Stephen. And I'm Sharon."

Ms. Kateb nods. "And I am Amira." Then she looks at me and offers a gentle smile, which I guess means I'm enough a part of the crew now to call her by her first name, too.

After that, our conversation circles the same subjects a few more times but gets nowhere because we still don't have any answers. Eventually, we fall into a silence that lasts for a while. I assume we're all imagining our own version of what might be happening elsewhere on the ship. I wonder if my dad has collapsed somewhere, having another seizure, or if he's still violent, ready to attack Evan and the captain.

When the comm pings, my mom leaps to her feet, head tilted upward. "Captain? Do you have him? Is he—"

"We . . . have him," the captain says, but her speaker voice sounds winded, blowing static every time she exhales. "We just . . . he made a run for it. But we have him."

"Are you okay?" Duncan asks.

"Everyone is fine," the captain says. "Dr. Mathers is secured in the br— In the storage room."

Mom moves toward the hatch. "We're on our way."

"Dr. Havilland," the captain says. "For the time being, I think it would be best if you remain where you are."

My mom laughs to herself, shaking her head as she reaches the hatch, and before anyone can stop her, she unlocks it and marches out into the corridor without looking back, even at me. I hurry after her.

"Dr. Havilland?" the captain says. "I repeat. Do not—"

"She left," Amira says.

Out in the corridor, I hear the captain say "damn it" through the comm, and a moment later, Amira, Duncan, and Liz are following behind me.

We rush down the hallway to the nearest spoke, where we catch up to my mom. Amira tries asking her to stop, but Mom's not listening, and all we can do is follow her up and along the ladder to the hub. Once we hit microgravity, I am clearly the weakest link, but my mom keeps the lead with graceful and effortless movements, like she can do this without even thinking about it.

We travel up the hub until we enter the sleek, bright section that I passed through when I came up here to find Liz. At the end of that stretch, we reach an open hatch. My mom dives through, and then the rest of us pile up in front of it, forced into single file, and I push my way ahead first.

In the junction beyond, the captain hovers in front of the hatch across the way from Brad the computer. Evan floats at her side, and my mom faces both of them. The space gets pretty tight as Duncan, Amira, and Liz climb into the junction from below.

"I assure you," the captain is saying, "he is sedated and safe."

"Let me see him," Mom says.

The captain glances at Evan, who still holds what I assume is a taser at his side, and then they both pull themselves out of the way. My mom lunges for the hatch, peers through its round window, and then immediately reaches for the console to open the door. The controls don't respond to her.

"You bastards," she says, and rounds on the captain. "Open it."

"No," the captain says.

"Open it!"

I push forward and sideways until I have a view through the window, into the brig. My dad appears unconscious, his head lolling to one side. He floats in the middle of the empty room, hands tied behind his back, a heavy strap around his chest and arms. Cords bind his legs together at the knees and ankles, anchoring him to the floor. He's like a limp balloon that's lost some of its helium.

My mom clenches her fists and shakes her head. "I knew you would do this."

"Dr. Havilland," the captain says, "I wish you would've stayed in the common room—"

"Why? So you could hide this from me? He needs medical attention!" She stabs a finger in Evan's direction. "You promised you would do right by him."

The engineer's mouth tightens. "We will. We are."

I can see why my mom is upset, and I wonder if I should be more upset than I am. Maybe it was the empty look in my dad's eyes, or what he did to Dr. Gutiérrez, or maybe it's because he felt like a stranger to me even before the seizures, but it's hard for me to see the rag-doll body in the brig as his anymore.

"What about the rest of you?" My mom sweeps a furious glare over everyone in the juncture. "What if that was one of you in there? Would you be okay with this?"

If anyone in that tight space is breathing, I can't hear it, but I can tell by their firm expressions and silence that no one is on my mom's side of this.

The captain lifts her chin. "You are on mutinous ground, Dr. Havilland. You will refrain from—"

"Fuck you!"

Mom pushes toward her in a threatening way. Evan raises his taser, and Liz flinches next to me. But then my mom wheels to the side and shoulders her way through the rest of us toward the hatch. Duncan and Amira move aside to let her pass, and then she drops through the floor and is gone.

I'm supposed to go with her. I'm her daughter. But she didn't even look at me or call my name. Or wait for me. And the truth is, I don't want to go with her. I want to stay here, with the people who can help me find out what happened to my dad. I can feel them looking at me, probably wondering what I'll do.

I keep my eyes down, and all I can think to say to them is "I'm sorry."

"You have nothing to be sorry about," the captain says without any hesitation, and I can tell she means it. She looks at the brig's window. "I truly wish this wasn't necessary, but until we determine—"

"I understand." I think about the body on the other side of the locked hatch. "What will keep him from waking up like he did before?"

"We put him to sleep all the way this time," Evan says. "Full sedation."

"It is only temporary," the captain adds. "We'll get some guidance from Earth soon. Then we'll know how to help your father."

"So basically eleven hours from now," I say.

Liz nods. "More or less."

That did not feel soon to me.

"In the meantime," Evan says, turning somber and quiet, "there is something I'd like to take care of. With your permission, Captain?"

"Of course," she says, like she knows what he's talking about.

"Thank you." He moves toward the hatch.

"May I help?" Duncan asks. He apparently knows what Evan is talking about, too.

Evan stops and glances at the captain.

She looks at Duncan, frowning in worry. "It's biowaste. You aren't certified—"

"Please, Mom," Duncan says, and I realize they're talking about Dr. Gutiérrez's body back in the medical bay. "Let me do this."

"I'm okay with it," Evan says. "I'll make sure it's done according to regulations."

The captain sighs and nods, but reluctantly. "Very well."

"Thank you." Duncan moves toward Evan.

"Can—can I help?" I ask.

They all turn to look at me, and I almost hope they'll say no, because it's not like I'm enjoying the idea of cleaning up a broken body. But I also feel like I should be a part of whatever it is they're doing, since it was my dad who caused it.

"You don't have to." Now Duncan is the one frowning at me with worry, and maybe doubt that I can be of any use. "You didn't really know him."

I don't think he means that in a hurtful way. "I want to help," I say, which is mostly true.

"Are you sure?" Evan asks.

I pause to really think about it. "I'm sure."

The captain looks like she wants to say no. Like if she'd known that saying yes to Duncan would lead to this, she would have said no to him, too. But she nods with a slight toss of her hands, and Evan tips his head toward the hatch.

"Okay, Mathers. Come along."

I follow him and Duncan down the hatch into the hub, and we sail through the long vault in silence. I can see Carver 1061c through the windows we pass, only now the planet feels like a huge eye that never blinks, watching me as much as I'm watching it. As if the violence in its orbit has awakened it to our presence. Duncan and Evan are moving at a slow, somber pace, which means I'm under the planet's gaze for longer than is comfortable.

When we get to the medical bay and open the hatch, the room smells of old spilled coffee and dried blood. Dr. Gutiérrez's body is lying on the floor just as we left it, and the stark reality of it takes me aback. But I work to steel myself as Evan goes to the storage compartments and searches them for something. Duncan steps closer to the body.

"Wait," Evan says, and Duncan stops. The engineer pulls a box of gloves out of a storage compartment and extends it toward us. "I told your mom we'd do this right."

Duncan pulls two gloves from the box. Then Evan swings the box toward me, and I do the same. The gloves squeak like balloons against my skin as I pull them on.

"Okay, what next?" Evan goes back to searching compartments and lockers. A few moments later, he says, "There it is."

He pulls a bundle out of a compartment near the floor and brings it toward us. As he shakes it out, I see it's some kind of pale, translucent bag about the length and width of a body. It makes a dull crinkling sound as he lays it out on the floor, unzips it, and opens it up. Then he moves to the body's head and gestures toward the feet. "I'll get his shoulders if you each want to take a leg."

As we lift, I find the body is heavier than I expect it to be, and its midsection sags as we swing it from the place where it broke to the open body bag next to it. Duncan crouches and takes hold of the zipper at the feet. Evan tucks the arms inside, and the way they flop reminds me of an empty puppet. The two of them are quiet and respectful as they work, closing the bag just as they would if they were packing away any of Dr. Gutiérrez's valued possessions, and after the zipper has come together over the nose and face, we grab onto the straps on the outside of the bag and lift again.

I'm on the left, near the shoulder, while Evan takes the right, and Duncan carries the feet. Together, we lumber from the medical bay out into the corridor. The bag helps distribute the weight of the body evenly, which makes it easier to carry, but it's still heavy, even in the partial gravity. Evan turns us downship and guides us to a rear section that I haven't seen since Amira gave me the tour.

Where our corridor ends, we come to a hatch that's twice as wide and tall as the others, like a loading dock. Evan taps its console with one hand while hanging onto the handle of the body bag with the other, and the hatch opens, revealing a metal cage like an elevator. It sits on a track that rises through a long tunnel at the angle of an escalator. A rush of cold air rolls over us, smelling of machine oil as we step into the cage and set the body down. My arm and shoulder are grateful for the rest.

"It'll be easier from here," Evan says. "We'll be in micro-g when we reach the top."

He works the controls on a pedestal, and the platform lurches with a hissing sound, followed by a loud, ratcheting clanking that follows us upward. The higher we rise, the less gravity I feel, and at the top of the ramp, our cage slides into a kind of air lock and stops with a shudder.

"You'll want to hold on to the side," Evan says.

There's a handrail, and I grab onto it. So does Duncan, and then Evan works some more controls on the pedestal. The cage shudders again, and in the next second, I go fully weightless, like I'm in the hub. The body bag is hovering above the floor, and it bumps into my leg.

When Evan opens the air lock and the cage, we're greeted by a very different kind of *Theseus* than I've seen before. There are no corridors or sleek panels here. Instead there is a network of color-coded handrails that seem to mark pathways up and down through a maze of pipes, conduits, instruments, machines, and computer terminals. Evan latches onto one of the bag's handles and tugs it with him as he pushes off.

"This way," he says.

Duncan and I follow him down a central channel, surrounded by the hum of the ship and the tang of metal and static in the air. A short distance on, Evan banks to the right, and we come into a wide alcove filled with what looks a trash compactor.

Its open mouth is large enough for a person to fit inside, and we all help to feed it the bagged body. The process feels surreal and solemn, but also wrong. Teleportation counselors would probably say it should feel no different from disposing of any other type of waste. But the three of us speak in whispers and work gently anyway, until the bag is settled inside, along with our used gloves. The mouth closes, and only then do I take a deep breath and sigh it out.

Evan looks at me. "Are you okay?"

"That was hard," I say, but I don't mean physically.

"You did well," he says. "Both of you."

"What is this?" I ask, looking at the compacter.

"Resource retrieval unit." Evan hits some buttons on the machine's display. "It'll extract all the useful elements and minerals, and some other compounds, amino acids and such."

"The cool thing is," Duncan says, "if we reestablish Dr. Gutiérrez here, we might end up using material from his old body to print him."

"One molecule is the same as another," Evan says, his voice flat, like he's saying what he's supposed to say. But then he turns toward us with a wry smile. "That is pretty cool, though. And I think Alberto would agree. What's that poem he likes? Something about stars?"

"He once quoted Shakespeare to me," I say.

"It was 'Sonnet Fourteen,'" Duncan says.

"Right." Evan nods. "'Sonnet Fourteen.'"

We wait until the resource retrieval process is well underway before heading back, but this time we don't take the lift, because Evan says that uses up energy unnecessarily when we can just climb down a ladder instead. He guides us through the rest of the engineering module until we arrive at a hatch, and on the other side of it, we enter the hub.

"You kids should go try to relax." Evan launches ahead of us. "This was a hard day. I'll finish cleaning the medical bay."

Duncan readies himself to push off and follow. "I'll help you—"

"I insist," Evan says, looking back. "It really is against regulations. But I appreciate the help getting this far. Now, go take a break."

I don't think Duncan wants to stay behind, but he doesn't leave, either. "Just let us know if you need help," he calls.

Evan is already a good distance up the hub, but his voice still reaches us. "I will."

After he's gone, I shake my head. "I don't know how he expects us to relax right now."

"Yeah," Duncan says, but he isn't looking at me. "I wonder when ISTA will tell his husband."

"Whose husband?"

"Dr. Gutiérrez. His husband is back on Earth."

"I didn't know he was married."

"His husband's name is Tom. Tommy." He pauses. "I wonder if we'll get to see him again."

"Dr. Gutiérrez? Why wouldn't you?"

"If his print orders give his husband the choice, he might just bring Dr. Gutiérrez home. It's already been two years."

I may not know Dr. Gutiérrez well, but my few interactions with him were enough to say that would be very hard for him. He wanted to write the history of humanity in the stars. "That would be like he never got the chance to come out here," I say.

"But if his husband gives us the okay to reestablish out here, then he'll be choosing to reset the clock on Dr. Gutiérrez's mission. I can't imagine that will be an easy decision for him to make." Duncan pulls his focus the rest of the way back onto me. "Is anyone on Earth missing you?"

It's a blunt question, and I feel awkward answering it as we float here in front of the hatch to the engineering and reactor module. I suppose this is as private as it gets on a ship like this, but I still feel the need to move the conversation to the side of the hub.

"I know my grandparents miss me," I say, stopping us far enough from the nearest window that I avoid the weight of the planet's direct view.

"How did they feel about you coming out here?" he asks.

"They didn't try to stop it, but I could tell they were upset. They knew I didn't want to go. They know all my friends. And one time I heard them tell my parents I was doing well where I was, on Earth. With them."

Duncan reaches out and lays his palm against the wall of the ship, like an anchor. "So your friends probably miss you, too."

I let out a little laugh. "Well I hope they do." Then my voice gets quiet. "I know I miss them. I miss Avery."

"Who's Avery?"

"Oh, you know. Just one of my best friends that I've secretly been in love with for like a year." It feels good to say this out loud to someone. "I had this plan to finally tell her, but then I found out I was coming out here, and there didn't seem to be a point anymore."

"So she still doesn't know?"

"Believe it or not, you are now the only other person in the universe besides me who knows. I'm . . . not very good at this kind of thing. Friends, yes. Relationships, no."

He bows his head. "I'm honored. And you can trust me. If I ever meet Avery, I will keep your secret."

"Thank you for that," I say, and then I ask, "What about you? Who misses you back on Earth?"

"No one," he says, looking me right in the eye.

That surprises me. I'm about to argue with him and insist that, surely, there must be someone, but I stop myself. It doesn't seem like he's trying to get sympathy or pity. He's telling the truth that he believes, and I feel bad once again for what I said before about his life on Earth. I decide not to argue with him and say instead, "The people on this ship would miss you—I know that."

He accepts this with a grudging nod, and then a half smile. "I'm lucky to have them."

"And they are lucky to have you," I say.

They're his family. And I need to somehow make sure my dad doesn't break any more of them.

## AFTER

AS I WALKED DOWN THE TUNNEL, IT GOT EASIER FOR my brain to use the flashing squiggles to find my way, and I felt more confident with each step. I started making sounds with my mouth instead of stomping and scuffing my feet. I even squeaked like a bat, wondering if my brain was perceiving the world the way they perceive it. But even though I could see, that didn't mean I was safe.

I'd never been so thirsty in my life. My mouth and my throat had never felt that dry. All I'd had to drink that day was a bit of water from the reclaimer and whatever liquid my body could get out of two packs of cold spaghetti. I didn't know what time it was, but it felt late at night, and not just because of the darkness. I was tired and weak.

The tunnel didn't lead me into another big chamber like the other corridors had. It just kept going. So I kept walking, passing dozens more skeletons on the ground. The squiggling lines made them seem animated in a freaky way, but I tried to ignore that and remember that they had been dead for a long, long time.

The way they lay scattered and sprawled reminded me of battlefield images from Earth's world wars. That's probably because there seemed to be two types of alien skulls. One type was smooth, like the bones used to build the towers. The other type had horns or spikes growing out of them, and it began to feel like I was walking through the casualties of a war between them. Without much evidence, I decided that the city had belonged to the smooth-heads, and the horns had attacked. The squiggly lines made it easy to imagine the fighting and the horror, but my exhaustion kept me from hurrying through it as fast as I wanted to.

When I finally came to the end of the tunnel, I entered a more open, more ravaged section of the alien city. It seemed the walls, balconies, and walkways had been shattered into rubble, as if struck by bombs. The squiggly lines turned messy and chaotic against those jagged surfaces, and I wondered if that was why all the walls in the city were rounded and smooth.

Then I came into a vast cavern that stretched ahead of me and to either side, beyond the reach of the sounds I made, so that the squiggly lines faded into the black distance. Without any tunnels forcing me to make a choice, I didn't know which direction to go, other than straight ahead. So that's what I did, and pretty soon the size of that room made me feel as if I could get lost in it as easily as in a maze of smaller chambers.

Broad columns supported the ceiling, made of stone like the towers and pillars standing in the lake. Several had fallen, and the damage to the city only got worse as I crept along. Whole sections of ceiling had come down, forming jumbled walls of rock that I had to pick my way around or climb over. Dangerous cracks and holes seemed to open up right in front of me where the floor had collapsed, and the squiggly lines revealed only hints of deeper levels below.

It went on like that for a while. When I finally allowed myself to consider the possibility that I couldn't, and wouldn't, find a way out, my exhausted legs and feet came to a stop. I slumped down onto a large rock, where I decided to sit and rest for a few minutes to clear my head, get some strength back, and maybe come up with an actual plan of escape.

I closed my eyes to shut everything out, but that didn't turn off the squiggly lines. So I went silent and slowed my breathing. That finally stilled the world enough to calmly add up everything I knew about where I was. Which wasn't much.

I knew I was underground, and I was pretty sure the city had always been underground, even before Mount Ida erupted. That seemed like the best explanation for the way the aliens had built it. Tunnels aboveground made less sense, and also, they had a substance down there that let me see in the dark. Maybe it did the same for them.

I assumed an underground city would have been built with exits to the surface, but those were probably buried under a layer of lava and dirt now. So even if I found the front door, I figured I probably couldn't get out that way. And yet the city wasn't completely sealed off. Water, at least, had found a way in. All I could do was hope there were other openings like the one that fed the big lake, and that one of those would let me climb out. If I could find it.

But that was the exact opposite of what I'd been doing. I had been choosing the driest path at every juncture, trying to find the front door, when I should have been following the water.

The thought of backtracking overwhelmed me. I felt almost suffocated by defeat, already exhausted to the point of collapse. I simply didn't have it in me to do what needed to be done, so I shut it all out and let myself drift off as I sat there, in and out of almost delirious sleep.

I imagined myself lifting out of my body, leaving it behind as I rose up, right through the rock and the dirt, past the purple ferns, then up into the sky, until I was floating in outer space, in weightless orbit above Hades, no longer tired and thirsty, no longer hurting.

And then I was suddenly in a ship I didn't recognize, sitting in a big room with windows that opened to the stars. The cosmos whirled around me as though I stood at the center of it, but after a few moments I felt dizzy and had to look away.

Then I was with my parents playing Magical Mountain, but I wasn't a kid, and we weren't at home. We were on the lander, and my dad was moving his yellow kobold. Then the mountain on the game board turned into Mount Ida, spewing a tower of smoke and ash.

Then a noise I hadn't made wrenched me back to alertness in the alien city. Without opening my eyes, I saw squiggly lines blazing. I blinked at them, feeling confused.

I heard the noise again, a kind of rumble from somewhere behind and below me, a deep, throaty growl that seemed to grasp me by the nape of my neck. It echoed in a way that suggested it had come from one of the lower levels, but I couldn't tell for sure.

Then I heard the sound of something scraping across stone, like a body much bigger than a ferret rousing itself, and terror made me want to run. But I didn't know where to run, and that kept me rooted, holding my breath, holding still, listening.

I didn't hear anything for what felt like a long time. But then that same low growl dragged itself along my spine, lighting up the squiggly lines even more brightly, and I could tell by the sound it wasn't below me anymore.

That shot me to my feet, and I scrambled behind the nearest pillar to avoid being detected. I didn't know if that would help, but I had to do something. I had to move, but slowly and quietly, using the squiggly lines made by the thing in the dark to keep pillars and piles of rubble between us. When the squiggles faded between its growls, I made a soft pop with my lips, hoping it would sound like water dripping, or some other underground noise.

With each passing moment, I found it harder and harder not to just take off running, but I didn't. I stayed at least somewhat calm, moving slowly and carefully. I even tried to peer in the direction of the growls when I could, to try to catch a glimpse of the alien, but it was always just a darting tangle of lines, about the same size as the alien skeletons.

Then I came to the edge of a cliff where the smooth floor had collapsed, endless blackness below and before me. I took a few steps along the ledge in both directions, but I couldn't see any way around or across the chasm. The alien growl sounded like it was behind me, louder, getting closer. I looked down into the abyss again, crouching and making my popping sound to get a better view, hoping to find a way out.

I noticed that where the floor had collapsed, it had snapped like a plank and settled at a steep angle, creating a broken ramp that descended deep into the city. I had no other options to escape the thing closing in behind me, and I had already decided I needed to find water.

I tried climbing down, which wasn't too hard, at first. I made it about ten meters before I hit a big crack where the angle of the ramp steepened, and it became harder for me to stay quiet. When one of my boots slipped a few centimeters on the dusty stone, it broke the silence like a harsh whisper. I froze, then heard a growl above me.

I looked up.

The alien loomed over the ledge, and I knew it saw me. It was too far away to make out much detail, but its outline looked more human than I was expecting. I tried to move faster, but my boot slipped again, and suddenly I was rolling and sliding straight down the slope, unable to stop myself. The sound and speed of my fall sent the squiggly lines into a frenzy.

I winced at the rock grinding against my back. All I could do was keep my feet pointed downward, bracing myself for impact. When I did hit the bottom, an almost electric jolt of pain rattled my legs and bit me in half at the waist. I pitched forward and fell hard into the ground, cheek to cold stone.

My whole body vibrated with shock, and I lay there trying to listen for the alien over the ringing in my ears. But I didn't hear it growling. I didn't hear it moving. I didn't hear anything.

I waited a few minutes, until all the squiggly lines faded away with the silence, before deciding that the creature must have chosen not to follow me. Or at least not by the route I had taken.

I rolled over, slowly, and nothing seemed broken. But one of my knees had started to throb, and I felt some piercing twinges up my back as I gradually got to my feet.

My grunts and groans made all the squiggly lines I needed to see where I had landed, and it looked like the chamber around me had been half destroyed by the collapsed floor. The parts still standing didn't look as much like a burrow as the other places I'd been in the city. The three tunnels leading away from me were broad and tall, more imposing than most of the passageways I'd traveled through. The metal patterns in the walls were also more intricate than what I had seen before, and the air felt much cooler.

I used my nose to choose one of the three tunnels, and I went with the passage that smelled dampest, hoping that my new strategy to find water would lead to a way out. I limped a bit from the growing pain in my knees as I walked, and I kept up the popping sound with my lips. But I tried not to be too loud, just in case the alien was looking for me.

The tunnel went on for a few dozen meters before joining with another passageway at an intersection. None of those branches seemed any more likely to point the way to water, so I kept to my course and entered a new section of tunnel lined with entranceways on both sides. I poked my head in a few and found a network of smaller rooms that felt more sterile or official to me than the housing I had seen.

That main tunnel crossed several more intersections and passed through a few empty chambers. At each turn, I followed the musty air, which eventually led me into the grandest chamber I had yet seen. It wasn't the largest, but it seemed the most refined. Hundreds of windows and doorways looked down on me from a height that would have hit me in the gut with vertigo if I'd had to cross it using one of the narrow bridges that spiraled and weaved overhead. All the bone towers put together wouldn't have filled it, but I did see a group of alien skeletons, the first down there in those deeper levels.

There were six of them in the middle of the room, and they were different from the others up above. They weren't broken or jumbled, and I saw no obvious signs of violence. They lay together on the ground like the spokes of a wheel, smooth heads pointed inward, three sets of limbs pointed outward.

They looked completely peaceful after the carnage I had seen, and they gave the room a solemn importance that hushed me into silence. But after a few moments, I noticed that despite my quiet, the squiggly lines had never fully faded from my view.

That was when I detected a low humming noise, a subtle vibration in the rock, almost too faint to hear, but loud enough that it kept the lines dancing in my eyes. It wasn't a threatening sound. It reminded me of something I couldn't quite place, and I decided to investigate it.

On the other side of the room, I found the tunnel where the humming seemed loudest. I followed that passage, and the humming grew louder as I walked, until the squiggly lines hung like a mist, clinging to the metal in the walls, which were covered with so much of the inlay that they glowed. A short distance on, I felt cool air stir against my cheeks and neck that almost smelled like sprinklers in the backyard during summer. I knew then that I wasn't imagining the dampness that I had been following. I was getting close to water.

Soon, the humming sound divided into layers that harmonized, like voices, filling the tunnel the way singing the right note in the shower sometimes turned the tiles into tuning forks. The walls shimmered and pulsed with the sound, and the mist of squiggly lines seemed to arrange itself in response to it, lining up in waves and swirls on invisible currents.

Then I heard something else on top of the humming, a rushing like a river, and excitement hurried me to the end of the corridor.

The sounds of the water and the humming hit me with their full power as I stepped out into the open, and my vision exploded. The squiggly lines became a churning kaleidoscope of geometric and organic shapes, fractals repeating infinitely in circles and spirals that flooded my mind.

The force of it drove me back a step and took my breath. I struggled to see through the storm of patterns to the chamber beyond. But

I seemed to be standing at one end of a long room with a high, vaulted ceiling. The walls narrowed, like in a theater back on Earth, pointing toward a tower at least ten meters tall. At first, I thought it was another bone tower, but as I looked at it more closely, I saw through the squiggly patterns and ribbons flying off it that it was something new, shaped like a mountain and made of what seemed like bells.

A heavy stream of water poured in through a crack in the ceiling and pounded the mountain's peak before cascading down its slopes. Something about the movement of the water over the bells rang out layers and layers of tones, all droning together in strange harmonies to make the hum I had heard. The water splashed against the floor, and some of it gathered in a shallow pool that surrounded the bells at the base, but most of it vanished beneath the tower.

It seemed that place had been designed to create the effects I was experiencing, almost like a temple or a cathedral. For a while, I just stood there, staring at the endlessly shifting, twisting, and whirling patterns. They were beautiful, but also strange and frightening in the way they seemed to hypnotize me. I think that's why it took me so long to notice something else.

Behind the churning fractals, I saw light. With my eyes. It came from little bioluminescent mushrooms that grew in some of the corners and cracks around the room. But they didn't light up the place. Their soft, subtle glow only seemed as bright as something pale placed under a black light. But they were the first living thing I had encountered down there, and I was glad to see them.

When I finally forced myself to approach the bell mountain, the humming seemed to take on physical substance, squeezing my eardrums, my eyes, the roots of my teeth. I blinked and shook my head against it. I covered my ears, trying to push through it, because I had to find out where the water was coming from.

I was reeling by the time I reached the base of the tower, and I was surprised to discover the bells felt slightly warm to the touch beneath the cool water flowing over them. They ranged in size, as big as bathtubs at the base and growing smaller toward the summit. I had no idea what they were made of, but it was apparently something that could withstand millions of years of erosion, and the humming vibration in them felt electric against my hands.

I looked up toward the source of the water, but I couldn't see a thing through the vortex in my eyes. I knew I would have to climb up there eventually if that was how I planned to escape, so I started up the mountain, hugging the bells like slippery beach balls, feeling my way.

My tired limbs trembled and wobbled, ready to give out, and my brain felt blended into soup by the humming. But I took the climb slowly, one bell at a time, and I stopped frequently to rest. The cool Hades water soaked me, but it also soothed my scrapes and sore muscles, and I was too thirsty to worry that some of it splashed against my lips and got in my dry mouth. It was hard to resist gulping it down.

The humming and the kaleidoscope faded a bit when I reached the peak and disrupted the flow at its source. The water pouring in threatened to knock me off my perch, but I could finally get a good look at the opening in the ceiling.

It was a meter above me, as wide and smooth as a waterslide, and did not seem natural. Its position over the bells suggested to me that it had been carved or built to guide the water to that exact spot. And the cascade didn't fall straight down but followed the angle of the chute, leaving it like water from the spout of a pitcher.

When I craned my neck to look up the shaft, I saw only a narrow tunnel of noisy lines tied together at a distant point that might or might not have been the end of it. I also saw no actual light, but I tried not think about that. Instead I focused on my relief that the chute looked big enough to fit me, barely, and the slope seemed gradual enough that I could climb it. I didn't know where the shaft would lead, or what I would find at the other end. But I had been looking for water, and I had found it. I could only hope it came from the surface.

I positioned myself behind the cascade, like I was behind a waterfall. Then I took a deep breath, and I stretched one hand toward the spout while keeping my grip on the mountain peak.

It was only a meter away, but the bells were slippery, and I knew the fall to the floor below would break me. I knew hunger and dehydration would break me, too, eventually, so I kept reaching. My stomach lurched every time I lost a bit of balance, or a bit of my grip, but my hand finally made contact with the lip of the chute. Then I managed to get my other hand up there, leaving me in a kind of crouching position behind the waterfall. To get myself up into the tunnel, I would have to push through the fire-hose torrent pouring out of it.

I firmed up my stance on the mountain, took a deep breath, and straightened my legs. That pushed my head and chest up through the cascade, and the force of it almost knocked me over backward. But I threw myself forward until I was lying facedown almost halfway inside the tunnel.

The water hammered against me, shoving me, charging up and over me, in my mouth and my nose. I sputtered and gagged, barely able to breathe, but unable to move or the tunnel might spit me out.

My feet still had contact with the top of the mountain, so I steadied myself, bent my knees as much as I could, and then pushed off hard. That second lunge got my waist into the tunnel but left most of my legs sticking out in the air. But I was far enough in I could roll onto my side, somewhat out of the main current. Then I wiggled and wormed myself upward, a few centimeters at a time, until finally my whole body was inside the shaft, and I could brace myself with both legs and both arms.

I paused then to rest, mostly out of the current, coughing and shivering. I looked down the spout at the mountain and the chamber floor far below, a little amazed that I hadn't just fallen. The kaleidoscope from the waterfall wasn't as bright up in the tunnel, but I could still see and admire its swirling shapes. But then I heard a distant, familiar growl that clawed through the fractals, shredding the pattern.

The thing in the dark had followed me. I squinted and peered into the room below, and I thought I saw something rush out of the passage-way I had used. But it stopped as soon as it entered the room, almost frozen in place, like it was just as overwhelmed by the bells as I had been.

I used that distraction to scramble higher, away from the spout. Then I got to my feet, hunched over, hands pressed against the sides of the tunnel, and I started climbing. I hoped the alien couldn't hear me over the ringing of the bells, but every moment that passed, I expected its growl behind me.

My fear and adrenaline found energy where I didn't think I had any left, and I made my way upward using a kind of four-legged waddle, back and forth. It was awkward, but it worked, and the squiggly lines returned to normal as I got some distance from the tower below me.

The squiggles guided me toward a distant dot that never moved or grew any larger, until time and distance didn't seem to matter or even exist in that tunnel. I just moved, and I kept moving. But soon it was like dragging myself through a nightmare, the kind where I was being chased, but running got me nowhere.

I started to shiver in my jumpsuit, and my wet socks chafed inside my boots. Muscles in my thighs, arms, and shoulders seized up, twisted in burning knots, and then my hands went numb. I felt dizzy. A few times, I lost the rhythm of my climb, and I almost stumbled and fell, which would have meant a fast ride down the waterslide, and a landing I didn't want to think about.

Eventually, the dot became a spot, and then the spot grew into an eye that stared at me just as hard as I stared at it, and neither of us blinked. The eye swelled, and then something came through the squiggly lines and into my vision that confused my brain for a second or two as it remembered what it was supposed to do with light. I saw stars in the eye.

I laughed out loud like I had never laughed before. It was an eruption, the only thing I could do with my pain, my exhaustion, my disbelief, and my joy. The squiggly lines jumped and danced to it, and the sound of it echoed in the tunnel.

I emerged from under the ground into a narrow, shallow stream in a deep riverbed. It was nighttime, and the sound lines attached themselves to the shapes and shadows of things I could finally see again with my eyes by faint, cold starlight. I felt a breeze of fresh, wild air blowing down the channel, and I took it deep into my chest.

I stood inside a thick ring made of solid stone, or something stone-like. It was about the height of my chest, and it surrounded the opening I had just crawled out of. Somehow it let a controlled amount of water through, which drained pure and clear down the hole into the alien city. The rest of the stream flowed around the ring downriver. I managed to pull myself up and over that final hurdle, and then I flopped into the water with a splash.

I stumbled toward dry land, and that was when my body finally gave out. I slumped against the embankment, my feet in the water. A moment later, I started crying for all the same reasons I had just been laughing.

I had made it out of the darkness. I was free. And I was alive.

DUNCAN AND I FLOAT IN THE HUB FOR A WHILE, talking about our lives back on Earth, and then he decides he's hungry. I don't feel like eating, after everything that's happened in the past few hours, but I go with him to the common room and sit down in the middle of one of the sofas while he heats up some food. It smells like teriyaki, and the smoky, sweet aroma does nothing to give me an appetite. I just feel tired.

A few minutes later, he carries a steaming bowl toward me by the rim, between his fingers, and he clears his throat and inhales, like he's about to say something. I wait and watch him as he takes a love seat near me and balances the bowl on the arm of the chair.

"Thank you for helping with Alberto," he finally says, and then he glances at me. "I think I owe you an apology."

"What for?"

"For what I said when I first met you. And after that."

I also still feel bad about some of the things I said to him. "So does this mean you don't think I'm a liability anymore?"

"No." He smiles and pokes at his food with his fork. "I admit I did think that at first. But I was wrong. I was just . . . jealous."

"I was wrong, too. What I said about your life back on Earth—"

"You weren't wrong." He brings his food closer and hunches over it, staring down into the bowl. "I don't have a life back on Earth." He takes a huge bite.

"That's not what I mean." I slide toward him along the sofa. "When I said that, I didn't know anything about you. I wasn't trying to say something that would actually hurt you. I wasn't . . . I'm sorry I said it. That's all."

"I know."

"And for what it's worth, if we were both back on Earth, right now? I would want you as a friend."

He looks up into my eyes. "Same." Then he goes back to his food, and when it's gone, he sighs and wipes his mouth with the back of his hand. "I think I'll do what Evan suggested and rest in my cabin for a while. You'll be okay?"

I lean back into the sofa, feeling exhausted. "Yeah. You?"

"I'll be okay." He gets up and takes his empty bowl back to the kitchen. "Everything will be okay."

"I know," I say, even though I don't. But I hope it will.

He gives a little wave, and then he leaves me alone in the common room. I know I should probably go check on my mom, but I don't have the energy for that right now. I just want to lie down on the sofa where I am and close my eyes and shut everything out. So that's what I do.

I fall asleep quickly, but then someone says my name and that wakes me up. It feels like only a few minutes have passed. People are talking about me, over by the kitchen, but they're using hushed voices. I realize they probably can't see me on the sofa, so they think they're alone. I don't move. I listen.

"Wait, are you serious?" I can tell that's Liz. "Do you really think it will come to that?"

"I do not know." And that's Amira. "This situation is without precedent, that I'm aware of."

"Damn," Liz whispers. "Have you ever been involved in . . . ?"

A moment of silence passes.

"No," Amira says. "Have you?"

"Refactoring is a bit above my pay grade, and I'd prefer to keep it that way."

"I wish that it were above mine."

Another moment of silence passes, and I wonder what refactoring means. It sounds like something to do with computers, but that doesn't match the tension and fear I hear in their voices. Even though they think they're alone, they're talking quietly, like it's a secret.

"I suspect the captain will insist on taking the burden," Amira says.

"Probably," Liz says. "I can't imagine . . . I mean, the parents are one thing, but Jessica? She's just a kid."

"She won't—"

"I know, Amira, I know. But knowing doesn't help. Maybe there are some lines that aren't meant to be crossed, you know? Maybe some leaps are just too far."

"Exploration has always come at a price."

"I know that, too. But maybe I'm not willing to pay it."

"You will not be asked, I assure you."

"But I'm here," Liz says. "On the ship. That makes me complicit, even if I'm not the one who—"

"Shh," Amira says.

I hear footsteps walking toward me, and I close my eyes, pretending to be asleep.

"What is it?" Liz asks.

"I think there is someone . . . Jessica?"

I can feel Amira standing over me, but I hold still and say nothing.

"Oh no," Liz whispers. "Did she—"

"Jessica?" Amira says again, a bit louder.

"Hm?" I fake a flinch and open my eyes, like I'm just waking up.

Amira frowns at me, hard. I know she's wondering what I might have heard, but she doesn't know how to find out. I need to throw her off before she tries, make her think I'm thinking about something else.

"Sorry." I blink and sit up, rubbing my head, and I try to look embarrassed. "Am I not supposed to sleep in here?"

The question seems to catch her off guard, and in the next moment she softens her severe expression. "No, that's fine, you—you must have been very tired."

"I guess so." I stretch and start to fake a yawn, but it turns into a real one. "I was pretty out of it."

"That makes sense," Liz says, walking over. "You've been through a lot."

I turn like I'm just noticing her. "After Dr. Gutiérrez, his body, I—I think I just needed to check out for a while." I swing my head back around and stare blankly at the floor, pretending not to notice the glances flying back and forth between them. "What time is it?" I ask.

"Almost five," Amira says.

"Really?" I stand, wanting to get out of there. "I'm glad you woke me up. I don't want to be in the way when the crew comes in for dinner."

They both step toward me.

"You're not in the way," Liz says.

"Are you okay?" Amira asks. "You mentioned Dr. Gutiérrez. That must have been difficult for you."

"It wasn't easy, but I'm feeling better now." I rub my eyes. "That nap really helped."

Liz reaches out and places her hand on my arm, not gently, but also not quite firm enough to hold me there. "Do you want to eat something?" she asks.

It's clear they are still very worried about what I might have heard, which means I really wasn't supposed to hear it. "Maybe in a bit," I say. "Right now, I think I need a shower to help me wake up."

A second ticks by, and Liz lets go. "Yeah, a shower usually helps."

Someone enters the common room then, one of Evan's crew, which draws their attention. I use the distraction to slip away, but I try not to hurry as I move toward the hatch.

"I'll see you guys later?" I say.

"See you later," Liz says.

Then I'm out in the corridor, and even though I'm alone, I walk like they might still be watching me. My heart is pounding, and I'm not sure why, because I don't really understand what I just overheard. But I know from the way they were talking about it that it can't be good, and the fact that they didn't want me to know about it scares me.

I could maybe ask Duncan what it all means, but he said he was going to his room to rest, and I'm not completely sure that I can trust him as much as I want to. I can't really trust any of the ship's crew, and I sure as hell can't ask my dad. That just leaves my mom.

She's had a few hours to calm down, and I hope I'm not about to make things worse by bringing this up with her. I hope it means nothing, and she'll chuckle at how silly I am for misinterpreting what I heard. But there's an alarm bell in my head telling me she won't.

I head for the lander, since that's where I told Amira and Liz I was going, and I find my mom sitting at the terminal where my dad had his seizure just a few hours ago.

"What are you working on?" I ask.

"Habitat diagnostics," she says. Then she spins around in the chair to face me. "Just making sure everything is up and running for us down there. Oh, and I gave you security clearance to access all its computer systems. In case of emergency."

"Oh. Okay." Our present circumstances already seem like a state of emergency to me. I don't know if she's in denial, or what, but habitat diagnostics don't seem like an especially high priority anymore, or even necessary, and I'm not sure what to say. "You think we'll—"

She holds up a hand. "I don't know when we'll go down there. But I couldn't think of anything else to do, and I'll go spacey if I don't do something."

I nod. "And I guess we wouldn't want to ignore protocol."

She opens her mouth to say something, and with a sad smile she settles on, "Yes, exactly."

"Have you eaten?"

"No."

I'm still not hungry, but I move toward the lander's little kitchen area. "That's something we can do."

"I suppose you're right." She stands and crosses the room toward me. "How are things out there?"

"On the ship?" I dismiss her question with a wave and pull out a couple of food packages without even reading the labels. "I think everyone understands what you're going through."

"I didn't handle myself well." She stands close to me, at my side, and leans forward, pressing the heels of her palms into the countertop. "Apologies are in order. Which I have never been very good at."

"I get that from you, huh?"

"I'm afraid so." She looks over, chin in her shoulder, and tries to smile. "But don't expect me to say I'm sorry."

"I won't."

She looks down at her hands. "I just . . . I can't let them take all these years from your father. From me." Her arms tighten as she shakes her head. "I can't—I won't allow it. If you knew what we've been through, what we've accomplished out here, it's . . . a part of who he is. Who we are. I'm not going to let anyone rob him of that without a fight, I'm not. Especially now that you're with us. That's why we wanted to bring you out here."

I'm trying to read the instructions on the packages, but the letters and words aren't getting through, because I think I know where this is going, and I don't want to talk about it right now, or ever. But especially not right now.

"So it could be a part of you, too," she says.

I drop the package, and it lands on the counter with a slap. "What if I don't want it to be a part of me?"

"What?"

I didn't mean to say that so loudly, but now that it's out there, I'm almost glad that I did. I push the package of food aside. "What gives you the right to decide what becomes a part of me?"

"That—" She pivots to face me, her head cocked in confusion, like the answer to my question is obvious. "That's what parents do."

"Is it?"

"Yes. I'm not saying it's fair. I'm not saying it's right. But whether you like it or not, when you are a child, your parents, grandparents, teachers, we create the experiences that will shape you."

"You know what shaped me? When you left. That's what shaped me."

She folds her arms and plants her hip against the counter. "I'm sure it did."

I glare at her and wait for more, but get nothing. "Is that it?" My voice is raised now. "It's been six years, and that's all you have to say?"

"I am listening to you. It isn't for me to say how it shaped you—"

"You just said that's what parents do!"

"No, Jessica. I said that we create the experiences that shape you, but how those experiences shape you isn't up to us."

"Oh, so it's my fault that I felt abandoned?"

"Of course not."

"Then what are you saying? Do you know how long I wondered what was wrong with me?"

"Wrong with you? Why would you—"

"Because you left me! What was I supposed to think?"

She unfolds her arms and takes a deep breath through her nose, eyes closed. Then she opens them and looks directly at me. "Jessica, I want you to listen very carefully. Your father and I did not leave because of you."

"You didn't stay because of me, either."

"We—" She stops and clears her throat. "Our decision had nothing to do with you, and that is the truth. I'm sure if you were to ask any of your friends' parents, or even Gram and Pop-Pop, they would tell you the same thing. They would tell you that I was simply being selfish. And maybe they would be right."

That was as close as I had ever heard her come to an apology, but I wanted her to go further. "Would you do it again?"

"What?"

"If you could go back, would you do it again? Would you leave me?"

She is silent for long enough that I know the answer. Then she says, "We can't change the past. We can only deal with things as they are."

She lays the words down like bricks in the wall that's holding her together, and I know I'm not going to be able to tear it down. Maybe she doesn't think it was wrong to leave me, or maybe she simply thinks it would have been more wrong to turn down a job in space. Whatever she tells herself, I have to agree with her about one thing: It was selfish of her to leave me, and it was selfish of her to bring me out here.

She turns away and reaches for one of the food packages. "Perhaps your father can do a better job explaining all of this after he recovers."

That shoves the argument aside and draws the conversation I overheard in the common room back to the front of my mind. "What does refactoring mean?" I ask.

"It's a computer programming term. It has to do with redundant code—" She freezes, and then her head snaps toward me. "Wait. Where did you hear that?"

"From the—" I swallow and flick a glance toward the hatch. "I overheard Amira and Liz. They didn't know I was listening—"

She seizes me by my shoulders and leans in close. "Jess, tell me exactly what they said."

Her reaction confirms that I was right to be alarmed. I stammer and wither a bit, truly frightened now as I repeat what I heard, every word that I can remember. By the time I finish, she is trembling, eyes wide.

"What does it mean?" I ask. "What is refactoring?"

She lets go of me and covers her mouth with her hand for a few moments. "It's a euphemism," she finally says.

"For what?"

She looks around, and then she steps in even closer to me. "Sometimes, under very rare circumstances, it is necessary to print someone back on Earth while they still have a body out in space."

"Why would they still have a body out in space?"

"Sometimes they can't bring that body home."

"But then—but that's illegal."

"It is. Which is why it sometimes becomes necessary to remove the redundancy from the system through other means."

"Other means?" I'm trying to put this all together, but it's like there's a waterfall up ahead that my mind doesn't want to go over. "So . . . ISTA destroys one of their bodies? That's what refactoring means?"

She nods. "It almost never happens. I only know of one case in the past six years, a liaison. Her older sister was dying of cancer, and she didn't want to wait for an origin ship with a scanner to return home."

I have so many questions, but I'm struggling to ask them, because I'm not sure I want the answers. "How do they . . . ?"

She shrugs. "Usually a lethal dose of a sedative. They select the redundant body and put it to sleep."

"But . . . Liz and Amira. I think they were talking about refactoring us. You and dad, and me."

"I know they were." A flash of her earlier anger returns. "Liz and Amira, the captain, they are preparing for the possibility that ISTA will declare this an emergency and order your father home using his old scan. That means he'll need to be refactored."

"What about us?"

"If they determine that our data was also potentially compromised, then we would be refactored, too."

"What if we just refuse? Can they . . . ?"

Her nod is grim. "Legally, refactoring does not have to be voluntary." She looks at the computer terminal where she was working when
I came in. "This settles it."

"Settles what?"

"We have to get off this ship."

# 22 — Hades

## AFTER

I HOPED THE ALIEN WOULD STAY BELOW, IN ITS UN-derground city, but I worried it could still come after me. I allowed myself a short rest against the embankment, listening for its growl, but after just a few minutes, that fear got me out of the riverbed and up onto dry ground.

I saw Mount Ida towering over me twice as tall and wide as it had before. I nearly lost my balance craning my neck to take it in. The squiggly lines had begun to fade and no longer attached themselves to the dark outline in the sky that parted the stars. It seemed that my trip through the alien city had brought me almost to the volcano's slopes. I should have been encouraged by that, but instead it filled me with a new dread, because I couldn't forget what lay deep beneath my feet. The bones I had seen turned the ground all around me into a vast graveyard, and the mountain stood over the land like a tombstone for the whole planet.

Regardless, Mount Ida was still where I had to go, and I wanted to get away from the tunnel behind me. But my body needed rest. I stumbled ahead a few hundred meters, until I was far enough from the river and deep enough in the ferns that I would be at least somewhat hidden from view if the alien crawled out looking for me. Then I slumped to the ground and stared up at the volcano in silence, feeling empty and alone.

I wished Duncan was there with me, with his white fur, feather-whiskers, and beady eyes. I even wished *she* was there, despite her lies.

A few minutes went by.

Then I noticed a distant light flickering, as if a single star had dropped out of the sky onto the face of the volcano. It blinked sharp and white against the immense shadow all around it, too regular and too bright to be caused by anything natural. It didn't seem like something that belonged to the alien ruins, either. It felt familiar, human, and its location meant it had to be the habitat.

That took away some of my dread, but not all of it. I was still incredibly thirsty, despite the water I'd swallowed. And I was starving. I had no strength left to travel farther that night. I could feel my body and mind switching off.

I laid my body down the rest of the way, positioned so I could see the light flashing above and between the ferns as the fronds swayed. I fixed my heavy eyes on that point so I could find it again in the daylight, and I locked my gaze there until I couldn't keep my eyes open anymore.

When I woke up, the sun had just started to rise. I sat up and shivered. My hair and jumpsuit felt glued to my skin, cold and wet with heavy dew that glistened on the ferns around me like costume jewelry. The sight of it made me wish I had the reclaimer. My dry tongue stuck to the sandpaper roof of my mouth, and I had to resist the urge to lick all that water right off the fronds. I'd seen people do that on survival shows, but I still had no idea whether the purple plants were poisonous.

When I stood up, aching and sore, I looked back and realized that I wasn't as far from the river as I had thought the night before. But I was still in one piece, so even if the alien had come out of the tunnel while I slept, it hadn't found me.

I felt grateful for that as I turned toward Mount Ida and set off in the direction of the light I had seen, and I felt pretty good for the first few meters. But it didn't take long to realize that the sleep I'd managed to get couldn't make up for the lack of water and food. I felt weak and lightheaded as I trudged along, almost stumbling with every step. Despite my slow pace, my heart fluttered, and my breaths came shallow and short.

The rising sun warmed me up and dried out my clothes, which felt good for a little while, but then it grew hot, and my socks were still wet inside my boots. I could feel the back of my neck turning red, and I tried flipping up the collar of my jumpsuit to shield my skin. Even my eyes dried out, smearing the mountain into a great big blur that told me I was still going in the right direction.

I don't know how far or how long I walked. I tripped several times, sometimes over a plant or a fold in the dirt, sometimes over my own toes when I couldn't lift my feet high enough.

When I came to a small rise, I had to struggle on my hands and knees to reach the top. But then I saw something on the other side that made me worry I had finally gone spacey.

There was a lander below me. Not a crashed lander like hers. A different lander, in one piece. I stood there for a while just staring at it, unable to accept it, waiting for it to change back into a big rock or whatever it was underneath my hallucination. But it didn't change, and my dehydrated brain couldn't figure out what it was doing there, or what it meant.

I lurched forward to get a closer look, but instead I stumbled into a hard fall that rolled me all the way to the bottom of the hill. After that, I didn't get up again. I just flopped onto my back and stared up into the sky.

I thought I was probably dying, but my thoughts were so fuzzy and scattered that I wasn't even afraid of it. I knew I shouldn't close my eyes, but I had lost control of them, and I drifted in and out of something like sleep, but emptier.

The sound of growling woke me. But I couldn't move. I couldn't run. The growling got closer, louder, until it wasn't the sound of an alien anymore, and it became the voice of an engine that rose and fell with purrs and rumbles.

A shadow passed over me, and I looked up into the face of a boy. I thought I was hallucinating. I tried to speak, but I wasn't sure if the words made any sense. I didn't even know if they made it from my brain to my mouth.

The boy spoke, but his words made even less sense. Then I felt myself lifted off the ground, and a few moments later I was sitting with the wind in my face and the sounds of a motor in my ears. The purple ferns sped past me, and I sank backward into a rigid seat.

I smelled mist in the air and felt wind against my face. Then I was hoisted and carried out of the mist into a place that was dry, cool, and dim. I was lying down again, and the boy was moving around me, still talking, asking me questions. I tried my best to answer him, but my voice felt seized up with rust and grit. When I finally heard a word I knew, I couldn't say whether it came from him or from me, but I listened to it.

*Sleep.*

So I slept.

When I woke up again, I was lying in a bed with blankets, my head on a pillow, in a small room shaped like a thick slice of pie. I didn't know where I was, but the boy I thought I'd dreamed or hallucinated was sitting in a chair next to me.

"It's okay," he said, holding up his hands. "You're safe. But don't move too much or you'll pull out your IV again."

I felt a pinching in my arm and looked down to find clear tubes taped to needles in my skin. "Wh—" I started to say, but the word scratched like a wire pipe cleaner as it left my throat. I swallowed and felt a headache setting in.

"It's okay," he said. "It's just fluids and a painkiller."

"Where am I?"

"The habitat."

A sudden flood of returning memories sat me upright. I looked at the boy again, at his longish, shaggy brown hair, and his sharp features. He wore a jumpsuit like mine, and he seemed tired, or sad, with dark circles under his eyes. There was something familiar about him, even though I didn't know who he was. But I did know there was only one ship he could have possibly come from, which meant he probably knew her, and probably thought I was her, and I wondered what he would do when he found out I wasn't.

"You tripped one of my perimeter sensors," he said. "Too big to be a ferret. I came out to investigate, and I'm glad I found you when I did. You were severely dehydrated."

Despite the painkillers he'd given me, the headache reached from behind my eyes to the back of my skull, and I cradled my head with both hands. My sluggish thoughts couldn't move fast enough through the pain to try to pretend that I was her. So I didn't. "Who are you?" I asked.

"I thought you knew."

I looked over at him. "Why would you think that?"

"You said my name."

"I did? When?"

"When I found you."

"What's your name?"

"Duncan."

A wave of tingly chills crawled over me. I didn't know how to explain to him that I'd given my ferret friend that name. I couldn't even explain the coincidence to myself.

"I thought maybe she had told you about me," he said.

He looked directly into my eyes when he said it, and he spoke in a way that convinced me he knew exactly who I was, and what I was, which meant the thing I had feared would happen had happened much sooner than I had expected it to. And I was right to fear it, no matter what she said about flavors of ice cream in different cones. I also knew that the human Duncan sitting next to me had met her first. She would be Jessica to him, not me. I suddenly felt the need to be very careful about what I said.

"She didn't actually tell me much of anything," I whispered.

He leaned forward in his chair, elbows on his knees, and shook his head. "You know, I thought you were her, at first. But then I saw your forehead." He glanced up at my hairline. "No scar."

"No scar." I glanced down at my hands, which were covered in scrapes and cuts from the crystals. It looked like Duncan had cleaned them up and closed them with some kind of medical sealant, and I wondered if any of them would become *my* scars. "Does she know you're here?" I asked.

"She does," he said. "How is she?"

There were so many ways to answer that question, but I settled on the simplest. "She was alive and healthy the last time I saw her."

"When was that?"

My headache made it hard to focus as I tried to count the endless hours I had spent underground. "It was . . . a couple of days ago, I think?"

"Where?"

"Not far from her lander. The crashed one. We had started to come here." I nodded around the room. "But we had a fight, and she went back."

"What did you fight about?"

I put my hand on my thigh and felt the vague shape of the kobold in my pocket through the fabric of my jumpsuit. "I realized she had been lying to me."

"About what?"

I didn't like all his questions. I didn't like that he was trying to find out about her through me. I also didn't know if I could trust him. So I decided to ask a question of my own, one that she hadn't really answered. "What happened to my parents?"

That seemed to surprise him. "You mean . . . she didn't tell you?"

"I know they arrived on the *Theseus*," I said before he could lie about it the way she had.

"Well, yes, they arrived, but . . ." He looked away, rubbing the palm of one hand over the calloused knuckles of the other. "They didn't make it off the ship. I'm sorry, I thought she would have told you."

I couldn't decide yet whether I thought he was telling the truth. "And what happened to the ship?"

"I don't know."

I scowled.

"It's true," he said. "We had to evacuate. At first it was just a fire, but then I guess something went wrong with the security overrides in the system, and things got out of control in the reactor. It all happened so fast. That's really all I know."

So far, his story lined up with hers. "Then what happened?"

"We used the landers. I ended up on your—I mean, on the lander assigned to your parents. Everyone else took the other one. The one that crashed."

"So you flew here by yourself?"

"No, the flight path was already programmed." His voice turned somber and quiet. "I don't know what went wrong with the other one."

I didn't know what it meant that he had used my parents' lander when they hadn't. Or why she had kept the existence of a second lander a secret from me. Or why she had said nothing about human Duncan. She had sent me off to find the habitat, so she had to know I would most likely meet him and discover it all eventually. I thought of the graves I had seen back at the crash and wondered if he knew the people whose broken bodies had been buried there. "What were you doing on the *Theseus*?" I asked.

He swallowed. "My mother was the captain."

I assumed that meant I had seen her name badge on one of the mounds of dirt. "I . . . I'm sorry. And your dad, is he . . . ?"

"Back on Earth. My father is a—" He stopped and looked at me, but I couldn't read his expression. He seemed almost irritated, or confused, or sad, or disappointed. Then he leaned back and stared at the ceiling, cheeks puffed out a bit, and when the words finally spilled out of him, they came like the air from a deflating balloon. "Don't take this personally, but I told her not to do it. Not to . . . print you."

"You told her— Wait. Wait a minute. You mean—" I tried to stay calm, struggling to think through the pounding in my head, and for a few seconds, I was too stunned to speak. If what he had just said was true, then I wasn't an accident, after all. She had printed me. On purpose.

"We argued about it for days," he said, looking at the floor. "She wouldn't listen. That's why I left her and came here. I didn't want any part of . . . that. Sorry."

Inside, I was reeling, but I worked hard to go along with him on the outside, to keep him talking. "If it makes you feel any better," I said, "I would have told her not to print me, too. But she wouldn't have listened to me, either. Which kind of means she wouldn't even listen to herself."

He chuckled. "That sounds like Jessica—" He stopped and looked up at me like he was thinking about what he had just said. "What I mean is, that sounds like . . ."

I waited.

But he didn't finish that thought. "I'm sorry, this whole situation is—"

"Fucked up?"

He sighed. "Yes."

"This must be weird for you."

He hesitated, then shrugged. "Probably not as weird as it is for you."

"It would be less weird if I knew why she did it."

He squirmed a bit in his chair. "I guess she didn't tell you that, either?"

"No."

"Well that puts me in an awkward position."

"What position is that?"

"Between the two of you."

"I didn't put you there."

"I know." He folded his arms. "So she didn't tell you *anything*?"

I shrugged. "She said there are things only one of us can know. That's it. Do you know what that means?"

He shook his head, but not in answer to my question. He seemed to be shaking his head in anger or frustration at her. "I assume she didn't tell you about your dad."

"What about him?"

He pressed his lips into a rigid frown.

"Whatever it is, I have a right to know," I said. "He's my dad, too."

"It's not that. I just don't know how to tell you."

But for the next few minutes, he tried. He explained that when my parents had arrived, everything seemed fine, at first. She had spent some time with them, which I'd figured out when I saw the kobold from Magical Mountain. But then Duncan told me about my dad's seizures, and other horrific, unbelievable things. Things I had a hard time even imagining. That my dad's data had been corrupted, and he had attacked someone, a doctor, and the captain had put him in the brig for it, which made my mom really angry.

"But then he escaped," Duncan said. "And after that, everything went to hell. I think he may have started the fire, but I don't know that for sure."

"What happened to my mom?"

"I don't know, I'm sorry. Several people got left behind."

As he told his story, I felt a strange detachment from it all. He was describing things that hadn't happened to me. They had happened to her. They were her memories, not mine, and I struggled to believe or accept them. I still hadn't seen my dad in years. But I knew he would never hurt anyone on purpose. That wasn't him. And so far, nothing in Duncan's story had explained why she had printed me, either.

"So you landed here. And the other lander crashed. Then what happened?"

"After I touched down, I used one of the habitat's rovers to go searching for the others. By the time I found them, she had already buried them. She was alone. I tried to get her to come back here with me, but she wouldn't leave." He kneaded his forehead with his thumb and index finger. "I assumed it was grief, or shock, so I tried to be patient. She didn't talk much, and she didn't really sleep or eat. A week went by. I was getting really worried, but then one day she said she wanted to print you, and I— That's when I came back here. She got so angry with me when I tried to stop her. She told me to leave."

"I'm sorry," I said, feeling bad for him. He seemed just as bewildered and scared and frustrated by her as I was. "I wouldn't have done that."

"Wouldn't you?" he asked in a way that made me stop and think about it, but before I could answer him, he said, "Can I be honest with you?"

I sighed. "Duncan, that is all I want from you."

"Okay, then." He leaned a bit toward me. "I don't know what to think about you. I mean, you're you. You're her. But you're the Jessica I met weeks ago when you first arrived, before anything happened. Right?"

For a moment, I wondered if that idea disappointed him, or if that's who he wanted me to be, but it didn't really matter. "No, I don't think I'm that Jessica anymore."

"Why is that?"

So I told him.

I DON'T COMPLETELY UNDERSTAND HER PLAN. I JUST sit beside her while she types and clicks at the computer until it's pretty late at night and the rest of the ship has gone to bed. Then, after she has double-checked and triple-checked a ton of details I can't follow, she says it's time to move and digs a couple of radios out of a locker. She hands one of them to me.

"We can't use the ship's comm, so you'll have to keep this with you. Do you know how it works?"

I don't, so she explains the push-to-talk button, and then she holds out a small micro drive.

"I need you to take this to the other lander," she says.

"What are you going to do?"

"I'm going to get your father. I'll meet you back here."

I think of him floating all tied up in the brig. "How will you get him here by yourself? Isn't he—"

"I have a plan," she says. "But I don't have time to explain it. You just need to trust me." She presses the micro drive into my hand. "Find a computer terminal on the other lander and plug this in. Wait a few minutes. You'll see a prompt come up asking if you want to execute the program. Click yes."

"What does it do?" I ask.

"It will create a sequence of competing commands for the docking gear. That will keep the lander in place."

"Why do we need to keep the lander in place?"

"Because I don't want them following us down to the surface right away. By the time they find the problem and fix it, we'll be secure, and ISTA procedure will require a tactical response the *Theseus* isn't capable of carrying out. They'll have to stand down, and we'll be safe at least until the *Clarke* arrives."

But that makes me wonder what will happen to us when the *Clarke* arrives. I don't exactly feel safe when I think about being trapped in a lander or a planetary habitat with my dad for a year. But my mom seems completely confident, and her confidence convinces me to trust her instead of listening to my doubts.

"Wait until the program finishes, and then remove the drive. Do not leave it behind. They could use it to fix the hack."

I already feel sick to my stomach, but I nod and fold the micro drive into my fist.

"Are you with me?" she asks.

I think I nod again, but she grabs my jumpsuit collar and pulls me close. "Are you with me, Jess?" she asks.

"Y-yes," I stammer. "I'm with you."

"It's this, or we lose your father. We get refactored. Do you understand?"

"I understand."

She releases me. "This will all be over soon. We just have to get through the next few hours. But first, we both have jobs to do. I'll be with you every step of the way over the radio, okay?"

"Okay."

After that, we separate. She goes upship toward the Belfry, and I set off down the curve of the barrel toward the lander on the other side of the *Theseus*.

It's late at night, and the passageways are all empty. The ship is quiet in a way that makes it eerie and turns up the volume on every noise that I make. I keep expecting the captain or Evan to appear and ask what I'm doing up so late, wandering around the ship. But they wouldn't need to ask, because I have a micro drive in my sweaty hand with all the evidence they'd need.

I'm thinking about turning back before I've made it even halfway. I consider waking somebody up to tell them about my mom's plan, but my fears about refactoring stop me. After the conversation I overheard between Liz and Amira, I don't know who to trust. But I tell myself I should trust my mother before anyone else.

When I reach the other lander, I climb down through its hatch into a darkened twin of our ship, and the lights flick on before I reach the bottom rung of the ladder. I beep my mom with the radio as I hurry to find a computer terminal, and a moment later, her voice comes out of the little speaker.

"Jessica? Is everything okay? Over."

"I'm fine." I lower my voice, even though I don't need to. "I'm on the lander. Where are you? Over."

"In the hub," she says. "Almost to the Belfry."

I reach the galley and sit down at the terminal. "Do I need to log in or anything? Over."

"To the computer? No. Just plug in the drive. I wrote security authentication into the script. Over."

"Dad said you've become an impressive hacker." I pop the drive into the port and wait. "Where did you learn how to do all this?"

There's a pause. "You pick up stuff out here. When something breaks, you're often the only one around to fix it. How's it looking? Over."

"It's still thinking," I say, and another minute goes by. Then a window opens just like she said it would. "I'm executing the program now. Over."

"Good. I'm outside the room they call a brig. I can see your father through the window, and he—" She grumbles something about the captain that I can't hear clearly, and then she says, "Okay, I need both hands now, so I'm going to sign off. But call me if you hit trouble. When you're done, take the drive and hurry back to our lander. I'll meet you there. Over."

"Will do." I still don't know how she plans to move my dad by herself. "Be careful, Mom. Over."

"You too, sweetie. You're doing great. Havilland out."

*Havilland out?* I look at the radio and assume that sign-off was automatic. But I doubt that's how she signs off with my dad.

A few minutes later, the program window closes, and the micro drive stops blinking. I hope that means my mom's hack has done its job, but I give it another minute before I pull the drive from the port. I stick it in one of my pockets as I leave the lander, where I find the yellow kobold I'd forgotten about. The game we played just last night already feels like a memory from a different life. With a different dad.

Back in the barrel of the DS *Theseus*, I creep along the ship's corridors feeling even more nervous than I did before. I know that what I did to the lander would be considered sabotage, and I also know that's a crime, and probably even more illegal on a spaceship. That means I am officially a criminal, and I'm probably old enough that I won't be able to blame my mom for it if I get caught. She didn't make me do it anyway. I chose to do it. But the weird thing is, that makes me worry less about running into the captain or Evan or Amira, and more about seeing Duncan. I care what he would think about me if he knew. But I manage to reach the lander without bumping into anyone.

I'm hoping my mom is already on board with my dad, but she's not. I pace around the ladder while I wait for her, and several minutes go by. Then I start to worry that something has gone wrong. I think about calling her on the radio, but I know she needs both hands free, and I don't want to interrupt and risk messing up her plan. Then more time goes by, and I wonder if maybe she got caught. I'm starting to freak out inside when she finally calls.

"Jessica?" she whispers, out of breath. "Jess, do you read me? Over."

"Yes, I read you," I say back, leaning into the radio. "Is everything okay? What's going on? Where are you?"

"I'm in the hub. I have your father. Are you on the lander? Over."

"Yes, I'm here. What is taking so long? Over."

"We're almost there. But I need you to hold on to something."

"What do you mean?"

"The ship's rotation is about to stop. You're going to lose gravity—"

"What?" But I press the button while she's still talking and don't hear her next few words.

"—way I could get your father from the hub to the lander. And the confusion will buy us time to take off. Do you copy?"

It sounds like the ship is about to lose gravity because of something she has done, or is about to do, and I'm too stunned to speak.

"Jessica, do you copy?"

"I—I copy. But . . . isn't that dangerous? Over."

"Almost everyone on this ship is in bed," she says. "Safest place they could be. I've thought this through."

I don't know how she can be sure that everyone is in their bed and not up getting a drink or using the bathroom. I worry people could get hurt. Everything feels out of control to me, but she sounds so in control, and that confuses me enough that I don't argue with her.

"Ship rotation will stop in just over three minutes," she says. "I want you to secure yourself to the ladder and wait there to help me with your father. Do you copy?"

I look around, not sure how she wants me to secure myself, or what she expects me to use.

"Do you copy?" she asks.

"I copy."

"You're doing great, sweetie. We're almost there. Havilland out."

I immediately start searching for something I can use as a strap or a tether, counting seconds in my head. But I don't know where they keep those kinds of things on a lander, and I quickly lose track of the time. In a panic, I run to my room and whip the sheet off my bed. Then I tie one end around my waist, and the other to one of the ladder's rungs. Then I grab the metal bars and look up at the hatch, bracing myself.

A few moments later, I'm hurled and pulled by powerful momentum as the rolling barrel eases to a stop, followed by a tidal wave of vertigo. If I had been in bed, I might have tumbled right out of it and puked. But my puke would have been floating, because in the next second I'm in micro-g, my feet off the floor.

The world has turned upside down.

## AFTER

I WORRIED THAT DUNCAN WOULDN'T BELIEVE ME, so I stuck to the basic facts, and I didn't say anything about the alien, at first. But he did believe me. Or maybe he simply couldn't imagine why I would make up an underground city filled with towers of bones, or cave glitter that turned sound into squiggly lines. Or maybe he had dreamed about finding an alien civilization since he was a kid, which is what he sounded like with all the excited questions he asked. He almost seemed to have forgotten the circumstances that had brought us both there.

"I knew it," he said after I'd finished, and there was a smirk in his grin. "I told you."

"Told me what?"

"Oh, right, sorry—" He scrunched his face in a slight grimace of embarrassment. "Not you. Back on the ship, I told her there might be more down here than the ISTA survey found."

I said nothing, skin crawling a bit at the way he confused me with her, but also at his excitement over a place that had almost killed me.

"It makes complete sense, when you think about it," he went on, apparently unaware of my discomfort. "This planet is old enough to have had advanced species, if we're comparing it to Earth's history. And it's in the Goldilocks zone."

"If you say so, pal."

"When you're feeling up to it, can you take me there?"

I almost laughed, even though there wasn't anything funny about it. "Um, fuck no."

"Why not?"

"Were you not listening to everything I just said?"

"Yes, but you went in unprepared. Next time, we'll—"

"There isn't going to be a next time." Just thinking about it turned my stomach into a blender. "I am never going back there."

"But this is exactly what the habitat is here for. We have equipment. We can—"

"I said no!" My ragged voice made it sound like a bark, loud and harsh, and Duncan looked suddenly wary of me. I didn't want him to think I was like her. "I'm sorry. But there's something else. Something down there. And it's not a ferret."

"Something living?"

I nodded, and he went still.

"What did it look like?" he asked.

"I couldn't see it that well. I mostly just heard it growling."

"Could you tell how big it was?"

I thought back to the silhouette I'd seen peering over the ledge at me. "I think it was about the size of a human. Why? Do you know what it is?"

He glanced toward the room's hatch. "I need to check on the perimeter sensors."

"Should I take that as a yes?"

"Not exactly."

"Not exactly?"

"I never got a good look. It always came at night, but it hasn't returned since I put up the perimeter. I thought maybe it had moved on."

"What do you think it was?"

He hesitated, and when he answered, he didn't sound confident. "Probably just a nocturnal species the ISTA survey missed." He stood and moved toward the door. "I'll be right back."

Then he left the room, and he closed the door behind him. I wanted to follow him, but I had an IV in my arm and a severe pounding in my head. A few minutes went by, and I lay back down with my eyes closed, hoping to ease the pain. When Duncan returned, the sound of the hatch opening startled me awake, and I was surprised that I had drifted off again that quickly.

"Nothing on the sensors." He came toward me holding what looked like some sort of medical device. "Let me check your status. Maybe we can take you off the fluids. Hold out your hand?"

I hesitated, but then I realized he had already stuck a needle in my arm without obvious trouble, so I sat up and did as he asked. He pushed two clips over my fingertips and pressed some buttons on the device. A few seconds went by. The device beeped, and his quick nod said he was satisfied by what he saw.

"Looking good." He glanced up with a sheepish grin and gestured at the display with his other hand. "That's what it tells me, anyway. And it doesn't show any toxins. So maybe that powder is out of your system."

"Or maybe that thing doesn't recognize alien toxins," I said.

"Or maybe that powder wasn't toxic. Either way, I think we can take the IV out."

I moved my arm closer to him. "Yes, please."

I could tell he tried to be gentle, but I still felt a couple of sharp pinches as he worked. I didn't want to make him nervous, so I kept talking.

"I wonder what that stuff was."

"That powder?" He pressed a wad of gauze into my elbow and had me bend my arm closed around it. "I've heard some psychedelics can cause synesthesia, where your senses get crossed and mixed."

"You mean like mushrooms?"

He shrugged. "Yeah, maybe."

I had never done any drugs, let alone psychedelics, but I thought maybe he was onto something. "I did see some mushrooms growing down there."

A moment later, he straightened my arm, and I felt his thumbs spread a bandage over my skin.

"There," he said. "All done."

I rubbed the place where the needle had been. "Thanks."

"Are you up for a tour of the habitat?" he asked. "Think you can walk?"

I pushed myself to the edge of the bed. "I have a headache. But I think I can walk."

I wasn't actually sure I could, but I wasn't going to say that until I'd tried. He stepped back to give me room, holding up his hands, ready to support me if I needed it. When I swung my feet out from under the blanket, I realized he had taken my boots off, and my saggy wet socks had dried stiff around my toes. The bed was higher than a normal bed, with built-in drawers and storage compartments beneath it, and I was already halfway to standing when my feet hit the smooth, beige, industrial textile that apparently passed for carpet in space. A wave of vertigo washed over me, and I steadied myself with a hand on the mattress.

"You good?" he asked.

"I'm good." I breathed through my nose until the wave passed, and then I blinked my eyes wide open. "Okay, ready for the tour."

He watched me for a moment, until I guess he believed it, and then he said, "Okay, this way."

I followed him out of the room into a juncture of three radiating hallways, which were all lit by track lighting both overhead and along the floor and smelled a bit like new car. Three hatches faced mine from across the intersection, marking slices of room between the three corridors.

"These are the sleeping quarters," he said, then pointed at one of the doors. "That's the bathroom. The others are bedrooms." He pointed down the hallway to my left. "Lab and medical module is through there." Then he hitched his thumb over his shoulder to indicate the passageway behind him. "Storage module is that way." He turned his body down the hall to my right. "The other living space is this way."

He led me along the passage, through an open hatch, and we entered a large, round common room. The light that came in through frosted windows in the domed ceiling seemed to settle in a muted haze. I noticed two other hatches across the room, mirroring the general layout of the previous module, but with different insides. A small kitchen occupied a wedge of floor space on the left, and six indifferent folding chairs sat loosely around a long table nearby. All the plastic and metal surfaces looked glossy and smooth, as if their protective plastic coating had just been peeled off. The same boring, industrial carpet from the bedroom muffled my steps, and it was silent, except for a low rumbling coming from somewhere.

The whole place felt empty and lonely in an eerie way that reminded me of this time I went with Gram to visit her sister. We stayed in a hotel near the hospital. But when we checked in, there were no other cars in the parking lot, and I never saw another guest. I kept wondering if there was something we didn't know. Something wrong.

I tried to imagine the habitat as it was supposed to be, with my parents there, the three of us sitting around that table eating breakfast or dinner, living together, crowded together, getting on each other's nerves in all the ways I had expected us to.

"What is it?" Duncan said.

I didn't know what he saw on my face that made him ask. "Oh, it's just . . . not that long ago, the idea of being forced to come here made me very angry."

He nodded, one corner of his mouth turned up, like he already knew that. "And now?"

"Now? I actually wish my parents were here. It feels empty without them."

"Like when they left," he said.

The blunt accuracy of that startled and unsettled me, and I wondered if she had told him something about it, or if he had just made a
really good guess. Either way, I didn't want to talk about it, and I turned
away from him without answering, searching for a change of subject.

My eyes landed on a mobile computer terminal sitting next to
a large, black screen mounted to a base with wheels. It reflected the
room, but only dim hints of it, more like a window into a dark parallel
universe than a mirror. I gestured toward it. "They have anything good
to watch?"

"I don't know." He sat on the edge of the table and folded his arms.
"I haven't been able to access any of the computer systems."

"Why not?"

"I don't have clearance. I was never supposed to be here. That's another reason I wanted her to come back with me."

"She knows you don't have clearance?"

"She does."

"And she has clearance?"

He paused. "*You* have clearance."

"Ah. Right. Assuming she hasn't changed the password." But then
something else occurred to me. "Wait, if you don't have access to the
computer systems, that means you can't use the Tangle."

"Nope."

"So ISTA still doesn't know what happened?"

He shook his head. "The beacon on the lander is sending an SOS,
at least. But that's it."

"We need to fix that," I said. "That's the whole reason she sent me
here."

He only nodded in agreement after a pause. "Yes. I guess we do
need to fix that. Eventually."

"What's wrong?"

"Honestly?" He reached for the nearest chair and dragged it to where he could sit down next to the table, but turned sideways to face me. "I've sort of been fine putting that off."

"Why?"

"Because I don't know what ISTA will do."

"About me?"

"No, not about you, about everything. There are only a couple of ways out of this for us."

"Such as?"

"Best-case scenario? The *Clarke* arrives a year from now, on schedule. They pick us up and teleport us home. The others get reestablished on Earth as soon as possible."

The idea of living on Hades for a year did not appeal to me, especially with an unstable version of myself that I couldn't trust, and an alien running loose somewhere, but at least it seemed doable. Survivable. But that was only the best case. "What's the worst-case scenario?"

"ISTA puts this system in quarantine."

I stepped closer to him. "What does that mean?"

"It means they'll divert the *Clarke* and suspend teleportation. No one gets in or out." He rubbed the table with his thumb, like he was polishing away a smudge. "ISTA will reestablish everyone back on earth."

At first, that didn't seem worst case to me. "Okay, so we . . . Wait. Everyone?"

"Everyone."

"You mean—"

"Yes, us. They'll declare us lost and print us with the others."

"But we're not lost."

"We are if they decide not to retrieve us."

I glanced around the room again, and I noticed for the first time how clean it was even though a teenage boy had been staying there. I didn't know Duncan well, but it looked like he had been keeping it tidy. Like someone taking care of a house he planned to live in for a long time.

I dropped into the nearest chair, hands in my lap. "Can they—they can do that? They can just leave us out here? Forever?"

He shrugged. "To them, a lost body is no different from a broken body. But it won't be forever."

"It won't?"

"No. Eventually, these bodies really will break. But they'll probably expect us to refactor ourselves before that."

I could guess what that meant, but I didn't want to. "Is there a third scenario between best and worst?"

"There might be." He propped an elbow on the table and leaned his head against his loose fist. "They might keep the *Clarke* on course to pick us up—"

"I like the sound of that much better."

"—but they'll still suspend teleportation. We'll be stuck on the *Clarke* until ISTA decides it's safe to try sending us home."

"How long would that take?"

"Who knows? Months? Years? Or maybe they'll divert the *Clarke* and send another ship to pick us up that's better prepared to study the anomaly. But that will take even longer to get here. Many years."

"Fuck."

"Yeah." He sighed. "So anyway, that's why I haven't been too worried about getting on the Tangle."

Nothing about that conversation had helped with my headache, and neither had the new-car smell in the habitat. "I need some air. Where is the front door?"

He nodded behind me, in the direction of the hatch that had been on my right when we first entered the common room. "It's a standard air lock," he said.

"Thanks." I stood, and I bumped my chair with my shin as I turned and headed toward the exit.

When I emerged from the exterior hatch, it was close to sunset, and

I discovered the source of the rumbling I had heard inside. The habitat sat next to a waterfall, right at the edge of a fissure that looked like a sharp, fresh gash down the face of the mountain. I took a few steps closer to it, and then I saw that part of the habitat seemed to be missing, as if it had been swallowed by the abyss. What appeared to be the tattered remains of another module still clung to the backside of the common room and hung over the edge of the ravine in shreds and splinters.

The waterfall poured down from the direction of Mount Ida, which was somehow still far away, still as high as a pile of skyscrapers. The cascade splashed white against sharp boulders and columns of dark rock below, spraying mist that I could smell in the air, before it trickled away in a winding stream. The land below the fissure looked turned over, like the dirt in Gram's garden when she's getting ready to plant something new.

Duncan came outside then, and he stepped up next to me. "There must have been a landslide," he said, raising his voice a bit to be heard over the rushing of the falls.

"When?"

"Hard to say. But obviously after the habitat arrived."

"What was in that module?"

"More sleeping quarters probably."

I looked down at the ground where we stood, at the cliff on which the remaining four domes of the habitat huddled together. "Why did ISTA put it here?"

"For the water." He said it like that should have been obvious. "For the hydropower. And the habitat filters it."

"But is the ground . . . stable?"

"I think so." He pointed at the far side of the ravine. "You can see from the erosion pattern where the water carved an underground channel. I think that weakened the rock above until it fell away. But this ground should be stable."

I felt only slightly reassured by that, and I turned away from the crevice to face a different view of Hades than anything I had seen until then. From the habitat's vantage, I could look down for the first time, and the terrain below seemed to tumble and fall away from me to the horizon. The later-afternoon light over the land had turned golden and red, and it occurred to me if that view, with a waterfall nearby, were back on Earth, it would be undeniably beautiful. People would probably travel from far away to see it. I took a few deep breaths, and then I turned back to Duncan.

"What if we don't say anything to ISTA?" I asked. "Just let the *Clarke* come on schedule. One year from now."

"I've considered that," he said.

"And?"

He folded his arms, his blue eyes turned brilliant by the sunlight. "The problem is, they already know about your dad and Dr. Gutiérrez. We told them that much before the evacuation."

"Oh."

"It's possible they've already diverted the *Clarke*. And besides, the others are counting on us. They've all got families and friends waiting for them back home. What if something happened to us before the *Clarke* got here? Or before we told ISTA what happened?"

"I guess that's a good point."

His arms fell loose at his sides. "You must be hungry."

"Very," I said, but the stuff in the IV had helped a lot with that.

"How about we get something to eat. Then we can go from there."

We went back inside, and he showed me the cupboard that he had stocked with rations. I saw some spaghetti but chose a beef stew instead, and he left me alone for a few minutes while I heated it up. I had just sat down at the table when he returned and put a small device on the kitchen counter, then went to the cupboard to pick his meal.

"What's that?" I pointed at the device with my spoon.

"Radio," he said. "It's connected to the perimeter sensors. Without access to the habitat's systems, I had to go pretty basic with the tech."

"So, if that thing goes off . . ."

"You'll know something bigger than a golden retriever is getting close." He put his ration package in the microwave.

"How close?"

"It's got a five-kilometer range." He glanced at the radio. "That's as far as I could push it. With the habitat's systems online, I think I could extend that a lot farther. So maybe after dinner, you could try logging in?"

"Sure," I said. "But I'm not quite ready to hop on the Tangle yet. I think we need to be smart about what we say and how we say it. Especially when it comes to . . . me. And her."

His gentle smile held sympathy, or maybe it was just pity. "Agreed."

We finished our meal, and then I ate a second package before I dragged my chair over to the computer terminal. When I switched it on, it booted up fast, which I took as a good sign, and then my login and password worked without any issues. But I was pretty lost from there, so Duncan sat down in my chair and took over. He quickly figured out how to navigate the habitat's complicated systems, and as he flipped through directories, I glimpsed some folders labeled with my name.

Duncan moved right past them, but the sight of them froze me. I assumed they held my pictures, my music, my life. Her life. I stood there at Duncan's shoulder staring at the screen, seeing a flood of memories instead of whatever he was doing.

"Jessica?" he said.

"Huh?"

"I said, it looks like I've got some work to do if I want to get the habitat and the sensors to talk with each other."

"Oh." I nodded like I had been listening. "Sure. Okay."

He frowned a moment, then waved off what he had just said. "Never mind, it's fine. I'll leave that for tomorrow. You seem tired."

"Sorry." I blinked and pushed the memories away. "I—I wish I was more help. I must seem like, I don't know, a liability to you."

"What?" He lifted his head without looking at me. "I didn't—"

"It's okay. You don't have to say anything. The truth is, I didn't come out here as prepared as I should have been, and I know that."

He was silent, and he was right that I was tired. The sight of those folders had rattled me.

"I think I'll go to bed early," I said. "Same room as before?"

He nodded.

"See you in the morning." I hurried away, but he called to me before I got to the hatch, and I turned back, lips tight, eyes closed at first. "Yes?"

"I just wanted to say good night." He had twisted around to look at me, hanging an elbow over the back of his chair. "And just so you know, I don't think you're a liability."

He seemed to mean that. "Thanks."

"Sleep well." He went back to the computer screen. "I'll lock up."

I left him there and found the way back to my room, where I threw myself onto the bed and buried my head under the pillow. I tried to fall asleep fast and shut off my brain. But I kept thinking about my files, even though my restlessness wasn't really about the photos and songs. It was about the life that was supposed to be mine—all saved and uploaded—that was also hers.

Then, even when I finally did fall asleep, I kept waking up from bad dreams I couldn't remember, drenched in sweat, thinking I had heard something outside my door, or outside the habitat wall. Something growling and prowling around in the dark, or the ground cracking and groaning, ready to give way and plunge us into the ravine. Each time that happened, I sat up and listened, wishing I could still see in the dark. But I heard nothing.

# 25 — Hades

## AFTER

IT WAS LATE WHEN I AWOKE THE NEXT MORNING, OR at least it felt late, and the sunlight through the windows in the dome of the common room looked full. I heated up some breakfast and coffee by myself, wondering where Duncan was. He didn't seem like the type to spend half a day in bed, but he still hadn't appeared by the time I finished eating, which meant he'd probably gotten up before me. I thought maybe he had gone out to do something with the sensors, and I decided to look around a bit more until he returned, to familiarize myself with the place. No matter which scenario played out, best case, worst case, or something in between, the habitat would be home for a while.

Before leaving the common room, I opened the third hatch to satisfy my curiosity. That door had obviously once led to the lost module and now opened directly onto the wide ravine in a way that could make sleepwalking deadly. The raging waterfall sent a cool, damp breeze against my face that smelled like wet rocks. It was loud, but not deafening, and I heard something else with it, a kind of ringing. I braced myself against the frame of the hatch and leaned out to see what it was.

The cliff below wasn't quite sheer, but it was steep enough to have taken most of the module straight down with the rest of the rockslide. What was left rested against the side of the ravine, some of it flapping, some of it jutting out. Not far below me, a crooked metal pole reached toward the falls and held a torn sheet of metal under the water. The pounding cascade struck it like a bell and reminded me of the tower I'd climbed to escape the alien city.

It seemed like the ringing grew louder as I stood there, and the height was getting to me, so I pulled back inside and closed the hatch. That shut out most of the noise, but it also restored a silence that was lonely and unsettling. I went to explore the habitat's other modules to see if I could find Duncan.

The laboratory next to the sleeping quarters felt sterile. A broad table stood in the center of the room beneath a bar of bright lights suspended from the domed ceiling. They flickered on automatically when I entered the room, and their glare reflected off the shiny floor in wavy ribbons. Six workstations circled the room, divided by clear partitions. The cubicles all had the same setup, with a desk and a long workbench that traced the outer wall of the module like a broken metal ring. None held any equipment yet, except for one, which had some tools hanging from a rack above the bench, and some electronic components spread across the desk around a computer terminal. I assumed that's where Duncan had been working on his sensors.

When I went to check out the storage module, I finally found him, standing among a dozen or more metal and plastic crates, all opened, their contents arranged on the floor. He glanced up from a tablet as I came through the hatch.

"Good morning," he said. "It's still morning, right?"

"It is to me."

"Did you sleep well?"

"I slept late."

"You probably needed it." He went back to his tablet. "I haven't been up that long, either."

"What are you working on?"

"Well . . ." He glanced at all the parts near his feet and let out a huff. "Apparently, the habitat requires some assembly. I guess ISTA didn't think perimeter sensors would be necessary on an uninhabited planet." He held up the tablet. "But I've got the instructions, and I should be able to wire this up to my array."

I folded my arms and nodded as if I agreed with his assessment. It looked like he had already put together several pieces of equipment, a couple of satellite dishes, some other components. Hundreds more crates stood in towers and mounds around the room, pathways winding between them, containing what I assumed to be a year's worth of food and supplies and all the scientific things my parents needed to carry out their survey of the planet. Unlike the other modules with their trio of hatches, the storage bay had a broad roller door on its far side, and a rover with dirty wheels parked by it. I realized that must've been how Duncan had brought me here.

"What about the Tangle?" I asked.

He pointed. "Over there. It seems to be up and running. Part of the systems check your parents performed from the *Theseus* to get everything ready. But I haven't done anything with it yet."

I left him to his tablet and wandered in the direction he'd indicated, through the stacks of crates, until I found what had to be the housing for the quantum channel. A copper-colored metal drum a meter and a half tall squatted on the floor, as big around as a small trampoline, looking solid and heavy. It was perfectly flat and smooth on all sides, without any seams, and above it towered a knotted bank of coiled pipes and conduit. I had always thought the Tangle got its name from quantum entanglement, but looking at that nest, I wondered if it had a second meaning. I couldn't see what gave the impression that it was working, because it showed no signs of life that I could detect. When I returned to Duncan, he was sitting cross-legged on the floor, bent over something with tools in his hands, the tablet at his side.

"Can I help?" I asked, which may have sounded like a dumb question to him, since I probably hadn't come across as capable of much, but I was sincere in my willingness to try.

He shook his head. "Nah. I should be done soon. If you want, there's a crate by the door with some fresh clothes. You could take a shower."

"Are you saying I stink?" I was sure I did but tried to sound offended.

"No, no," he said in a rush. "It's a decent shower, that's all. Much better than what we had on the *Theseus* . . ." He seemed to realize I was giving him a hard time. "But if you're asking, then yes, you do stink a bit."

"Noted," I said as I walked away.

When I located the crate, I dug through the plastic-wrapped packages until I found clothing in my size. Then I walked to the bathroom, which stood between two of the bedrooms, long and narrow, made from white molded plastic floor to ceiling, with a shower stall at the far end.

Before I undressed, I took the yellow kobold out of the pocket of my dirty jumpsuit and set it on the counter next to the sink. I stood there staring at it for a few moments, full of memories and nostalgia, thinking of my dad and wishing my parents were there to play a game with me.

Then I stepped into a shower that surprised me. I had expected it to be highly efficient, meaning not very comfortable, but it seemed that filtering water from the river allowed for heat and pressure like a normal shower back on earth. The weight of the water may have come partly from Hades's gravity, but either way, I enjoyed it and took longer in there than I needed.

When I finished, I returned to the common room wearing a clean jumpsuit, the kobold back in my pocket, with wet hair and fresh socks on my feet. Duncan hadn't come in yet, so I figured he was still working, and I walked over to the computer terminal. I felt able to confront whatever had freaked me out the night before, so I opened up my files to make myself look at them.

It wasn't as painful as I worried it would be, at first. I watched some of the videos I had uploaded, like the one with the guinea pig on the goat. They made me smile, but not in the way I had thought they would when I chose them. I smiled at myself for thinking that was the type of thing I should bring to an alien planet. I smiled at the music I'd picked and only wished I could play it for my parents, not to annoy them, but to have them there to annoy.

But then I saw the photo of Avery, the one with the green pepper in her nose, and that's when I finally confronted what I'd tried to avoid the night before. The sudden contact with my own life took my breath like that plunge into the underground lake, and that was when I broke down. I had done some crying on Hades, but nothing like that. I sobbed with my eyes open, hands covering my mouth, shaking as I stared at the screen. Just the memory of that moment, eating pizza and laughing, somehow felt more real than anything I had experienced since waking up in the printer.

I hadn't told Avery how my feelings for her changed after that day, and I knew I never would. Because even if the *Clarke* came on schedule, and we teleported home in a year, I knew it wouldn't be a scan of me. I was redundant. Nothing of me, not even my data, would leave that planet. It would all be hers. Teleportation philosophers would probably try to tell me that sending her data would bring me home, too, but I knew that wasn't true. I wasn't convinced it had ever been true, even in the very first second after I'd woken up.

I had a sudden and frightening urge to just delete the picture, erase all my files, but I fought it back and quickly shut off the computer. I stared at my snotty reflection in the dead screen for a while, until Duncan entered the room. I had fortunately stopped crying by then, but I looked like a mess, and he noticed. I could tell by his silence, and I watched his smudgy form ease closer to me in the dark mirror until he stood close enough that I could see his reflection next to mine.

"Are you okay?" he asked.

I sniffed. "I'll be fine."

He frowned. "You can tell me if you're not."

I wondered if he said that because she would have confided in him. "Are your perimeter sensors working now?" I sat up straight and swept under my eyes with my fingertips. When he didn't respond, I stood and faced him to let him know I expected an answer.

"Almost finished," he finally said, his brow still wrinkled. "I need to take the rover out to reposition and recalibrate them . . . Are you sure you're okay?"

"Yes. You don't need to worry about me like you worried about her."

His forehead relaxed a bit, but he kept looking at me for long enough that I wondered if he would let it go. "Want to come with me?" he finally asked.

"What, on the rover?"

"Yes."

I opened my mouth to say no, but then I changed my mind. I didn't like the idea of going out there where an alien might be running around, but I also didn't feel right letting him go by himself. "Sure," I said. "When do you want to leave?"

"Pretty soon." He glanced at the computer. "I think we need to send a message to ISTA first."

My voice faltered. "Wh-why?"

"Just a precaution. Since we're both leaving the habitat. In case something happens to us. But also . . . it isn't fair to the others to put it off anymore, no matter what ISTA decides to do."

I couldn't disagree with either of those points, and I didn't really want to. I just had no idea where that left me. "What should we say?"

"I've been thinking about that, and I've decided to keep it factual and brief. For now, we'll say there was a critical system failure on the *Theseus* that forced an evacuation. All hands lost, except for—"

"Who?"

He inhaled. "Myself, and Jessica Mathers."

That was a partial truth I could live with. For now. I hoped Duncan could, too, even though the full truth would have to come out eventually.

"Thank you," I said.

He nodded, then stepped around me to sit at the computer. I told him my login and password, and he had the Tangle system opened up a few moments later. I peered over his shoulder without making it obvious, and I saw the message he typed. It said exactly what he had told me he would say. Then he closed the system and stood with a deep sigh.

"Okay, that's done. We've missed the noon opening, but it'll go out when the quantum channel opens at midnight. That's actually a big weight off my chest."

"Mine too." That message was the whole reason I had left the lander to come to the habitat in the first place, and it was done. "Now we just wait to see what ISTA says."

He shrugged, and his hands slapped the sides of his legs as they fell. "I'm going to try not to worry about that until noon tomorrow."

I wasn't sure how successful I would be at doing that, but I knew it would at least help to have something to take my mind off it. Like the perimeter sensors.

Back in the storage module, the rover waited by the roller door where I had seen it earlier. Up close, the vehicle reminded me of an Earth ATV, except larger. Its four meaty wheels stretched outward on curved arms, like it was doing push-ups. It had two narrow bucket seats, side by side, caged inside a sleek metal frame.

"Do you want to drive?" Duncan asked.

I appreciated the offer, and I probably would have taken him up on it back home. "Maybe later," I said, and I stepped around the rover to the passenger side.

As I climbed in, Duncan went to the roller door. He bent down to pull free a manual bolt lock near the floor, and then he heaved upward. The door rattled over my head, loud inside the domed module, and dusty sunlight poured in from outside.

"It's actually pretty fun," he said as he came to the driver's side. "The motor has a lot of torque." Then he grabbed the upper frame and swung himself into the vehicle next to me.

"Maybe on the way back," I said.

He pressed a large button, and the rover's center console lit up with an array of gauges and meters. "Seat belt," he said with a glance over my shoulder.

I twisted and pulled the strap across my chest to buckle in, but Duncan paused in the middle of doing the same, like he'd just thought of something. Then he hopped back out of the rover.

"What did you forget?" I asked.

He hustled over to a crate that opened like a suitcase and pulled out a large, steel-gray handgun. When he came back to the rover, he slid the gun into a sleeve behind his seat and then climbed into the vehicle.

"What's that?" I craned my neck to get another look at the weapon. "I mean, I know what it is, but—"

"Just a precaution," he said. "And it's loaded with pellets. Painful. But nonlethal."

The gun got me thinking about possible dangers, simply by being there. It also reassured me, but not completely. It was too easy to imagine something a nonlethal pellet wouldn't stop.

The steering mechanism in front of Duncan looked like two joysticks attached to the ends of a big video game controller. The motor was silent until he did something to ease the rover forward, and then we purred out of the module, into the full light of the sun.

"Right trigger to go forward," he said, flapping his index finger as we rolled out. "Left trigger for brakes. Turn like a normal steering wheel." He cranked it to the left to demonstrate, and we swung around the lab module, heading downhill. "This switch flips it into reverse." He pointed at a little lever near the base of the controller between the joysticks.

"What's all that other stuff?"

"I don't actually know. The rover is designed for all kinds of planets and conditions. Low gravity, no atmosphere. We won't ever use a lot of what it can do."

The uneven ground tipped us back and forth a bit, but the flexing of the arm-wheels seemed to take most of the bumps. After circling the lab module, we passed the sleeping quarters, and then came to the habitat's front air lock.

I smelled mist from the waterfall and had twisted around in my seat to look back at the ravine when we jerked to a stop. The seat belt pulled against me, and the motor went quiet. Duncan gripped the steering wheel with rigid arms, staring straight ahead. Then I saw her, too.

She stood about ten meters down the hill from us, dirty and disheveled, her scowl furious as she glared back at me.

"So!" she shouted. "You're alive! That's great!" She threw her backpack on the ground, but then I realized it was my pack, the one I'd left beside the river. "That's just fucking great!" She turned around to storm away, back down the mountain.

"Wait!" Duncan said.

He scrambled out of the rover and rushed toward her, kicking up dirt. She spun to face him with her arms folded. The look on her face would have stopped me in my tracks, but he kept running, and when he reached her, he stepped in close, as if he meant to hug her. I couldn't hear the words he said, but I heard the urgency in his voice. A moment later, she threw her hands up and backed away from him shaking her head. He leaned toward her, gesturing in my direction, and she glanced at me, then folded her arms again.

At first, I stayed in the rover, hunkered low in my seat, like I was embarrassed by an argument that was none of my business. But then I realized I was being an idiot, and it was totally my business, so I climbed out to join them.

"... not about you!" she was saying when I got close enough to hear. "And, yes, I am leaving."

"No, you're not," Duncan said.

"Excuse me?" She moved toward him, and I thought she might shove him or punch him, but instead she just jabbed his chest with her finger. "You don't tell me what to do. I go where I want, when I want."

"I'm not going to let you push me away." Duncan kept his voice calm, but I could see his cheeks getting red. "Not this time."

"Oh, you're not going to *let* me?" she said.

"No," he said.

"Okay, space brat." Her laugh sounded bitter and angry. "How are you going to stop me?"

His chest rose and fell with a deep breath. "We are going to talk about this."

"What is *this*?" She spread her arms. "There's nothing to talk about. What do you mean, *this*?"

"Me," I said, finally speaking up. "We're going to talk about me."

They both turned toward me, and their irritated looks said they hadn't even realized I was there, and what the hell was I doing listening in on a private conversation, and I should have just stayed in the rover.

"Oh, you want to talk about her?" she said, nodding toward me.

"No." Duncan blinked hard. "Yes. I want to talk about all of it."

She shrugged. "What you want doesn't matter. You weren't even supposed to see me again. I'm only here because I had to make sure she got here alive."

I wanted to say that I almost didn't make it to the habitat, because she had lied to me and abandoned me, but Duncan spoke before I could.

"What do you mean?" he asked her. The tone of his voice had changed suddenly, no longer angry, but frightened. "Why wouldn't I see you again?"

She clamped her mouth shut, put her hands on her hips, and looked down at the ground, shaking her head. She had done the same thing to me, refusing to answer my questions, willfully holding back the truth.

"Tell me," Duncan said, the fear in his voice turning to panic. "Why wouldn't I see you again?"

"You know why." She looked up at him, chin out, eyes wet and defiant. "It's nothing ISTA wouldn't tell us to do, anyway."

He took a step backward from her, mouth open, and I remembered something he had mentioned to me earlier, when he said ISTA would expect us to refactor ourselves if they decided to print us back on Earth.

"Were you planning this all along?" he asked, almost whispering.

Her chin fell. "Don't look at me like that."

"Like what?"

"Like this isn't how it works."

He glanced at me, and then back at her. "How what works?"

"All of it! Fucking teleportation!" She stepped toward him, pointing at me. "She is me!"

"No," he said. "She is not you—"

She slapped him across the face. Hard. I flinched at the sound, and he touched his cheek with his fingertips, eyes wide in shock.

"I'm sorry." She pulled her hand into a tight fist against her chest and stepped backward, away from him. "I'm sorry. This is why I—I didn't mean—"

"Yes," Duncan said, "you did."

He turned and stalked away from us, back up the hill toward the rover. When he reached the vehicle, he pulled himself into the driver's seat, and in the next moment the rover charged toward us.

I didn't believe he would actually hit us, but I still jumped out of the way as he sped by, and then I watched the vehicle careen down the slope, spitting chewed-up dirt and rocks into the air behind it.

"Where are you going?" she shouted, and then she asked me, "Where is he going?"

"Probably to finish setting up the perimeter sensors."

"Why does he need perimeter sensors?"

I turned to face her, fully expecting to get a slap like Duncan. "He's not wrong, you know. I am not you."

But she didn't slap me. She just stared at me. And then she broke down and started crying.

I almost rolled my eyes. I was past feeling bad for her. I just stood there and watched her hugging herself, and when I finally spoke, I sounded even colder than I meant to. "Come inside. You have some explaining to do."

I STAND NEAR THE GRAVES I DUG WATCHING DUN-can drive away. I want to run after him, but I don't, because he would think I've changed my mind when I haven't. I just feel horrible for how I treated him, and I want to somehow make him understand. But I know he won't, so I let him leave, and I stay there until he's gone and the dirt cloud behind him has settled.

When I finally go back inside, I feel even more alone than I did when I thought I was the only one who had survived. But I'm hungry for the first time since the crash, so before I do anything else, I eat. There are plenty of rations. I rip one open and dump it into my mouth, leaning backward against the counter in the lander's kitchen. When I'm done chewing, I go to work.

The body printer needs a power source, and I think I have one. The beacon on my lander has its own fuel cell with plenty of energy, enough to shout a continuous signal deep into space for years. But I don't re-ally need it, since Duncan got the beacon on his lander working, which makes it my best option. And my only option.

I get some tools and make my way through the lander's battered corridors to the front of the ship, and then I climb inside the cramped, reinforced compartment that houses the beacon. It's not much bigger than the inside of a refrigerator, but I spend the next few hours work-ing to extract the fuel cell. Every panel, bracket, and component that I remove seems to reveal three more pieces blocking my way. Before long my knuckles are covered in scrapes and cuts from reaching into tight spaces full of rough edges, and the sweat dripping into my eyes makes it hard to see what I'm doing.

I'm sure there's a simpler, easier way to accomplish this, like when they need to swap out an old fuel cell for a new one. Based on the location of the beacon, I'm guessing the access point is somewhere outside and under the lander. That would be great if the landing gear had deployed, but instead I'm forced to spend the day trying to break in another way.

By the time evening comes, I surrender and accept that the fuel cell will have to stay where it is, which means I'll just have to run a line to carry its power to the printer at the other end of the ship. That will take time, but I remember how the electrical cables are marked, so it shouldn't be too difficult.

I climb out of the beacon's compartment, back into the cool air, and I start pulling panels away from the bulkheads. Where I can leave the existing wire in place, I do. Where I can't, I rip it out, and I cut and twist a new power line, one gradual meter at a time. It weaves in and out of the walls, and where the course of the wire crosses a corridor or junction, I splice in a section of cable to bridge the gap and keep going. I work late into the night, until I'm so bleary I worry I'll make a stupid mistake, and I lie down in the corridor to rest.

A few hours later, I wake and pick up the loose ends where I left off. The wires are thin and sharp, and they wear the tips of my fingers raw. Sometimes they jab up underneath my nails. I stop to eat again. Later I stop to sleep again.

On the second day, I reach the printer room, and it takes some time to figure out where the power goes into the machine. When I think I have it, I get everything ready, but I leave it disconnected. Then I return to the beacon's fuel cell, and I attach my power line to its auxiliary contacts. The wire should be live at the other end.

As I return to the printer room, I check all my connections down the line. I'm not sure what problems I need to look out for, other than sparks or smoke, but everything seems fine, and soon I'm kneeling in front of an open panel at the base of the machine. Very carefully, I use a pair of pliers with rubber grips to twist the negative lines together, and when I bring the two positive connections together, there's a crackling, popping sound until I pinch and twist them tight. I think that means the wire is live.

I stand and move to the control panel at the foot of the printer, where I'm relieved to see a few basic indicator lights are now blinking. I find the main power button and push it. For just a fraction of a second, but long enough to panic, nothing happens. Then I hear a whisper and murmur rising inside the machine, and then the touch display lights up with a boot screen before switching to a login.

"Damn it," I whisper.

It made sense for there to be security. I just hadn't anticipated it.

I go ahead and try mine first, but of course it doesn't work. My mom said she gave me access to the habitat systems, but apparently that permission does not apply to the body printers. I tap the username field, and I can see all the people who have logged in before, including Liz and Dr. Gutiérrez. I don't have anything to lose in trying to guess, so I pick Liz, and I try multiple variations on the few possibilities I can think of.

*Star Splitter.*

*Brad.*

*Robert Frost.*

*Telescope.*

My fingers leave smears of grease and dried blood on the screen, and nothing works. But I have an idea for Dr. Gutiérrez's password, so I pull up his login and type *Sonnet 14*, first with numbers, and then with Roman numerals. The Roman numerals work. The system welcomes me in with a soft glow inside the dome of the printing chamber that lights up the room.

My smile cracks my dried lips. "You all really like your poetry out here," I say.

From there, things appear straightforward, and mostly automated. I assume that's partly because the laws don't allow for any changes to the body being teleported, but it's mostly because there are plenty of times when the destination ship has a limited crew, or it might even be empty, waiting at the end of a long, lonely journey for its passengers to arrive. All I have to do is find the right file and execute the process, which will establish her here, exactly as I was when I left Earth. My heart is beating all over the place, and my body is trembling by the time I get her data loaded and press the button.

The printer goes into a calibration mode, and its arms leap out of their cradles. They whip up and down the length of the chamber with inhuman speed and precision, the sound of their motors a muffled chittering between them as they prepare to fabricate a body together.

The process will take a while. And I am suddenly exhausted. I go to the galley, where I've been sleeping, and I gather up my pillow and blankets. Then I grab a couple of food rations, and I haul it all back to the printer. I make myself a little nest on the floor nearby, and I tear open a package of spaghetti with my teeth, which I eat cold. The printer will take nine days to establish her here, but I can wait. I feel more at peace watching its jerky dance than I have since arriving on the *Theseus*. Before long, I fall asleep to the sound of it remaking me.

I sleep a lot over the next couple of days, but then the nightmares come back. During one sleepless night, a Hades rainstorm thunders through, pounding the lander. It kind of scares me until I realize it will cover up Duncan's tracks, which means one less thing I need to worry about explaining right away.

The printer's display keeps me updated on the stages of the process, system by system, layer by layer, which is both fascinating and disgusting to watch. At each new phase, the machine's arms lay down the scaffolding first, a lattice of crystal fibers that are so thin they're almost invisible, like a spiderweb. That framework will end up dissolved and absorbed into the tissue that is then laid down inside and around it, gradually forming a body that is disturbingly recognizable as human early on.

I've taken biology classes, but the color-coded pictures in text-books, and smooth, digital animations don't show the truth. Bodies are not that clean. They really are just bags of fluids and substances hanging from bones and wrapped up tight in skin. I can't help looking down at my own body like I'm seeing it for the first time.

When the printer shifts to the brain, the scaffolding it spins out in-side the bowl of the cranium is dense, and incredibly fine and intricate, like a thin puff of shimmering cotton candy. I lean in closer to look at it, pressing my hands against the glass, which is wet with condensation from the cold temperatures inside.

That is the shape of my brain. I wonder what would happen if just one of those ghostly threads got bumped. I wonder what the lattice of my mind would look like if I were scanned now, and if the differences between it and the one being printed in front of me would be visible. I think they would have to be.

The scaffolding gets filled with brain jelly, and then the printer moves on to the rest of the skull, and then the face. By day seven, the body inside the printer is basically me. The display identifies this as the final curing stage, so I assume the tissues under the skin are still grow-ing and knitting together. But the body is me, unharmed. It has my face, my eyes closed and peaceful. Oblivious. She is completely ignorant of everything that has happened, or what she will face when she wakes up.

I appreciate that about her.

But I also kind of hate that about her.

She knows almost nothing about deep-space travel. She knows nothing about Hades, or what it takes to survive out here. Worse than that, she doesn't even know enough to care that she doesn't know. She's a liability, just like Duncan said. She's a whiny, arrogant, self-centered bitch who doesn't realize how good she has it.

Maybe Duncan was right, and this was a bad idea. I think I can still stop it. I go to the control display, where I find the abort button. But then I look at her again, and I can't bring myself to push it. She's basically alive in there. Whatever I might think about her, and even if what I think is true, I still need her. I need the very things that I despise about her. But she doesn't think she needs me, which is kind of the whole point, and I wonder if that's another reason I hate her.

I force myself away from the controls before I do anything stupid and impulsive, and I busy myself looking for underwear, a jumpsuit, socks, and boots in her size. She'll need those when she wakes up. I just have to decide if I want to be here when she does, and exactly what I will say to her.

There are a few things she will need to know.

AFTER

WE SAT ACROSS FROM EACH OTHER AT THE TABLE IN the common room. She slumped low in her chair, chin almost against her chest, looking sullen. I waited until she stopped sniffing to pull the yellow kobold out of my pocket. Then I put the wooden game piece in the middle of the table and leaned forward on my elbows, hands interlaced near my chest.

"Let's start with that," I said.

She glanced at the kobold. "What about it?"

"You tell me. Did you play a game with them or something?"

She folded her arms and tightened her lips, glaring at me like a stubborn child.

I couldn't take any more of her secrecy, and I blew up. I slammed the table with the flat of my hand, bouncing the game piece, and shouted, "Tell me!"

She flinched, then stammered, "Y-yes, okay? We played the game. So what?"

"So what?" I scooped up the kobold and held it out between my thumb and index finger. "You played Magical Mountain with them. Not me. You. And you know what this means to me. What it meant to—"

"It doesn't matter what it meant or what it means," she said. "And it doesn't matter which one of us played some stupid game with them. They're not going to remember it anyway. They won't remember any of it."

"Any of what?"

"Their time on the ship."

"Why not?"

She threw back her head and let out a growl of frustration. "Don't you get it? Their data is old! When they climb out of the printers back on Earth, they won't remember the last six years!"

I frowned at that. "Six years?"

"That's right."

I frown, and she adds, "They never got scanned out here."

I leaned away from her, clutching the kobold in my hand, and thought through everything that had been explained during my orientations. I recalled the travel itinerary that had been repeatedly outlined for me, because things were not adding up. "I thought they were supposed to get scanned when they left New Beijing," I said.

She didn't answer. Instead, she looked away, and her knee started to bounce.

"They *did* get scanned," I said. "They had to if they teleported to the *Theseus.*"

"Right." She nodded, but more to herself than to me. "Yes, that's right. I guess they were scanned."

"Then why would they lose the last six—"

"I don't know. Just forget that."

"But you said—"

"I got confused, okay?" She sat up higher in her chair. "I misspoke."

I could believe she felt confused, but I did not believe that she had misspoken. I knew she was still lying to me, and I knew that six years meant something. My parents had obviously been gone for six years, and it was possible they hadn't been scanned in the time between leaving me on Earth and their recent scan before leaving New Beijing. The only reason they would lose those six years would be if something went wrong with that last scan. I looked down at the kobold in my hand.

"Is this about Dad's data?" I asked.

Her knee stopped bouncing. "What?"

"Duncan told me something went wrong with Dad's data. Something in his brain."

"Now I'm glad I slapped him."

"He also told me I wasn't an accident. That you printed me on purpose."

"Duncan should know when to keep his mouth shut." Her voice sounded brittle, like an icicle.

"What did you think he was going to say when he met me? You knew he was here." I tossed the game piece back onto the table, where it made a clicking sound as it bounced and settled in front of her. "What was your plan if I hadn't found that, and we hadn't split up?"

"I don't know." She looked down her nose at the kobold. "I didn't have it all worked out."

"Obviously. But you had something worked out. You had some kind of plan."

"I did," she whispered.

"What was it?"

A moment went by, and she picked up the game piece. She held it pressed in the middle of her gathered fingertips, staring at it. I thought she was about to answer me, finally. But then her jaw tightened, and the kobold disappeared into her palm.

"What was your plan?" I asked again.

She held up her fist and gave it a shake. "This is just a piece of wood, you know. It means nothing."

"It means something to me."

"I'm glad. But you should let it go. The real game is waiting back home."

Even though my dad hadn't given the kobold to me, he had printed it for me, and I did not like the way she sneered at it. I held out my hand. "Give it back."

"This is basically just a piece of garbage. It's worthless."

I jumped to my feet. "Give it back!"

Then she stood to face me, slowly, and I didn't recognize the look in her eyes, anger mixed with hatred or pity or both. "This is for your own good," she said.

I flew at her, right over the table, so fast I surprised myself. She tried to get away from me, but she stumbled over her chair and ended up on the floor. I pounced, fighting to claw the kobold from her grasp.

"Give it to me!" I shouted.

She grunted and grimaced, and then she punched me in the face with her other hand. I fell to the side, stunned, tasting blood. She scrambled to her feet, casting around, frantic. Before I could get up, she raced for the nearest hatch, the one she didn't know led to the ravine.

"Wait, stop!" I shouted.

She opened it, about to step through, and my breath caught as she teetered right at the edge, arms floundering in the mist and the wind and the roar and the ringing of the metal. But she managed to catch her balance against the frame of the hatch before she fell.

"Be careful." I sighed as I stood. "Part of the mountain collapsed."

"I can see that." She leaned out to look down and then glanced back at me. She tossed the kobold out into the ravine.

"No!" I shouted.

But it was gone.

She stood up tall and lifted her head, like she was waiting for me to yell at her so she could say she'd done nothing wrong. But I couldn't speak, and after a few moments went by, she shut the hatch, pushing us into silence.

I blinked at tears, searching for words to express my rage, my loss, my confusion, my sadness. I finally settled on, "That's how I know I'm not you. I would never have done that."

She exhaled, almost a gasp, like I had just punched her the way she had punched me.

"Why?" I spread my hands wide, shaking my head. "Why do you have to take everything from me?"

She swallowed. "I— I'm not—"

"You are!" I pressed all the fingers of both hands hard against my chest. "I don't get to go home! It doesn't matter what you say—I'm redundant. I don't get Magical Mountain, or Avery, or Pop-Pop's spaghetti, or any of it! I don't get Mom and Dad! And you just threw away the one piece of—"

"Jessica, stop. You have it all wrong." She stepped toward me. "I'm giving you all of that. I'm giving you everything."

That brought my rant to a halt. "What?"

"I'm not going home." She looked directly into my eyes. "You are. That's the whole reason I printed you."

I didn't trust her, especially after what she had just done, and I was still looking for the lie, the trick. "I— I don't understand."

"I know." She laughed, but sounded weak and exhausted. "That's kind of the whole point. I don't want you to have all the . . ."

"All the what?"

She closed her eyes, grabbed her hair at the side of her head into a tight fist and pressed hard against it. "All the shit in here."

"What shit?"

Her eyes flew open. "Why do you think I haven't told you? I don't want it to be in your head, too! You're me before it all happened. And I want you to stay that way for when you go home."

That was when I finally realized what she really wanted from me. She was using me as a way to erase the memories that she didn't want, making it so what happened didn't happen.

I had to sit down under the weight of all the things that were finally starting to make sense. But not really make sense. I understood why she had printed me, at least. I certainly wished I could go back to when I was eleven years old and erase the pain of my parents leaving me, and if

I had gone through whatever she went through on the *Theseus*, I might have printed me, too. But it was a doomed and terrible idea from the beginning because ISTA would never let it happen, and I also knew I couldn't be what she wanted me to be, because what she really wanted was to *be* me.

"Jessica," I said, hands clasped in my lap, "please, listen to me. I am not you—"

"Stop saying that! You are!"

"But I'm not. Maybe I was in the beginning. Maybe I wasn't—I don't know. I only know I'm me now. And I'm not you."

"That doesn't make any sense. You just woke up a few days ago. How can you possibly be that different?"

"How long did it take for you?"

She didn't answer that, but she didn't need to.

"After you abandoned me, I went through my own shit." I tapped the side of my head. "It's all in here. I've been through things and seen things that you haven't."

She drew closer to me. "I'm sorry. I should have stayed to protect you."

"But that's ridiculous. How can you protect me? We're on an alien planet. And that's not even my point."

"Then what is your point?"

I sighed. "My point is, you've been through shit, and I've been through shit. Shit will always happen, and you can't stop it." I glanced over at the computer terminal. "But the truth is, it's not even worth arguing about."

"Why not?"

"Because I don't think either of us will be leaving Hades. ISTA is probably going to reestablish us back on Earth from our first scan."

"What?" She started to shake her head but stopped, and she seemed to be thinking about what I had just said. "But they can't do that . . ."

"You know they can. Duncan says there are some other possibilities. They might still send a ship to come get us and teleport us home. But I'm not very hopeful, and I don't think he is, either."

She dropped into a chair near me, eyes vacant, head a bit wobbly. "Well shit."

"We'll see. Maybe ISTA will surprise us."

"I don't think ISTA surprises are ever the good kind."

"That's probably true."

She sat forward in her chair in a posture that mirrored mine and stared straight ahead, with occasional glances at me, until she finally said, almost with a laugh, "This is pretty fucked up. Isn't it."

"Yup."

"So now what?"

I wanted to say I had no idea. And why was she asking me, because this was all her fault. This was her plan that was never going to work. But instead I just shrugged. "I'm not sure we have much of a choice. Until ISTA decides what they're going to do with us, we have to figure out how to live with each other."

Her reply came after a long silence. "I guess you're right."

I don't know if she really agreed with me, but I didn't care, and I was done talking about it. I needed space from her. "Are you hungry?" I asked.

"Probably."

"There's food. You should eat."

"What are you going to do?"

"I think I just need to be by myself for a bit." I got up from my chair and walked away, ignoring something she started to say but didn't finish.

I marched toward the hatch that led into the sleeping module, but I didn't go to my room. That wasn't far enough away from her, because the more I thought about everything she had said, the angrier I felt. She thought she could decide who I was. She thought she knew who I was, but she didn't even ask about what I went through.

I kept moving, into the lab module. Then I went to sit at Duncan's desk, and I put my head down in front of the computer terminal, surrounded by electronic parts. Eventually, I turned the computer on and started recording.

I know what I went through, and I know it mattered. I don't understand everything that happened. I don't know exactly what it all meant. But I know it happened to *me*. It's my story. It's what makes me different from her, even if she won't see it. And she has her own story. And both our stories make us different from the Jessica back on Earth that ISTA might already be printing.

But maybe all our stories can go together somehow to make us who we are to each other.

One Jessica.

I MAKE MYSELF EAT, AND THEN I LIE DOWN ON THE floor and look up at the domed ceiling, fingers linked over my stomach. The food isn't sitting well, but nothing sits well anymore. Especially not what she just told me. Like how different she says we are. I mean, I know we're different. That's kind of the whole point. But I don't see how she can be that different from who I was when I first woke up on the *Theseus*. She is still me.

The afternoon light coming in is yellow and warm. I'm sure the habitat has beds somewhere, but I'm too exhausted to go looking for them, and the floor isn't much different from the ground where I've spent the past few nights. I don't even plan to sleep, but before long, my eyes are trying to close, and I let them.

When I open them again, the room and the windows are dark, but there's a knife of sharp light slicing the floor in half from a hatch that just opened, which must be what woke me up. Apparently, she has returned from wherever she went to be by herself, and her shadow passes over me as she approaches and taps my boot with the toe of hers.

"Wake up," she says. "Have you seen Duncan?"

"No." I sit up. "How long have I been out?"

"Hours."

"What have you been doing?"

She doesn't answer right away. "Thinking. I lost track of time." She leaves my side, and a moment later the room's lights switch on, making me squint until my eyes adjust. I remember what she said as we watched Duncan drive away outside the habitat, but I still don't understand.

I get to my feet. "Why do we need perimeter sensors?"

"To let us know if something is close to the habitat."

"Obviously. But what kind of something?"

She opens the external hatch and steps into the air lock without answering me. Then she's gone, and I'm left alone in the silence of the common room.

She probably believes I deserve to have my questions ignored for hiding things from her, and maybe I do. But she seems worried about Duncan, so I follow her outside into the night.

A chilly wind is sliding down the mountain behind us, over and around the habitat's domes, and it carries the waterfall's mist along the edge of the ravine in ghostly billows. Where we stand, just outside the air lock, we're mostly sheltered from the breeze, but I don't think that's why neither of us strays very far from the hatch. The light of the habitat falls on our backs and not much farther. Beyond it, Hades is a featureless black sea all the way to the horizon, and the stars are the only way I can tell where the land stops and the sky starts.

"I was hoping we could see his headlights or something." She stands with her feet apart, hands on her hips. "Do you see anything?"

"No, I don't."

She points up into the sky. "Do you remember the name of that constellation?"

"It's not a constellation."

"It has a story."

"Are you really going to make me ask again?"

"Ask what?"

"What is out there?" I face her, but I keep glancing at the darkness. "Why do you need perimeter sensors?"

She puts her hands in her pockets and glances down for a moment. "We don't know what it is. But it's not a ferret. It's as big as a human.

Duncan saw it when he came back from the lander. I saw it in the underground city."

It takes me a second to register that last part. "The *what*?"

"The underground city. Which you would already know about if you had asked me about what I've been through."

I hadn't asked because I didn't think it mattered. I didn't want it to matter. But maybe it does. "I guess I'm asking now."

She makes me wait a bit longer. Then she tells me a story about falling into an underground lake and finding a buried alien city filled with towers of bones, and I want to call her a liar. I want to tell her that if the planet had anything like that, it would have been in the reports Dad put together for me, that not even an ISTA survey could miss something that big. But I don't have that kind of faith in ISTA anymore. Then she says she saw something down there, an alien. It all sounds unbelievable, impossible.

"Did you, uh, tell Duncan about all this?"

"Yes." I can tell that she's glaring at me, even though most of her face is in shadow. "Why? You don't think he'd believe me?"

"No, I just—"

"I'm not making this up. And he saw the alien, too." She gestured at the landscape below us. "You think he'd go out there to work on the sensors for no reason?"

"No, I guess not."

"Okay, then."

She's acting like that settles the matter, and I'm fine letting her think that, because the more important thing right now is to figure out where Duncan is.

"Is there a way we can contact him?" I ask. "Like a radio or something?"

She seems to think about that for a few seconds. "Maybe. I saw him with a radio once before, and there might be a radio on the rover."

She turns and goes back into the habitat, and I follow her. She secures the hatch behind us, and then she looks around the common room. When she doesn't find whatever she's looking for there, we leave through another hatch that leads into the next module, past what I assume are the sleeping quarters. We make a turn and enter a storage room filled with a maze of stacked boxes and crates. It's colder in here, and I smell fresh Hades air.

"Oh no," she says, and she rushes over to a wide-open roller door.

I see some dirt and tire tracks on the module's floor nearby. "I guess this is where you park the rover."

"Yeah." She reaches up and grabs a cord, and then lets her knees bend to pull the door down with her body weight. "We forgot to close this earlier."

"Is that a big deal?"

"It is if we want to keep things out."

The door rattles overhead, and after it slams closed, she slides a bolt near the floor with her foot to lock it. Then she weaves back through the crates to where I'm standing, in a clearing where several containers have been opened, their contents spread on the floor. She looks around, and then she spots something and bends to pick it up.

"Here we go." She turns a small radio over in her hands, studying it. "I don't know how to—"

"Can I see it?"

She frowns at me for a few seconds before offering it to me, like she's skeptical and wants to know how I know about radios when she doesn't. But I am not going to answer that question, so before she can ask it, I find the dial-switch that turns the radio on.

As soon as I do, the thing shrieks in my hand with a piercing siren, and I'm so startled by the sound that I fumble the radio and almost drop it. I hurry to turn the volume down, but the wailing goes on, like somebody's distant car alarm.

"Why is it doing that?" I ask.

She's staring at the device in my hands, holding still, not blinking. "Before, he—" she says, but something seems to catch in her throat, and she swallows. "Before I got here, Duncan linked the sensors to the radio. But once I logged into the computer system, he needed to recalibrate them. That's why he went out in the rover."

Now I look at the device in my hands. "So is it doing this because Duncan is out there messing with stuff? Or did something cross the perimeter?"

"He—he didn't really explain it."

I still don't know what she and Duncan saw, but if Duncan felt the need for a security system, then I'm going to take it seriously. "This could have been going off for a while."

She nods, but her shoulders are riding high, and her head is low, and she's looking all around us like a skittish animal.

"I'm sure it's just a glitch," I say, trying to reassure her, even though I have zero confidence that what I'm saying is true. "Let's go figure this out in the common room. It's warmer in there."

"Okay."

Now she's the one following me back through the sleeping quarters. My mouth has dried up, and my palms are sweating against the radio's plastic shell. Even turned down, the siren is starting to feel like a drill in my ears. I want to turn the thing off, but I know that silencing a smoke alarm doesn't make the fire go away, and I think it's probably better to know.

When we reach the common room, she goes to make sure the front hatch is secure, even though she already locked it, and then she turns and asks, "What about Duncan?"

The radio has twenty channels, which isn't too many to check, even if I have to try every frequency. The alarm goes quiet as I leave that channel to switch between the others, and a soft hiss replaces the wailing, somehow sounding just as ominous.

I walk over to the table and sit down, resting my arms on the smooth metal surface, and on each channel, I press the button and say, "Duncan? Are you there?"

Then I wait. Then I say the same thing again. And then I say it a third time before I try the next frequency. I cycle through a dozen of them, and each time I'm afraid of hearing something that isn't Duncan on the other end.

She paces around me while I work, hugging herself and rubbing her arms like she's still cold. As I watch her, I decide she's not faking her terror, which means that she probably believes she saw everything she said she saw. Even though I don't want to fully join her in that belief just yet, I'm starting to.

On the eighteenth channel, on my second try, we finally get a reply.

"Duncan?" I say, and she's at my side, leaning over the table even before I can ask, "Is that you?"

"It's me," he says, sounding crackly and distant. "Are you both okay? Over."

"We're fine," she says at my shoulder, leaning in close, but he can't hear because I'm not holding down the button to talk.

"We're okay," I say. "Where are you? Over."

"I'm stuck out here for the night," he says. "It's my fault. I was distracted and not paying attention. Battery ran out of juice. It was too dark to try walking back. Over."

I assume I was the distraction, his anger at me when he left. "No, that's my fault. I'm sorry, Duncan." I paused, not wanting to say more than that with her listening. "So what are you going to do? Over."

"I'll sleep here," he says. "It's not too cold. I was dozing off when I heard you over the radio. Good thinking, by the way."

"Duncan?" she says, leaning in close to the radio.

I scowl at her. "I have to press the button for him to hear you. What is it?"

"I just want to know how he'll get back tomorrow," she says, her voice low.

I press the button. "Duncan, can you charge the battery? Do you have to walk back?"

"There's an emergency solar panel," he says. "I'll set that up at first light. Should get me back by early afternoon. Over."

"Ask him if he's really okay," she says.

I already did, but I ask again, for her sake. "Are you sure you'll be okay out there tonight? Over."

"Yes, I'll be fine," he says, but I think I hear some doubt and fear in his voice. "I'm pretty hungry, though. And I'm sure I'll be sore in the morning from spending the night cramped in this seat. But I'll live. Over."

"We'll stay on this channel," I say. "If you need anything, call us. You copy?"

"I copy," he says. "But you guys just try to get some sleep. No sense staying up and worrying."

"Okay," I say. "But, Duncan? There's one more thing. An alarm is going off on the radio. Is that something you did? Over."

The radio hisses softly. "Let me check that channel on my end. Stand by."

He's gone for a few moments, and we both lean toward the little speaker, staring at it while we wait in static.

"That isn't from the recalibration." His voice is sudden and loud when he returns. "Something crossed the perimeter before I switched the sensors over to the new system. But it's possible I tripped it by accident. Over."

"Possible?" I ask. "Over."

"Yeah," he says. "That's probably what it is, but just to be on the safe side, make sure the habitat is locked down. Check the storage module. I think we left the rover door open. Over."

"We took care of that," I say. "We're secure here. Over."

"Good, then you've got nothing to worry about," he says. "It would take an industrial cutter to get through the habitat's carbon-fiber shell. But call me if anything else does happen. I'll see you soon. Over."

"See you soon," I say, but I feel her leaning in, so I hold the radio closer to her, wondering if he can tell which of us is which.

"Good night, Duncan," she says. "Call us if you need us. Over."

"I will. Duncan out."

The line goes back to hissing, and then to silent idle.

"Do you feel better?" I ask her.

She pushes off from the table. "Not really. He's still out there, and the alien is out there with him."

I stay in my chair and set the radio on the table. "I know you just met Duncan. But trust me. He is very capable. I'm sure he'll be okay, and we're safe in here."

Instead of saying something in response, she marches over and checks the air lock hatch again. There's probably a part of me that would do the same, but since she's doing it, I don't have to. I don't have to care about anything as long as she's safe, or at least, that's what I thought until she told me ISTA might leave us both here. That was a possibility I never considered when I came up with this idea, and I feel pretty stupid for not thinking of it. But until we get an official response from ISTA, nothing has changed. I just have to stick around longer than I planned.

"There's no way I'm getting any sleep tonight," she says. "What about you? Are you . . . sleeping better?"

She's talking about the nightmares. I thought they might stop once I printed her, but they haven't. I'm still angry she saw that, but I am not going to talk about it with her, and I give her a backhanded wave. "Don't worry about me."

She walks over, right toward me in a determined way, and I ready myself to defend against her annoying questions and demands. But she doesn't say anything. Instead, she leans down and pulls me into a hug, her cheek on the back of my shoulder. I freeze.

"I'm sorry," she says.

"For what?"

"For what happened to you. What you went through. In a weird way, I wish I had been there."

"What?" I shrug out of her arms and stand up. "Why?"

"So—so we could go through it together." Her hands are still out-stretched, awkwardly. "You know, be there for—"

"Are you serious?" I step away from her, not sure if I want to laugh, cry, or punch her again. "What aren't you getting? I did this so you wouldn't have to go through what I went through. How many times do I have to explain this—"

"You don't have to explain it. I get why you did it."

"Then what is your problem?"

"I don't have a problem." Her hands fall to her sides. "You do. Because it doesn't matter how many times you explain it to me, you're never going to be right."

I shake my head, rage swelling inside me. "Then it's a good thing I don't actually need you to agree or understand. You just have to be you, so you can be me."

"But it doesn't work that way!" she shouts. "Don't you think I wish it did?"

"Do you?"

"Of course I do! Don't you think I would go back and be who I was before Mom and Dad—" She stops, and her bottom lip quivers. "Before they left? You, of all people, should know that . . ."

Her voice trails off like something is squeezing the air out of her chest, and her pain puts out the fire of my anger in an instant, because that was my pain, too. It still is when I look deep enough, but less so now.

I step closer to her. "I know you think we're different, but in this way, I promise you, we are the same. They left both of us."

She sniffs and nods. "I know that."

I act on an impulse, maybe the same impulse that drove her just a few moments ago, and I reach out to put my arms around her. Now she's the one who goes rigid, but only for a moment. Then she relaxes, and I feel her hands on my back.

"They didn't leave because of you," I say into her jumpsuit's collar.

"They didn't stay because of me, either."

"It had nothing to do with you." I lean out of the hug to look directly at her, at myself, wishing I could go back and say this same thing to eleven-year-old me. "They were selfish, okay? Ask anyone. They made a selfish decision that had nothing to do with you, and you need to believe that."

She has tears sitting on the edges of her eyelids. "Do you believe that?"

"Almost. Maybe if I hear it that you do."

She wipes her nose. "It had nothing to do with you."

I lower my chin. "Or you?"

A few seconds go by. "Or me."

"There. Now I believe it."

She nods, and the corners of her mouth turn up, just barely, and I envy her even that small amount of relief.

I let her go, and as I watch her dab her eyes with her sleeve, I feel for the first time that it might be possible for us to live together, but I also know what that will require of me. I'm tempted to get it over with right now, and finally confess the truth of what happened on the *Theseus*, because I don't know how much longer I can suffocate under the weight of it all.

I don't like hiding things from her. I don't want to hide things from her. I want to trust her. But as soon as the words start to take shape in my mind, to actually say the things I'm hiding, panic seizes me. Everything freezes up, my tongue, my thoughts, even time seems to get stuck. I'm perched at the edge of the cliff, one foot in the air. All I have to do is lean forward, and there's no going back. Like when I used to imagine telling Avery how I felt, only this is much worse.

"What now?" she says.

"Now?" The word comes out like I'm asking what it means.

"Yeah, what should we do now?" She glances at the radio where it rests on the table. "I think I'm going to eat something, and then I think I'm going to do what Duncan suggested and try to sleep. You?"

Her question wrenches me back from the edge and pulls me into the next moment where I would never even think of telling her anything. My confession can wait for another time. "I guess I could eat," I say.

We heat up some ration packages, and I finish mine first. She's taking longer to eat her eggs, which reminds me of her pet.

"You know," I say, "that mole-snake of yours was hanging out by your backpack."

"He was?"

"I warned you about feeding him. He followed me the whole way here."

"Really?"

I glance at the air lock. "I'm sure he's out there somewhere close by."

"And he followed you?"

"I think he thought I was you."

"Did you feed him?"

She's grinning at me like she already knows the answer, and I decide to let her have the victory. "I gave him some scraps," I say.

She keeps smiling until she's finished her eggs. Then I grab the radio, and we leave the common room through the hatch that leads into the sleeping module. She directs me to one of the empty rooms, and then she points at another nearby.

"That one is mine," she says. "Just in case."

I assume she's thinking about the night we shared a bed on the lander, but she leaves that unsaid. I give her a nod. "Good to know. I'll keep the radio with me and let you know if Duncan calls again."

"Okay."

She goes into her room, and I go into mine, and we both close our hatches. The bed is a bit softer than what they had on the *Theseus*, and the room is much bigger. It's comfortable enough that if things had gone the way they were supposed to, I would not have been completely miserable calling it my bedroom for a year. But that doesn't matter much now.

I lie down facing the door and set the radio on the mattress next to me, in easy reach. I don't expect to fall asleep quickly, since I just woke up from a nap a short while ago, but before long, I do.

Her scream wakes me up.

I JOLT AWAKE.

I'm facing the wall, but my body knows something is wrong. My muscles are all tense and burning, and I feel my heart thumping in my throat. The habitat is quiet, but I know I heard my hatch open, and now there's someone, or something, in the room with me.

I roll over to face it, and I recognize the terrifying silhouette of the alien looming in the doorway. I scream as it advances toward me. But in the next moment I see the figure more clearly, and I'm stunned into silence.

"Dad?" I whisper. But it can't be him. "How—"

He leaps on top of me, and before I can react, his hands are around my neck, choking me. He squeezes hard, his fingernails digging into my skin, and I can't get air in or out. I feel a popping and crunching in my throat. I try to spit words out, begging him to stop, but he doesn't. He's staring down at me, face half-concealed in shadow, skin like water-stained leather, eyes so cold and vacant I'm not even sure that he sees me.

This is a nightmare. I need to wake up.

But my body screams this is real. My vision is fading, and every-thing is going cold, like I'm back in the narrow shaft above the ringing tower, trying to claw my way to the surface, but I know I'm not going to make it out this time. I thrash, hitting his arms and his head with my fists, but my blows are weak and pointless.

Then I see another figure rise up behind him, and I hear a loud crack. His head falls forward, and he grunts, then releases me. His weight leaves my chest, and I gasp and gurgle. The shape of my throat feels wrong in my hands. I can barely get air in, like I'm breathing through a straw.

She's holding something in her hand, the radio, or part of the radio, ready to strike again. He spins to face her, blood on the back of his head, growling. When she sees his face, she almost seems to collapse.

"No." She shakes her head without taking her eyes off him. "Not—"

He lunges toward her, and she flees from the room. I hear their footsteps thudding down the corridor, her screams, and then the hatch into the common room opens.

I stagger out of my bed, clutching my throat. I taste blood. I can barely breathe. But I force myself to follow them, bumping along the walls, still trapped inside the underground shaft.

When I get to the common room, I see he has her cornered on the far side, near the hatch that opens out to the ravine. She's up against the wall, but holding a chair over her head, ready to smash him with it if he comes closer. That seems to have stopped him for the moment, only a few paces away from her and the hatch. She looks over at me as I stagger toward them.

"What are you doing?" she shouts at me. "Get out of here!"

But I'm not going to leave her, and I don't know how far I would get even if I tried. I still can't breathe. The shaft is tightening, the light too dim and far away. I stumble closer, and my dad turns his head to look at me, but also not look at me, and the empty way he's staring gives me an idea.

I point at the hatch and call out to her, but my voice won't work. It comes out a mangled wheezing sound, and when I try again, louder, my dad turns his body to face me instead of her.

"No!" she screams.

She's about to charge at him from behind with the chair, but I wave for her to stop, and I point at the hatch again. I try to say the word, but all I can get out is the last sound. But it seems to be enough because she stops and looks at the doorway. I nod as vigorously as I can, and even though she seems confused, she rushes to the hatch and opens it.

Outside, the night is black, and the roaring of the falls and the ringing of the metal fill the room, stopping my dad like he hit a wall. He swings around from me to face the opening, distracted, overwhelmed, and I know I was right. He was down in that underground world with me, and a tangled mess of squiggly lines is all he can see.

I can't feel my legs anymore. My throat is swelling shut. I'm about to pass out, so I use the few seconds I have left to rush him. It's not a fast rush, but it's hard, like a fall. I feel like I've slipped in the shaft, and now I'm careening down it, back into the alien city, back into the dark.

I slam into him from behind, and he gasps, too stunned to do anything about it. I drive him forward with my shoulder, straight toward the hatch just a few paces away, and he trips along with me. He doesn't even put out his hands to catch himself when we reach the ledge. He just goes right over it, out into the ravine.

I've got too much inertia behind me, and I'm going over too, but I feel her grab for me. She snags a pocket of my jumpsuit, and as I fall, I twist and hit the rocks and the remains of the module hanging below the habitat. I'm dangling, getting soaked by the mist from the waterfall, and when I look up, I can see she's already halfway out of the hatch and still slipping. If she holds on, we'll both fall.

My throat can't make a sound, and I don't have the words. But I know she has to let me go. I grab her hand and pry her fingers from my jumpsuit, just like I tried to pry the kobold away, but this time, her hands are wet and slick.

"Stop!" she screams, but she sounds far away. "What are you doing?"

I break free of her. My face and chest smash against rock, and then I tumble into an icy, grinding torrent of water and wind and

# 30 — Hades

## AFTER

I WATCHED HER BODY PINWHEEL AND VANISH INTO the mist. I couldn't hear anything over the roar of the falls and the ringing of the metal scraps, but I knelt there and sobbed her name into the ravine for a long time, like I was pleading with her. I don't know what I was begging her for, or even who I was begging, because I knew she was gone.

After I had worn my voice out, and my face had gone numb in the cold spray, I stood and stepped right up to the ledge, ready to follow her. I couldn't be alone again in the prison of my own head, and that would force ISTA to reestablish me back on Earth. I just had to take one more big leap. But I made the mistake of looking down first, and the height gave me an automatic twist of vertigo. Then some survival instinct rebelled, holding me back just long enough to think of Duncan.

I realized that if I was gone, and she was gone, then he wouldn't know what happened. Even worse than that, I knew he would probably blame himself for driving off and leaving me a second time, and I couldn't do that to him. I couldn't leave him all alone on this planet without an explanation. I had made a promise. But I'd smashed the radio, so I couldn't call him.

That's why I came over to the computer. I was going to leave a message for Duncan. That's all. But when I logged in, I saw her recent activity, and her recording showed up as a new file. I decided I needed to listen to it. And now I'm adding my story to it, because I've realized she was right.

I tried to pretend that what she went through didn't matter, because

I didn't want it to matter, but now I know it does. And what I went through matters. Because if Amira was right about time and quantum ghosts, then maybe I am all my past selves, and my future selves, and my possible selves, all at once. Maybe it's like that "Star-splitter" poem. If you look closely enough, maybe we're not just one star. Maybe we're all constellations, and we only make sense if you listen to the stories, and tell the stories, and write new ones.

I wish so badly that I had told her everything when I had the chance, but I was scared, and ashamed. I'm still scared. I'm terrified, actually, especially when I think about what Duncan will say when he learns the truth. I mean the whole truth.

But she had a right to know, and I guess this is my way of telling her.

The truth is, I killed the crew of the *Theseus*. I didn't mean to. But I knew what I was doing, and they are broken because of me. I want to be clear—my mom didn't mean for any of it to happen, either. She thought her plan would work.

So did I.

## BEFORE

AN ALARM WENT OFF ALMOST IMMEDIATELY, A SIREN like an ambulance or a fire truck, and then the captain's voice cut in over the comm.

"Code red," she said, sounding much calmer than I would've been if my ship had just stopped working. "Designated emergency crew members will report to your stations. Everyone else, secure yourselves where you are and report your status to the Belfry. If you are experiencing a medical emergency, responders will come to you. I repeat: This is a code red. Stick to your protocols, and we'll get through it. Captain Sharpe out."

The alarm returned as soon as she stopped talking, but I noticed she hadn't said anything about a security threat. I hoped that meant she hadn't learned yet that it was my mom who had sabotaged her ship and freed my dad, but I knew that secrecy couldn't last much longer. The brig was right by the Belfry.

I was still anchored to the ladder, so all I could do was stare at the hatch as the minutes stretched way too long. I expected to see my mom come flying in at any moment, tugging my dad behind her. But she never came, and a few minutes later, the captain came back over the comm sounding much less calm, and a lot angrier.

"Attention! All personnel! We have a security threat, level one. I repeat: We have a security threat, level one. All personnel will initiate lockdown measures. If you see Dr. Mathers or Dr. Havilland, retreat and report their location to the Belfry. Do not engage. I repeat: Do not engage. Captain out."

I ripped the sheet from around my waist. Then I hauled myself up the ladder to poke my head into the corridor. I didn't see or hear any-one coming, but I knew the captain would be on her way toward our lander, with tasers or worse, and I was there alone.

I risked beeping my mom over the radio. "Where are you?" I said, my whisper loud and desperate. "Mom, are you there?"

"Jessica, be quiet," she said, but I could barely hear her, and she sounded different. Her hushed voice had a high-pitched edge, like a mouse. "Stephen . . . got loose. He—he attacked me—"

"Attacked you?"

"Be quiet!" she said. "He's . . . looking for me."

I had never heard her sound so fragile, so frightened, so small.

"Sweetie, I—I love you," she said. "I'm hurt . . . I think it's bad. And I was wrong, that—that is not your father. Don't let them say it was your father."

"Hurt how?" I couldn't help asking, but I forgot to press the button, so she didn't hear me.

"You need to hide," she said. "Don't worry about me. Lock yourself in the lander. The captain needs to—"

The channel went dead.

I cradled the radio in both hands like it was an injured animal. I waited for her voice to come back. I wanted to call her, but I worried she was hiding from my dad, and I didn't want my voice to give her away. Then a tortured screech erupted from the little speaker, and I didn't know what was going on, until I realized the sound was coming from my mom. She was screaming, but I had never heard a human make a sound like that. She must have clenched her fist in pain and pressed the button on the radio. Her shrieks went on and on, with horrible ripping and popping noises behind it.

Then the radio went dead, and a sudden avalanche of silence buried me. I could hardly breathe, and when I finally let myself press the but-ton, I had almost no voice.

"Mom?"

No reply came. Just the shush of static.

"Mom, are you there? Over."

The silence wore on, and the longer it lasted, the heavier it weighed on me. She was gone, and the memory of her screams still rattled my bones, wrenched my guts.

Then I heard something down one of the corridors, and I panicked. My mom had told me to hide, so I dove back into the lander and locked the hatch, sure that my dad had come looking for me. I imagined him drawing closer, covered in whatever he had done to my mom. I flinched at a knocking and banging sound as someone repeatedly tried to open the door. Then a loud voice bellowed over the comm inside the small ship.

"This is Captain Sharpe. Dr. Havilland? Jessica? I know you're in there." She paused, but not for long. "Listen to me very carefully. This path will not end well for you. Do you really think you can lock me out of my own lander? We'll cut our way in if we have to."

I wanted to open the hatch to warn her about my dad, but I was so frightened and shocked by what he had done to my mom that I couldn't even think in words. So I didn't say anything. I didn't do anything. I tried to be small, to stay hidden.

The captain made a few more threats over the comm before she either gave up or got called somewhere else. I stayed near the hatch because I had to know if my dad tried to get in. But then I started to think maybe he had somehow already gotten inside with me, that he was lurking somewhere. I couldn't shake that idea, so I ended up cowering in a corner, eyes wide, covering my ears to keep out the screaming that wouldn't stop in my head. I lost track of time. I lost track of everything, but at one point, I heard the captain call a code orange in the hub, and I didn't know what that meant.

A while later, her voice came back over the comm again, but she didn't call any codes.

"Attention, all personnel!" she said. "This is Captain Sharpe. I hereby give the order to abandon ship. This is not a drill. Abandon ship. The reactor has failed. I repeat: The reactor has failed. All personnel will proceed to *Lander Two*. *Lander One* is not accessible. Proceed to *Lander Two* for immediate evacuation."

She said that because I had locked them out of *Lander One*. I was the reason it wasn't accessible.

"Do not enter the hub," the captain went on. "I repeat: Do not enter the hub. Find alternate routes to *Lander Two*. You have twelve minutes. I repeat: You have twelve minutes to board *Lander Two*."

The comm went quiet, but I didn't move. I felt detached from my body. Nothing had seemed quite real since my mom's screaming. It was as if I had lost my center of gravity, just like the *Theseus*. I'd heard the captain's words. Something had happened to the ship. The reactor was failing. That meant radiation, or an explosion maybe. But none of those words meant anything to me.

The captain's voice over the comm returned, now ten minutes until evacuation. She repeated her orders, calling all personnel to *Lander Two*, and I gradually became aware of what I had done.

They thought they had a lifeboat. But I had sabotaged it with the micro drive in my pocket.

That finally roused me. I pulled myself up the ladder to the hatch, but I was so terrified of seeing my dad on the other side with his empty eyes and his snarling face that it took me at least another minute to find the courage to open it. When I finally did, I smelled burning rubber and climbed into a thick, black haze that burned my eyes and my throat. The ship was on fire.

I coughed and covered my mouth with my sleeve. Red emergency lights strobed and spun in the smoke as I flew toward the other lander, gasping, my eyes watering and half shut. I got disoriented and took a couple of wrong turns, flapping and bumping hard into the walls the whole way, and something in the caustic air made me dizzy.

When *Lander Two*'s hatch finally came into view, I saw a shadowy figure hovering near it, and I jittered to a stop with my heels against the floor.

"Who is that?" Evan said. "Mathers, is that you?"

"Yes!" I said, my voice a ragged croak. "It's me!"

He coughed and waved me toward him. "Hurry up!"

I launched myself forward, but I misjudged the speed and distance, and I collided with him. His elbow hit my jaw, and we both grunted, but he managed to wrestle me into formation and send me down the hatch. I dropped into the lander feeling stunned and confused, and before I had my bearings, the captain flew right at me.

"Where's Duncan?" she asked.

It took a moment to realize she was talking to me. "I—I don't know," I said, blinking. "Why—"

"He was coming to get you!" she said. "He left against my orders!"

Guilt hollowed me out. "I'm sorry, Captain, I didn't mean for anyone to—"

"Duncan," the captain said into her comm. "Son, report. Where are you?"

"Captain." Evan's head poked down through the hatch. "We've got three minutes."

She gave him a tense nod, and she seemed about to bellow into her comm a second time when Duncan's voice came back.

"I'm on *Lander One*," he said. "The hatch was open. But Jessica's gone."

The captain scowled at me. "That's because she's here."

"Wait, she's there?" I heard his sigh of relief as a crackle through the speaker. "I'll be right back. I can—"

"There's no time." The captain closed her eyes and pressed her forehead into the crook of her thumb. "You'll have to evacuate on *Lander One*. Do you remember what you're supposed to do?"

"Yes."

"Get started," she said. "Call me if you run into any trouble." Then she opened her comm ship-wide. "Attention, all personnel! This is the final warning. You have two minutes until evacuation. *Lander One* is now available. Board either lander immediately. You have two minutes."

I looked around to see who was already there, who else blamed me. I saw Amira floating next to Liz, holding her close. Amira was crying, pressing a blood-soaked towel against a gaping wound in Liz's side. But Liz did not appear conscious, or even alive. Hundreds of glistening red pearls hung in the air around them, and I didn't know if my dad had attacked Liz, or if she had suffered some other accident.

I gripped the micro drive in my pocket. "Where is everyone else?" I asked.

The captain ignored me and soared up to the top of the ladder. "Mr. Martin," she said, peering through the hatch. "We need you in the cockpit now. It's time. I don't think anyone else is coming."

She moved aside, and a moment later Evan dove into the lander, his jaw clenched. Then he kicked off down the corridor, leaving the metal rungs of the ladder vibrating. The captain stayed where she was, watching the hatch and the time despite what she had just told him.

"Where is everyone else?" I asked again.

Amira answered me, barely above a whisper. "They're all broken. Trapped or poisoned by the fire. Or they—" She stopped and looked down at Liz's side. Droplets of floating blood polka-dotted their jumpsuits.

"I'm sorry," I whispered, thinking about all those people, and their suffering, and their fear. "I'm so sorry."

"It is not your fault," Amira said.

I looked away. Her trust in me turned my shame into something I couldn't even face.

"Our grief will have to wait." The captain pulled the hatch shut and locked it in the same way I had locked *Lander One.* Then she spoke into her comm. "Duncan, status report."

"Still here," he said. "I had a slight delay."

The captain frowned. "Elaborate."

"I could've sworn I closed the main hatch, but it was still open. I'm initiating the launch sequence now. Looks like they had the ship ready to go."

"Good," the captain said, but the glare she gave me felt accusatory. "We'll see you down on the surface, son. I love you. Fly safely."

"I love you, too. Duncan out."

I knew Evan would be initiating the launch sequence for our lander, too. Any moment, I expected him to call the captain to inform her of a problem with the docking gear, and I had the solution in my pocket.

But I was a coward.

A lot of people had broken horrifically because of me. Liz's body was still leaking blood into the air. And if I pulled out that drive, I would have to confess what I had done, and everyone would know it was all my fault.

So I left the micro drive in my pocket, and when Evan called the captain up to the cockpit, I said nothing and hoped that maybe my mom's hack would fail, or maybe Evan would be smarter than my mom and figure out how to stop it. And if he didn't, then I would break, too, and we would all wake up back on Earth, reestablished, and everything that had happened would be like a nightmare we couldn't remember. Or at least, that's what I hoped. But then the lander shook all around us, violently, and I heard metal squealing. It got so loud I had to cover my ears, and then it just stopped, and everything went still.

A few moments later, the captain came back. She explained that the docking mechanism had malfunctioned, but Evan had somehow torn us free of the *Theseus*. We were clear of the radiation danger, but the lander had suffered catastrophic damage. We would have to make an emergency descent, which would be very dangerous.

I nodded along through everything she said, trying to tell myself the drive in my pocket no longer mattered. Then the captain asked me to follow her.

I didn't know what was happening, but she led me to the rear section of the lander, into a room with a body printer. She walked over and leaned against it with her back to me, arms planted wide, hands flat against the glass. Her body shook for a few seconds, and I realized she was crying, but she had it under control when she spoke.

"I don't know what happened to my ship," she said, head bowed so low I could barely see it over her shoulders. "I don't know what your mother did. I don't know what part you played in her scheme. At this point, I don't care. I only know that someone needs to contact ISTA to give them the names of the broken so they can be reestablished. I have decided that someone will be you."

I did not want that responsibility and I wasn't worthy of her trust. "What happens if no one contacts ISTA?"

"Without official confirmation, we go into limbo." She dipped her head even lower, shaking it. "Fucking bureaucratic red tape limbo." Then she stood up straight and hit some buttons on the printer's control panel. The lid popped open with a familiar hiss of air, and she turned to face me. "Get inside," she said.

"What?"

"The printer is the safest place to be during an emergency landing. It's durable. It's contained. It's practically an escape pod."

"But why me? What about you? Or Amira? I don't deserve—"

"Stop." She took a step toward me. "This isn't because you deserve it. This is because I'm not leaving my engineer to fly this ship without his captain. This is because I'm not leaving my liaison alone holding the broken body of someone very important to her. And this is because neither of them would take this spot from a seventeen-year-old kid. No matter what she's done."

"They would if they knew—"

"Jessica, please! There isn't time." She sighed. "Just get inside. That's an order."

I didn't know how to argue with her. So I did what she said. I climbed into the printer, and I kept still as she moved up my body, tightening straps around my legs, my arms, my chest, like she was tucking me in.

"Remember," she said, "ISTA needs to know what happened. We're all counting on you."

I swallowed and nodded.

"And I will ask one more thing from you," she said.

"What?"

"Find my son down there and—" She broke off. Her bottom lip quivered, and she bit down on it. Her eyes glistened. "Just promise me you'll look out for each other until you're rescued. Okay?"

"I promise," I said.

She hit some buttons on the controls, and the lid closed with a sucking of air and a whump, sealing me in. She looked at me through the glass, gave me one last, sad nod, and then she left the room.

I was almost back where I had started, and all alone. I couldn't hear anything outside the printer, just my own rapid breathing that fogged against the curved glass. I felt cut off, trapped, with no way of knowing what was happening. A growing panic in my chest tightened the air in that small tube, so I closed my eyes to try and calm my body. I pictured myself somewhere else.

The straps allowed me to twist and get my hand inside my pocket, where I felt around the micro drive for the yellow kobold. As the lander began to shake, and I heard a deafening rumble even from inside the printer, I grabbed that game piece tight in my hand, and I imagined myself before my parents had ever left, my hair still wet from my bath, sitting in my pajamas, begging for just one more game of Magical Mountain.

But then another memory invaded my thoughts. It trapped me in the game we'd played on the *Theseus* and forced me to relive everything that came after. I let go of the kobold and pulled my hand out of my pocket, and as my mind came back to the body printer, I realized I would never be able to look at my parents or think about them the same way again. I thought about the people who had suffered because of my mistakes, and I didn't know how I would be able to live with myself.

An alarm blared on the lander, muted inside the printer. To keep myself from thinking about what was happening to the captain, to Amira, to Evan, I closed my eyes again. But that time, I simply imagined myself in another printer, back on earth, reestablished.

But not as me. As the me I used to be. I imagined what it would be like to wake up without the memories of what had happened, without the shame for everything I had done. To be the me I was before. The me I might have been.

That is what I held on to as the lander crashed.

## AFTER

I AM THE FIRST THING I REMEMBER.

Me.

I'm me.

And I'm here. In a tube of glass, lying naked on a warm, contoured metal plate.

Then I remember the moment just before that, back in the teleportation room on the *Liverpool*. Jim tucked me in, and then the scanning chamber closed. The stasis drugs obviously went to work almost immediately, because I don't remember anything else. Now I'm here in this body printer, remembering myself.

The room beyond the glass is filled with a harsh, bright light. I can see a couple of people moving around at the edges, maybe doctors, or technicians, and I cover myself with my hands. At that point, one of the figures approaches the body printer, a woman I don't recognize with wavy blond hair. She pushes a button, and I hear her voice through a speaker near my head.

"Jessica, welcome home. I'm going to open this up so you can get dressed, okay?"

I nod, confused why she welcomed me home. I was supposed to wake up on the *Theseus* with my parents, light-years from Earth, in orbit above a barren planet with a volcano problem.

I hear a gentle pop and the hiss of releasing air, and then the glass lid lifts away. The woman wraps me in a blanket as I sit up, and then she supports me as I climb out of the printer. I get goose bumps all over as my bare feet touch the cold, smooth floor, and it takes a moment to steady myself. But I manage the walk to a large changing booth without stumbling too much, and inside I find underwear, a tank top, and a jumpsuit, all of which I put on. The suit is made of a thick, warm terry cloth, like a body-sized hoodie, and when I'm dressed, the woman finds me some slippers in my size.

"How do you feel?" she asks.

"I'm fine. But I'd feel even better if you told me what's going on."

"Your liaison is almost here," she says. "I think it would be best to leave the explaining to him."

I don't want to wait for answers, but it seems I don't have a choice. She goes back to her crescent-shaped workstation with the other technicians, and I sit quietly but impatiently until Jim Kelly enters the room. He strolls toward me wearing the kind of friendly, propped-up grin that doesn't seem like it will last long once we start talking about whatever he's come to tell me.

"Jessica," he says, extending his hand. "It's a pleasure to see you again."

"A pleasure to see you, too." I give his hand a shake. "But I have to admit, Jim, I wasn't expecting to see you so soon."

He chuckles. "Nor I you."

I look around the room. "Am I still—"

"On the *Liverpool*? Yes."

I remember getting into the scanner, and I know I just woke up in the printer. But I have no memories of anything in between. "So . . . did I leave?"

He hesitates a few moments, which isn't typical of the Jim Kelly I remember from our brief interaction before my scan, and I'm not sure why that question would be a hard one to answer. I either teleported, or I didn't. My lack of memories would suggest that I did not leave. But Jim seems to know more than I can remember.

He turns to address the woman with the blond hair and the other technicians. "Could I have the room for a few minutes?"

The workers all glance at each other, then gather their things and file toward the hatch. The blond woman is the last one out, and she smiles at me one last time before leaving Jim and me alone to talk about something that apparently requires privacy.

"Seriously, what is going on?" I ask.

"That will take some time to explain," he says. "But don't worry. You and your parents will get a full briefing, along with the rest of the *Theseus* crew."

"My parents? They're here?"

"They are."

I don't know what the hell has happened, but if my parents are here, I wonder if that means their plan has changed. Maybe I won't be going to Carver 1061c to spend a year imprisoned in a planetary habitat studying rocks and primitive alien life-forms. Maybe instead, they are finally coming home. "Where are they?" I ask, looking around. Mine is the only printer in this room.

"Right now, they're probably asking their liaisons the same question about you."

"Can I see them?"

"Soon. But let's take a seat for a minute."

He motions me toward the technician workstation, and I frown as I cross the room and sit in one of their swivel chairs. "You've got me a bit worried, Jim. Are my parents okay?"

"They're fine. That is, they're healthy." He sits in the chair next to me, arms folded, and leans toward me like he's about to tell me a secret. "Whether or not they are okay, well, that will ultimately be up to them."

"What does that even mean?"

His brow wrinkles, and he looks at me like he's trying to figure out a math problem in his head. "You know, you were a singular traveler even before your scan, Jessica Mathers, so I'm going to be honest with you."

"About what?"

"There was an accident on the *Theseus*. The investigation is ongoing, so we're still piecing together what happened. But ISTA has brought everyone home, using each traveler's most recent scan. Including your parents."

"Wow." I've learned about some famous space disasters, like the Europa colony that flooded, and the OS *Conrad*, but nothing recently. Space travel is supposed to be safe. "Okay. Is this bad? Because it seems pretty bad."

"It is a significant and consequential event," he says. "ISTA hasn't lost a ship in a decade. But that's not really what I'm here to tell you. The thing is, Jessica, the last usable scan for your parents was old."

"How old?"

He pauses. "Six years."

"What?" I stand, but I'm still a bit dizzy from the body printer and sit down again. "But that would mean . . ."

"It's the scan from when they left. And right now, they are being told that their eleven-year-old daughter is seventeen. For them, it will be as if the last six years never happened."

"But it won't be like that for me."

"No, not for you."

I don't know what to think or how to feel. I've often wondered what my life would have been like if they had stayed on Earth with me, but I never imagined it happening this way.

"Your life is going to be quite different from this point forward," Jim says. "But you'll have people who understand. Others who are going through similar experiences. They could even be your friends."

"What people?"

"Liz Kovalenko," he says. "Alberto Gutiérrez. Evan Martin. Amira

Kateb. Rebecca Sharpe. The rest of the *Theseus* crew. And there's a young man about your age. Duncan."

The last name is familiar to me, even though I don't think I've ever known a Duncan.

"You met them all before the accident," Jim says. "But that all happened after your scan."

"So, wait a second. I did teleport?"

"You did."

"And I was on the *Theseus*?"

"You were."

It's strange to think that I did things out there in space that I can't remember, because I never really did them. But a version of me did, and I wonder what that means for me.

"There's something else I need to tell you," Jim says.

I almost laugh. "You mean there's more?"

"There is. I have something for you. Some recordings. I'm confident that ISTA wouldn't want me to give them to you. But I researched the regulations, and it seems that by sending them directly to me, as a private communication, you either cleverly or luckily found a loophole. But you'll need to keep them a secret, just in case. For both our sakes."

"You're saying I sent you recordings? From outer space?"

"You did."

"Recordings of what?"

He leans back a bit and tips his head to the side. "Do you remember before your scan, when we were going through your paperwork? I mentioned that your parents seemed very excited to finally have you with them. Do you remember that?"

"Yes, of course." It feels like that conversation just happened, even though I know it didn't.

"Do you remember what you said next?"

"I think I said they're excited about having a free research assistant."

"Right, exactly. And then I asked you if that's the story you tell yourself. Now, I'm not a therapist or a counselor. But as a liaison, I have had some training in human psychology and behavior. I know the stories we tell ourselves are powerful. They're how we know who we are, and they make us who we are. But it's important to remember that we can change our stories. Sometimes, all we need to do is start telling ourselves a new one. Does that make sense?"

"Honestly? No."

He grins and hands me a book. A collection of Robert Frost poems.

"It will," he says.

# ACKNOWLEDGMENTS

*Star Splitter* was a challenging book to write for many reasons. Nearly five years of slow, methodical work stand between first contact with Jessica and now, a far lengthier time than any of my previous books have taken, and throughout that long process, I had the support of many.

The inimitable Richard Peck once said that we write by the light of every book we've ever read. I don't have the space here to list all my literary heroes and inspirations, but I think it important to mention James Patrick Kelly. I encountered his brilliant short story "Think Like a Dinosaur" as an undergrad, and his solution to the "teletransportation paradox" has haunted me ever since. (I later encountered Mr. Kelly himself at the International Conference on the Fantastic in the Arts, and his kindness and encouragement also left a lasting impression on me.)

DaNae Leu, Walter Eddy, James Wright, Carolyn Frank, Wendy Toliver, and Dan Wells all read the first pages of *Star Splitter* as it took the shape it now holds, and their input helped me find my footing. Christopher Chambers had no idea when he invited me to speak at his library that I would end up reading from an unfinished draft of *Star Splitter*. I would not have made that choice without the magical atmosphere he creates with twinkle lights and teacups, and the enthusiastic audience response from friends like Bill Dunford and Jennifer Adams gave me a boost of confidence I didn't know I needed. Cory Myler and Tim Wynne-Jones later read complete drafts and provided valuable insights that guided my early revisions. Fellow wizard Christian Heidicker went with me to the bottomless well, and our conversations never failed to bring up gold (let's meet there soon, brother, we got work to do).

My agent, Michael Bourret, continues to provide me with wise and valued counsel. My editor, Julie Strauss-Gabel, understood this book from the beginning and asked the exact questions needed to bring Jessica's story to completion. Both showed faith in me for which I struggle to express my gratitude. This book would not exist without them.

As always, my friends and family remain an infinite source of love and strength. Jaime, especially, bore with me through all manner of challenges that this book brought our way. Her boundless insight, patience, optimism, and grace are behind every page I write. I am the luckiest.